P9-DVQ-684

EX
LIBRIS

THE ROMANCE TREASURY
ASSOCIATION

TORONTO · NEW YORK · LOS ANGELES · LONDON
AMSTERDAM · PARIS · SYDNEY · HAMBURG
STOCKHOLM · ATHENS · TOKYO · MILAN

These stories were originally published as follows:

SECOND BEST WIFE
Copyright © 1978 by Isobel Chace
First published by Mills & Boon Limited in 1978

THE HUNGRY TIDE
Copyright © 1975 by Lucy Gillen
First published by Mills & Boon Limited in 1975

WILD INHERITANCE
Copyright © 1977 by Margaret Pargeter
First published by Mills & Boon Limited in 1977

ROMANCE TREASURY is published by
The Romance Treasury Association, Stratford, Ontario, Canada.

Editorial Board: A.W. Boon, Judith Burgess, Ruth Palmour,
Alice E. Johnson and Ilene Burgess.

Dust Jacket Art by Wes Lowe
Story Illustrations by Wes Lowe
Book Design by Charles Kadin
Printed and bound by R.R. Donnelley & Sons Co.

ISBN 0-373-04098-9

Printed in U.S.A.   A098

CONTENTS

SECOND BEST WIFE

Second Best Wife
Isobel Chace

All her life Georgina had been eclipsed by the sunny disposition and luminous beauty of her sister, Jennifer. While she was ignored, men flocked to Jennifer's side in droves.

Somehow it never bothered Georgina until one too many suitors turned her capricious sibling's head, causing her to break her engagement to the autocratic William Ayres. For since Jennifer refused to deal with anything unpleasant, it fell to Georgina to inform him.

Everything would have been fine, had not William blamed her for his rejection and insisted that she come to Sri Lanka with him in Jennifer's place. William needed a wife for reasons of his own, and even if she was second best, Georgina would have to do!

CHAPTER ONE

Georgina had first met the redoubtable William Ayres when she was ten years old. She had disliked him on sight, mostly because at fifteen he hadn't looked like a boy at all but a fully grown man. Worse still, he had made his reputation locally as a wit at her expense and she would never, never forgive him for that, not if she lived to be a hundred and one.

It had been at a village children's party which, as far as she was concerned, had begun badly and had got steadily worse as the afternoon had gone on, until that brief, devastating moment when William had made her the laughing-stock of the whole community. Georgina had been told to look after her nine-year-old sister, as she always was, and had been taking the duty as seriously as she always did. This had largely consisted of defending Jennifer from the village bully, a boy named Duncan Radcliffe. She had been remarkably successful too, for her flair for organisation and her practical way of going about things in general had already been in evidence at that tender age. She had only turned her back once in two hours, but it had been enough for Duncan to pull Jennifer's skinny plaits and twist her arms, and then, of course, half a dozen adults had stood between him and the revenge Georgina would have meted out to him then and there.

So Georgina had bided her time. She had waited for the inevitable game of Postman's Knock—a game she thought remarkably silly at the best of times—and had

waited her turn to choose Duncan as her victim. She
had even pretended to kiss him, but at the last moment
she had drawn back her fist and had hit him, hard, on
the nose. And Duncan had cried and she had been *glad*
he had cried.

And then it was that William, bored stiff by the do-
ings of his juniors, had opened his mouth and drawled,
    *"Georgie Porgie, pudding and pie, Kissed the boys and
made them cry!"*

A roar of laughter had greeted this sally, the more so
for Georgina was a solid little girl who had not yet fined
down into the slim, well-made woman she was now.
The nursery rhyme had followed her wherever she
went. Even Jennifer had begun to shorten her name to
Georgie, accompanied by a silly giggle that never failed
to make the discomfited Georgina see red. One day,
she had vowed to herself, *one day* she would teach William Ayres a lesson he would never forget and everyone would laugh at *him* as they had laughed at her!

Now, thirteen years later, the instrument of his punishment had fallen into her hands and the unassuaged
bitterness of years rose in her throat, blinding her to
the difficulties that still lay ahead of her. It had not
taken her very long to discover that William disliked
her almost as much as she disliked him. She had
thought it a pity that that dislike hadn't been extended
to Jennifer as well, but her sister had blossomed into a
frail, gentle young woman, unable to make up her
mind about anything, but so sweet-natured that nobody minded her ineffectual ways. As far as boys were
concerned she was a regular honeypot, which Georgina
was not. Perhaps to make up for her sister's lack of
character and push, Georgina had a practical streak that
verged on the managing and a defensive attitude to life
that made her as prickly as a hedgehog and not sweet at
all.

It had been last year that William had asked Jennifer to marry him, and Jennifer, unwilling as ever to hurt him by telling him that she wanted to marry someone quite different, had blurted out her consent and had then run to Georgina to get her out of it, just as she always had.

Georgina's moment of triumph had been sweet. She had tasted it on her tongue and had found it good. Not normally vindictive, she had known she was going to enjoy telling him of her sister's defection. Her moment of complete, devastating revenge had come!

Georgina stared at herself in the looking-glass, pulling a face at the strongly defined features that stared back at her. Where Jennifer was so fair as to be almost wholly pink and white, broken up only by the pale blue of her eyes, Georgina's hair was black, her eyes the grey-green of a stormy sea, and her face as tanned as any gypsy's—and she had known a few for, once upon a time, they had been allowed to camp quite close to the village where she had been brought up. They never came now, for the police had long ago been given orders to move them on as fast as they had arrived in the district and, as far as Georgina knew, she was the only person who missed them.

She sighed, wishing her chin was a little less square and her mouth a little less firm, even if it did kick up at the corners when she smiled. Her father had once told her she had a passionate mouth, but he had been laughing when he had said it and she had known in her heart of hearts that he, too, secretly preferred the rose-bud curves to Jennifer's lips, often left slightly open to accommodate her slightly prominent teeth and to relieve her neat but not very practical nose.

It was no wonder that William had fallen for Jennifer, Georgina thought. There was no danger of Jen-

nifer challenging any of the dictates he had handed out
to them both during the years of their adolescence. It
had always been she, Georgina, who had fallen foul of
the temper which she had taken some pleasure in provoking whenever she could, frightened as she had been
at times of the cold rage that had possessed him,
swamping his normally excellent judgement, and closing his mind completely to the reasoned practicalities
she had deliberately offered him, fanning the flames of
their mutual dislike.

But Jennifer had not fallen for William. Georgina
had feared she would, for Jennifer liked what she called
"strong" people, but in the end she had chosen someone almost as gentle and undefined as herself, a man
Georgina had despised from the first moment she had
set eyes on him. Imagine her astonishment, therefore,
when Jennifer had introduced him as the grown-up
version of that juvenile bully, Duncan Radcliffe, of
whom she had been so afraid when they had been re-
spectively nine and ten years old.

"*You're* Duncan Radcliffe?" Georgina had accosted
him in accusing tones. "You can't be! Duncan was a
beast!"

Duncan had smiled sweetly back at her. "People ignored me," he had explained diffidently. "I was always
trying to get them to listen and they never did. *You*
always made me cry, I remember. I was scared stiff of
you. Whenever I managed to say a single word to Jennifer you would come up and bash me."

"You bullied her!"

And Jennifer had gone a delicious pink and had said,
"Yes, but I liked it, Georgie. He never hurt me as you
did. I told you so at the time, but you were too busy
quarrelling with William to pay any attention to anyone
else." She had giggled suddenly. "Duncan and I
thought it awfully clever of him to bring out that funny

rhyme at that party! We laughed about it for months afterwards!"

Months? It had been *years* before Georgina had heard the last of that particular nursery rhyme, years in which she had seen to it that even if nobody had forgotten it, just as she had never been able to forget the burning humiliation of that moment, they never dared to repeat it any more in her hearing. It had cost her dear, but she had come out on top in the end. Even Jennifer had received a black eye when she had repeated the offending verse in an incautious moment.

Georgina had given them both a bewildered look. "But what about all the time he pulled your hair and twisted your arms?" she had asked Jennifer.

They had both of them smiled at that. "You wouldn't understand, Georgie," they had said together. "It only meant that we liked each other."

Georgina didn't understand now, but she had understood at once when they had, both of them, shuffled their feet and looked slightly pathetic and had asked her if she would mind breaking the news to William.

Georgina's eye had gleamed with a long-awaited triumph. "That will be a pleasure," she had said. And she had meant it, every word of it.

But walking along the short distance between the Perry household and the much grander residence where William Ayres' parents lived, she began to wonder if it was really going to be the kind of revenge she would enjoy after all. She had never felt sorry for William before and it would ruin everything if she were to feel any sympathy for him now. He hadn't felt sorry for *her* when he had made her the butt of the whole village's somewhat simple brand of humour!

Georgina opened the gate and walked into the pleasant garden that surrounded the rose-pink brick building that she had always thought wasted on anyone as undis-

cerning as William. She stood for a moment, running
her eyes over its familiar features with a hunger she
would have spurned had she been aware of it. The
Perry house where she lived was as bleak and bald as
this one was gracious and welcoming.

"Well, if it isn't Georgie Porgie," William's voice
broke into her thoughts, making the hairs prickle on
her neck with hatred for him. "What's brought you
into the lion's den?"

"Certainly not your charm, William Ayres," she
snapped back at him. "I was wondering how you could
have lived in such surroundings all these years and yet
be so uncharming." She wanted to tell him that he was
more like a scorpion than a lion, but her innate honesty
of mind forbade the attack. He did look remarkably like
a lion, with lion-coloured shaggy hair and eyes the colour sometimes of warm toffee and sometimes of sun-
burned grass.

"What do you want?" he asked her wearily.

It was so unusual for William to be anything but
terse and faintly taunting when he spoke to her that she
was thrown off balance by the dullness of his tone of
voice.

"I'd hardly have come for my own pleasure," she
retorted tartly.

He leaned on the spade he had been wielding, looking her up and down. "Give it a rest, Georgie. I could
see from the cut of your jib the moment you opened
the gate that you'd come to give me a set-down. Why
don't you get it over with?"

She narrowed her eyes, resenting the intimate way
he was looking at her. He didn't see her as a desirable
female, so he shouldn't look at her as if he did. "It's
too good to hurry," she murmured, forcing a smile.
"Much too good to hurry!"

He picked up the spade and dropped it into the

ground. The metal cut through the hard ground as easily as a hot knife through butter. Unaccountably, Georgina took a step backwards, knowing that that was what he'd like to do to her and feeling suddenly unsure of herself.

"Well?" he said.

"It isn't really good," she contradicted herself. She took a deep breath, averting her eyes from the mockery in his. "Oh dear, I wish she'd told you herself now, but Jennifer would just leave you hanging on for ever—"

To her surprise William grinned at her. "She hasn't your gift for quick surgery," he agreed. Then he sobered, his mouth settling into a grim line. "Get on with it, girl! And don't look at me like that! If you think I'm going to bleed all over the garden for your delectation, you're wrong. I wouldn't give you the pleasure of sharing my wounds with you!"

"No, of course not! You've never been vulnerable like the rest of us, have you?" Georgina returned hotly. "You're as arrogant now as you were *then*! In fact, I think you're worse now, if you want to know."

"I don't."

She twisted her fingers together in an agitated movement that betrayed her inner torment. She wasn't enjoying this half as much as she had thought she would. She spent a long moment trying to find the right words to soften the blow she had waited so many years to deal him, but there was no way she could find of wrapping up the unsavoury truth that she had to deliver. Besides, it wasn't her way. She had always looked facts straight in the eye herself and she thought that William did too.

"In ancient times the bearer of bad tidings was often killed for bringing them to the ear of the king," she said at last.

"Is that why you're nervous? Because you think I

might murder you for enjoying sticking pins in me? Not in cold blood, my dear Georgie. Of course there's no saying what I might not do in a rage—"

"Jennifer isn't going to marry you."

His face hardened. "On your say-so?"

Georgina opened her eyes wide. "Why should you think that?"

"Because you've bossed the poor girl about unmercifully ever since I've known you! It was one in the eye for you when we got engaged, wasn't it? Did you have to break it up? Couldn't you have contained your jealousy for your sister just this once?"

Winded, Georgina stuttered a denial which withered on her lips as she read the full depth of his contempt for her in his expression.

"She's going to marry *Duncan*," she explained.

"Oh, is she? We'll see about that!"

Georgina recovered a little. "You mean it's all right for you to bully her, but not for me?"

He pulled the spade free of the earth and slammed it down again. "Heaven give me patience, for you'd try the patience of a saint, Georgina Perry! What made you pick on Duncan of all people?"

"I didn't!"

But she might just as well not have spoken. "I suppose you found out long ago that he couldn't stand up to you?" he went on nastily. "Well, I can, Georgie Porgie, and I will. I'll make you rue this day for as long as you live, if it's the last thing I do!"

A shiver of fear ran up Georgina's spine. "Why me?" she asked almost humbly. "Why are you always so beastly to me? All right, I wanted to be the one to tell you because—because I've never forgiven you for making everyone laugh at me, and this was the best opportunity I've ever had to hurt you as I was hurt then. But it wasn't anything to do with me that she preferred someone else to you! Anyone would! But you can't take it like a man, can you? Well, I don't believe your silly threats, so there!''

"So there?'' There was a trace of cold steel in his amusement. "How are you going to stop me taking it out on you?''

She faced up to him, swallowing down her momentary fear. "I'll stay out of your way.''

"Much good that'll do you!''

"It'll be a pleasure!'' she told him passionately. "I don't like you at all—I never have!''

"Because I called your bluff when you made that poor little rabbit of a boy cry? Little girls should be taught early in life to keep their fists to themselves.''

"That was Duncan,'' she retorted. "Duncan Radcliffe. He's the man Jennifer is going to marry instead of you! He was a horrid boy, always pulling Jennie's hair and pinching her.'' Her brow wrinkled as she remembered her earlier bewilderment. "Only Jennie doesn't remember that now.''

"Probably because it never happened outside your imagination. It was most likely the excuse you invented in case anyone asked you why you'd punched the poor little devil. Usually you didn't bother with any excuse. You even took me on once, my girl, and you narrowly missed a good thrashing as a result. If I'd given it to you then, you might not stand in such need of one now!''

She was offended. "Oh, I *hate* you!'' she declared. "You don't *know* anything about me at all, but you've always pretended you do, and it was never anything to my credit. Jennifer could do no wrong, but I could do no right, could I? Well, for what it's worth, you can do no right as far as I'm concerned either!''

"Pity.''

"And what does that mean?''

He brushed the mud off his fingers, ignoring her.

She had a good view of his face in profile and she wondered, briefly, how she would have felt about him if she hadn't learned to hate him so many years before. He had a lot going for him in the way of looks. It was a good, strong face that turned slowly towards her and the eyes that met hers were well-shaped even if they were as cold as a winter's day.

"I'll tell you after I've seen Jennifer and heard her side of this affair. But I warn you, Georgina, if I find you're the cause of things having gone wrong between us, you'll pay for it. If you've messed things up for me, I'll have you instead!"

Her mouth fell open. "What on earth do you mean by that?"

"I mean," he said with such restraint that she found herself believing every word of it, "that you may not be my ideal woman, but you belong to the female sex, more or less, and that's all that's necessary for you to take Jennifer's place and come with me to Sri Lanka. I don't intend to go alone and you, my dear, will hate every moment of it, and that's good enough for me!"

"You're mad!" she gasped.

"If I am, it's because you've driven me round the bend," he responded with a grunt. "You've nobody to blame but yourself!"

"If you think—"

He put a hand on her shoulder, his fingers biting into her flesh. "I don't think, I know. Come along, Georgina, we're going to have a talk with that sister of yours—*both* of us!"

"She's with Duncan," Georgina protested. "Can't you see, William, she was afraid to tell you herself? I wish she had! I thought I'd enjoy hurting you—"

"It won't be me who receives the lasting hurt!"

"No, but why hurt me? Why did you have to make them all laugh at me at that party? People went on about it years later, still quoting that stupid rhyme at me. It was so unfair!"

"Life is unfair. Besides, you deserved it and you know you did. A tomboy is one thing, but a termagant is another."

"I never hit you!"

"Not for lack of trying." He glanced down meaningly at her clenched fists. "Are you going to try it now?"

Georgina forgot that discretion is the better part of valour. Her temper flared and she took careful aim, judging her distance nicely. She made exactly the right allowance for him to dodge her blow and caught him fair and square in the eye. At the moment of contact her anger seeped away and she withdrew the guilty fist to cover her mouth, her eyes wide with contrition.

"You dared me to!" she defended herself.

"I can't say I thought you'd do it all the same," he muttered. He put a hand up to his eye and swore briefly. Georgina was horrified to see that it was already discoloured and more than a little red.

"I'm sorry, but you shouldn't have made me lose my temper. If we went inside I could bathe it for you." The colour drained from her face. "It might look better then before your mother sees it."

He was startled. "Does her opinion matter to you?"

Georgina nodded. "I like her," she said simply. "I've always liked her. You're not at all like her."

"No," he agreed with feeling. "I never allowed you to pull the wool over my eyes! Well, now she'll see you as you really are, won't she? As an intemperate, vicious little thug!"

"Because I got the better of you? It was your own fault, only of course you won't admit it! You dared me to hit you, you know you did! I suppose you didn't think I would, that I would slap you or something silly like that, and now you don't like it because it was as good as anything you could do! A fine flush hit! It's made a pretty good mess of your face, let me tell you, and I'm completely unmarked!"

He uttered an exasperated laugh. "Only because I didn't hit you back!"

"You might not have succeeded," she pointed out. "*I* would have dodged out of the way!"

He turned to face her, reaching out for her and, with a gasp, she rushed out of arm's reach and ran down the garden path towards the gate and the comparative safety of the public highway. William caught her up halfway down to her parents' house.

"Have you forgotten I'm coming to see Jennifer?" he asked her sweetly. "Or did you hope I'd give you time to tell her what to say? Not on your life, my girl! This time you won't shift the responsibility on to anyone else, least of all that long-suffering sister of yours. Jealousy is a very nasty thing and, if you allow it to, it will warp your whole nature. You ought to be grateful to me for making you face up to your motives for doing your best to ruin your sister's life. The only thing I want to know now is did you make Jennifer agree to marry me in the first place so that you could have your moment of triumph, or are you making her marry Duncan?"

"I suppose you won't believe I've had nothing to do with anything Jennie chooses to do?"

"That would be stretching my credulity too far," he agreed.

Georgina's eyes stung with tears. "All right, *ask* Jennifer! I hope you'll feel as much a fool as you'll look when she's told you how wrong you are!"

"*If* she tells me I'm wrong. I've known you both for years, remember, and you've always made Jennifer go your way. You won't do the same to me, so make up your mind to it, Georgina."

"I wouldn't want to try," she countered dryly. "I've never pretended to know everything as you do. I wonder you mix with us lesser beings at all!"

William favoured her with a cold, blank look. "Nor will that sharp tongue of yours help you. It doesn't cut any ice with me."

"No," she said, not without bitterness, "it takes a pair of bright blue eyes to do that!"

His face flushed with anger. "Georgina Perry, I'm warning you! Another crack like that and I'll put you across my knee in the middle of the road! It's more than time you learned to control that jealous temperament of yours! Is it Jennifer's fault that men find her more attractive than they do you?"

Georgina formed her lips into a smile. "Do they?" she tempted him. "How can you possibly know that?"

"Jennifer—" He broke off, his eyes narrowing.

"Jennifer told you!" Georgina finished for him. "Such a reliable source of information, I'm told. Still, it's something that you don't pretend to be privy to my love life as well as everything else—it might surprise you, it might even shatter a few illusions, and that would never do, would it?" She was rather proud of the note of mockery she had achieved, knowing he found it as objectionable as he did everything else about her.

"I have no illusions about either you or Jennifer," he answered her. "I've known you both far too long."

"So you have," she agreed with a light laugh. "There's none so blind as he who will not see, though. Even the mighty William Ayres isn't always right! And, before you decide it's my vindictive nature that makes me say such a thing, it was your mother who said it first. She said it to comfort *me*. She said when I grew up I wouldn't care what you thought about me—"

"Why do you?" he interrupted her.

She thought of denying that she did, but William was no fool and she knew he would recognise it for the lie it was.

"I don't know," she said at last. "Because I'm a fool, I guess. Because you hurt me so badly and I wanted to change your mind about me. *I don't know!*"

"Because you're jealous of Jennifer and you hated anyone to like her better than you. Isn't that the squalid little truth that's driven you on to seek your revenge on me all these years?"

"No, it had nothing to do with Jennifer," she claimed, but she knew he wasn't even listening. There was an eager look to his face as he marched up the path by her side towards the front door. He had probably forgotten all about her, so intent was he on getting to Jennifer. For the first time she wondered if he were really in love with her sister and she was a little shocked that the question should arise in her mind at all. Why else would he have asked Jennifer to marry him?

Jennifer and Duncan were still sitting in the sitting-room where she had left them. They looked ill at ease when they saw her, glancing at her guiltily out of the corner of their eyes. Georgina felt the old, remembered irritation with her sister that she could never come out into the open and say what she meant. One always had to dig everything out of her bit by bit and, truth to tell, it was seldom worth the trouble when she did finally make her views known.

"Didn't you tell him?" Jennifer asked Georgina now. "You said you would, Georgie. You said you'd enjoy it!"

"No, I didn't," Georgina returned calmly.

"It's what you meant, though, you know you did! Why bring him here? I can't possibly see him now. You'll have to get rid of him, darling. He frightens me."

Georgina turned her head to William who was still waiting in the hall. "She says you frighten her," she repeated. "She'd prefer it if you went away."

"Or is that what you would prefer?" he demanded. He took a step forward into the doorway, reaching out a hand to Georgina and spinning her out of his way. Unfortunately she lost her balance and collided with the rising Duncan. "That's right, knock him out too!" William jeered at her.

Jennifer gazed at him with stricken eyes. "William, your eye! Did Georgie do that?"

"Who else?"

"Oh, how awful of her! I only asked her to—"

"Yes, what did you ask her to say to me?" he asked grimly.

Jennifer fluttered her lashes, glancing briefly at her sister. "Oh, William, you know I wouldn't have hurt you for anything in the world! I can't help it if I'm easily persuaded, can I? Georgie could always make me say and do anything she wanted me to. I know I ought to stand on my own feet more, but you don't know what it's like when you have a big, overbearing sister like mine! She doesn't mean any harm, only she can't understand that anyone should want to do something else but carry out her commands. You mustn't be angry with her, William dear, or with me either."

William's mouth set into a dangerous line. "Meaning that you do want to break off our engagement?"

Jennifer nodded. "I never wanted to get engaged in the first place! I wouldn't have done if Georgie hadn't—"

Georgina pulled herself up on to her feet, unable to believe her ears. She felt as though she were drowning and the harder she tried to breathe normally, the worse she felt. She felt dizzy and bells rang in her ears.

"If I hadn't what?" she pressed Jennifer.

"Oh, Georgie, I know you think I'm betraying you to the enemy, but you shouldn't have suggested I did it in the first place. It wasn't a worthy revenge for you to take. You knew I always wanted Duncan and you should never have persuaded me to lead William on. He has every right to be angry with both of us!"

William's hand closed round the nape of Georgina's neck, holding her in a painful grasp. "I've heard enough!" he declared with a suppressed violence that made Georgina shiver. "Don't worry, Jennie, I don't blame you for anything. I hope you'll be very happy with your Duncan, though I doubt you will be unless you can find some way of getting Georgie out of your life. I may help you do it! I may very well help you do it!"

Georgina tried to break away from his bruising fingers, but he shook her like a cat does her kitten, reducing her will-power to zero.

"William, please!" she begged him.

"Oh no, you don't, my girl. You're coming with me! For once in your life you're going to pay in full! I'm going to render my account in person and you are going to pay it! Understand?"

Georgina's senses swam. She had seen William in a rage before, but she had never seen him like this, and she was afraid. She was scared silly of what he might do to her and even more scared as to how she might react to whatever he was going to do.

It was then that she knew that she didn't hate William Ayres at all.

CHAPTER TWO

Georgina could hear the laughter behind her as she struggled against the iron grasp of the man who held her, yanking her out of the room behind him and hauling her through the hall and out the still open front door.

"*Georgie Porgie, pudding and pie, Kissed the* boys *and made them cry!*"

"You see!" she ground out. "*They've* never forgotten either!"

"How childish can you get?" William asked of no one in particular. "It must be true for you to mind so much. Is it?"

"No!"

"Then why all the fuss? Why try to ruin Jennifer's and my life for such a trivial reason?"

Georgina slowed her pace in an attempt to retrieve some of her dignity which he was doing his best to destroy, jerking her after him as she vainly tried to keep up with his much longer legs.

"I suppose it's useless to say that I didn't?"

"Completely useless."

They went on in silence with her half-running to keep up with him. "You're hurting me," she complained.

"No, I'm not. You're not going to wriggle out of it this time, Georgina, so don't go all soft and feminine on me. It won't work. And *don't* cry! I can't stand whining females!"

Georgina had never whined in her life. "I'm not crying!"

"Good. Keep it that way. You can cry as much as you
like when I've finished telling you what your meddling
has got you into. Come to think of it, Meddlesome
Matty would have suited you as well as Georgie Porgie.
But *this* time *you're* going to pick up the pieces of your
own demolition job! I don't see why anyone else should
suffer, do you?"

Georgina made another futile effort to ease her hand
out of his. "Just me?" she asked bitterly.

His expression was as bitter as her voice. "And me.
I'll be there, right beside you, and it won't be much fun
for me either. But if I can't have Jennifer I'll get what I
can out of you—"

"But you don't even like me!"

"No, I don't like you at all, but I'll have the satisfaction of knowing you won't be hurting Jennifer all the
time you're with me—and that you'll be hating every
moment you find yourself stuck with my society."

Georgina's legs refused to carry her any further. She
came to an abrupt halt, ignoring the searing pain in the
muscles of her arm as William tried to force her on-
ward.

"William, don't be daft! I know you're angry at
what's happened, but, truly, none of it was my fault.
There's no need to behave like a bull chasing a red rag.
Sooner or later you're bound to recover yourself and
then you'll regret—"

"The regrets will be yours!"

She eyed him cautiously, remembering the results
of earlier rages when, blind to everything but the impulse of the moment, William had had every child in
the village trembling with fear at what he might do
next. His tempers never lasted long, however, and she
of all people should have been able to understand

them, for she lost her own temper with all the frequency and heat of a redhead. William's rage was never a hot emotion, however, it was cold and deadly and all the worse because he looked so normal all the time he was in the grip of the need to savage anyone who came near him.

"William," she pleaded, "remember what happened last time!"

"Tell me about it," he invited her.

"I wasn't here," she said uneasily. "I was away at college. Jennifer told me about it. When I came back you'd moved out of your parents' house—for ever, I hoped!—and Jennifer was in a state that bordered on hysteria because of what you'd said to her. She swore she'd never forgive you!"

"A nice story," he commented. "And just what is it I'm supposed to have said to her?"

Georgina pursed up her lips. "You cast aspersions on her virtue."

"On *her* virtue? Come off it, Georgia! I never said any such thing. We quarrelled about you as usual and if Jennifer was 'in a state', as you put it, it was because she'd just received a letter from you telling her what you would do to her if she got engaged to me. I told her she could leave your reactions to me, but she could never escape from your influence, could she? She didn't believe me and she resented that I had to go away because of my job. How you do twist everything to your own ends!"

Georgina could have cried then. She could feel the tears stinging at the back of her nose and eyes. "But Jennifer said—"

"She was afraid of you—and she had good reason to be! If you can black my eye, what could you do to her?"

"All right," Georgina shouted at him. "I didn't like

the idea of your marrying Jennifer. I *hated* the idea! But I wouldn't have done anything to stop it—my quarrel has always been with you, not Jennifer. *Her* I love, and nothing would induce me to do anything to hurt her!''

"You're not going to get the opportunity," he retorted.

It was strange, but miserable as she was, Georgina could still feel the warmth of the red-brick house's welcome as she reluctantly followed William inside. There was a pleasant smell of furniture polish and pieces of well kept copper twinkled at her from their place on the wall. Unlike the Perry house, it was warm too, with a promise of comfortable chairs and hot crumpets for tea. She had once in her life been invited to tea with Mrs. Ayres and that was what she had been given to eat, with piles of home-made jam and a great deal of shared laughter. William hadn't been there. He had just started to travel extensively in his job and Mrs. Ayres had been proud of his achievements at such a young age. He had been working on a Commonwealth health project, she remembered, and he seemed to have been doing that ever since. It was a pity he was home at the moment.

"You can't make me do anything I don't want to," she remarked as he pushed her ahead of him into the sitting-room. "I'm not afraid of you!" There was a quiver in her voice that belied her words, but she held her head up high and gave him look for look. "Just because you're as mad as hell—"

"Children, children," Mrs. Ayres rebuked them gently, coming in from the garden at the same moment. "What are you bickering about now, you two?"

"Do we have to be bickering?" William asked her, his lips quirking with what could have been amusement.

"When have you ever done anything else?" his

mother returned placidly. "My dear boy, what have you done to your eye?"

"Ask Georgina!"

Mrs. Ayres clicked her tongue, her eyes twinkling. "Georgina, you *didn't*? It seems to have been remarkably effective."

"He dared me to do it," Georgina defended herself, trying not to allow her embarrassment to show. "I'm terribly sorry, Mrs. Ayres."

"My dear girl, I'm in your corner! William has done nothing but provoke you ever since we first came to live here."

Georgina cast a doubtful glance at William, but it was impossible to tell what he was thinking. His expression was sober and completely calm, not at all as though he was still in the grip of one of his cold rages.

"I've been provoking her to some effect this afternoon," he told his mother, sounding almost amused. "Didn't I tell you I hoped to marry the Perry girl?"

It was hard to tell who was the more astonished, Georgina or Mrs. Ayres.

"Marry?" Georgina gasped, but the sound of her comment was completely lost in Mrs. Ayres' whoop of joy.

"Darling William! I never thought you'd show so much sense! I'm ashamed to say that when you told me you were thinking about the Perry girl I jumped to the conclusion you meant Jennifer. I couldn't be more pleased!"

"Thank you, Mother." His tone was so dry that Georgina blushed for him. "I'm glad it meets with your approval."

Georgina thought that Mrs. Ayres, who must have known her son better than anyone else alive, should have been warned, but she was far too relieved to attempt to hide her joy from him—or Georgina.

"I know it's your life," she rushed on, kissing her son warmly on the cheek, "but Jennifer would never have been *my* choice for you. She would have bored you to death inside a fortnight of close proximity, whereas one never knows what to expect from Georgie, does one? So *much* more interesting! But I'm surprised you realised that for yourself, dear. I was so afraid you were blinded by Jennifer's fragile beauty—it won't last!—and would mistake one of her little girl's appeals for masculine sympathy as true love. The girl has never yet formed a stable relationship and, in my opinion, she never will."

Georgina watched William's nostrils flare with fascinated dismay. Indeed, so intent was she on his reactions that she missed her own cue to deny the quite preposterous suggestion that she would ever marry William while she was still in her right mind and had breath in her body.

"We'll leave Jennifer out of this," William said sternly to his mother. "It's easy to see you don't know her at all—only what you've heard about her from Georgina, who has never made the faintest effort even to be kind to her! That's something I mean to put a stop to in the future."

The pleasure drained out of Mrs. Ayres' face. "William, you're not doing something foolish, are you?"

"Certainly not! It's all arranged, Mother. Jennifer is going to marry Duncan Radcliffe, and Georgie Porgie is going to marry me."

"Have you asked her?" Mrs. Ayres returned coldly.

"Georgina will do as she's told!"

"And put up with you calling her by that ridiculous name as well, I suppose? You should have grown out of teasing defenceless little girls by now, William. I'm disappointed in you."

Georgina groaned inwardly. This was making bad

worse with a vengeance. "Mrs. Ayres," she began, "I don't mind! I'm used to it! And—and William doesn't mean anything by it." May God forgive me, she added to herself. "Besides," she went on, trying to sound lighthearted and able to take a joke against herself, "the sting went out of that particular nursery rhyme a long time ago. Who wants to kiss the boys anyway? I'll settle for a grown man myself."

"William?" his mother demanded caustically. "You must be dotty, darling. If I were you I'd black his other eye for him and give him more of the same until he behaves himself." A faint smile twisted her lips. "I must say you did a good job. He's beginning to look like a prize-fighter—and not a very successful one at that! Does it hurt?" she asked, all concern, and then, when he nodded, briefly and without enthusiasm, "Good!"

"I don't know about William," Georgina said, intent on her own thoughts. "He doesn't really mean to marry me, you know, and I certainly don't want to marry him!"

"Enlisting my mother's sympathy won't help you!" William shot at her. "You'll marry me, Georgina—"

"You can't make me!"

"You think not?" Georgina's eyes fell before the dangerous glitter in his. "I think I can. I can make things so hot for you you'll be glad to marry me!"

Mrs. Ayres looked so appalled by this claim that Georgina felt sorry for her. She put a comforting hand on the older woman's arm and said, "You mustn't mind so much, Mrs. Ayres. William never means anything he says in a rage—you know that."

"I mean it this time, Georgie Porgie. This time you're going to have a man to kiss and it won't be he who ends up in tears. You're going to marry me and come with me to Sri Lanka—"

"That'll be the day!" she scoffed.

"Indeed it will!" he retorted.

William would do nothing to put his mother's mind at rest.

"Don't hide behind her skirts," he advised Georgina. "It won't do you any good."

"But, William, I *like* your mother. Why do you have to hurt her too?"

"She'll get over it. She'll forget *why* we got married once the deed is safely done. By the time we present her with her first grandchild she'll be convinced that the whole idea was her own. She's always preferred you to Jennifer."

Georgina tried not to allow the barb to hurt her. "Is that so odd?"

"To me it is. You have none of Jennifer's gentle and appealing ways. Mother doesn't usually approve of violent people."

"How she must dislike you!" Georgina exclaimed.

He cast her an angry look. "If I am violent with you it's no more than you deserve," he bit out. "You'll find me quite reasonable as long as you behave yourself. I think I know how to handle you so that neither of us gets hurt too badly. It's more than time that someone took you in hand!"

Georgina set her mouth in a stubborn line. "I'm not going to marry you. I plan to marry someone else, as a matter of fact. I may have my faults, William dear, but your kind of arrogance is not part of my make-up. How will your pride enjoy having a wife who's in love with somebody else?"

"With whom?" He laughed without humour. "Are you trying to tell me you have a boy-friend?"

"Why not?" she countered in commendably cool tones.

"Who is he?"

She opened her eyes wide, beginning to enjoy herself. "Peter Anthony. I don't think you know him. Jennifer and I met him at a dance—"

"And you took him away from her, I suppose?"

Georgina sighed. "I didn't have to. Impossible as you find it to believe, there are a few men in the world who don't give Jennifer a second glance. Not many, I grant you, but there are one or two."

William frowned at her. "And how far has this romance gone?" he demanded.

"That," said Georgina, "is none of your business."

"It is now! Marry me you're going to, Georgina Perry, and although I don't relish the prospect of second-hand goods, it isn't going to put me off, if that's what you're hoping?"

Georgina's face flamed. "Think what you like! I don't care!"

William raised his brows thoughtfully. "I wonder why you do?" he murmured. "You've always cared what I think. Why not admit it?"

Georgina shrugged. "You flatter yourself—as always!" She flicked her fingers as close to his face as she could get. "I don't care that much for what you think! And you won't find Peter as easy to bully as you do me. He's more of a man than you'll ever be!"

William threw back his head and laughed. "Tell me that when you've been married to me for a week or more," he said nastily. "I've never had any complaints before."

"I daresay nobody dared voice any," Georgina retorted. "Like Jennifer, they probably told their troubles to someone else. You're not a very sympathetic listener, William Ayres. In fact I don't find you sympathetic at all!"

"You don't have to, though, do you? Bullies in my

experience always complain of being bullies when any-one dares put a stop to their activities. If you want me to be kind to you, the remedy is in your own hands. I'll be as kind to you as I think you deserve, no more, no less."

Georgina rose to her feet. "Thanks very much," she said, the bitterness she was feeling rising like a geyser to the surface. "I don't want you to be kind or not kind, or anything else! I just want you to leave me alone! I'm going home!"

He took her hands in his, pulling her into the circle of his arms. "You're not going anywhere, my sweet—"

She stamped her foot at him, trying vainly to free her wrists from his clasp. "Really, William, don't you think this joke has gone far enough? All right, you've given me a fine fright, which is presumably what you wanted to do, but I'm not frightened now. I've had it, and I've had you too!"

"Not yet you haven't, but you're going to." He smiled at her with a gentleness that belied the pressure of his hands in the small of her back. "You won't hanker after your Peter for long, Georgie Porgie, I pro-mise you. If you'll let me, and by that I mean if you don't fight me every inch of the way, I'll make you very happy. It's a long time since I took a good look at you, but you're not as bad looking as I thought. Jen-nifer is so delicate-boned and fragile that she makes you look too solid and robust by comparison—"

Georgina achieved her ambition of stamping hard on his toe, followed by a fierce kick on the shins. She might just as well have saved herself the trouble, for William's only reaction was to laugh.

"Don't you want me to kiss you?" he teased her.

"I don't want to have anything to do with you!"

But she was very much aware of his hands on her back. They were warm and competent, holding her with an ease she had never come across before. Struggle as she would, she could not gain her freedom from him, and yet it was no effort to him to bring her closer still against him. Her heart beat increased its rhythm in a sudden excitement that she found quite inexplicable.

"You see," he said in her ear, "it isn't quite as you thought, is it? How do you like being on the receiving end for a change?"

It was a kiss such as she had never experienced before. His mouth commanded hers, parting her lips, and ignoring her spluttered protest. And then she didn't want to protest any more, nor did she want to escape from the pressure of his hands, or from the earthy, male smell of him at close quarters. It was as if she had no will of her own, but that her whole being had merged with his to give them both the greater satisfaction.

When he let her go, the reality of her position came rushing back to her and the tears came brimming into her eyes and down her cheeks. She wiped them away impatiently, hating herself for the feeling of acute loss that afflicted her.

"I told you it wouldn't be I who cried," William's mocking voice reminded her.

"But you didn't say you wouldn't be able to resist saying I told you so!" she flared up at him. "Nobody has ever kissed me against my will before, if you want to know. Are you surprised I'm upset?"

A crease appeared between his eyes, which were more green than gold at that moment. "Peter can't be much of a man if he lets you make all the running. A woman has to be wooed, not left to take the initiative herself. Is he afraid of you too, Georgie Porgie?"

"Peter isn't afraid of anyone!"

He was silent for a long moment and Georgina eyed him covertly, wondering what he was thinking.

"In the same way that you're not afraid of me?" he questioned her at last. "You can't make up your mind, can you? You're more attracted by my handling of you than you'll admit, Georgie. I don't believe anyone has assailed your heart and come close to bringing your defences tumbling down, my innocent. Tell me more about this Peter of yours."

"There's nothing to tell." Georgina gave him a mutinous look, recovering herself sufficiently to whip up her anger to boiling point again. "I love him and I mean to marry him. That's all you need to know." She hoped she didn't sound as guilty as she felt, for she could well imagine the unfortunate Peter's consternation if he could hear her. She thought it unlikely that he wanted their easy-going relationship to turn into anything more than the unemotional friendship it had been so far. He wouldn't like her using him as a defence against William, but, once she had explained things to him, she thought he would back her up until the danger was over. Peter was the most reliable person she knew and one of the best friends she had. It was true that sometimes she suspected he had got to know her in order to get closer to Jennifer, but she had never held this against him. He had seen through Jennifer with the greatest of ease and had pronounced her both shallow and wilful. Georgina hadn't wholly agreed with him, but she had been grateful that for once she had been found to be the greater attraction for one of the more personable young men of their mutual acquaintance.

"You must introduce him to me," William suggested. "I don't suppose you want to break it to him yourself that you aren't going to marry him after all?"

"But I am!" she protested.

"Oh no, my dear, you're not. It wouldn't *be* him for long, would it? You'd soon be casting an envious eye over Duncan, and we'd all be back where we started, making the best of things after you've broken them into little pieces. No, Jennifer won't be safe from you until I have you firmly shackled to my side. I may not be able to give her anything else, but at least I mean to give her that!''

Georgina felt obliged to argue the point with him just one more time. "What did I do to spoil things between you two?" she demanded. "It wasn't I who forced Jennifer into Duncan's arms!"

"No, it was my arms you pushed her into, not Duncan's, but it all comes to the same thing. You've pushed Jennifer around for far too long. I'm going to give her her freedom. What she does with it is her own affair. I shall be occupied with controlling my own wife." He smiled slowly, looking surprised. "I even think I may enjoy it, young Georgie. Whatever else it is, it certainly won't be dull!"

"But William, I don't want to marry you!" Georgina wailed.

"You will when you get used to the idea," he returned calmly. "My dear girl, susceptible to your own passions you've always been, but I don't believe anyone else has ever stormed your selfish little heart before today. Take care you don't lose it to me entirely if it amuses me to turn you into a loving wife after all."

"William, I *hate* you!"

"Of course you do," he answered in soothing tones. "But hasn't anyone ever told you, Georgina dear, that hatred is the other side of the coin of love? Now, calm down and listen for a change. I have to be in Sri Lanka in three weeks' time. Can you be ready by then?"

Georgina seethed with frustrated fury. "Am I supposed to answer that? How can I make it any clearer to you? I'm *not* going to marry you!"

"We can be married that same day in the morning," he went on unperturbed. "That'll give you the flight to get over the shock of finding that for once you haven't got your own way about something. Cheer up, Georgie, I won't hurry you into the responsibilities of married life once we're safely away from here. You'll have all the time you need before we come back to England and Jennifer. By that time you'll have forgotten that you were ever a reluctant bride and wife."

"And what about Peter?"

William had the audacity to grin at her. "I think I'll see Peter myself. If he's really set on marrying you, he'll probably take it better from me that you've changed your mind about him. I have an idea that you wouldn't throw your heart into the chore of telling him you're about to jilt him for another."

"You're right! Nor am I going to jilt him! I refuse to allow you to take my life over in any way. This is the twentieth century, William Ayres, and you'll soon find out you can't do it!"

For an instant he looked almost sorry for her. "But I can, Georgie, that's the whole point. I can do it because you're the kind of girl who has been brought up to believe that she ought to marry her lover." His eyes narrowed, giving him a wicked look that made her tremble inside. "Would you prefer me to take you without marriage?" His eyes never left her face which he had forced up at an uncomfortable angle to make his point the more brutally. "No, I thought not," he said at last. "At least you don't pretend that I couldn't do that too if I had a mind to! You're a poor loser, but you have a proud spirit. When I've finished with you, my sweet, you're going to be quite a woman!"

A lump formed in her throat and dissolved into a ball of hot wretchedness that robbed her of speech. All she could do was to thump her closed fists against his chest.

She would have given anything to have poked him in
the other eye at that moment, but her tears defeated
her. Boxers wouldn't be boxers if they ever cried, she
thought. Nor were they ever overwhelmed by a sense
of desolation that occasionally afflicted all her sex. Life
was so unfair!

"William, please let me go," she whispered.

"I'm sorry, Georgie, but I can't do it. You won't find
it so bad once you're used to the idea. And you'll enjoy
living in Ceylon for a few months, if you'll allow yourself to. It's a beautiful island and a beautiful people to
go with it. You'll love it!"

At any other time, under any other circumstances,
that might have been true, but he must be mad if he
thought she would enjoy anything in his company
when she had thoroughly disliked him ever since she
could remember. She opened her mouth to tell him so,
but somehow the words didn't come out as she had
intended. Instead a quite different question came tumbling out.

"What do you do when you go abroad for months
together?"

He gave her a startled look. "Don't you know? I'm
an engineer. This time I'm going to Sri Lanka on a
Commonwealth project to do with irrigation. It's one of
the most interesting jobs I've ever tackled. I like having
Commonwealth backing too. It's the sort of thing we
ought to be doing to help the poorer members in the
Third World, not making the gap ever wider between
us. One day we'll pay for our greed and stupidity in the
West if we don't do a great deal more of this sort of
thing." His golden eyes mocked her. "One way or
another, the selfish always pay in the end, or hadn't
you noticed?"

Georgina's mouth trembled, betraying her hurt.
"Isn't there a parable about removing the beam from

your own eye before you attempt the mote in your neighbour's? It could have been meant for you!"

He laughed out loud. It was a great gust of mirth that made her want to join in. "My word, you never give in, do you?" The words ended in another bout of hilarity. "Who ever would have thought the elder Perry girl had so much to her? Yet perhaps I should have guessed. You have a passionate mouth and enough fire in your belly for any man to handle. I wonder why I never noticed it before?"

Georgina made a face at him. "My virtues will fade like candlelight before the sun when next you see Jennifer, no doubt. You can keep your compliments to yourself! I don't want to hear them!"

He kissed her lightly on the cheek. "Jealous?" he asked in an intimate, deep murmur. "You don't like it that I kissed Jennifer first, do you? Never mind, my sweet, at least you have the comfortable knowledge that from now on it will be you I'll be kissing."

"Without love—"

"Love is only the icing on the cake," he cut her off, his good humour gone. "A good cake doesn't need to be covered in sentimental nonsense. It matures with time and never goes stale."

"Cut and come again?" Georgina suggested wryly. "That would never suit Jennifer, I'm afraid. She has a very sweet tooth."

"It isn't Jennifer who has to be suited. All that matters on this occasion is what sort of a cake are you?"

Georgina thought she knew. A badly baked fruit cake that had sagged in the middle was how she felt. She could only hope that William would choke over one of the half-cooked crumbs!

CHAPTER THREE

Georgina studied her husband sitting in the seat next door to hers, but the dreadful unreality of the day refused to go away. Not even the solid bulk of William's body could make her believe she had given way and had acutally said the words that morning that had transformed her into being his legal wife.

She would have held out if Peter hadn't betrayed her so thoroughly and with such a lack of subtlety that she still cringed when she thought about it. He had completely ignored her frantic signals that she would explain matters to him later. With a stupidity she had found deplorable, he had willingly confessed to William that he had no romantic interest whatsoever in Georgina Perry.

"We're just good friends," he had said. Georgina had told him afterwards that he might have found something more original to say than that, but her erstwhile suitor had merely looked hurt and puzzled and quite definitely lacking in push.

"But, Georgie, you know we don't feel that way about each other," he had defended himself.

"*I* know," she had agreed on a sigh. "I would much sooner that William hadn't known, though. If I don't look out, the wretched fellow really will make me marry him!"

Peter had been embarrassed. "How can he unless you let him?" he asked unanswerably.

Georgina still didn't know how he had done it, but

the gold band on her finger refused to go away no matter how often she tried to blink it out of sight. There was no doubt about it, in the eyes of the law and in the sight of men she had been transmogrified into Mrs. William Ayres and it felt as though the whole bottom had fallen out of her world with a vengeance.

And vengeance had been what it was all about. She was too honest with herself to pretend that William's first judgment of her had changed to liking in the past few weeks. Far from it. If anything, he seemed to dislike her more now than ever. She wished she could say the same about him. She had disliked him, more had loathed everything about him, but in the whirlwind of the last few days, somehow she had found herself beginning to look for his arrogant presence. At first she had thought it was because he afforded her some protection from the avid curiosity of her whole family, but she had soon learned better. For some reason best known to her subconscious self, she just liked to have him around. Could it be that she was beginning to enjoy the verbal battles that was the only way they seemed able to converse with each other? If so, she had got everything she deserved: a marriage that was no marriage, and a husband who didn't even accord her the most grudging respect.

Her mother had been the other traitor who had made no bones about her joy in going over to the enemy's camp.

"My dear, I couldn't be more pleased!" she had crooned in ecstasy. "I've always had a soft spot for William. Dear boy!"

"You don't think it might be a trifle awkward as he's only just stopped being engaged to Jennifer?" Georgina had said practically.

"I never took that particular relationship very seriously, dear," her mother had replied, quite unperturbed. "And nor should you. William knows what he's doing, I'm sure. Jennifer would never have done for him. Why, he looked and sounded like a grown man when he was only fifteen, and Jennifer—well, Jennifer is Jennifer, and we all love her dearly, but no one could describe her as *mature* yet in her love affairs. Why are you laughing, Georgie? Don't you think that's why William decided not to marry her after all?"

Georgina had regarded her mother with a little less than the usual affection she had for her. "It wasn't William who broke things off, it was Jennifer. She prefers Duncan, or so she says. Hasn't she told you yet?"

Her mother's brow had creased thoughtfully. "Duncan? You mean that little boy who was forever making her cry when you were all children? No, she hasn't said a single word to your father and me. She probably knows we wouldn't approve of her chopping and changing every few minutes—and certainly not to someone like Duncan! What a repulsive little boy he was!"

"I thought so," Georgina admitted. "Jennifer says she always rather liked him, only I used to bully them both into behaving badly. Is it true, Mother? Did I bully Jennifer?"

"Whoever gave you that idea? Your father used to say I made you look after Jennifer too much, and it would serve me right if you went through one of those tiresome bossy phases elder sisters do sometimes, but I can't say I ever noticed that you did. The only person you ever fought with was William. You turned into a regular shrew every time he came around." She had laughed softly. "The magic chemistry already beginning to work between you seems the most likely solution to that! It seems ridiculous now, but when your father and I were courting we used to fight like wildcats too, but since we got married we've seldom had a cross word. *That's* how it will be with you and William, you see!"

Georgina, unable to follow her on this particular romantic flight of fancy, had merely looked sulky. "A quiet wedding would be much more suitable. I'm sure William would prefer a register office—"

"Certainly not! This is your big day, darling! William and I have already agreed you'll be married in the village church with all your friends about you. He doesn't approve of hole-and-corner weddings any more than I do. They lack conviction."

"I lack conviction," Georgina had said sadly.

"Very proper in a bride," her mother had put in quickly. "You can rely on William to more than make up for any reservations you have, however. I do like a man who knows his own mind!"

Georgina had made one last attempt to win her mother over to her side. "What about Jennifer?" she had asked bluntly. "She won't like it—"

Mrs. Perry hadn't even bothered to look up from her sewing. "Jennifer will have to live with her own decisions," she had said. And then she had looked up, holding her daughter's whole attention by the simple expedient of waving her needle in her face. "If you let Jennifer ruin this for you, Georgina, I'll never forgive you!" she had declared with unusual vigour. "William is everything I hoped for you, and if you throw his love away in a foolish gesture of concern for Jennifer, he's unlikely to give you a second chance to make a fool of him. Be happy with him, darling, and forget all about everything else. If you don't, you'll be storing up a great deal of unhappiness for yourself. Love denied turns to bitterness more often than it can be sublimated into service for others."

"I haven't said I'm in love with William," Georgina had protested.

"I can't imagine your marrying him for any other reason!" her mother had retorted. "Don't be a silly girl! Of course you're in love with him! So marry him and be happy, and give over worrying about Jennifer, do! The Jennifers of this world are very well able to look after themselves."

Georgina hoped she was right. She had been too busy bending to the wind that was William these last few days to have given much thought to her sister, but she had spoken to her the night before. Jennifer had been out with Duncan and had come in late. There had been a hectic flush in her cheeks and her eyes had sparkled with the excitement of the evening's dancing.

"Will you give this letter to William tomorrow?" she had asked Georgina.

"You'll probably see him before I do," Georgina had answered. "Mother has an idea it's unlucky for a bride to see her groom before they meet in church."

"But the letter is for afterwards, darling," Jennifer had drawled, a malicious smile on her lips. "We don't want him to carry you off to the wilder shores of the Indian Ocean still wondering about his first love, do we? It's only to say I don't bear either of you any resentment for leaving me behind without giving a thought as to whether I shall be happy without you both."

"But if you're going to marry Duncan—?"

Jennifer had shrugged her shoulders. "Am I? William was a lot less boring than Duncan, if you want to know, only he was always going away. You're welcome to him!"

The letter. Georgina hadn't given it a thought from that moment till this. She opened her handbag and scrabbled round inside looking for it.

"Are you going to be sick?" William asked her.

"No. Why?" She found the pale mauve envelope with a sigh of relief. For a moment she had thought she had forgotten to transfer it from one bag to the other, and she could well imagine Jennifer's anger if she had forgotten to give her precious letter to William.

"You look a trifle green," he observed.

"I thought I'd lost Jennifer's letter." She handed it to him. "It's for you."

"So I see," he said dryly. He examined the envelope with care, noting the way the flap had been tucked into the back and the way Jennifer had written BY HAND in the top left-hand corner, in huge, flamboyant capitals, and William down below, underlining it with a strong double line. "Have you read it?"

"Of course not. It's addressed to you."

"You might have been curious as to what she had to say to me now that I'm your husband." He pulled the single sheet out of the envelope and opened it slowly. "Weren't you a little bit curious?" he asked Georgina, a funny little smile playing round his lips.

"If I was, I managed to restrain it by forgetting all about it. I thought I'd left it in my other handbag—" She broke off as his expression changed to one of cold contempt.

"I don't believe you," he said.

"Why not? What does she say?" Georgina demanded. She snatched the letter out of his hand and began to read it for herself. It was dated the day before yesterday and began, Darling William— "I don't understand!" Georgina said brokenly. "I don't understand it!"

"Don't you? It seems quite simple to me. Jennifer changed her mind again and tried to let me know she'd made a terrible mistake and very much hoped I would take her back after all. Why did you do it, Georgina? Why? It wasn't as though you wanted to marry me yourself. Or did you? Is that why you deprived us of our chance of happiness?"

"But it wasn't like that! She told me to give you the letter *after* the wedding. I made a point of telling her that Mother wouldn't allow me to see you before the service began. Jennie said it was to tell you that she didn't bear you any resentment for marrying me."

"That isn't what she says there," William pointed out.

"I can't help what she wrote to you! I'm telling you what *happened*!"

"And I don't believe you."

Georgina went very white. For one awful moment she thought she was going to faint. "I don't care what you believe! I don't tell lies!"

"Meaning Jennifer does? Forgive me, my dear wife, if I choose to believe the woman I love. Her record gives her a credence which yours does not!"

"You don't have to stay married to me!" Georgina cried out. "An annulment would suit me just fine!"

"Oh Georgie, stop whistling in the dark! Why suppress the letter and marry me in the first place if it's an annulment you want?"

Georgina gave way to an hysterical laugh. "Why indeed? That ought to prove it to you that I didn't read the letter in advance. If this isn't just like Jennifer! How she loves to stir things up!"

"And you don't?"

She sobered. "No, I don't think I do. I haven't the imagination to make the most of my chances. If I had, I would have read your letter then and there and found out what Jennifer was up to. One is at such a disadvantage when one expects everyone to behave by one's own standards. You'd have thought I'd have learned better by now." It was a cry from the heart, but William showed no sign of taking it as such.

"Very clever," he remarked. "If I didn't know you better I might have believed you. God, Georgina, I didn't think even you hated me as much as that!"

"You've never done anything to make me like you very much, so why shouldn't I? Not that I did! Not because of you, but because of me. I wouldn't *stoop*—"

"Words, Georgie. I think you'd do almost anything to get even with me—perhaps you think you're justified, who knows? But I can promise you you won't enjoy the fruits of your triumph! Marriage can be heaven or hell, my dear. I was going to try and make it as pleasant as possible for you; I now feel relieved of any such obligation. My vengeance can be as bitter as yours—and a great deal more intimate!"

She closed her eyes, trying not to listen. "Why don't you let me go and marry your marvellous Jennifer, if that's what you want to do?" she asked him.

He was quiet for so long that she thought he hadn't heard her and she opened her eyes to see what he was doing. His face was very close to hers in what could easily have been mistaken as a loving gesture. she could see the cold hardness of his eyes.

"What I have, I hold, Georgina Ayres," he said slowly. "Isn't that what I promised you this morning? *To have and to hold, from this day forward?* For ever? For the rest of your life, my dear, dear wife!"

She closed her eyes again, giving herself up to misery. What a fool she had been to marry him, she thought. What a *fool*! Perhaps she had said it aloud, though she had said it to herself.

"Why did you marry me, Georgie?" he asked her. "I couldn't really have forced you to it, as you very well know. What made you actually say the fatal words?"

The pain of her unhappiness collected as a lump in her chest and the back of her throat felt as stiff as a board.

"I think I wanted to," she answered. "I wanted to see Sri Lanka."

"And to be my wife?"

"I don't know," she confessed. "I tried not to think about it. I thought you'd find out—I thought you might be kinder once we were away from home. I don't know what I thought!"

To her surprise he smiled at that. "Very likely! Poor Georgie, do you always hit out before you think, even when it's yourself who gets hurt?"

Her gaze flew to the yellow smudge that was all that was left of the black eye she had given him.

"Only with you," she confided. "You're the only person I've ever hated." She swallowed, summoning up all the reserves she had at her disposal. "I wish I were as nasty as you think me," she said passionately, "and I'd make you wish you'd never been born!"

His smile widened. "You can try," he invited her.

He turned away from her, settling back in his seat, and began to read the printed menu he had found in the pocket in front of him. "Good lord, they don't mean us to starve! Two dinners and three breakfasts! That ought to hold us for a few hours after we get there!"

Georgina slept fairly well until the vast aeroplane prepared to come down at Bombay. She had watched the pirate film that had been provided for their entertainment, but had been unable to keep her mind on the rather trite story. She had enjoyed the fencing, though. She had done some fencing herself while she had been away at college and she found that that knowledge added to rather than detracted from the carefully staged fights on the screen.

She had taken some pleasure in telling William that the heroine was very much better with the foil than the hero.

"Are you a female chauvinist as well?" he had asked her.

"I am when she has to work quite so hard not to disarm him entirely," she had retorted. "She could take him apart any time she chose!"

"It wouldn't do much for the story line," he had observed. "The helpless maiden rescuing the knight in shining armour doesn't sound right. That's the trouble with women these days, they won't stick to their own role in life."

"Wailing and weeping on the sidelines went out with crinolines," she had said with satisfaction. "We've learned it's better to rely on ourselves since then. It's better to make one's own mistakes."

"And have two heads in every household?"

She had considered the point carefully, sure he had laid a trap for her. "I suppose it works better when the man is the head and the woman the heart of the family, but some men abdicate their responsibilities and then the woman has to step in or the children suffer."

He had picked up her hand in his, examining the ring on her finger. "I shan't abdicate my responsibilities," he had said.

It wasn't possible to get any accurate impressions of what Bombay was really like. Circling over it as they came down to refuel at the International Airport, it looked much smaller than Georgina had imagined it to be. But then, from the air, all India looked the same dun colour and practically uninhabited. The teeming millions of India were nowhere to be seen.

"Next stop Colombo," said William.

"And then where?"

"Nowhere today. I'll be picking up a car tomorrow and then we'll drive up to Kandy and settle in. Today, we'll sleep off the flight and catch up with ourselves."

"And see Colombo?" she prompted him.

He shook his head. "There'll be plenty of time for that. Don't look like that, Georgie. We're going to do things my way and it simply doesn't pay to rush about the moment you get off an aeroplane after a long flight. You'll see the whole island before we go home, I promise you. Only not today."

She looked up at him through her lashes. "You're still angry," she accused him. "It will take more than that to spoil my pleasure, though. Everyone says Sri Lanka is a beautiful place, and even you can't make it ugly just to spite me!"

He was taken aback by the attack. "My dear Georgina, hasn't anyone ever told you about the effects of jet lag? If you want to make yourself ill, by all means take yourself off and visit the museum, or anywhere else you want to go. I'm going to bed!"

She wondered if she wanted to brave an unknown city in an unknown world by herself and came to the conclusion she didn't.

"You're sure it isn't because you want to ruin things for me?" she demanded, still suspicious.

"My revenge will be a great deal more subtle than that," he told her. "Enjoy Sri Lanka all you can, it's your marriage to me which is going to be your prison. For once, you're going to pay for taking something away from Jennifer out of the rather despicable envy you've always had for her. To be an unloved wife is more of a punishment than to deny you any amount of sightseeing, as you'll find out!"

He made a formidable enemy, she thought. "You mean we're each going to live our own lives—?"

"What on earth makes you think that?" he exploded.

"You said unloved. I thought you meant—unloved."

"I see." His grim amusement cut her to the quick. "Making love is a euphemism that should never be used in our kind of marriage, but I don't see why I should deny myself the pleasures of your body for such a quixotic reason, do you?''

"I think you're horrid!"

"So you've said before. It becomes tedious. It would be more wifely if you kept your opinion of me to yourself in future.''

"While you can say what you like about me? You'd better look out that I don't black your other eye for you! A fine fool you'd look if I did!"

"By all means try if you think you can, but to be forewarned is to be forearmed. I might get in first. Have you thought of that?''

"You mean you'd hit *me*?" She could scarcely believe her ears. Surely William wasn't the kind of man who would hit a woman?

"There are times when I'd give anything to wallop you black and blue, but I don't suppose I will unless badly provoked, and you won't do that, will you, Georgie Porgie? I'll make a pact with you: if you keep your fists to yourself, so will I. Agreed?''

She sniffed. "You talk as if I were always punching you in the face," she complained.

"Once was enough," he said dryly. "I won't be as forbearing another time, my ruffian wife.''

"No? I suppose you'll think of Jennifer and let fly? What a pity she won't be there to see it!''

He snorted in derision. "Could be! And you won't have my mother in your corner to cheer you on either, which should reduce your chances somewhat. You'd better make up your mind to behave yourself like the lady you were brought up to be!''

She managed a wide, insouciant smile, to show him how little she cared about his threats. "I'll see," she compromised. "It was such a splendid black eye last time that the joy of it may last me for a long time to

come, but I'm not making any promises, you understand? Even ladies slap down their menfolk when the
occasion demands it, you know.''

''The operative word is slap, my dear, not punch in
the eye!''

The wry humour of his words appealed to her, but
not for worlds would she have let him see it. ''Why
don't you go outside and stretch your legs?'' she suggested to him.

His only answer was to sit down again in the seat
beside her, hunching his shoulders in an attempt to get
a little more comfortable. She sank back herself, pushing her legs out in front of her. Why it should matter to
her that he should choose to stay, she could not tell,
but his presence lit a small candle of happiness inside
her. If he would only forget Jennifer for a few days he
might see her as a person in her own right. If only— It
was the most useless phrase she knew. He didn't want
to forget Jennifer and, now that he couldn't have her,
he was intent on exacting his revenge for his disappointment from her. If only he would believe her about
the letter! If only—

''I'm going to write to Jennifer,'' she said aloud. ''I'll
tell her you got her letter safely. You can read it before
I send it, if you like.''

''I don't believe in flogging dead horses. Put Jennifer
out of your mind, Georgie, and I'll try to do the same.
We're stuck with each other, so we may as well make
the best of things.''

She pursed up her lips. ''And know you're wishing I
were Jennifer whenever you come near me? Why
should I put up with that?''

''I'm more likely to treat you gently if I do imagine
you to be Jennifer! But you needn't worry. No one
would mistake you for her in their right senses. And you
won't mind half as much as you think you will. If you

were honest, you would admit you liked my kisses very
well indeed. Nor have you any excuse for mistaking my
intentions towards you, like you did Peter's. A trifle slow
in the uptake, your gentleman friend, wouldn't you
say?''

Georgina would have said a great deal more than
that, but she restrained herself nobly. "He's not such a
fool as all that!"

"My dear girl, you should have seen his face when I
suggested to him you were hoping to marry him. He
wasn't worthy of your undoubted talents!"

She blushed with pleasure. "What talents?" she
asked hopefully.

"That would be telling!" His mouth twitched. "You
haven't had as much experience of the opposite sex as
you pretend, Georgie Porgie. The time for kissing mere
boys has gone now you have a man of your own. You'll
need all the talents you possess to cope with him!"

"With you?" She felt suddenly humble in the fact of
the challenge he held out to her. He must feel *something* for her after all.

"Since Peter failed you, I'm the only man you've
got," he drawled, getting slowly to his feet. "I won't
have you playing around with anyone else."

He disappeared down the aisle towards the open door
of the plane, exchanging a laughing word with one of
the fresh hostesses who had come on board a few minutes before. Georgina saw the quick interest on the
hostess's face and wondered if every female felt the
same way when they saw his shaggy good looks and
the distinctly masculine look in his gold-brown eyes.
Was it no more than the automatic, feminine reaction
to any personable man that she felt for him? Was that
what had been the matter with her ever since she had
discovered she didn't dislike him half as much as she
had thought she did? But no, that was ridiculous. He

wasn't the kind of man who had ever attracted her in the past. Her type had always been the well-read, gentle, academic sort, not an engineer who liked to get his hands dirty and who didn't give a damn how he won just as long as he did. That was the William she knew! A man too arrogant to be borne!

Yet when he came back to her there was no doubt but that her heart beat faster.

"We're about to have breakfast again," he said, throwing himself back into his seat.

"*Again*?"

"It's the last time before Colombo," he said solemnly. "You'd better make the most of it."

She giggled in a way she seldom did, but which Jennifer did all too often, and was rewarded by a sharp look from her husband.

"You don't do that often enough," he told her.

"There hasn't been much to laugh about recently," she reminded him.

"We'll have to change that." His eyes lit with a purely masculine glint that shook her to the core, it was so unexpected. "What kind of things do you find funny, Georgie?"

"Not you!" She turned her head away and made a play of fanning herself with the paperback she held in her hand. "It's hot in here, isn't it?"

He put out a hand and took the book away from her, glancing at its title as he did so. Apparently he approved of the title, for he turned it over and began to read the blurb on the back.

"Coward," he murmured. "What do you think I can do to you in a public plane?"

"I hadn't considered the matter," she replied with a lift to her chin.

He chuckled. "Liar! Are you reading this?"

"Yes, I am!" She took it back from him and, finding

her place, buried her nose in it to such good effect that she barely noticed the shutting of the doors and consequently missed the last sight she might have had of Bombay as they took off and circled southwards over the city.

It didn't seem long after that she had her first glimpse of Sri Lanka. The white sands that fringed the coconut plantations shone brightly in the sun, promising a welcome of the kind that usually only travel brochures can offer, and then only by dint of some very careful photography.

Georgina put her hand on William's arm, shutting out the scene down below her. "Is it all like that?" she breathed.

"Round the coast it is." He looked at her more closely. "What's the matter?"

"I'm frightened," she said. "I wish I hadn't come! And, more than anything, I wish I wasn't here with you!"

"It looks pretty good to me," he said.

It looked better than that to her. That was the trouble, though she could hardly tell him that. She was afraid of losing her heart to both the island and to him. *If she hadn't done so already.*

"I want to go home," she said.

CHAPTER FOUR

The hotel was, frankly, a disappointment to Georgina. She had expected something more in keeping with the way of life she had glimpsed from the minibus that had taken them from the airport into Colombo, but once within the air-conditioned portals of the hotel they could have been anywhere in the world.

"You'll feel better when you've had some sleep," William told her with such confidence that a little of her own fright ebbed away. "Sit down over there while I check in and cash some money and then we'll go upstairs to bed."

But even that promise seemed to hold overtones of other, less desirable, possibilities, and she was a little afraid she would lose sight of him altogether in the comings and goings of parties of French and German tourists who seemed to be constantly on the move in the gigantic foyer of the hotel. She wished she had asked William if she could have had a cup of tea while she waited, for despite the many meals of the night, she was thirsty, but she didn't like to join him in the queue where he was standing.

When he had finally finished his business and came over to her waving the key, she was obsessed by the idea of having something to drink.

"William, do let's have tea out on the terrace," she suggested.

"We will this evening," he promised her. "Right

now I want to get upstairs before the luggage arrives. You'll have to make do with water."

"From the tap?"

He shook his head. "Maybe, here, but don't even drink from the tap outside of Colombo. You can tell, more or less, if the water is potable or not by whether the hotel provides a flask in the bedrooms. Coming?"

She went with him to the lift, a trifle bemused by the many exhibitions that were being housed in the various public rooms of the hotel.

"Still wanting to go home?" William inquired as they stepped into the lift.

She watched him press the button, knowing that he thought she was being silly. "I suppose you feel at home in places like this?" she hazarded. "I don't think I've ever stayed in a large hotel before. I read somewhere that such places have a well-oiled cosmopolitan atmosphere, but I've never been part of the international jet set before, so it just seems frighteningly impersonal. Positively gruesome!"

He laughed. "Still hankering after going sightseeing?"

"No," she admitted, "I'll settle for some sleep. I expect the beds will be comfortable anyway—" She broke off, playing nervously with the strap of her handbag. "Have we got two rooms?" she asked abruptly.

"Married couples usually share a room," he responded calmly. "But cheer up, Georgina, you'll have your bed to yourself for today and tonight."

She expelled her breath in a sigh of naked relief. Indeed, she felt sufficiently reassured to answer him in his own manner. "I hope you don't snore," she said. "Jennifer does. When we've been away together, I never would share a room with her because of it. But perhaps no one has told you whether you do or not?"

"I've never had any complaints," he said dryly.

The lift doors opened and he stepped out before her, marching off down the red-carpeted corridor with an air of knowing exactly where he was going. Georgina followed more slowly. It came to her that she really knew very little about her husband, or the kind of life he led when he was away from home. There could have been any number of women who had shared more with him than she ever would. The thought of them disturbed her, distressing her out of all proportion to their probable importance to him and therefore to her.

He unlocked and threw open the door to their room, waiting for her to come up to him. When he touched her arm she felt a wave of excitement shoot through her and she hastened her step to get away from him. She was being ridiculous! More men than she could count had made a similar gesture towards her and she had never felt the slightest thing more than a brief gratitude for their courtesy. Her innards had never, *never* turned to liquid fire, not even when some of them had kissed her.

It was a typical, impersonal hotel room, and yet she thought she would never forget the way it had looked to her then. William swept back the curtains to reveal a view of the sea and the Parliament buildings outside the double-glazed windows. There was a small notice stuck on to the glass asking guests not to open the window when the air-conditioning was switched on, and she examined it with a care that she hoped would hide her nervousness from him.

"William—"

He looked up, his eyes quizzical. "Georgina."

"I'm sorry I'm not Jennifer. I mean, I know you're not getting any more pleasure out of this than I am. Wouldn't it be better—"

"No."

"*Why not?*"

"I'm not pretending Jennifer wouldn't have been a better choice, but you'll do, Georgie Porgie. I'll see that you do!"

"One can't make oneself love to order," she said, rubbing at the paper notice on the window with her finger.

"Who said anything about love?"

She sighed. "It's hopeless trying to talk to you," she complained. "If you aren't in love with Jennifer why did you want to marry her?"

"I don't consider that any of your business," he returned coolly. "If you want to use the bathroom first, my dear, you'd better hurry up before my chivalrous instincts are overcome by need."

"Have you got any?"

"Chivalrous instincts? I have a few. If you give up your bossy ways, you may be surprised." He grinned maliciously at her. "Are you going to try me out?"

Tears—tears, she hoped of fatigue—flooded into her eyes and she blinked them angrily away, disappearing into the bathroom. For a long time she stood in the small space that was all that was provided and fought to regain control over herself. She would feel better after a good sleep, she told herself, and therefore the sooner she got into bed the better, but until the luggage came up she had no nightdress with her. She undressed to her petticoat, paused, and then went the whole hog, taking a quick shower while she was about it. She put her petticoat back on, draping her towel about her shoulders for added protection.

William's eyebrows rose when he saw her. "Is that for my benefit?" he asked. "The female form holds no surprises for me, Georgie Porgie."

"It's for *my* benefit!" she retorted.

His eyes travelled over with appreciation. "Your modesty becomes you, but it doesn't cover you very well." He watched the burning blush travel up the back of her neck as she turned away from him, seeking the safety of the bed nearest the window. "Relax, Georgie. In that department, at least, you're every bit as good as your sister!"

She flung herself into bed. "I'm better, if you want to know!" she declared violently. "Even Jennifer admits that!"

"Does she, though? Then why try to hide yourself away? I wouldn't have said timidity, or coyness either, was a vice of yours."

She gritted her teeth, hiding her face in the pillow. "I'm not accustomed to sharing a room," she said in muffled tones. "Leave me alone!"

He stood over her, laughing. "Very affecting. You'll get used to it, Georgie Porgie." He bent down and kissed the exposed skin below her ear, ruffling her hair as he did so. "Sleep well, little one!"

"I'm not a child!" she flared, frightened by the burning excitement his touch induced in her.

"No, you're not, so if you want to sleep don't press your luck, my girl!" He placed the back of his hand against her cheek in a surprisingly tender gesture. "We'll talk this evening if that's what you want. I don't suppose you've ever seen the famous green flash that follows the sun's going down in the tropics? That'll be one thing you can look forward to without any fear of the consequences."

She wanted to put up her hand to his, but she had no right to do so. Instead she turned on her back and looked steadily up at him.

"I'm not afraid of you, William Ayres. I'll never be afraid of you! So don't flatter yourself that I am!"

He smiled. "If you were, you'd die sooner than admit it, wouldn't you, Georgie Porgie? What a strange girl you are! I'm glad I brought you with me if I couldn't have Jennifer. Life with you is unlikely to be dull, whatever else it may be!''

Her eyes followed him as he walked away from her and went into the bathroom in his turn. Would she be second best for ever and ever? she wondered. As far as he was concerned it seemed likely. What a fool Jennifer had been to want someone else when she could have had him and his love as well! How could anyone prefer a man like Duncan when they could have had all that? Georgina fingered her cheek where she could still feel the sensation of his touch and marvelled at the painful surge of emotion that engulfed her. She didn't even like him! She must concentrate on that and on all the things about him that had never failed to irritate her in the past. But she could still feel the gentleness of his skin against hers when she fell into an uneasy slumber, and it was of him that she dreamed until his hand on her shoulder shook her awake many hours later.

"Is it time to get up already?" she asked, confused.

"If you want that cup of tea it is." He shook her again. "No going back to sleep again now! You didn't even wake up when the suitcases arrived. Do you always sleep like one dead?"

She blinked, her dreams merging into real life for a delicious, uncertain moment. But then she saw that he was already dressed and that his expression was one of impatience rather than tenderness.

"You should have woken me sooner," she said. "Why don't you go down and order the tea and I'll follow as soon as I'm dressed?"

But still he lingered. "How long will you be?"

She glanced at her watch. "Ten minutes?"

He smiled at that. "That'll be the day! If you're much over half an hour there won't be any tea for you; an hour and I'll come up and get you!"

"I'll be ready in ten minutes!" she claimed. She

screwed up her eyes, watching him through her lashes to see what his reaction would be to that. It was impossible to tell. She hoped that her own racing pulses were as invisible to him. She had been so sure that he had been about to lean over and kiss her, which was ridiculous in itself, but what was worse was that she had wanted him to do exactly that and she had wanted it in every fibre of her being. "You'd have made a good slave master," she added, "only slaves are self-made, you know. I read an article about it. If you think free, you are free!"

"Stone walls do not a prison make—and all that? I shouldn't rely on the theory too heavily if I were you," he advised.

"But you're not me! Will you kindly stop standing over me in that impossible way and go away! I'll never get dressed with you looking on. I'm entitled to my privacy and I mean to have it!"

His eyebrows rose, a gleam of amusement entering the gold of his eyes. "My dear girl, if you carry on like this often I shall begin to think I've disappointed you in some way. What were you dreaming of when I woke you, or would that be telling?"

She cast her gaze down to his neatly polished shoes. "You'd find it a dead bore if I did tell you," she said. "There's nothing more boring than other people's dreams. Besides, I can never remember mine."

"Pity. They might tell you something interesting about yourself—"

"Am I so difficult to understand?"

"You'd best ask yourself that. Do you understand yourself?" His lips twitched. "Do you begin to know what it is you want out of life?"

"Oh yes," she answered gravely. "I've always known that. William—"

"Uh-huh."

"Go away."

But when he had gone she didn't get straight out of bed. She lay there, with her hands under her head, wondering what it was he had said that she had found so shattering. Or was it what she had said? Or dreamed about him? That was the most likely explanation! Her whole being had been expecting his caress and it had been like falling into ice-cold water to have it denied her when she had been jolted out of her sleep into reality. Had he known? Was that what he had meant when he had asked her if she knew what she wanted from life? The thought was humiliating in the extreme, in fact it was quite unbearable and most unlikely. If she were sensible she would put it out of her mind and go and join him on the terrace for tea. There was nothing in their last exchange for her to get hot and bothered about; it was merely her imagination playing tricks—

But William had known many, many women. He probably knew better than she did the unconscious signs a woman made when she was attracted to someone, even if she didn't want to be attracted to him. Well, she would just have to disabuse him of any thought that *she*— Supposing he had kissed her? It would have been no big thing in her life! *She didn't like William!*

She chose a pretty flowered dress from her suitcase and donned it in a rush, determined not to give him cause to gloat over being longer than she had specified before she joined him on the terrace. It was a very feminine dress with frothy lace at the neck and cuffs. Surely no one could think her hard and bossy in such a dress? To her own eyes she looked as vulnerable as she felt: afraid of William and afraid that she was going to get hurt, but when she smiled she looked a shade more confident. She would have to smile a great deal that evening, she recommended to herself. She would be cool, casual, and charming, and he would never suspect the turmoil that was going on inside her.

She squirted some scent on to the back of her neck and down the front of her dress and then sniffed the air anxiously, afraid she had been too lavish. Some people had an aversion to the cheaper scents that flooded the world's markets and she had never been able to afford anything else. What did William think about things like that? She tossed her head at her reflection in the glass, telling herself it was sheer snobbery to care, and hurried on her way downstairs before she could think of anything else to worry about. She could do without such niggling doubts if she wanted to carry the day with William. With him, she needed every scrap of confidence she could command. And yet—and yet it felt that her whole being burgeoned into a new life when she saw him, his long legs stretched out in front of him, sitting at one of the far tables on the terrace.

"Eleven and a half minutes," he growled at her as she sat down beside him.

"One and a half minutes to find you sitting right over here," she retorted, flashing a determined smile in his direction, and then wishing that she hadn't, since he was bound to know that it was as false as was the lightness of her tone.

"You still look a bit washed out," he commented, looking her over.

'How charming of you to notice," she returned. "I could say the same for you, but I won't. I'll compliment you on your choice of shirt instead."

"Meaning that you hoped I'd notice you had on a Jennifer-style dress? Well, I had noticed. Did you steal it out of her wardrobe when she wasn't looking?"

Georgina looked far out to sea, her whole attention on the setting globe of the sun, now gold, now enormous and scarlet as it slid down into the purple-grey water.

"Jennifer's clothes don't fit me," she said mildly. "Hadn't you noticed that I'm larger round the bust?"

"It can't make that much difference!" He studied her with renewed interest. "Perhaps it does at that! You haven't Jennie's delicate air, but you make an exciting handful for all that!" He noted her blush with satisfaction, his smile adding a cruel twist to his lips. "Is that what you really wanted me to notice?"

"No, I'm quite indifferent to your excitements." She leaned forward, staring so hard at the setting sun her eyes hurt. "When does the green flash come?"

"Just as the sun disappears. Any second now. Wait for it—*now*! Did you see it?"

"Yes—yes, I did." She sounded almost as surprised as she felt that she had actually seen the flash on the horizon that had saluted the departure of the setting sun. "I didn't really believe it would happen. Why does it?"

He started to explain it to her, but soon realised she wasn't listening to him. "You don't really want to know, do you?" he muttered, disgruntled.

"It might destroy the magic," she explained.

He gave her a wry look. "Who would have thought our Georgie Porgie was a romantic at heart? You've given few signs of it before! What did you learn at that college of yours, by the way? Jennifer seemed to think it was something about making bricks without straw? Not very likely, I thought."

Georgina deliberately relaxed her clenched fists. "Women seldom take up building," she said.

He laughed. It wasn't a pleasant sound. "I can well imagine you as a 'bricky', though, carrying hods of bricks through the mud and wet concrete of a building site, proving yourself as good or better than any man!"

Georgina forced a smile. "A regular Amazon, in fact? I rather like that! When one's small, one likes to be thought bigger than one is, and to be a pint-sized Amazon is better than to be a quart-sized, besotted humbug—"

"Like me?"

She shrugged. "If the cap fits," she suggested sweetly, "you know what to do with it."

He looked suddenly thoughtful. "I hadn't realised how small you are," he said at last. "How tall are you? Five-one? Five-two? Jennifer must be a good three inches taller—"

"She weighs more too!" Georgina pointed out, not without malice.

"Not when I first knew you," William remembered. "You were a very solid little girl."

"That," Georgina said briskly, "was a long, long time ago. You should catch up with the times, my lad. You live far too much in the past. Anyone would think you were middle-aged, you're so nostalgic about the days of your youth! Still, I suppose everyone feels the same about their first love—only most of us grow up and go on to bigger and better things."

William eyed her soberly. "What did you learn at college?"

"Not psychology. Design and commercial art." She lifted her chin, congratulating herself on getting the best of the latest skirmish between them. "Hence the bricks without straw, I suppose. Jennifer doesn't approve of artists selling their talents on the open market. In her opinion they ought to be starving in a garret, or living in the shadow of some patron. I'm not that romantic!"

"Nor am I," he agreed unexpectedly. "That's why I became an engineer. I like to see good, solid, practical results to my work. You don't get that with pure science. It's the technicians, the engineers, who've made civilisations work, right from the very beginning—far more than the so-called scientific bods. Nor do I live in the past much. My work is fashioning the future, and that's where most of my thoughts are."

"And in your private life?"

"That's a more difficult question to answer," he admitted. "One gets caught up in things. That's why I wanted to bring Jennifer out here." He hesitated, chewing on the inside of his lip. "She has a gentle, loving nature and that's what Celine needs most at this moment." His lips tightened. "Celine is the past all right. She lives there all the time, no matter what anyone does to try and give her a future." He sighed. "Jennifer would have been good for Celine."

"Celine?" Georgina felt completely lost. "Who is Celine?"

William stared morosely out to sea. "I inherited her from her father. He was a good friend of mine until he was killed by a flash flood in Australia. I'd promised him if anything happened to him I would take care of Celine for him. She's a pretty girl, but not quite all there, if you know what I mean. She was completely normal when her mother was alive, but her death affected her very badly. After that she never seemed to grow up. She's nearly twenty now, but she sounds and behaves as if she were half that age. I thought Jennifer would be good for her."

Georgina spread her fingers on her knees. "Did Jennie know about Celine?"

"No. I thought it would be enough for her to find out about her after we were married. Whatever happens, you see, I can't ditch Celine now."

Georgina surveyed him in silence for a moment. "It's a good thing you married me and not Jennie, then," she said. "Jennifer is used to being the baby and the most precious member of the family—"

"Come off it, Georgie! Jennifer is grown up and has

been for a long time now. She would have shouldered the responsibility of Celine easily enough. Celine could have done with her kind, gentle ways too. It was a risk bringing you in your sister's stead, but if you so much as touch that girl you'll have me to answer to. She needs loving, not bullying, and that's what she's going to get from both of us."

Georgina sighed. "How did her mother die?" she asked.

"In a fire. Celine was got out of the house by some neighbours, but they couldn't get her mother out. Celine's father tried to make the child talk it out of her system, but she wouldn't say a single word. Whenever he mentioned Alice, his wife, the child shut up like a clam with a dreamy look in her eyes, and she's been like that ever since."

"Poor girl!"

William glanced at Georgina and it seemed as if a reflection of that fire was lighting his eyes. "I'd give anything to make that girl happy," he said abruptly. "I owe it to her father—and the girl herself. She's beautiful, Georgie, the most beautiful creature I've ever seen."

Georgina raised her eyebrows. "More beautiful than Jennifer?"

"Good lord, yes! Jennifer has a fragile prettiness, but this girl is out of this world!"

"And you think Jennifer would have tolerated comparison with a raving beauty?" Georgina was stung into asking. "She'd have got rid of Celine somehow—especially if she knew how fond of her you are! Her gentle ways wouldn't have lasted two minutes after she realised she was expected to share your attention with somebody else. You've had a lucky escape, William, my lad!"

"By being stuck with you? Don't you ever have anything pleasant to say for your sister?"

Georgina bit her lip. "I've known Jennifer all her life," she reminded him. "She doesn't share things—with anyone."

"Only because she's had to put up with your petty jealousies whenever she wanted to strike out for herself. Older sisters can have one hell of a lot to answer for when they constantly resent being put in the shade by their younger siblings. Still, it's a risk I've chosen to take with Celine. You might say the choice was forced on me: either I got married to make a home for her, or I should have had to put her in a home and visit whenever I could. I chose to marry you—and I'll make it work if it's the last thing I do! You won't make Celine suffer for your inadequacies as you did Jennifer, my girl. I've got your measure, and if anyone can handle you, I can!"

Georgina bent her head. "What will you do if Celine recovers? She may not stay a child for ever. Have you thought of that?"

"I can't afford to," he dismissed the question. "I have to think of her as a child. One can't think of her as anything else."

But he already did, Georgina thought, surprised by the insight he had given her into his feelings. It had been Celine all the time! Was it possible? Could he really have decided to marry Jennifer for no other reason but that she would be kind to Celine? If so, where did she stand herself as Jennifer's substitute?

"A child in a woman's body," she mused aloud. "Does she know I'm coming?"

He nodded. "I had her brought over from Australia last week. She's already installed in the house at Nuwara Eliya where we're staying while I'm working on this irrigation project."

"Alone?" Georgina gasped.

"Of course not! She has her nurse with her—a

woman I very much want to get rid of, incidentally. If you can do that for me, I'll be eternally in your debt."

Georgina eyed him covertly. "Are you afraid of this dragon? I don't believe it!"

"You needn't. Miss Campbell doesn't alarm me, she bores me with her baby-talk and her upsy-daisies! Celine doesn't understand much, but she's a human being and should be addressed as such."

Georgina allowed herself a faint smile. "All right," she said, "I'll get rid of your Miss Campbell for you. Anything to oblige and all that."

His eyes narrowed, openly mocking her. "Anything?"

"Almost anything," she amended, and yawned to show she didn't care what he thought. But she did care! And she was alarmed too, because now she was back at the beginning with him, not knowing or understanding him at all. She had got used to his being in love with Jennifer. Now she didn't know if he was in love with anybody at all—and she had to know! She had to know *something*!

She cleared her throat, hesitated, and then started again in a now or never voice that betrayed her nervousness. "William, why did you marry me? As an alternative Miss Campbell?"

"Does it matter?" He stood up, pushing back his chair with a vigour that had the backs of her hands tingling.

"It matters to me," she said.

He bent over her, leaning his hands on the arms of her chair. "Does it? Why did you marry me, Georgie Porgie? You see, you can't answer that either, can you? It's better not to ask questions that have no answer to them. It'll have to be enough for you that you're here— that in itself fulfils one of your ambitions, doesn't it?

Haven't you always wanted to travel and see the world?"

"Yes," she admitted. "But I want to know where I stand too. Was all you wanted a nursemaid for Celine?"

His face was unreadable, at least to her. "I wanted a wife. Wives are usually expected to share their husband's responsibilities, aren't they?"

She made a last effort to explain her anxieties to him. "I don't resent Celine—"

"You haven't met her yet. You resented Jennifer all right and with much less cause. Where do you want to stand, Georgina?"

She shrugged her shoulders. "I want adventure!" she burst out. "I don't know what exactly!" Only she did. She wanted the whole of her adventuring to be with him! "Are you in love with Celine?"

His fingers brushed her cheek. "My dear girl, are you going to be jealous of her too? I don't kiss Celine like this—at least you can be sure of that!" He bent his head and put his lips to hers, kissing her hard and with an expertise that rendered her breathless and made her heart pound against her ribs. "She won't be taking anything away from you, Georgie Porgie, and you'll fight with her at your peril! If you want to let fly at anyone, you'll have to make do with me. Okay?"

It was so unfair! But then she caught sight of the slight yellowing that was all that was left of the black eye she had given him and her conscience was aroused, making her feel both uncertain and tearful.

"I don't want to fight with anybody!" she exclaimed.

He straightened his back, looking down at her with amused eyes. "That'll be the day, my dear. Come and eat. You'll be meeting Celine soon enough and then you can make up your own mind about her. The only thing that's wrong with your fighting instincts right now is that you're half asleep." A smile flickered across his lips. "Shall I carry you, or will you walk?"

She stood up quickly, avoiding his helping hand with a disdainful gesture. "You'll never have to carry me, William Ayres!" she declared. "I can look after myself, just as I always have!"

"But you have a husband now," he reminded her. "Won't you allow him to look after you?"

If she only could! "A husband is as a husband does," she answered pertly. "I don't need a keeper too, you know, so you'd better keep your care for Celine— and Jennifer if you have any over. I'll pull my own weight, thank you very much!"

He stopped her with a touch of his hand. "Not against me you won't, my love!" He pulled her close against him and kissed the tip of her nose with a mockery that made her want to cry. "Little Miss Independence!" he added on a laugh.

CHAPTER FIVE

The road to Kandy enchanted Georgina. She loved the changes in the scenery as they climbed further and further away from the sea. First there had been the coconut palms, their trunks weaving gorgeous patterns against the vivid blue sky; then there had been the paddy fields, some of them bright with water and some of them covered with the vivid green of the rice; and then, finally, there were the first of the tea plantations, hundreds of ruthlessly clipped back bushes marching their way across the higher slopes of the hill country, their lines keeping a military precision.

There were the changes in the people too. In an island noted for its beautiful women, most of them seemed to be out in the streets that morning, smiling and waving and dodging out of the way of the constantly hooting traffic as they went about their tasks of the day. The clutter of shops, single-storied and bursting at the seams with fruit and coconuts and other local commodities, came and went, giving way to long stretches of teak forest, rubber plants, and other crops. But it was the rice fields that appealed most of all to Georgina. To see the water-buffaloes doing their twice yearly task of ploughing the inundated mud of the terraced fields, their owners urging them on to greater effort, was for her symbolic of a whole way of life she would never have seen anywhere in the familiar world of the West. This was what she had dreamed would be the stuff of the intriguing East.

"Still want to go home?" William's voice cut across her contented thoughts.

She shook her head. "No wonder they thought this must have been the Garden of Eden. Is it always so beautiful?"

"Probably. The Buddhist temples help the scene along, don't you think? The shape of those stupas must be one of the most satisfactory ever invented by man."

Georgina followed to where he was pointing to the domed buildings surmounted by a steeple, pencil-thin and narrowing towards the summit, and had to agree with him. "Some of them are very old, aren't they?" she asked.

"Before we go home I'll take you to Anuradhapura and Polonnaruwa where you can see some really old ones. They were building these huge domes here when we in Europe were congratulating ourselves on managing a few arches. Originally, they were built over a relic of the Lord Buddha, or of one of his more renowned followers, together with the treasures given by whoever had had the temple built as an act of devotion. I can't believe there were enough relics to go round for all of them, however, but it doesn't matter, for Buddha and his teachings are brought to the mind whenever one sees a stupa, or dagoba, or pagoda, as we call it in England, after a while."

"I'm surprised no one thought to steal the treasure," Georgina remarked.

"I've never heard that they ever did," William told her. "I rather like to think the Buddhist philosophy precludes such reprehensible vices as greed and violence. Sometimes it does, and sometimes it doesn't."

Georgina gave him a saucy look. "I didn't know you had pacifist leanings. They don't show much, if you don't mind my saying so?"

"It takes two to make peace, just as it takes two to

quarrel," he observed. He grinned suddenly, taking her breath away. "Besides, I shouldn't like my warrior wife to find it dull living with me. As far as you're concerned, my girl, I give as good as I get!"

It was strange to feel such a strong liking for her old enemy as she did now. "I'm still one black eye to the good," she reminded him. "Perhaps it doesn't count," she added, "because I repented it almost at once. And it was partly your own fault. You practically dared me to hit you!"

"I can't say I thought you would," he retorted dryly. "You won't get through my defences as easily another time."

"I may not want to hit you again," she murmured.

"You will! *One little kiss*—that's all it takes with you, Georgie Porgie! But I'll tame you in the end. I'll have you eating out of my hand, a reformed character, you see if I don't!"

She was silent. Back in England she might have argued the point with him, mostly because she was afraid that she already liked the feeling of his hands on the reins far too well, but here it would have seemed strident and out of place to have denied the possibility that there might come a time when she wouldn't want to fight him—if that time wasn't already upon her.

One little kiss!

The memory of the brief kiss he had given her the evening before stirred her blood and she found herself speculating on her reactions if he should want more than a few kisses from her. The thought of it made her burn with an emotion she had never experienced before.

The Moslem women in the village they were passing through covered their heads with the loose folds of their saris, but they too were out in the street doing their shopping and standing in little groups exchanging the day's gossip. She felt very close to them. She felt very close to all women at that moment, for they too, some of them, had been caught up in the tide that held her in its grip for the first time in her life. They too knew what it was like to be submerged in a need for someone else— only why did it have to be *William*? How much easier life would be for her if she could have gone on hating him in peace!

"Kandy isn't far now. We'll stop there for lunch and go on to Nuwara Eliya afterwards," he told her.

"Is that where you're going to be working?"

"Fairly near. I'll be able to get back most nights. I was fortunate to be offered the use of this house on one of the tea plantations there. It'll be more comfortable for you and Celine than anything the site will be able to offer."

"I don't mind roughing it," Georgina asserted. "I don't want any favours from you!"

"You won't get many, but Celine deserves something better than the dust and grit of a dam in the building. Her father always gave her the best, and so shall I!"

Which meant that Georgina would be expected to do so too, she thought wryly. Oh well, it wouldn't be new to her to come second to someone else. What else had it ever been with Jennifer?

"Have you seen the house?" she asked, making conversation because she didn't want to be left to think her own thoughts an instant longer.

"No. I've only been to Sri Lanka once before and that was on a brief trip from a job I was doing in India. I thought I'd like to spend longer here, so I applied to help build this dam. I was very interested in the historic aspects of their irrigation systems here. They're absolutely fantastic!—and built long before our modern machinery came along. I want to make a study of how they were done, to see what we can learn from it. It's a pity they were so neglected later on, but the European conquerors weren't interested in rice or the hinterland, they were attracted by the cinnamon and other spices and weren't any too nice in their methods of getting as much of the stuff as possible. The 'bunds', as they call the dams here, and the 'tanks', or artificial lakes, fell into disrepair and are only being put right now. At one time Ceylon fed twice the population she has now and still had rice over for exporting, now she has to import about a third of what she eats. It's getting better, but they still have a long way to go to catch up with their own history."

"But surely nowadays—"

"Don't underrate the men of old," he said dryly. "We have the technology to do wonderful things nowadays, but have we the will? They lacked our machinery, but their deeds survive them to tell of their genius. We haven't yet built any comparable irrigation system in our time."

Georgina was impressed. "Was it very long ago?"

"I'm afraid it was. Europe had a long, long way to go in those days."

Georgina made a face. "I'm suitably chastened," she said. "Does it give you a good feeling to be treading in such august footsteps with your own project?"

He flushed absurdly, looking young and eager. "It does, but I hadn't expected you to understand something like that. You're a much more complicated person than I thought!"

"Perhaps we all are," she suggested. "I mean, I don't think I know you very well either. I thought I did, but we're strangers really, aren't we? First impressions aren't always the most accurate after all. How I hated you that day!"

He laughed. "It showed!" he said. "You've been try-ing to hate me ever since, haven't you?"

"Not more than you despised me. And I still hate you! I hate you every moment of every day!"

He slowed the car, his eyes flicking to her face and back to the road. "Who are you trying to convince, yourself or me?"

She clenched her fists and found one of them covered by his own, much larger hand. "I don't know what you mean," she declared. "I don't have to con-vince anyone about that! Ask anyone!"

"Funnily enough, I did. I asked my mother." His eyes flicked over her face again, noting the strain be-neath her hardly won composure. "Did you know she prefers you to your sister any day?"

"Yes."

"Ah, but did you know why?"

She shook her head, not trusting herself to speak.

"She thinks you have courage. I hope you're not go-ing to prove her wrong by continuing to insist you hate me, because you don't, do you, little Georgie? She doesn't think you ever have."

Georgina chewed frantically on her lower lip. "I don't like you!" she managed at last.

"Liking is a very pale emotion. It doesn't warm the blood—as I can warm yours any time I choose. *That's* something else!"

Georgina lifted her chin. "Any attractive man could do the same! It doesn't mean anything. I don't think it's anything to congratulate yourself about. It—it doesn't make me like you any more!"

"Nevertheless," he said with a smile she could only think would have done justice to the Bad Baron in a pantomime, "it gives me a great deal of pleasure to know I have you at my mercy—"

She trembled. Was it possible he knew of the strange

excitement that burned inside her whenever he came near? If he did, she would have to make it equally clear to him that she was ashamed of all such emotions. But how to do it?

"You're making far too much of very little! What makes you think I shall ever change my mind about you? I'll fight you to the last ditch! Just because you took me by surprise and—and *kissed* me, and I didn't *say* anything, it didn't mean I *liked* it!" She took a deep breath, preparing to hurry on with her castigations of his behaviour, but he seemed totally unperturbed. The hand that was covering hers patted her lightly on the knee.

"Took you by surprise? My dear girl, husbands are usually expected to kiss their wives. Indeed, the complaint is usually that they don't do it often enough!"

"In the normal way." She cast him a glowering look. "Ours isn't a normal marriage! Do you think I *want* to be kissed by someone who is obviously wishing I were somebody else? You should have put up more of a fight for Jennifer. Haven't you always thought of her as a nice, biddable girl? Well then, why didn't you make her change her mind about Duncan? She would have done if you'd pressed hard enough."

His lips twitched. "Somehow I prefer greater enthusiasm in my wife—"

"Then you shouldn't have married *me*!"

He grinned. "But I did marry you, my dear, and now I'm looking forward to the rewards of having done so."

She swallowed the lump in her throat, making a supreme effort to keep her voice light and airy. "What makes you think I shall be any more loyal than Jennifer?" she taunted him. "We are sisters, after all! And *I'm* not at all in love with you!"

His hand closed over hers, his fingers as hard as steel bands. "Try it and see what happens to you. I'm not the type of man who competes for the favours of his wife, Georgina, and you are my wife, whether you like it or not."

"Only because—"

"You can't argue your way out of this one, Mrs. Ayres. You're caught in a snare of your own making when you said the words that made you a wife. *My* wife!"

"I didn't have much choice," she protested, but there wasn't a great deal of conviction in her words. Nobody could have *made* her say the words, nobody but herself, so why had she?

"Your jealousy of Jennifer *made* you," he countered dryly. "You never count the cost when it comes to the long-standing rivalry between you! However, I'm not complaining. Haven't you promised me that you're better than she is?"

She flushed. "I only meant—" She broke off, finding it impossible to discuss with him whether she or Jennifer had the better figure. When one was loved such things hardly mattered, and if one was not loved it mattered even less.

"Yes?"

"I'm not jealous of Jennifer!" she protested in a whisper. "Why should I be? She hasn't anything I want and she never has had!"

"Not even the ability to attract every man in sight?" he put in dryly. "When she was around nobody ever looked twice at you, did they, Georgie, not unless you forced yourself on their attention with your fists! Going away to college should have given you the space to find yourself. I wonder why it didn't. Away from your sister, you're not as strident as you are in her company. When you hold on to that temper of yours you're quite an attractive girl. Why didn't you take the opportunity to make your own friends?"

She uttered a mirthless laugh, hunching up her shoulders and refusing to answer. How could she tell him that most of the friends she had shared with Jennifer had been hers in the first place? He would never believe that it wasn't she, but Jennifer, who had resented her popularity and had done everything she could to subvert her friends to herself. Georgina had never cared sufficiently to bother about her sister's activities, but now she wished she had. She would have liked to have flung half a dozen potential lovers in William's face! It would have given her a most rewarding pleasure to have flicked her fingers at him and gone off with somebody else—somebody who would have more charm in his little finger than William had in his whole body, a fact she would have brought home to him with the kind of insolent derision to which he frequently treated her!

When the haze of tears cleared from her eyes she found the car had stopped and they were parked in the centre of a town whose buildings could only have been built by the British but which, nevertheless, was completely foreign to the English high streets it so closely emulated. Of course the people who thronged the pavements could never have been English. There were the men, spare and narrow-hipped in their sarongs, and the women as bright as butterflies in their distinctive saris if they were rich enough to wear such a costume; some of them seemed to have no more than a much washed skirt, similar to those worn by the men, and a bolero top that accentuated their very feminine figures.

"Never mind," said William, "you have me now."

She jumped, wringing her hands together. "What?"

"You may have few friends, but you've landed yourself a husband, Georgie Porgie." He stroked her cheek with his forefinger. "Wake up, Madam wife, this is Kandy. Are you hungry?"

She stared at him, not really seeing him at all. "Really, William, how Victorian can you get? Madam wife, indeed!"

"Why not?" His smile forced a shiver up her spine. "I have very Victorian ideas about marriage. He for God only; she for God in him! It goes with the decor the British Raj left behind!"

"That was in India," she pointed out in husky tones. The shiver had settled into a space round her heart, increasing in intensity until she was afraid it would explode inside her. "Yes, let's go and eat! And may we stop for a while to see the Temple of the Tooth? Is it genuinely a tooth from Buddha himself? I'd love to see that!"

"A whole lot safer than crossing swords with your husband?" he suggested, mocking her hurried, breathless speech.

"Not at all! I'm hungry!"

He shrugged his shoulders. "Why not? The rest will keep until after you've met Celine."

Georgina's spirits deflated with all the speed of a pricked balloon. *Celine!* How could she have forgotten all about her, even for a moment?

"I suppose Celine is your Victorian romantic dream?" she murmured, and then almost immediately, "I shouldn't have said that. I'm sorry—only you did ask for me to say something nasty. You seem to enjoy getting me all riled up about nothing at all."

He studied her closely and she could feel herself colouring angrily under his regard. "I like to have my first impressions confirmed. They're not as inaccurate as you would like me to believe, my Georgie Porgie! You never miss an opportunity to rise and snap, do you? But be careful! There's a hook in the bait when you play such games with me. I always play to win and, unlike the Duncans of this world, I never, never cry!"

"You may do one day," she muttered, put out. "Everyone cries sometimes!"

His eyes narrowed. "I shouldn't bet on it."

She would have liked to have turned away and have talked about something else—anything, as long as it didn't mean they had to go on fighting. But she was far too stubborn to allow him to see she was worsted.

"Are you as nasty to poor Celine too?" she asked him, looking him straight in the eyes.

"You'll have to judge for yourself," he said, and added, "Celine doesn't answer back. She's all woman in that way, having learned that more victories are won with soft words by the fair sex. Why don't you try it some time?"

"I wouldn't be so patronising!"

He placed a finger across her lips, effectively silencing her. "Is that what it is? My, my, but you tempt me to teach you better! *All* is fair in love and war, my dear."

"And which is it in Celine's case?" she demanded, resisting the temptation to bite his finger. "I already know which it is with me!"

"Do you? I wonder?" He reached into the car for his coat and shut and locked the doors. "Come along and we'll eat! I'd like to show you the Temple today, Georgie, but we haven't any time to spare if we're to get to Nuwara Eliya before dark."

Georgina was unbearably disappointed. "Does it matter?" she pleaded.

He nodded. "It's raining in the hills and that may delay us considerably as it is. I'm sorry, my dear, but there'll be other times."

But she wouldn't be alone with him then, she thought, and wondered why it should be so important to her that she should have his full attention all to herself. She gave in with a good grace, however, accepting the inevitable with a gallant smile that he found touching in its insouciance. It was a little surprising too, he reflected, for he had always been led to believe that Georgina would bear a grudge for years, sulking over what everyone else had long forgotten. But this Georgina had courage, as his mother had suggested, and scorned to fight with weapons others might well have seized upon, fair or not. This Georgina had a tough, honest quality that he found he admired almost as much as it amused him.

They had lunch at a small local restaurant overlooking the lake which lends an air of enchantment to the whole city. William advised Georgina to follow his example and eat one of the curries that had pride of place on the menu. Georgina, who had a taste for hot, spicy foods, agreed readily and was delighted with the result. Half a dozen dishes were brought to their table, some of them familiar and some of them not, and she had an extremely agreeable half-hour tasting them all one by one.

William eyed her with a tolerant air. "I don't believe it's even occurred to you that you might upset your tummy with all this strange food," he observed.

"Why should it?"

"It has been known to. A change of germs more than a change of food probably, but the results are the same."

"Pooh," said Georgina. "A few germs? I won't allow them to get the better of me! I'm enjoying myself far too much!"

"I hope you're right," he said dryly.

The rain had already started when they left the restaurant. It was more low cloud that had got trapped between the hills than actual rain, but there was a distinct dampness in the air and the sun had completely disappeared for the day.

"It's still beautiful even in the rain," Georgina sighed, turning round in her seat to see the last of Kandy. "Did you see those gorgeous flowering trees? The university campus is full of them! I've never seen anything like it!"

"The mauve ones are jacaranda, the scarlet flamboyant—no, that one is a flame tree, I think. The pink ones are new to me too."

"And the bushes?" she asked eagerly.

"Bougainvillea. I can remember a time when they trailed over things, but they seem to have got them to stand up by themselves nowadays, and to come in so many colours that they're a feast to the eyes all by themselves." He pointed with a finger at another, darker tree in the middle distance. "There's an ebony tree."

Georgina sat back, contented. "It was worth coming just to see the flowers and the paddy fields and—and everything," she said.

"But it would be better still without me?"

Georgina was surprised by the question. She averted her face and stared out at the grey drizzle. "No, you make a good guide," she said grudgingly. "I wouldn't have known what anything was by myself."

"A good book could have told you."

She moved uncomfortably. "I never recognise flowers and birds in books. They always look different somehow."

He grimaced at the wet road ahead. "Well, thank you for that recommendation at least," he drawled. "It doesn't say much for my personal qualities though, does it?"

"You don't think much of mine," she retorted.

The rain grew steadily heavier as they climbed higher. It was strange to see the heavy grey skies dominating the countryside that always, in pictures, was bathed in eternal sunshine. The hairpin bends became more and more slippery too, demanding William's total concentration. Georgina was glad of the silence. She had thought the lower slopes spectacular, but the higher they went, the more beautiful it became. There were waterfalls everywhere and glistening white stupas of Buddhist temples hidden away in unexpected valleys. Sometimes, too, the heavily carved square towers that tapered inwards towards the top that marked the Hindu temples rose above the simple buildings of the villages, lending an exotic touch in contrast to the down-at-heel squalor of these high country villages. The Tamil workers, imported from South India for the back-breaking endless task of picking the tea, were the poorest people in the land, and it showed.

The tea factories were the largest buildings to be seen now. They all looked much the same, several stories high, with square, impersonal windows that gazed out across the miles of tea which surrounded them. Sometimes a plume of smoke rose from an asbestos pipe that served as a chimney, but on this wet, gloomy day few of the factories were working as hardly any tea had been picked.

"They'll be glad of the rain all the same," William said with satisfaction. "It's been a very dry wet season and tea needs a certain amount of moisture to flourish as it should." He went on to explain that the higher it grew the finer was the tea obtained. "But you'll find out all about that for yourself once you're settled in. Some of the best tea in the world is produced on the plantation where we're living."

Georgina looked at the green bushes with renewed interest. It was funny how one took things for granted, she thought, recollecting the number of times she had made the tea at home without ever giving a thought as to how it was grown and prepared before it arrived on the shelf of the nearby supermarket.

"Jennifer doesn't like tea," she said, apropos of nothing.

William favoured her with a blank stare. "Jennifer isn't here to dislike it right now. Can't you leave her where she is, at home in England?"

Georgina pulled in her lower lip, looking away from him. "Can you?"

"Easily." He changed down to negotiate a particularly awkward corner. "Have a look at the map, will you? I think we're nearly there."

Georgina did as she was told, but the criss-crossing black lines on the plain white paper seemed to bear little relation to the road they were on.

"It's so smudged," she said, "it's impossible to tell where we are. Is this the best map you've got?"

"The only one." He stopped the car and took it from her, huffing and puffing over the almost illegible names. "Not much help, is it?"

Georgina pointed hopefully ahead. "Let's go on and hope for a signpost," she suggested.

He shrugged, putting the map back on her knee. "We'll try it," he agreed.

They rounded the next corner to be faced by a very English scarlet letter-box, bearing the insignia of Queen Victoria. There was nothing else, not so much as a single house, anywhere near it. William got out of the car, pulling his collar up against the rain, and went to take a closer look at it. He came back almost immediately.

"We're here," he announced. "I reckon the entrance must be just along the road."

And so it proved. A tree-lined earth road led several miles through the tea gardens, went past a Hindu temple made of corrugated iron down below, but with a truly handsome painted and elaborately carved tower that marked it unmistakably for what it was. Beyond were the lines, where the Tamil workers lived. To

Georgina's relief they seemed to be better housed on this estate than most of the others they had seen. And then, when they were least expecting it, the grey stone house, set in a charming English-style garden, came into sight and a few moments later they were drawing up outside the porch that sheltered the front door.

The doors were flung open and a servant came out with an umbrella to usher them into the house.

"Tea is waiting for you in the drawing-room, sir, madam," he murmured to them. "The two ladies are waiting for you there."

Georgina hung back, regretting the loss of the intimacy of the interior of the car. Here, in a strange house among strange people, would she ever have William to herself again? But even as she was wishing herself back on the rain-sodden road, a young girl every bit as fair as Jennifer but much, much more beautiful came rushing across the polished floor and flung herself into William's arms.

"Darling William, this is some bungalow!" She kissed him warmly, arching her body against his as a cat does when it winds itself about one's legs. "I thought you were never coming! Am I still the prettiest girl you know?" This last was said in such soft, seductive tones that Georgina blushed for her.

"You're still the most beautiful by far!" William answered laughing. "Now, calm down and say hullo to Georgina, minx."

Celine looked straight through Georgina, her eyes completely blank. "Who is she? Why did you have to bring her here, William?"

William patted the girl's shoulder, a great sadness crossing his face.

"Georgina is my wife," he said.

CHAPTER SIX

Miss Campbell was tall and statuesque with one of the ugliest faces Georgina had ever seen. It wasn't any particular feature that ruined her looks, but an unfortunate combination of them all, coupled with a colouring that was sallow to the point of being yellow.

She remained seated as the party moved into the drawing-room from the hall. Indeed, she barely looked up as they entered, preferring to continue a rather high-pitched conversation with the only other occupant of the room, a young man who was standing behind the comfortable sofa on which she was sitting, nursing a cup of tea.

"You underrate her understanding," he was saying angrily.

"Do I?" Miss Campbell rejoined. "Then what am I doing here?"

"I've been wondering that ever since you both arrived." His tea-cup rattled precariously as he changed it from one hand to the other. "You never let her out of your sight!"

"That's what Miss Campbell is paid for," William said dryly from the doorway. "You are speaking of Celine, I take it?"

The young man stood his ground. "She's not a child! Why discuss her as if she were?" He looked from William to Georgina. "Is this another gaoler for her?"

"I hope not!" Georgina exclaimed.

The young man managed a smile. "I'm sorry," he said, "but it makes me angry to see wild animals confined in cages."

Celine appeared pleased by this. "Am I a wild animal?" she demanded eagerly. "Stuart, am I?"

The young man tousled her hair. "A very beautiful one!"

"Wild animals are dangerous!"

He grinned at her. "Are you dangerous?"

Celine lowered her lashes, peeping at him through them. "Not with you, darling Stuart. *Never* with you!"

William cut her off with a brusqueness that Georgina thought both unnecessary and unkind. "Celine, behave yourself! I don't want to forbid Stuart to come to the house—"

"What nonsense!" Georgina put in hastily. She moved closer to Stuart herself. "I'm Georgina Perry," she said, holding out her hand to him.

He shook it gravely. "Mrs. Ayres," he corrected her, amused by the slip. "My name is Stuart Duffield. I work here on the estate."

"He's the most important person here!" Celine claimed. "They couldn't do anything without him!"

Georgina raised her brows in silent enquiry and the young man laughed. "I'm the fellow who tastes the tea," he explained. "Every estate has one who makes sure that the tea doesn't undergo any process for too long, thus spoiling it. It's a bit like wine tasting. They'll be getting a local chap in to do my job before long, but meanwhile, I enjoy it here. The manager is a good friend of mine. You must meet him and his wife as soon as I can arrange it. His name is Peter, Peter Kotalawala."

"He has an English name because he's a Catholic," Celine chimed in. "His wife is sweet!"

"Only because she allows you to do as you like,"

Miss Campbell said with menace. "She has no control over you at all!"

"She's not my keeper. She's not a spoilsport either." Celine turned a blank stare on Georgina. "What are you?"

Georgina opened her mouth to answer, but William did it for her. "She's my wife," he said.

"And too pretty to be a spoilsport," Stuart added.

"She's not as beautiful as I am!" Celine spat at him, annoyed.

"No one could be that," he agreed cheerfully. "But beauty isn't everything, duckie. Georgina is very much my type!" He flashed a meaning look at the surprised Georgina. "Pity she's already taken!"

Celine was furious. "You mean you prefer Georgina to me?" she demanded.

"It's a different thing. You can't compare the two. You're my friend; Georgina—well, she could be something else!"

Georgina swallowed hard, not daring to look in William's direction. "No, she couldn't be!" she stammered out. "I couldn't!"

To her surprise William laughed. "You're embarrassing my wife," he said wryly to Stuart. "She isn't accustomed to compliments from the opposite sex. You'll have to go easily with her."

Georgina could have stamped her foot with sheer, unreasoning rage. Did he have to make it so blatant that she had no attraction for him? And how could one deny such a slight? She couldn't insist that she had had her share of compliments without sounding a boastful fool, and yet it hurt to let his disparagement go by as if it meant nothing to her. The trouble was that she wanted William's regard, wanted it badly, and was in danger of getting everything else out of perspective in consequence.

Happily, Stuart shook his head in stunned disbelief. "What's wrong with the men back home?" he wondered.

Georgina forced a wavering smile. "I have a sister—"

"And she takes everyone's eye?" Stuart whistled in derision. "She didn't take your husband's, did she, or you wouldn't be here!"

Georgina's heightened colour and obvious distress was an answer in itself. She saw the baffled expression on Stuart's face and wished the ground would open and swallow her up before she was forced ot hear William's rejoinder. Would he admit that she was only his wife as second best?

"Jennifer has the looks, Georgina the character," William said steadily.

"I wish more people thought that way," Miss Campbell approved. "But there, most people waste their time spoiling the beautiful while we plainer mortals have to make do with the crumbs. Mrs. Ayres is lucky to have found a perceptive man who doesn't think beauty is everything—"

"Am I so ugly?" Georgina burst out.

"Not in my book!" Stuart replied promptly. "Some kinds of beauty are extraordinarily dull, and you would never be that! Give me warmth and generosity any time!" He bowed with a play-acting formality to Georgina, his hand on his heart. "You're my ideal woman, Mrs. Ayres. Call on me any time!"

She made him a curtsey. "Thank you, Mr. Duffield, I'll bear it in mind."

"You'll do nothing of the sort!" William's anger was as unexpected as it was forceful. "Shall we change the subject before one of us says something we'll regret? Perhaps you, Miss Campbell, would be good enough to show my wife round the bungalow. You stay here, Celine. I want to talk to you!"

Celine smiled sunnily up at him. "I want to go with Georgie! Stuart isn't the only one who likes her—I like her too. *She* won't make me do things I don't want to do!"

"I shouldn't be too sure of that," William retorted.

Georgina held her head high. "My husband thinks I'm a bully too," she said to no one in particular. "I think it's because I succeeded in giving him a black eye not long ago. You can still see the remains of it if you look carefully."

It was Stuart who laughed. "A nice plush one! What a girl!"

William grinned reluctantly. "She won't do it again. We have better things to do nowadays."

What a pity he didn't mean it, Georgina thought, and wondered why it should hurt so much that he didn't. She smothered a sigh and turned to Miss Campbell, whose look of pure hatred caught her unawares. Why? she wondered. Why should Miss Campbell dislike her with such intensity?

"Come this way, Mrs. Ayres," the older woman bade her. "We've prepared the master suite for you and your husband. It looks over the garden with the tea gardens in the distance. I hope you'll like it."

Georgina was astonished by the magnificence of the house. To call such a dwelling a bungalow seemed to her to verge on the ridiculous. Each of the bedrooms she glanced into was spacious and beautifully fitted out, but the master suite was out of this world. There were two bedrooms, one feminine and flouncy, the other decorated with a more masculine restraint, joined together by a bathroom full of solid, Edwardian equipment such as she had never seen before.

"The water doesn't often get hot," Miss Campbell sniffed, "and, as you can see, the roof leaks, but I suppose one can't expect anything else so far from civilisation. Seeing that you're practically on your honeymoon, I don't suppose you'll notice our inconveniences, but I'm used to something better, I can tell you. I've given up a great deal to stay with Celine, poor child! I knew her father very well, but I suppose Mr. Ayres will have told you all about that?"

Georgina frowned. "No, he hasn't said much. What a lovely place this is! What about Celine's father?"

"I was called his housekeeper, but of course, I was much more than that. It was a tragedy when he died."

"It must have been." Georgina sat down on the edge of the bed. "Did you know Celine's mother?" she asked.

Miss Campbell went a mottled red. "That bitch? Celine takes after her. She hadn't a moral to her name!"

Georgina froze her with a look. "Nevertheless, she was married to Celine's father and you—were not."

"If you care to put it that way. He was well rid of her!"

Georgina looked down at her shoes. "Were you in the fire too?"

"I got out. I was lucky. Celine was got out too."

"But her mother died."

Miss Campbell shrugged. "I wasn't going back inside for her. She deserved to die."

"No one deserves to die in a fire like that," Georgina said gently. "Miss Campbell, are you sure you're the right person to care for the daughter of someone you hated so much? It must be difficult to be constantly seeing her mother in Celine."

"It doesn't matter with Celine. The child's simple, or hadn't you noticed? No man will ever make the mistake of marrying her!"

"I hope you're wrong, Miss Campbell. Meanwhile I have nothing to do with my time and I rather want to look after Celine myself. I imagine you could get another job quite easily?"

"You're asking me to go?"

Georgina looked her straight in the eyes. "I'm telling you to go, Miss Campbell. Shall we say a month's notice and an extra month's pay at the end of that to tide you over until you find something else?"

Miss Campbell made a strangled sound. "We'll see what Mr. Ayres has to say about that! You won't get rid of me so easily, my fine madam! You'll never get rid of me!"

"We'll see." Georgina crossed her fingers surreptitiously, praying that William would back her up and insist that the woman went. He had said he wanted to be rid of her, but not, perhaps, the minute of their arrival.

"You'll have to persuade Celine too," Miss Campbell said, her twisted smile more confident. "You've yet to see her in one of her states. It isn't a pretty sight and I very much doubt if you could cope with her single-handed as I've been expected to do these last years. We shall see, Mrs. Ayres, whether I go or not after you've had to put up with her screaming for hours together. We'll see if you change your mind then!"

Georgina could only think how much she disliked this woman. "I shan't."

Miss Campbell tossed her head. "Very sure of ourselves, aren't we? Well, you won't find Mr. Ayres at all pleased by this day's work, young lady. *He* knows my value and remunerates me accordingly, and *I* didn't have to put myself out to attract him either! What did you offer him? A young, nubile body—"

"And a black eye," Georgina muttered under her breath.

A look of venom crossed Miss Campbell's face. "Poor Georgie Porgie, did she hope to wear the trousers and did she get a shock when she found her William has a mind of his own?"

"No, Miss Campbell, I did not. I've known William since I was ten years old, so I think I may be said to know exactly what he's like. Nor do I relish being called Georgie Porgie—"

"*He* calls you that!"

"He has privileges I don't accord to anyone else!" Georgina snapped. She felt both exasperated and weary. "Please go away!"

"Very well, Mrs. Ayres, but I shall be speaking to *Mr.* Ayres about this, you may be sure!"

"About what?" William asked, coming into the bedroom through the bathroom door.

Absurdly, Georgina felt guilty at the sight of him. "It doesn't matter now," she began.

Miss Campbell folded her hands across her stomach, bridling with displeasure. "Your—*wife* has taken it upon herself to give me notice, sir. She seems to think she can manage Celine all by herself! She has also been unpardonably rude, but I can hardly expect you to defend me from that now, can I? A strong-minded young lady, if you don't mind my saying so! She'd have us all bending to that will of hers if we allowed it, and that's the last thing Celine needs, as you very well know. I may be exceeding my duties, sir, but I will not have that poor girl bullied—not while I'm still in charge of her welfare!"

William's face froze. "She won't be, Miss Campbell. I will see to that. Please leave us alone now, will you?"

"Of course, sir. But I should like to know whether I am to be dismissed or not? Mrs. Ayres—"

"The decision is mine, Miss Campbell. It's true I've been thinking Celine might benefit from being treated more like anyone else than is possible when she is in the constant care of one used to very young children, but I've yet to make up my mind as to what future arrangements I shall be making for her. I'll let you know."

"Yes, sir. Thank you, sir."

Georgina made a face at her departing back. "Three bags full, sir!"

"*Georgina*! I warned you—"

"You said you wanted to be rid of her!"

"Not if you're going to bully Celine in her stead. I won't have it, Georgie. What have you been saying to that woman?"

Georgina checked the hot words that threatened to pour from her. Losing her temper would not help her now. She spread her hands, wishing she were less vulnerable to his opinion of her.

"I gave her a month's notice. Apparently she doesn't think I have the right to employ whom I please in my own household, but I thought you'd back me up over this at least! She's a horrible woman and can't be doing Celine any good. Nor was I rude to her—not until she called me Georgie Porgie. I won't stand for that!"

"Was that all?" She could tell he didn't believe her and she was doubly hurt that he should prefer the word of that dragon of a woman. "It wasn't, was it?"

Georgina sighed. "She said Celine has crying fits when she screams for hours together. But why does she have them, William? There must be some reason for her to behave like that. She was sunny enough when we arrived just now."

"Hmm. She didn't like it when Stuart obviously preferred yourself to her."

"Oh, that." Georgina dismissed Stuart Duffield with an airy wave. "She knew he wasn't serious. With her looks, she'll never have to worry about competition in that department!"

"She's too young in herself to worry about things

like that,'' William answered. ''Thank goodness that she is! We've problems enough without her getting ideas about boyfriends or marriage!''

''Why shouldn't she?'' Georgina asked. ''Her body is quite grown up and there doesn't seem to be all that wrong with her mind. If she talks like a child, couldn't that be having to live with that impossible Miss Campbell?''

William put his hands on his hips and glared at her. ''D'you think you can do better?''

Georgina nodded. She pressed her lips together and straightened her shoulders. ''I'd like to try.''

Exasperation gave way to a more hopeful expression. ''Yes, but, Georgie, it won't do to bully her. You have to admit that Miss Campbell was pretty quick to sum you up. Celine wants a more gentle touch than yours. Jennifer—''

''Jennifer isn't here and I am! I think I can make Celine like me—I think she does already!—and I can't think Miss Campbell is the answer to anything. Where did Celine's father find her?''

''She found him. She's the old retainer type, devoted and selfless, though I have to admit I find her rather trying too.''

Georgina slanted a look up at him. ''I think she was in love with him,'' she hazarded. ''She certainly hated Celine's mother.''

''Rubbish, my dear. The Miss Campbells of this world can't afford the luxury of falling in love with their employers. They know nothing will come of it.''

''Knowing doesn't always have the desired effect,'' Georgina remarked wryly. Knowing that William was in love with Jennifer hadn't stopped her falling for him. Hope could survive on very little encouragement, or even none at all. ''William, I know my opinion doesn't count for much, but she was telling me about Celine's mother's death. She was in that fire too, but she didn't go back for that poor woman. Perhaps the fire was already too bad, but supposing it wasn't. I wouldn't put it past her to have stood by and watched her rival die." She shuddered. "Worse still, she says Celine is just like her mother. If she hated the mother so much, how does she feel about the daughter?"

William sat down on the bed beside her. "My dear little Georgie, how your imagination runs away with you! What do you want me to do? Tell the old harridan to go? Celine can be quite a responsibility, you know. She has frequent nightmares and she can be spiteful if you cross her. Are you sure you want to take on all that single-handed?"

Georgina looked at him, her eyes pleading for something she thought he didn't have it in him to give. "If I have your support," she said. "I thought you'd back me up with Miss Campbell, but you didn't. Okay, I know you don't trust me not to impose my ideas on other people, but you owe it to me to pretend we're a team in public. Or is that too much to ask?"

William's face softened. "I can't afford to make a mistake, Georgie, not with someone as helpless as Celine. But I promise you, I'll back you all the way for as long as you restrain your tendencies to play the bully. Play fair with me and I'll play fair with you, but if you once try to manipulate that girl to suit yourself, I'll take you apart, piece by piece! Try a little feminine gentleness and see what wonders that works for you!"

"Try leaving me alone and see what that does!" she snapped back.

His expression changed to one of amusement. "But I have no intention of leaving you alone, my pet. *That's* what I came in here to talk to you about." He studied the stubborn lines of her face for a moment. "Aren't you interested?" he enquired.

"Should I be?"

"Most brides are."

"But I'm not most brides! And I'm not Jennifer— I'm *me*!"

His amusement increased. "You're you and you won't change, is that it?"

"People don't change much," she sighed, "and you won't allow me to change the image you have of me, not that I care what you think! You always were prejudiced against me."

His eyebrows rose. "Was I?" He leaned closer. "Shall we call a truce until we've settled down into being man and wife?"

"You never play fair!" she complained.

"A truce," he said dryly, "binds both parties, Georgie Porgie. Come on, love, give a little bit! I don't want to have you in tears every time I kiss you, and I mean to kiss you frequently in the near future. You are my wife after all."

"You don't have to remind me of that! What a prize— to be the despised wife of Mr. William Ayres, the man who's never wrong about anything! Well, you can take whatever you feel you have a right to, but if I want to cry, I'll cry all the time, and *you* won't be able to stop me!"

"It sounds like a lachrymose evening," he drawled. He rolled away from her across the bed and went across the room to stare out of the window. "You can always try and make me cry instead?" he invited her.

"That'll be the day! You don't care a toss what I do, or how I feel. You never have!"

He turned quickly. "Should I be shedding tears over your fate, my Georgie? Are your tears shed for me rather than for yourself?"

She didn't know how to answer. She made a gesture of defeat. "I don't expect love, but you're not even kind! Nor do I think making love should be reduced to a legal obligation.''

"Good lord!" he exclaimed. "What do you expect? Bells ringing and violins playing off stage? Surely you, with your vast experience, must know it just doesn't happen like that?''

She ignored his sarcasm, wishing she had a small part of the experience he credited her with. "Perhaps you've never had the right partner," she struck out at him. She cowered away from the glint in his eyes, wishing herself anywhere else but there. "If you had, you wouldn't behave as though it were nothing more than sharing a cup of tea!''

"Well, if one's wife isn't the right partner, who is?'' he demanded softly, advancing towards her with such steely purpose that she shivered despite herself.

"One's beloved," she insisted.

He came to a stop in front of her, their knees touching, and looked down at her, his eyes burning a deep gold. He was even larger than she had remembered, standing over her like that, and he looked more than capable of holding his own in any battle with her. Not that she would be putting up much of a fight, for she had never felt more weak and feminine, with a tingling fear that might have been mistaken for joyful anticipation of the coming struggle. Was it possible that she wanted to lose to him?

"William, we have to go back to the others! Please don't! Not *now*!''

"Why not now?" He sounded triumphant and very much in control of the situation.

"I'm not ready—'' By contrast her own voice was ragged and unsteady. "I'm tired and—and I'm hungry too.''

"Are you now?" He swept her up on to her feet and into the circle of his arms. She looked up at him fearfully and was astonished to find he was smiling. "You seem smaller than ever. You fight like a heavyweight, so it comes as a constant surprise to find you such a small handful!"

"I haven't any shoes on," she found herself explaining, "and I stopped growing a long, long time ago, so I doubt I'll grow any larger—"

"I expect I'll get used to it in time," he mocked her. His hand went to the collar of her dress and trailed an intimate line down to the hollow between her breasts. He unbuttoned the first button, and then another, ignoring her hesitant attempts to prevent him. "Where's all that experience you were boasting about now?"

She clenched her fists, battering them against his chest. The blows wouldn't have hurt a fly and despair mingled with a burgeoning excitement that threatened to betray her into openly inviting his caresses. Even so, she was unprepared for the moment when he bent his head and his lips claimed hers with a force that made her glad of the strength of the arm that held her close up against him. She made a last, feeble protest before flinging her arms round his neck with an abandonment that would have shocked her to the core at any other time.

The harsh urgency of his kisses bewildered her as much as her own response, awakened new emotions she had never known existed inside her. When he pushed her gently back on to the bed, she clung to him as if her life depended on it.

"Don't go!" she flung at him. She buried her fingers into the hair at the nape of his neck and arched her body invitingly against his.

"I'm not going anywhere, my sweet." He stripped off his shirt in a single movement and took her back into his arms. "I want my wife and, it would seem, she wants me too! I can't say I believed I'd ever think you

lovelier than Jennifer, but you have a beautiful body."
His mouth travelled from her lips to her breasts and
back again, smiling deep into her eyes. "Aren't you
going to kiss me too?"

She shook her head. "I can't."

She felt his laughter rather than heard it. "All those
claims, my dear little Georgina, and you're as innocent
as a young girl. Confess, you've never felt like this before, have you?"

She shook her head again. "I've never—"

He turned her face gently towards his, exploring her
mouth with his own. "Never? Oh, Georgina! Why
didn't you say so before?"

"You didn't ask me."

He leaned up on his elbow, smoothing her hair away
from her face. "I still mean to have you, Georgie
Porgie. I'll be as gentle as I can—"

His words were cut off by a yell of anguish from
some other part of the bungalow. It came again and
again, rending the air with its piteous sound.

"Celine!"

Georgina felt cold with shock. "Celine? But it
doesn't sound human! William, why?"

He pushed her away from him. "How should I
know? I'd better go to her. Sometimes, if one gets in
early enough, one can stop her before she really gets
started. You'd better get dressed too."

Georgina pulled her clothes together with a heightened colour. "If I'm going to look after her I ought to
go to her now," she insisted. "Poor girl! She sounds as
though she's having a terrible nightmare, as if she's
really asleep. I wish we could wake her up!"

"To her it's a nightmare, a nightmare of fire and
death, but she won't talk about it. She never has."

They went together to Celine's private sitting-room,
where the girl sat for long hours on her own, refusing

any company or occupation, preferring to spend her time staring with unseeing eyes into space. Now she was struggling to get away from Miss Campbell, who was attempting to calm her.

"I won't! I won't!" she was screaming. "I won't tell them anything!"

Miss Campbell looked grim. "Who would believe such nonsense? No one has ever seen a demon a hundred and twenty feet high, you stupid girl! Certainly not one with the head of a bear! I never heard such nonsense!"

"It was there!" roared Celine. "I saw it! It had a thing like an elephant in its hand—an elephant-shaped cup! And then there was the fire again!"

Georgina pushed Miss Campbell to one side, taking the girl into her own arms. "Shall we look for this demon together?" she asked her, hugging her tight. "It's all right, Celine. I believe you!"

"It won't be there now," Celine sobbed. "It never is. Before, it was something else, but now it wears a mask and it drinks blood. I couldn't have imagined that, could I?"

"No," said Georgina carefully, "I don't think you could."

Celine stopped yelling, amazed by this reaction. "Nobody ever believed me before!" she sobbed. "Never! Never! Only I've seen a demon like this one before. He was *horrible*!"

Georgina's eyes met her husband's. "William will find out his name and, when you know who he is, you won't be afraid of him any longer," she promised soothingly. "I'm sure he has a name."

"They never have names!" Miss Campbell snapped.

"The first one did," William remembered, sounding surprised himself. "The first one was an Aborigine character."

Miss Campbell sniffed. "She shouldn't be encouraged in her fancies, sir. If you ask me, she frightens herself deliberately. I've no sympathy with her!"

"So I've noticed, Miss Campbell," William returned smoothly. "Happily, it seems that my wife has. Shall we leave her to finish calming Celine by herself? We would be better employed discussing the terms of your notice, I believe."

Miss Campbell turned venomous eyes on to Georgina's startled face. "You'll regret it!" she spat out. "You'll both regret it!"

CHAPTER SEVEN

The atmosphere at dinner was decidedly frosty. Georgina tried to tell herself that the depression was centred on Miss Campbell, but it was finally borne in on her that Miss Campbell was completely herself again, as was Celine, and the only person who seemed to be suffering from reaction after the scenes of a couple of hours earlier was herself.

She did her best to respond to Celine's overtures of friendship, but all she really wanted to do was to escape from the lot of them, to shut herself in her room and to howl herself to sleep.

"What are those masks in the hall?" she asked the girl—unwisely, she thought, the second the words had left her mouth.

"There's a whole craft industry centred round them in Sri Lanka," Celine told her shyly. "Do you like them?"

Georgina wondered how to answer. "They're very colourful," she said guardedly.

"I like them," Celine volunteered. "I like the small ones and the ones that don't move. They're different from—from—" Her mouth quivered and she looked fearfully across the table at Miss Campbell.

"Madam shouldn't have reminded you," Miss Campbell reproached Georgina. "Now, now, chicken! You don't want to water down your soup with your tears, do you? You get on with your food, my dear, and forget all about your little adventure. We don't want you having nightmares in the night, do we?"

The blankness came back into Celine's eyes. "The moon is getting full now," she said.

"That's right, dear. *Girls and boys, come out to play, The moon doth shine as bright as day!*"

A brand new suspicion crossed Georgina's mind. She turned impulsively towards her husband. "Did you know Miss Campbell when you were fifteen?" she demanded.

His lips twitched. "No, that was my own inspiration," he answered. "It was a long time ago, Georgie. Isn't it time you forgave me for that?"

"Never!" She glared at him, but a little giggle inside her betrayed her. "It wasn't funny, William. It wasn't at all funny for me!"

"You made far too much of it—then and now."

"*You* didn't have to listen to that dreadful rhyme being whispered by all and sundry every time you appeared anywhere. It hurt badly for years and years, especially as I was only trying to defend Jennifer from that little creep. It hurt terribly! I'd liked you up until that moment, you see, and then that had to happen!"

"My dear girl, you didn't like me at all! You were as prickly as a hedgehog."

"I was ten years old."

He smiled slowly. "Is that an explanation or an excuse?"

She smiled too. "You were so large. It never occurred to me that you might be feeling out of place at a children's party. All I was thinking about was how much I hoped you'd like me! You had a beautiful bicycle and I wanted to go for a ride on it. I thought you might take me upon the crossbar—"

"I invited you for a ride later on," he reminded her. "You refused."

She flushed, looking young enough to be ten years old all over again. "I had to refuse! I didn't want to have anything to do with you after—after coming out with *that*!"

"It could have been worse, my dear. I might have said: *There was a little girl who had a little curl, Right in the middle of her forehead. When she was good, she was very, very good, But when she was bad, she was horrid!*"

"That wouldn't have done the same damage," Georgina said at once. "I wouldn't have minded that half so much."

"Why not?" he asked, intrigued.

"That could have been anyone, the other one everyone knew to be me!"

He shrugged, losing interest. "You do have a little curl, though. You had it then, and you have it now. Mother used to refer to it as your 'kiss-curl'. You have pretty hair, Georgie Porgie, even if it does lead a life of its own. It never stays put like Jennie's does."

Georgina could have told him that she didn't use hair lacquer as her sister did, but she didn't. She sighed instead, wondering rather bleakly if there would ever come a time when he would cease to compare her with Jennifer all the time. She glanced out of the window at the steadily falling rain and took consolation from the thought that her sister would have hated everything about the bungalow and the sodden scenery. Jennifer was a fair-weather person in all senses of the word. She hated wet weather as much as she hated having to put herself out on another's behalf. Nobody could be more pleasant while everything was going well, but when she was crossed nobody was safe from her ire.

"It's all right," she muttered inelegantly. "It suits me as it is."

His eyes mocked her. "It certainly does!" he agreed. Celine came suddenly to life, pointing her knife at

Georgina in a manner which caused Miss Campbell to click her tongue disapprovingly. "Georgie Porgie ran away when the others tried to play! Did you run away, Georgina?"

"Not she!" William said on a laugh. "She gave them all a bloody nose!"

"*I did not!*" Temper flared inside Georgina. "You and Duncan were the only two—ever!"

"The others must have been wise enough to keep their distance!" William taunted her.

To everyone's surprise and to her own consternation, her eyes brimmed with tears and they ran unchecked down her cheeks. She wiped them away with an angry hand, ashamed of displaying such weakness before her tormentor. But he was already on his feet, standing over her with his arm round her shoulders.

"Georgina, you little fraud! You've never cared before when I teased you! What did I say?"

"Nothing, nothing at all!" she sniffed dismally. "I *like* being told how unattractive I am!"

Celine's eyes were as round as saucers. "Georgina's crying!" she announced. "Nobody ever cries here but me!"

"I'm sorry," Georgina muttered.

"I think you're nice!" Celine crowed. "You can't help being in love with William. Most married people fall in love—Stuart told me so. He says I'll fall in love one day and I won't have any more nightmares." Her face flickered with a new anxiety. "But I don't want to cry about it, I want to be happy! Why doesn't William make you happy?"

"He does," Georgina claimed, her voice muffled by her hand.

"Do I?" There was a note in William's voice Georgina had never heard before. "Then what are you crying about?"

Her face crumpled. How could she possibly tell him that? She scrubbed angrily at her cheeks and fell back on the oldest excuse in the business. "I'm tired and I have a headache!"

He pushed the curl back from her forehead. "Crying won't make you feel any better, my sweet. Why don't you skip the rest of dinner and go to bed?"

Georgina was very conscious of Miss Campbell's silent contempt, pointing out the inadequacies of the new mistress of the household as eloquently as if she had enumerated them one by one.

"I can't understand it!" Georgina said on a desperate note. "I don't usually cry at all!"

Celine stabbed her knife excitedly in the air. "You're pregnant!"

"I can't be!" Georgina wailed.

"Not yet," William confirmed, failing to control a yelp of laughter. "Celine, behave yourself! You're embarrassing my bride of a couple days!"

"Is that all it is?" Georgina murmured, surprised. "It feels much longer."

"An old married lady!" William mocked her, but there was a new gentleness in his voice that made her heart thump so hard she felt quite faint.

"It feels like for ever!" she moaned.

The glint in his eyes was for her alone. "It is for ever! Off you go, my sweet. Sleep tight."

Once she was in her room, however, she didn't know what to do with herself. The sound of the rain on the roof was like distant applause and oddly soothing to her. She tried to tell herself that the rain was doing the tea a tremendous amount of good, but she didn't really care. She liked the noise it made and that was enough for her. For a few moments she sat on the edge of her bed and made herself think about William. It took all her determination and concentration not to dwell on the good bits and ignore the bad. She wanted to live again those few minutes she had spent in his arms before Celine had started screaming. Then she remembered that even then he had had Jennifer in his mind, though for once she had come out of the comparison the winner in her husband's eyes. Never had she longed more for the delicate, fair beauty of her sister than now! Just for once it would have been nice to have been Mount Everest looking down on Snowdon, instead of the other way round. Or, better still, to have been the only person in the world for William for a little while, instead of always being an also-ran, tagging along behind his greater desire for her sister.

She picked up her night things and went into the bathroom. The light spluttered and flared when she switched it on and a long peal of thunder warned of a coming storm. Hastily she switched the light off again, afraid that the whole system would blow up when she saw the stream of water that was running down the walls. There was no hot water. It was very nearly the last straw, but she calmed herself and washed as well as she could in cold water and in the dark. Thoughts of various horrid insects she had read come out of their corners in tropical rain-storms happily remained only on the fringes of her mind. What she couldn't see, she wouldn't believe in!

But she did see the gigantic shape that fleetingly went past the window. She was rooted to the spot in horror. It was taller than the house and made a peculiar rattling noise as it passed.

She flung open the window and saw it again, disappearing down the tree-lined driveway. To her relief she saw it was nothing to be afraid of after all. It was nothing more than a gigantic stuffed scarecrow with a mask instead of a head.

"Hey there!" she yelled out of the window.

The masked figure wavered to a stop and then came slowly back towards the bungalow. "Excuse me, madam. Did you want me or something?"

"Yes. What are you doing with that thing?"

A thin, wiry man stepped from under the plaited figure. "Excuse me, madam, someone take it away. I take it back again."

Georgina eyed the figure with distaste. "What is it?"

"Mahasona, madam."

"It's hideous!"

"Oh yes, madam, but it mean nothing nowadays." The tone was so soothing that Georgina suspected that the man wasn't half as sure about that as he pretended to be. "We need it for the dance. This is the demon Mahasona. He gives you bad stomach, make you very ill—cholera, dysentery. Very bad demon!" He smiled with an effusiveness he obviously hoped would soften Georgina's stony expression. "After the dance he go away and everyone keep well!"

"I hope so," Georgina observed. "But surely you're not going to dance now, in this rain?"

The man shook his head. "The dance is finished, but someone took Mahasona away. Nobody mind that—but, excuse me, madam, the mask is very valuable. It is very old. It has always been used in my village. Now we don't know if the dance work." He looked up into the skies. "The rain brings bad stomachs, madam."

"Will you hold the dance all over again?" Georgina asked him. If Celine were to see this plaited demon for herself, perhaps she would lose her fear of it.

"No, madam. Did madam wish to see the dance?"

Georgina nodded. "I thought most of the dances were held down at the coast?"

"They dance too," he agreed vaguely. He picked up the huge figure of the demon, now collapsing against the stick that formed its backbone. "Come to the temple, madam. We make *puja*, very strong against this demon. Madam has no need to be afraid!"

Madam was not afraid. Madam was extremely angry, on the other hand. No wonder Celine had been frightened out of her wits!

"Is it heavy?" she asked suddenly. "Could I carry it?"

The man grinned through the open window. "Madam wishes to try?"

She climbed through the window without a second thought and struggled to hold the grips that the man pointed out to her. It was only then that she saw there were cords too that were attached to the mask and that when they were manipulated, the mask opened and shut, rolling its eyes and poking out its tongue. It was a horrible sight indeed in the almost total darkness. The whites, or yellows, showed up against the blackness of the reds and greens that only showed when they caught the light from her bedroom window. The tongue was like a snake's and, sure enough, there was a faint resemblance in the face to a bear which, coupled with the elephant-shaped head that was attached to it, was one of the most hideous sights Georgina had ever seen.

"Why, anyone could lift this," she remarked. "I wonder who did?"

"Very bad thing, madam."

"Very!" she retorted with feeling. "I'd like to see it again in the light of day. Would your village mind?"

"No, Madam. Mr. Kotalawala will bring you to the village if you ask him. I will tell the priest you are coming."

"Thank you. I'll be bringing another girl with me. Will that matter?"

"Madam Celine." He grinned, rolling his eyes. "Madam Celine is always welcome among us. The little madam too!"

Georgina found herself laughing with him. "My name is Georgina. I'm married to William Ayres."

"The man who makes the river flow backwards? A good man!"

"Yes," said Georgina, and was surprised to find she meant it, "he is a very good man—and a generous one too. I'm sure he'll be properly grateful if we can reassure Celine that what she saw was this and not some figment of her imagination. Only who can have wanted to scare her with such a silly trick?"

The man looked puzzled. "My name is Rabahindre, madam."

Georgina shook him warmly by the hand. "I'll be seeing you, Mr. Rabahindre," she said.

The man laughed and wagged his head. "Not Mister— Rabahindre only. Madam and I are friends, no?"

Georgina smiled back at him. "I hope so," she said.

It was much more difficult getting back through the window. She made one or two abortive attempts and then gave up the struggle and went round to the front door, hoping she would find it open. It was not. Feeling rather foolish, she banged on the solid wood portals, now wet through from the rain. The door swung open and William stood in the floodlit doorway, staring at her in open astonishment.

"How did you get out?" he demanded.

"Through the bathroom window." She slipped past him into the hall, dripping water on to the floor. "I saw Celine's demon. He's the demon of cholera and dysentery and his head has to be the most hideous thing I've ever seen. Rabahindre says we can go and look at in in daylight if we want to. He said someone took it away from his village and brought it up here. He wasn't best pleased about it."

"And you went out like that?"

Georgina looked down at herself, noting the way the

wet cloth of her thin dress clung to the shape of her body. "He'd have gone if I'd waited to get a coat," she said defensively. "Besides, it's dark outside."

"Well, it isn't dark in here," said William. He put his hands on her shoulders, turned her round until she had her back to him and forcibly propelled her down the wide corridor to her bedroom door.

"Aren't you pleased?" Georgina shot at him over her shoulder. His hands felt warm and intimate and hard and masculine against her shoulders.

"That you're doing your best to drown yourself when you ought to be tucked up in your bed?"

"No, silly, that Celine *did* see her demon!"

His hands dropped to her waist. "Damn all demons! For heaven's sake, go to bed, Georgina, and this time stay there! Can you manage, or shall I send Miss Campbell to you?"

She leaned back against him, weakened by his touch. "I can manage. I don't require Miss Campbell's services ever! William, are you coming to bed too?"

His hands squeezed her so tightly she cried out. "Not tonight, Josephine," he said, turning on his heel. "Tonight you look like a cross between a drowned rat and my canary—"

"Charming!"

"More charming than you know!" he flung over his shoulder. "All the curves in the right places and our marriage lines in my pocket."

The tip of her tongue protruded against her upper lip. "Well then?"

"Go to bed, Georgina. By yourself!"

Her eyes fell before the look in his. "Because I'm not Jennifer? I'll never be she, though! Can't you—"

"Not tonight, Georgina!"

"Then I'd rather you didn't come calling at all!" she shot at him mutinously. "I don't like you any better

now than I did when you were fifteen! You were horrid
as a boy, and you're equally horrid now!"

He was graceless enough to laugh at her. "I haven't
got a scarlet racing-cycle now. Is there some new attraction?"

She was down the corridor towards him before she had
thought, intent only on wiping the smile off his face, but
this time he was ready for her. He caught her up between
arms of steel and carried her into her room, dropping her
from a height on to the centre of her bed.

"Be thankful you look enough like Little Girl Lost in
the storm for me not to turn you over my knee, Georgie Porgie!" He bent down and kissed her hard on the
mouth. "*Goodnight, Georgina*!"

Her lips felt stiff and the warm masculinity of his
lingered long after he had gone. "Goodnight, William," she said to the empty room, and her voice
sounded as weak and vulnerable as she felt. And still
the rain came down, pounding a tattoo on the tin roof
of the bathroom. Georgina lay there and listened to it
for a long, long time before she struggled off the bed
and changed out of her wet clothes into her nightdress
and, pulling the sheet up over her head, went fast
asleep.

Stuart Duffield stretched his legs out in front of him
and allowed Celine to press some lemons into a glass
and add iced water and sugar for him. He watched her
every movement, Georgina noticed, an oddly contented expression on his face.

"So you girls want me to escort you down to the
village?" he said. "How did you get to hear about their
dances? I shouldn't have thought either of you were
the type to be interested in demonology."

"Not as such," Georgina affirmed. "Just one demon, Mahasona, whose image apparently walked out

of the village and all the way up to the bungalow by itself. It scared Celine silly, and I'm not at all surprised. It has the most hideous face I've ever seen."

Stuart's interest was caught. "You saw it too?"

"I saw it being taken back to the village by one Raba-hindre. I want to see it again in daylight when it will be a lot less scary. I'd like to know who played such a silly trick on us too, but I'm not hopeful about that."

"What did Rabahindre say?"

"Nothing. But he did invite us all to a ceremony at the Hindu temple. I don't think he knows how it got here any more than we do. His chief concern was the mask the creature wore. Apparently it's old and valu-able. It's certainly hideous!"

Celine's hand shook, clinking the ice in her glass. "I didn't see a mask, Georgina. I keep telling you, it moved! It drank some red stuff that looked like blood out of an elephant's head. A mask couldn't do that!"

"We'll see," said Georgina. "I'm almost sure this one could."

Celine looked unhappy. "But I'm always seeing things like that. It's nothing new. I'm touched in the head—I have been ever since my mother died in that fire. My father took me from hospital to hospital to find out what was the matter with me, but none of them ever found out. Mostly they thought it was caused by guilt because I wasn't sorry when my mother died."

The look of shock on Stuart's face was enough to tell Georgina that this was far more than Celine had ever said on the subject before. What was more, she had said it in the lucid terms an adult would use to describe her case, not at all as the child she usually pretended to be.

"I never believe in figments of the imagination until there's absolutely no other possible solution," Geor-gina answered in matter-of-fact tones. "Your other demons probably have a similar explanation if anyone had cared to look for it.''

"But I wasn't sorry when Mother died," Celine told her.

"I don't suppose you felt anything. One doesn't when one's shocked. Everyone knows that, Celine!"

"Father thought I was mad. He didn't like being with me afterwards. He was never at home, though Miss Campbell was always telling him I would be better if I saw a little more of him. She was in love with him."

Stuart hooted with laughter. "Miss Campbell?" he snorted.

Celine opened her eyes very wide. "The ugly have to make up in other ways," she explained carefully. "She wanted him for herself long before Mother died. I felt sorry for her. Mother didn't lift a finger where Father was concerned—she was always out with other men and things like that. It didn't seem fair. You wouldn't understand, Georgina, because men like you, but if they don't, what does one do then?"

Georgina was shocked into spilling her drink. "Darling, anyone as beautiful as you are—"

"Has to look out!" Celine finished for her. "I've known that for a long time. Beauty inspires hatred, not love. That's why Miss Campbell hates me. She was jealous of my mother, but she can't be jealous of me, can she? I'm not likely to take any man away from her."

Georgina stared at her. "Does she hate you?"

Celine nodded. "She only stayed to be close to Father."

"Then why stay now?" Georgina prompted her.

But Celine's glance wandered away from hers, whether deliberately or not it was impossible to say. "William says she's going away!" she remarked in delight. "I hope she does go, but she never has gone in the past. Sometimes I think she'll stay with me for ever and ever!"

Georgina made to speak, but Stuart stopped her, putting his hand over hers, his fingers tightening to gain her attention.

"Celine, why do you stay with her?" he asked.

She smiled a wry smile. "How unobservant you are! Because I'm only ten pence in the shilling, or whatever the expression is. I'm afraid of being on my own. I see things that scare me, and I have frightful nightmares and, when that happens, even someone one hates is better than nobody at all!"

"You ought to get married," he suggested.

Her mouth trembled and she shrugged her shoulders. "Nobody'd have me!" she said.

It was Georgina who was first aware that William had come out on to the verandah to join them. She hadn't seen him since the night before and the colour rose like a tide in her cheeks as she realised he had seen the way Stuart had his hand on hers. She snatched her own away, looking inexplicably guilty.

"The sun's shining," she said foolishly. "It all looks different in the sun, doesn't it?"

William tossed a letter down on to her lap. "Does it look more or less romantic?" he challenged her.

She had no answer, so she busied herself opening her letter, delighted to have one so soon from her family. "Goodness!" she exclaimed as she read the opening paragraph. "Jennifer wants to get away from Duncan's reproaches. She wants to come and visit us here. She's hopeful!"

William took the letter from her and began to read it aloud: "Poor Jennie misses you unbearably, my dear, as she always did when you were away. She has so few friends of her own and yours seldom come when you're not here to receive them. I wonder why? Your father and I have always thought she has by far the nicer nature. Perhaps we were wrong to insist she always looked up to you as the elder sister. Poor poppet, she was dreadfully upset over your marriage to William and she never let anyone guess it at the time. I must say, Georgie, I think you very wrong to have come between them. I know she thought she wanted Duncan, but you might have known that would never come to anything. None of us can understand why you let her talk you into telling William in the first place, unless of course you wanted him for yourself? One can't help feeling sorry for him when you think what he might have had!"

"It's from my mother," Georgina said unnecessarily. She snatched the letter back from him. "And it's addressed to me! If I want to tell you what's in it, I will when I've finished it. You may be my husband, but you have no right to read my letters in my book!"

William's eyes narrowed. "Is Jennifer your father's favourite too?" he asked her.

Hurt to the quick, she refused to meet his eyes, but buried herself in her letter instead, mumbling something about her father not playing favourites. "One can't help liking one person more than another, though" she added. "You should know that!"

He relaxed, throwing himself into the nearest canvas chair. "I do," he admitted. "Are you going to let Jennifer come?"

Georgina hunched her shoulders. "Have I any choice?"

Stuart finished his drink and rose quickly to his feet. "I'm off," he announced. "Thanks for the drink. I'll call for you around tea time, girls. Will that do?"

He smiled at Georgina, ruffled Celine's hair with a friendly hand, and was gone, leaving a silence one could cut with a knife behind him.

"What attraction is bringing him back this afternoon?'' William enquired, his gaze noting with interest the fluctuating colour in his wife's face. ''You?''

''He's taking us to the village,'' Celine answered him. ''To see if the demon Georgina saw last night is the same one that I saw.''

William raised a thoughtful brow. ''Good. I think I'll come too and keep an eye on this wife of mine.''

''You don't have to,'' Georgina protested.

''Don't I? What I have, I hold, Georgina Ayres. You won't cuckold me lightly, not even with such an easy-going partner as Stuart Duffield—''

Georgina raised wide, astonished eyes. ''But—''

''I should have accepted your invitation last night, shouldn't I, my sweet? I didn't awaken you to love to have someone else steal the cream! Stuart will have to look elsewhere—''

''What about Jennifer?'' Georgina cut him off, hotly embarrassed.

''What about her?'' he retorted. ''*She* isn't my wife!''

''But how you wish she were! Do you want her to come, or not?''

''Invite her by all means,'' he answered smoothly. ''It won't make any difference to us, I assure you. Much as I hate to ruffle your romantic dreams, my dear, her coming won't alter the fact that *you* are mine. Hanker after Stuart all you please, you're staying mine! He and Jennifer will be the ones who'll play games to-gether—''

''Then I don't want her here!'' Celine burst into the argument. ''Stuart is *my* friend. I don't like the sound of this silly Jennifer! Why can't she stay in England?''

Georgina could only wonder the same, but she knew her sister well enough to know that nothing she could say or do would make her stay away if she had made up her mind to come.

"I'll write to her," she said dully. "With any luck she won't come!"

But that was too much to hope for, just as William may have said that she was his, but would never, never admit that he was in any way hers. If he did, just once, a hundred Jennifers could come to Sri Lanka and be welcome!

CHAPTER EIGHT

Georgina was glad to be quiet for a few moments. She had never had an easy chair in her bedroom before, but these last few minutes had convinced her that it was a very good idea. Nobody would disturb her in her own room and she needed some time by herself to calm down and do a bit of hard thinking about what she was going to do about Jennifer. When she thought of her mother's letter she still burned with embarrassment, and that William should have read it was the last straw! He would think all the worse of her now that he knew that even her parents thought more highly of Jennifer than they did of herself.

There was Celine to be considered too. Georgina had been on the receiving end of Jennifer's sharp tongue too often not to know how she would make the younger girl suffer for having the kind of beauty that Jennifer had always been led to believe she possessed herself. Only when the sun shone, as Shakespeare had pointed out, the light of a candle paled into insignificance. Jennifer would not like Celine at all!

Then there was William. He might be possessive, but he was far from loving as far as Georgina was concerned. Jennifer was a different cup of tea. Jennifer was the love of his life and only Georgina would stand between them and the consummation of that love. And she was not such a fool as not to know that Jennifer would give him every encouragement. The mere fact that William was her husband would be enough to force her sister to go to any lengths to get him away from her. One way and another, it wasn't a very pleasant prospect actually to have her in the same house, the first home she had ever tried to share with William.

Outside the window was a frangipani tree, or temple tree as it was more often called locally. Georgina watched the white flowers dance in the light breeze and thought how different today was from yesterday. The sun was shining, for one thing, drawing some of the moisture out of the fertile ground in little puffs of steam. Otherwise the rain of yesterday might never have been. When she stood up, she could see a sloping garden, very English in character, that led down to a hollow where a table and chairs were permanently laid out, taking it for granted that most meals would be taken out of doors. Was that where they would have lunch? she wondered.

"Georgie, are you in there?"

If she kept very quiet perhaps he would go away. She had not yet forgiven William for reading her mother's letter. Besides, she felt too raw to embark on another skirmish with him before lunch. She would say something she would regret, something that would confirm him in his belief she was jealous of her sister, when she truly didn't think she was, not while she was thousands of miles away and there was no possibility of her benefiting from William's decided partiality for her rather than for his own wife.

The door opened and William walked in, taking in her small figure seated on the rather large chair in a single glance.

"What are you doing?" he asked her. "Sulking?"

She shook her head. "I was wondering what to do about Jennifer."

He gave her a long, hard look. "Wouldn't it be more

to the point to wonder where you're going with your husband?"

Her eyes fell before his. "You had no right to read my mother's letter without my permission," she said stiffly. "How would you like it if I were to read your letters?"

He shrgged. "You can read them any time you choose. You do anyway."

"I do not!"

"No? Do you still claim you didn't read Jennifer's letter to me, or hold it up until it was too late for me to do anything about it?"

"Yes, I do. Anyone would think it was I who forced you to the altar instead of the other way round!"

"Oh, not that again! Really, Georgie, nobody could have made you marry me if you hadn't allowed them to."

"I wish I hadn't!"

His expression took on a grimness she had not seen before. "So I noticed. Somehow I'd never thought of you as being particularly susceptible to the blandishments of my sex. Jennifer yes, but not you."

She looked up at him then, giving him a roguish look because, at that moment, it was the best defence she had. "Why not me?" she asked.

"Maybe you had no opportunity before to bask in the admiration of your male acquaintances because Jennifer was always in your way, but things are different now. I don't know how it is, but there's something different about you since we came to Sri Lanka. You're inviting trouble, do you know that? I'm not surprised young Stuart can hardly keep his hands off you!"

Georgina summoned up a laugh. "Don't be ridiculous! He can't take his eyes off Celine—and a very good thing too! She's much more normal when he's around, and she likes him very much. That's what bothers me about Jennifer coming here. It wouldn't occur to her to notice how Celine feels about Stuart. She'd dismiss her as a child and her feelings as being of no account to anyone! Jennifer never sees anyone's point of view but her own.''

"Meaning she's never worried much about yours?" he ground out.

"I never minded before!" she answered.

"Never?" His disbelief was total. "What about her engagement to me?"

Had she minded? Honesty forced Georgina to admit to herself that she had, though at the time she would have laughed any such idea to scorn, but she would not admit as much to William.

"It was a way of getting back at you when it was all over. As far as I was concerned that was all there was to it!"

"You took Jennifer's place—"

"I didn't think I had any choice!"

He put a hand on either arm of her chair. "You didn't. I meant to have you, and have you I will, my Georgie Porgie! What's more, I'll break your pretty neck for you if I see you playing patsy with Stuart again!"

His closeness made her heart pound. She tried to breathe normally, but somehow she couldn't get any air into her lungs.

"You wouldn't dare say such a thing to Jennifer!" she challenged him in a small voice.

"You underrate me! No woman will ever rule me, Georgina, however much they might like to. Not Jennifer, and not you!"

She had never lacked courage, but it was put to the test then as she stared back, deep into his golden eyes. "You take too much on yourself, William Ayres. If you think I'm going to sit down under such a Victorian attitude, while you read my letters and vet my friends, you're very much mistaken! I'll make my own decisions!"

"Will you, my Georgie?" His face softened into amusement and she hated him for it, for it was the amusement of the victor when he knows that nothing is going to stop him from getting his own way. "Women are at a bioligical disadvantage when it comes to some decisions. Diana the Huntress remained a virgin goddess, if you remember—"

"Perhaps I may choose to do so too!"

"You can try!" he mocked her. "But I'd hedge my bets if I were you. You may have got away with it at one time, little one, but that was before I had your measure. Are you afraid I'm not going to be man enough for you?"

She couldn't have answered to save her life. "Well?" he prompted her.

She swallowed, averting her eyes from his. "This is an impossible conversation!" she declared. "Why should you want to make my decisions for me anyway?"

He bent his elbows, bringing his face very close to hers. "Because you prefer it that way, little fraud. You'd run even now, if I let you, wouldn't you? Cutting off your nose to spite your face? What a girl! I won't fancy your kisses any more if you spread them around the neighbourhood in a series of trial runs. I'll teach my own wife all she needs to know, and I won't hesitate to call her to heel if she strays too far away from me—"

"I see!" she cut him off. "It's a matter of pride and I'm cast in the role of propping up your ego! What if I won't do it?"

His lips parted in a smile. They were so close to her that she could feel his breath on her own. "Care to try it?" he murmured on a note of laughter.

Her heart turned over within her. "No," she whispered.

"I thought not." His lips touched hers and drew back again. "*Sugar and spice and all things nice, that's what little girls are made of*, Georgie Porgie. Don't spoil it by overdoing the spice. It's the sugar that turns me on!"

She put up a hand and touched his cheek. "That's all it means to you, isn't it? A turn on?"

His lips took a long, slow toll of hers. "I'll let you know," he murmured. "Damn it all, Georgie, you are my wife!"

"Big deal!" Her other arm slipped up round the back of his neck. "How much will that mean to you when Jennifer gets here?"

He released himself with the greatest of ease. "That depends on you," he answered, walking over to the window and standing there with his back to her. "You have the advantage if you care to use it, but do you?"

"What advantage?"

He cast her a mocking glance. "If you play your cards right Jennifer could be just a memory by the time she gets here. Until I have to report on site for my work, I'm all yours!"

"Oh yes?" Her tone was every bit as dry as his. "Don't you mean that I'm all yours? Or at least, isn't that what you'd like to mean?"

"I mean we're stuck with one another," he answered, and quoted softly: "*As unto the bow the cord is, So unto the man is woman; Though she bends him, she obeys him, Though she draws him, yet she follows; Useless each without the other.*"

"Only if they're tied to one another," she objected.

'And aren't we tied by marriage?"

She sniffed. "I might have known you'd like Victorian poets as much as you do their ideas of male superi-

ority. Nobody quotes *Hiawatha* nowadays!'' She took a
deep breath. ''You're not stuck with me, William, unless you want to be. I'd never hold you to such an un-
profitable arrangement. I want to be the only woman in
the world for my husband, not a piece of tatty string!''

He turned and faced her. ''Poor Georgie! Ever the
romantic under that practical exterior of yours! It's an
intriguing combination. Dream your dreams, my dear,
and who knows, they may come true for you. Perhaps
you approve of Nietzsche more than you do of Longfel-
low? *Only he who is man enough will release the woman in
woman*, and Stuart and his kind will never be man
enough for you!''

''But you are?''

He was openly amused. ''At the risk of your thinking
me even more conceited than you do now, yes, I am.''

''You can't know that!''

He put his hands on his hips and laughed at her, a
great bellow of sound that rang round the silent bungalow.

''For heaven's sake!'' she rebuked him. ''What did
you have to do that for? Miss Campbell will wonder
what on earth we're doing!''

That made him laugh again. ''Do you care?'' he
asked, his eyes dancing.

''Yes, I do,'' Georgina answered him soberly. ''I think
Miss Campbell is a dangerous woman and I wouldn't
want to stir her into any further activity like the demon
of last night.''

''Miss Campbell?''

She nodded. ''Who else, William? Who else would
want to frighten Celine into a scene?''

''I don't know, my dear, but do you think Miss
Campbell has the imagination to make use of such a
thing? She and Celine haven't been here long, only a
few days before we arrived ourselves, and she's not the

type to go down to the village by herself. It was probably just a coincidence."

Georgina had her own doubts, but she was not prepared to give voice to them. "She looks like a witch," she said instead. "Perhaps she is one."

William gave her a startled look. "If she is one she'd have had a job to persuade the Aborigines to allow her to make use use of their sacred objects. It was the sound of a whirring rope that set Celine off in Australia. It always began the same way—and ended in her being frightened into a fit. One of the Australian doctors we consulted suggested she might have witnessed some Aboriginal ceremony as a child, some thing she wasn't supposed to see, and that it had haunted her ever since."

"That's no excuse for Miss Campbell telling her she's touched in the head!" Georgina said sharply. "That was cruel!"

William studied her face with a thoughtful look. "Women don't always examine their weapons with sufficient care before they throw them, Georgina. You should know that!"

"I've never tried to drive anyone mad!"

They stared at one another in mutual consternation, but Georgina couldn't bring herself to take the words back.

"But why?" William asked.

Georgina laced her fingers together. "I don't know. Celine says she was in love with her father. William, that woman has to go!"

"She'll expect to serve out her notice and I have no reasonable excuse for sending her away before the month is out. I agree she has to go, but don't overrate Celine's lucidity, will you? She'll never be more than a little girl at heart—that was about the only thing the doctors were agreed about! There's no point in encouraging her to start thinking of love and romance when she can never be a wife.''

"I don't see why she can't be. She's a lovely girl."

William's lips twisted into a wry smile. "A man wants more than mere beauty in his wife," he said.

But *he* didn't! He wanted Jennifer, and what for, if not for her delicate beauty? The answer to that hurt so badly that Georgina felt it like a physical pain inside her. When one loved, beauty didn't matter, *nothing* mattered except the joy one felt in the beloved's presence. That was how she felt about William. That was what was so awful about it, that he didn't feel the same way about her and he never would.

"Celine has a lot more than beauty to recommend her," she said aloud. "I'm sure Stuart sees her as something more than a little girl. I know I do."

"Despite the scene last night?"

Georgina nodded. "That was fright. We're none of us ourselves when we're badly frightened. At other times Celine is as lucid as you or I. That blank look she puts on is probably a defence she's grown up with. Anyone would if they had to put up with Miss Campbell all day and every day."

William grinned. "So you don't like Miss Campbell, Georgie Porgie, but I couldn't have managed without her—nor could Celine's father! How d'you suppose he would have looked after Celine on his own? He had his work to do. He couldn't have had a retarded daughter hanging on to his sleeve all the time."

Georgina looked down at her hands, trying to stop herself from entering into an argument on such slight evidence that even she could see she had formed her opinion largely on guesswork and a hunch that, despite its implications, wouldn't go away.

"And what were Miss Campbell's rewards?" she asked.

William froze. "What do you mean?"

"Only that her major interest doesn't seem to be money, does it?"

William hauled her up on to her feet and into his arms. She hid her face against him, trying to still the trembling that had seized her limbs. He smelled nice, she decided, but then she liked everything about him. His attraction for her was so strong she felt quite dizzy with it. His fingers found the nape of her neck and closed about it, before entangling themselves in her hair and forcing her face up to meet his.

"Why is it never the right time for me to kiss you properly?" he demanded in her ear. "I can't and won't wait for ever, Georgie Porgie!"

She shuddered against him, saying nothing. There was a lump in her throat the size of a tennis ball and she swallowed helplessly, trying to make it go away. It didn't. On the contrary, it grew so large she was afraid it would dissolve into a flood of tears and he would think it was something he had done to her.

"Don't you want me to kiss you?" he asked, smoothing the curl away from her forehead. "Don't you think you could try to kiss me too?"

"I—" She swallowed again as he bent his head bringing his lips within half an inch of her own. "I can't!" she blurted out.

"Why not?" he murmured, touching his mouth to hers. "You like that well enough, my Georgie!"

She liked it far too much! "It's lunchtime—"

"I'd rather have you for lunch!"

"*No*! Oh no!" She stepped back from him in a panic and found herself still held by her hair. "William, we can't! Not now!"

His lips twitched in ready amusement. "I won't let you go until you kiss me, Georgie Porgie." He wiped away a tear from her eye with a gentle finger. "And this time there'll be no tears from either of us, huh?''

She wriggled desperately, found she couldn't get free from him that way, and tried kicking his shins instead. It was a mistake. His fingers tightened in her hair and his other arm lifted her clear off the ground, placing her firmly on his knee as he collapsed into the chair she had only recently vacated.

"Still determined to be the little thug we all know and love?" he taunted her. "You ought to know by now it won't work with me, my Georgie! Now kiss me properly, my love, or take the consequences!"

"I won't!" She glared at him, her heart beating so fast she thought she might faint and that she might even welcome such an escape at that moment.

"You will if you want any lunch, my pet." A smile flickered across his face and the unwelcome suspicion crossed her mind that he was enjoying himself. "How will you explain your non-appearance at the village?" he added in the same, conversational tones. "Young Stuart will be disappointed."

"He's not all that much younger than you are!" she declared.

"You think not?" He turned the matter over in his mind. "He's young enough to let you make the running, but you're too feminine to put up with that for long! Aren't you, Georgie?"

"I prefer it to being patronised!" she shot back at him.

"Ah, but you are mine to treat with as I please," he teased her, his eyes alight with laughter as he waited for the coming explosion.

"Then you can't complain if I treat you just as I like!"

"You can try!" He lifted an eyebrow in derision. "You should listen more closely, sweetheart. I did say 'treat with', but I daresay one way is as good as the other with you."

"I won't be browbeaten—"

"My dear little Georgie, what's much more to the point is neither will I! Come, kiss me of your own free will and we'll cry a truce for the afternoon, if that will please my lady?"

She brooded over his words, knowing herself to be caught in a cleft stick. Nor was she as reluctant as she pretended. She leaned away from him, gazing at him thoughtfully, liking her position far better than she would have him know.

"And if I do kiss you? Will you be content with that?"

"For now," he drawled. He looked sleepy and not at all dangerous. "One good kiss on the lips, Georgina!"

Her eyes widened as her one line of retreat was cut off. She spread her hand across the opening of his shirt, giving herself a little more time to make up her mind what to do next. The hairs on his chest created a *frisson* of pleasure against her fingers.

"You're easily pleased if that's all you want," she said at last. "Wouldn't you rather wait until I offer to kiss you without being forced?"

He shut his eyes entirely. "When will that be?"

A cautious reconnoitre informed her that he was confident enough to have relinquished his hold over her. She patted his cheek gently, delighted with her own cleverness, and made to get off his knee, only to find herself caught more firmly than before.

"Cheat!" he said mildly. His eyes opened and they were full of a lazy amusement that brought the colour to her face and a singing to her ears. "Give in, Georgina," he recommended her. "You're not going to get your own way this time no matter how you twist and turn." He smiled at her outraged expression. "What's a little kiss between friends?"

"We're not friends!"

He gave her a quizzical look, but he said nothing, waiting for her to make the next move. And she would have to, she thought, for he plainly meant to go on sitting there until she did.

"I think you're mean!" she informed him roundly. "Why should you want me to kiss you?"

"I wonder!" he mocked her.

She tried another tack. "I think you should woo me a little first," she said.

"My dear girl, what else have I been doing ever since we arrived in Sri Lanka!"

Had he—? Was it possible—? His laughter demoralised her completely and she thumped him on the chest.

"Oh, *you*!" she exclaimed. But she was half glad he had defeated her. Her body tensed as she put her mouth to his and she kissed him as a child might kiss an adult under protest. "There!"

"That was a kiss? You have a lot to learn, Georgie! Come back where you were and I'll show you what I mean by a kiss!"

She relaxed into a delicious surrender that only wanted to please him and thereby herself. She felt his hands on her back and on the soft curve of her breast and dug her own fingers into the hair of his chest.

"That's better!" William murmured. His voice sounded husky but the mockery was still very much in evidence. "Who said you couldn't kiss if you tried?"

"But it wasn't me kissing you!" she crowed in triumph.

"No?" The flecks of gold in his eyes reminded her of fireworks. "Then what were you doing?"

She decided it was a rhetorical question undeserving of an answer. "May I go now?" she countered on her own behalf.

He raised his hands, freeing her from his embrace. "If you want to."

It wasn't fair, but then he never did play fair. She could only hope that he didn't know how little she wanted to drag herself off his knee. She went over to the dressing table and seated herself in front of the looking-glass, running a comb through her hair without bothering to see what she was doing. There was no reason why she shouldn't kiss her own husband, she comforted herself, annoyed by the guilty excitement that had reduced her to an eager participant in the embrace. What was there in a kiss to make her want more and more of the same?

William came up behind her and took the comb from her hand, finishing off the job for her, a half-smile curving his lips as he did so. His eyes looked her over with appreciation in the glass.

"Did you mind so much?" he asked her, when he had finished and was putting the comb down on the table in front of her.

She made a gesture to avoid answering, but as her eyes met his in the glass, she knew she was being less than generous. She turned away, fingering the ring on her finger with a nervous touch.

"No," she said at last and, jumping to her feet, she practically ran out of the room.

Celine was waiting for her on the verandah. She looked up anxiously as Georgina hurtled through the French window, her cheeks flaming with a very becoming colour.

"Georgina, may I speak to you now?" she begged. "You do like me a little bit, don't you? I mean, you don't like anyone here better than me, do you?"

Only William. "No," Georgina agreed vaguely.

"That's good! I was afraid you liked Stuart." Celine frowned. "William thinks you do."

"I like him well enough," Georgina admitted. "I hardly know him."

"Oh dear," said Celine, "I was afraid of that. I think— I think he likes you too."

Georgina gave her an impatient look. "What are you talking about?" she demanded.

Celine's face crumpled. "I thought you'd understand!" she wailed. "But you're just like all the rest of them. You don't think I can feel anything, but I do!"

"Oh, Celine, I'm so sorry," Georgina said at once. "I wasn't really listening. I was thinking about—something else. I didn't mean to be nasty, or to snub you or anything."

Celine smiled, the sunshine breaking through the threatened shower of rain. "I was talking about Stuart. Georgina, have you ever been in love?"

Georgina was on the point of saying no, but something in the other girl's face prevented her. "Why?" she asked instead.

"Well, you can't be in love with William. He'd know if you were because he's married to you. And *he* thinks you and Stuart might fall in love with each other. He said so! Only I couldn't bear it if you did!"

Georgina's look was scandalised. "How many men do you think I want?" But Celine was unamused. "Oh, Celine, really! William was talking about something else. He knows as well as you do that I'm not going to fall in love with Stuart! And as for him I hardly think my looks would appeal much when he has only to turn his head and look at you. You're the one who's beautiful, my pet, not me!"

"But you have something else—"

"*Me?*" Georgina laughed at the very idea. "You should ask my sister about that! She's the one who has the looks in our family and attracts all the attention, though even she would pale into insignificance beside you! I think you're the loveliest person I've ever seen."

Celine looked merely uncomfortable. "It's nice of you to say so, Georgie, but I don't think you know much about things like that after all." She looked up appealingly. "You're welcome to William, but not to Stuart as well! I wasn't going to tell you—I wasn't going to tell anyone because they'll only laugh at me, but I love Stuart and I want him to love me."

"If you ask me, he hasn't far to go! Why don't you tell him how you feel, Celine?"

"If it's true and your demon is the one I saw, I'll think about it. I won't otherwise. Stuart deserves the very best, not a retarded idiot—"

Georgina put on a severe expression. "I won't have you speak of yourself like that!" she cut in. "Don't ever say such a thing again, Celine!"

"Don't you believe it?" the other girl asked.

"No, I don't! And Stuart won't either!"

"Then you don't mind, Georgie? I know you only have to lift your little finger—" She bit her lip. "I expect it's always been the same for you!"

Coming on to the verandah, William caught Celine's last plea. He put his arm round the girl's shoulders, smiling down at her.

"Surely you're not afraid of competition from Georgie?" he teased her. "Jennifer never had any trouble from her."

"Then Georgie wasn't trying! I don't like the sound of Jennifer anyway. She sounds silly and spoilt, and Georgie isn't either of those things. I'll bet most people prefer her really!"

"Do you?" William appeared to have lost interest. "I shouldn't put my shirt on it, if I were you."

CHAPTER NINE

Georgina had never stood back and compared William to any other man before, but she did so now, watching him and Stuart as they stood side by side, making desultory conversation while they waited for Celine and her to join them. To an objective observer, the slighter man had to be considered the more handsome, but she was far from being able to make such an objective judgment. It was William who tugged at her heartstrings and whose smile reduced her knees to jelly. Besides, she liked his largeness, both in mind and body. Indeed, she couldn't think of anything she didn't like about him! Bad luck to her, she thought, if she couldn't keep her emotions under better control. Under the very best of circumstances William would be a hard man to hold, and her circumstances could hardly be worse.

Stuart had brought his jeep and they all piled in, the women sitting in the back to allow the men more leg room.

"Are you all right back there?" William asked, smiling an ironical smile at his wife.

"Would it matter if we were not?" she returned.

"You could always sit on my knee!"

She blushed. "And what about Celine?"

"I hardly think there would be room for both of you."

"Then I'll stay where I am!"

Having got that settled, Stuart drove off through the close by tea gardens, some of them planted on such steep hills that Georgina wondered that the Tamil women could balance themselves to pick the precious leaves. In their brightly coloured saris they looked as pretty as butterflies, making their way up and down the long lines of bushes, picking with both hands as they went. They wore some specially made baskets on their backs which they filled up at lightning speed, untiring in their urgency to earn the extra bonuses that were paid to anyone who picked more than the minimum weight required.

"Do they all come from South India?" she asked Stuart.

"Originally. I daresay a high proportion of these were born here in Ceylon, but they still think of their home as being in India. It's hard to believe, but many of their relatives back home in the mother country are even poorer than the Tamils here. Many of them send a large proportion of their earnings back to India. That's part of the trouble, because Sri Lanka can't afford the drain on her resources and the Tamils get caught between the pressures on both sides of the argument. Someone will have to think of an answer soon, though. Many of them are worse than poor—the whole island is poor!—but some of the Tamils are actually starving."

"Why did they come?" Georgina asked.

Stuart made a wry face. "We, the British, imported them to work the tea estates. They're much more amenable to long hours of repetitive, dull work than are the Sinhalese—especially the women. There's no doubt they've been let down somewhere along the line. Tea is very important to the Lankan economy and they ought to benefit accordingly. But when one tries to apportion the blame it becomes much more difficult. All kinds of political platforms are mounted by all kinds of people and they all make a great deal of noise. Meanwhile the Tamils fall further and further behind in the subsistence stakes."

"Can't we do something?"

Stuart pooh-poohed the idea. "Our hands are hardly clean enough for anyone to want to listen! Until recently many of these estates were British owned and nothing was done then for them. It would be a case of the pot calling the kettle black with a vengeance!"

Georgina sighed. "But on this estate—"

"Things are pretty good here," Stuart agreed. "The best tea is grown high up, and one can hardly get higher than here. We get the best prices and offer our workers the best conditions accordingly. Some of our tea is so highly thought of that if one were to buy it in London it would cost all of seven pounds a pound. Nobody will pay that, so it gets mixed in with other grades. When I take you over the factory you'll be able to try your hand at my job and find out how good your taste-buds are. I never drink alcohol or eat spicy food in case I lose my touch, but it has other rewards. Tea is a fascinating crop."

Celine leaned forward eagerly to catch the full import of his words. Her eyes were bright and alive with interest. It was a far cry from the apathetic, lacklustre child she sometimes appeared to be.

"I didn't want to leave Australia, but I'm awfully glad now that William made me come. He doesn't usually want Miss Campbell and me around when he's working and we just stick at home. But I wouldn't have missed all this for anything!"

"Miss Campbell might have been happier back home," William said dryly.

"Who cares? I love it here! She's cross because you only gave her a few hours to pack up all our things. She didn't want to come."

Georgina laughed. "I'm glad she hasn't succeeded in putting you off Sri Lanka," she said. "It wouldn't be the same here without you."

Celine blinked with pleasurable disbelief. "I didn't want to come because *she* didn't," she blurted out. "She doesn't like it when William comes the heavy guardian, you see. She likes to be the only one to tell me what to do."

Georgina put a comforting hand on the girl's shoulder. "If William comes the heavy guardian too often you should send him about his business," she advised. "You're old enough to make your own decisions. Don't you agree, Stuart?"

Stuart cast a quick look at the lovely, fair girl, giving nothing away. "I like her the way she is," he said.

Celine giggled nervously. "And how am I?"

"Gentle and biddable," he replied promptly. "I can't abide pushy women!"

"Like Georgina," William put in at once.

"*Georgina*?" Stuart exclaimed, almost running the jeep off the road. "There's nothing wrong with Georgie."

Georgina cast her husband a look of malicious triumph. "Thank you, Stuart," she murmured meekly. "It's nice to be appreciated for a change."

William uttered a snort of laughter. "Oh, I appreciate you all right, Georgie Porgie, but not for any milk-and-water blood in your veins."

Georgina looked warningly in Celine's direction, but William paid no attention at all. His eyes slid over her, their meaning perfectly plain to any observer, and then he turned round in his seat again, saying something *sotto voce* to Stuart that Georgina couldn't quite catch.

She was glad when they reached the Hindu temple and Rabahindre came running forward to meet them. He put the palms of his hands together and lifted them high in front of his face. "We are all ready, madam," he said to Georgina. "Everyone is very pleased to have you visit us!"

And sure enough, it seemed as though the whole village had turned out to mark their arrival. The children stood in neat lines on one side of the open space in front of the temple, watching eagerly as the visitors were divested of their shoes and led into the first of the chambers inside. There they were met by the local priest, a member of the lowest of the Hindu castes as were his flock, dressed in a white garment that was already stained with the mud of the evening before.

Georgina's first discovery was that the concrete floor was as slippery as glass. The roof had leaked in places, allowing the rain to come flooding in, and they were up to their ankles in muddy water long before they had passed through the outer room into the inner sanctuary.

The priest began a long sustained chant, the meaning of which had been lost in antiquity. Georgina remembered someone at college telling her that Hindu gods were some of the oldest in the world and that there was a school of thought that thought the gods of ancient Greece had originated from the same source, travelling to Europe by way of the very island where she was standing now.

The white-robed figure advanced towards them with a tin plate on which were mixed a number of coloured pastes. With infinite care he marked their foreheads and garlanded them with chains of marigolds and gold and silver decorations of the kind that are put on Christmas trees in England. Then with half a coconut in their hands, filled with flowers and the leaf of the betel-nut, they were led forward until they were almost touching the table that served as an altar and which stood in front of three curtained cubicles in which were hidden the representations of three of the most important members of the Hindu pantheon.

When the first curtain was drawn back, the elephant-headed son of Shiva and his consort, variously known as Parvati, Durga, Kali, etc., was revealed. Ganesha, as the remover of obstacles, is propitiated by every Hindu before every major undertaking and is much more popular than his warlike brother, Kartikeya, who is more generally known in South India by the name of Subrahmanya.

The central curtains revealed the more important god Shiva, the third member of the Hindu triad, the destroyer and the lord of the dance and who is sometimes worshipped for his sexual proclivities also. This last was brought home by a curious iron object on the altar in front of him that Georgina only belatedly recognised to be some kind of phallic symbol. Incense was burned before him and the chanting increased in intensity until one of the poorest-looking members of the congregation went off into a trance and began an erratic kind of dance that made Celine ask nervously, "Is he all right?"

"It can happen to anyone," Stuart reassured her. "If he gets out of control, they'll touch him with some of the sacred ashes and he'll come out of it. It can happen to anyone. It could even happen to you."

Happily, Celine had no time to express any further doubts before the priest was holding out a bowl of smouldering coals towards them and, following Stuart's example, they cupped the smoke into their hands and brought it up to their faces and down over their heads.

"What does this do?" Georgina asked in a whisper.

"You're receiving the power of the god," William answered her.

She hoped it would work for a non-believer and doubled her cash contribution to the proceedings as a kind of insurance that it would. She knew little or nothing about Shiva, but she was attracted by his dancing figure with its many arms and one leg raised, while the other stood on some diminutive figure down below.

The children had crowded into the limited space behind them, their dark eyes large with curiosity and shining with the reflected light of the candles. They were beautiful, well-made children, much given to laughter and with all the curiosity about visitors that is universal among the less literate, who get their news by word of mouth rather than from the written word. It seemed to Georgina that there was no air at all left inside the temple and she began to hope the ceremony would soon come to an end.

When it did, it was with a suddenness that made her forget all about the slippery floor, and she very nearly fell as they turned and made their way outside again.

"The priest doesn't speak English," Stuart warned her, so, as something was expected of her, she turned to Rabahindre and asked him to thank him for them.

"It was a great honour for us," she insisted. "I wouldn't want him to think us ungrateful. You will make sure that he understands that, while we're not Hindus ourselves, we're proud to have been allowed to visit his temple."

Rabahindre grinned. "He knows, madam. I have told him all about you and everyone is happy you came to see our gods. Now he has seen you for himself, he will allow you to see the demon as you asked. Excuse me, madam, if you will follow me, we will go now."

He led the way through the pitiful houses of the lines where most of the workers on the estate lived. Children abounded, falling in and out of the puddles that had not yet dried out, and thoroughly enjoying the novelty of having these strangers among them. Yet they made little noise. No one cried out, as they would have done at home in England; they watched and giggled in almost total silence, nudging each other if anything of particular interest happened.

The masks and home-made dancing figures were kept in a shed at one end of the village. Rabahindre unlocked the rusty padlock on the door and, gesturing them to stay outside, went in himself and came out again carrying several highly coloured ancient masks in his arms.

"But they have no bodies!" Celine complained.

Rabahindre waggled his head. "Not now, Miss Celine. Every year they have a new body specially made for them. They are made of palm leaves, plaited together, and are beautiful. But they last only a little time. These ones are not used at this time of year. They have their own festivals at other times." He turned back to the shed with an unconsciously theatrical air. "Now you will see Mahasona!"

There was a lengthy pause, disturbed only by the sounds of activity from within the shed, and then the mask that Georgina had seen the night before emerged from the battered door, rolling its eyes and opening and shutting its mouth, looking exactly as though it were indeed drinking the blood of the elephant's head that was raised again and again to its lips. Georgina found it hideous, the more so now that she could see the vivid colours in which it was painted: scarlet, green, yellow, and white, outlined in black. The body followed more slowly, its plaited shape catching in the light breeze and making it difficult to control. Finally it stood beside them, towering up into the sky, the result of many hours of work and startling in its evil aspect.

Georgina turned to Celine in time to see her normal pink and white complexion turn to a sickly green.

"Is that what you saw?" she demanded.

The younger girl put out a hand which was immediately captured by one of Stuart's. "I can't look at it! Please, Georgina, don't make me look any more!"

"But is it the same?" Georgina insisted.

Celine closed her eyes and swayed in time to the gigantic figure in front of them. "Take me away!" she pleaded to Stuart.

"But you haven't said if that's what you saw!" Georgina objected. She felt William's hand on her shoulder and tried to shake it off. "Celine, you *must*—"

"Leave her alone, Georgie," William bade her. "Can't you see she's in no state to be asked anything now?"

"But—"

"Georgina, don't bully her now!"

Georgina turned outraged eyes on to him. "I was not—"

He pushed her hair away from her face. "You've made your point, sweetheart. I'll do the rest. Okay?"

She didn't know whether she would have given in to him or not, because at that moment her attention was diverted by some of the men from the village gently lowering the plaited figure to the ground and releasing an excited Rabahindre from underneath.

"Come closer, madam," he invited Georgina. "You can see now how clever this mask is, yes? Hold it here, and here, madam. Now you can work it too! Excuse me, madam, like this!"

Georgina tugged on the ropes as she was bidden and found the mask less revolting when she was in charge of its movements. Indeed, she was beginning to see the fascination of an art form that at first she had found shocking and rather frightening. It was very cleverly made, fitting together as beautifully as if it had been made with precision instruments rather than the adze and clumsy knife that were the tools of the village carpenter.

She pulled on another rope and the mask rolled its eyes with devastating effect. Celine uttered a scream of fright and hid her ashen face against Stuart's shoulder. "Take me away!" she moaned.

He went with her without a backward glance. Georgina, beginning to enjoy herself, made the mask stick out its tongue at William, and she grinned at him happily.

"Isn't it clever?" she remarked. "Do you want to work it?"

He shook his head. "Aren't *you* clever!" he mocked her. "It would seem you were right, if Celine ever recovers sufficiently to confirm the fact. And not only about that. She's cut you out with Stuart, my poppet, and I don't think he looks on her as a child either. What are you going to do about that?"

She returned the mask to Rabahindre, giving her husband an uncertain smile. "Encourage it?" she suggested hopefully.

"You may be right." He dug a few coins out of his pocket and handed them to Rabahindre.

"Of course I'm right!" She picked a few more coins out of his hand and added them to the pile on Rabahindre's palm, enjoying the intimate feeling it gave her. Indeed, she felt so comfortable with William at that moment that she completely forgot to guard her tongue and said impulsively, "If only Jennifer doesn't upset everything when she comes! I could almost wish that she's still on about you, but that would be too much to hope. She'll probably want both of you!"

"Celine has no reason to be jealous of your sister," William rebuked her. "I hope they'll be friends."

Georgina's spirits sank. It was impossible for her to explain to William that Jennifer scorned to have friends of her own sex and that she certainly wouldn't have any time for Celine, except to try and belittle her shining beauty. She would have plenty of time for Stuart, though, and she wouldn't be happy until she had him dancing attention on her. Even if she had come for William, she would still want Stuart too; it was the way she was made. Georgina had long ago accepted the fact that she would never change and she had spent so many years protecting Jennifer from the consequences of her own actions that it was second nature to her now. Even the best juggler in the world would occasionally let a ball drop, and Georgina had been cast in the role of the assistant who picks it up and sets it spinning in the air again so often that she had never resented that all the applause for the act had always been reserved for Jennifer. It was only now that she had found someone even more vulnerable, who needed protecting far more than Jennifer ever had, that she knew that this time she couldn't allow Jennifer to purloin Stuart away from her. Jennifer played with men's hearts as if they were toys created especially for her pleasure, and Stuart would be no different from any of the others. But to Celine he was the one person in the world who could give her a normal life, putting the tragedy that had marred her life behind her for ever. *This time she couldn't allow Jennifer to do it!*

"I suppose she has to come?" she sighed.

"Why not?" he returned indifferently. "It will be on your own head if she takes anything you value away from you, Georgie Porgie. You have no reason to be jealous of her unless you want to be."

Miss Campbell was waiting for them back at the bungalow. She took one look at Celine's pale face and turned on Georgina.

"I told you she wouldn't be able to stand up to seeing that—*thing*! I hope you're satisfied now! I shouldn't be surprised if we have more than a few nightmares tonight! Come along, Celine. Say thank you to Mr.

Duffield for looking after you nicely. *He* wasn't to know that you aren't up to that kind of thing. We know whom to blame, don't we, dear?"

Celine clutched at Stuart's arm. "I don't want to go with her!" she breathed, swallowing convulsively. "I want to stay with you!"

"Oh, quite," Stuart agreed, putting a matter-of-fact arm about her and hugging her in much the same way as he would have done a child. "You can't go yet! You haven't told us if that was the same demon as the one you saw last night?" Celine shuddered visibly, but he went on speaking to her in the same calm tones. "Georgina went to a lot of trouble to show you that it wasn't something in your own imagination which you saw. I think we ought to talk about it now, don't you?"

Celine's eyes were troubled, but there was none of the blankness of former times about them. "Yes," she said simply.

"Then you'd better sit down and tell us all about it." Her fingers tightened on his shirt-sleeve. "It's all right," he soothed her. "I'll be here."

"Always?"

"As often as I can be. I can't always be with you, though. You'll have to get used to that. It won't matter, you know, once we've talked about it."

"Won't it? You'll go on liking me—"

"Nothing could make me dislike you. You have my word on that."

Apparently she believed him. "It was the same demon," she said on a sigh. "But it wasn't the same as the one I saw before. He always burst into flames. There was always fire everywhere, just as there was when Mother died. I liked fires before that. I had some matches and I was lighting them one by one. I may have started the fire that burned down the house."

"Was the demon around before the fire?" William asked suddenly.

Celine's eyes never left Stuart's face, but they widened with fright as she made a conscious effort to remember the night her mother had died.

"Yes," she said at last. "Mother saw him too—I'd forgotten that. All these years I'd forgotten that! I tried to tell Father that he'd been there and that Mother was frightened of him, but he and Miss Campbell said I'd imagined him—that there never had been anything."

"Interesting," William commented.

Miss Campbell's hand shot out and she slapped Celine hard on either side of her face. "You're as mischievous as your mother! She was always trying to turn your father away from me too!"

Stuart moved towards the hysterical woman, but William was even faster. "I think we've heard enough," he said, bundling Miss Campbell into the house before him. "I'll take Miss Campbell into Nuwara Eliya straight away and put her in a hotel. The rest is best forgotten once Celine has got it out of her system. Georgina, you'll look after her until I get back, won't you?"

Georgina started and nodded. "How long will you be?" she asked.

He turned and looked at her, but she couldn't read the expression in his eyes. "Who knows?" he said.

"*Girls and boys, come out to play, The moon doth shine as bright as day.*"

Georgina could hear Celine's pretty young voice rising and falling as she sang the old nursery rhyme to herself out on the verandah. But she had not been singing earlier; then she had been distressed and grey with fatigue.

"You can't possibly understand how it was," she had

said. "You see, I've always thought I killed her. If I had, I wouldn't deserve any happiness, would I?"

"I don't know," Stuart had murmured thoughtfully. "Who gave you the matches to play with? I'd say the blame was largely theirs."

Celine had responded with all the eagerness of a young puppy. "But I can remember it all now!" she had exulted. "I never did light any of the matches because I heard a funny, whirring noise. I looked out of the window and there was this black man with paint all over his body and he was whirling something round and round his head. Then everything went up in flames. I climbed out of the window and ran round to the front of the house, where Miss Campbell was standing. She was calling out something to the black man and he went inside the back door, but the fire must have come rushing out towards him when he opened the door, because I remember him being surrounded with flames—and he never came out again. I wanted to go inside to my mother, but Miss Campbell wouldn't let me go. She kept saying she was glad she was dead. It went round and round in my head until I thought I was saying it too."

"I never did like Miss Campbell," Georgina had said with distaste.

"No," Stuart had agreed, "but we'll never know now what her part in the fire was. Perhaps it's best that way."

Celine had nodded decisively. "Poor thing, she thought she would have Father all to herself, but all he wanted from her was a nurse for me. Funny, I might have hated her if we'd never left Australia, but now I know how she must have felt. Sometimes one can't make do with less than everything from a particular person. She should have gone away long ago."

"And allowed you to grow up?" Stuart had said very gently.

Celine had looked at him, her heart in her eyes. "I'll try," she had said.

Stuart had gone away shortly after that. Georgina and Celine had waited for William until they were both rubbing their eyes to keep awake, it was so late. Georgina had insisted that they dined at their usual hour because there were the servants to consider, but still William hadn't come.

"You go to bed, Georgie," Celine had suggested, after they had finished their coffee out on the verandah. She had stretched, holding her arms high above her head. "I feel so much lighter! I'll wait up for William, shall I?"

Georgina had thought the younger girl might have wanted to speak to William on her own, so she had gone meekly to bed, but that had been a long time ago now. Celine began the nursery rhyme all over again, a note of irrepressible laughter in her voice.

"Do you like that one?" she asked when she had finished.

"It's not my favourite," William answered her.

"No," she agreed, "but I know what is! *Georgie Porgie—*"

"Where is she?"

"She was tired. She went to bed."

"Good idea! Off you go too, Pussycat! Oh, and Celine, don't worry about anything any more. It will all come right now."

"With Stuart too?" And then, when William didn't answer, "Georgie doesn't want him. She said she doesn't. Besides, she's married to you!"

Georgina craned to hear William's answer, but it was lost on the evening breeze. All she heard after that was Celine's footsteps in the hall as she went to her room and the sound of William locking up the French windows for the night.

He came into her room through the bathroom. She had not expected him and she lay very still, half hoping he would go away again.

"Georgie?"

"Go away!" she said.

His laughter gave her a winded feeling, as if she had been hit hard in the solar plexus.

"Georgie my love," he said, "you've done it again! All the way home I've been telling myself how pleased you'd be to please me, that there wouldn't be a word of argument from you, only a soft, gentle woman welcoming me home—"

Georgina sat up in a rush. "You should have known better!" she began.

He sat down on the bed beside her. "Will you always want to fight, my Georgie?"

She hugged her knees tightly, considering whether she should turn on the bedside light or not. If she did, she would be able to see him the better, but that went both ways and he might discover the traces of tears on her cheeks and draw his own conclusions. He had been gone so long! But she would much rather he didn't know how his absence had affected her.

"Georgina—"

"If you come any closer, I'll—I'll black your other eye for you, William Ayres!" she threatened.

She heard his breath catch. "You can try!" he retorted. "Because I'm coming a whole lot closer, Georgie Porgie. Move over!"

She stared at him through the darkness, her heart taking up a new and exotic rhythm within her. "What happens if I don't?" she asked him.

He scooped her up into his arms and deposited her on the far side of the bed, holding her hands in one of his behind her back. "I've waited for this moment for a long time," he said, and his voice made her tremble much as his kisses had earlier. "You're not going to spoil it for me, are you?"

She stopped struggling. "William?" she said on a note of wonder. "Is there anything to spoil?"

She felt his laughter against her ribs and she gave way willingly before his questing hands. "As if you didn't know," he said softly. And he kissed her.

CHAPTER TEN

Georgina felt as contented as a well-fed cat. It was bliss. For a week she had done nothing but purr with pleasure at the new turn in her relationship with William. What did it matter if he didn't love her? It seemed no more than an abstruse philosophical point when she lay in his arms at night, or when he looked at her in that certain way of his in the daytime and she knew he was remembering, just as she was, the delights of the passion that flared so easily between them.

Of course, it wouldn't always be like this. She knew that, but she wasn't going to think about it now. Soon William would be away all day working and she would have to pay more attention to Celine and her problems. And then there was Jennifer—

"If you screw up your face like that you'll get terrible wrinkles," Celine broke in on her thoughts. "Think pleasant thoughts if you want to be beautiful! I remember my mother saying that."

"If she was anything like you she didn't have much to worry about!" Georgina remarked dryly.

Celine laughed. "Well, she wasn't. She wasn't at all like me—I mean, she wasn't beautiful in any way. Her face was a jumble of features and her teeth were all crooked. But she was never without a man at her side. They all loved her, even Father, though she made no effort to be faithful to him. Beauty hasn't anything to do with it."

To Georgina, this was heresy. "Wait until you meet Jennifer," she said on a sigh. "She's not as lovely as you are, but she's well enough to have put me in the shade all my life."

"Perhaps she has something else as well. *You* have. You're nice."

Georgina was about to say that Jennifer was not nice, but she stopped herself in time. It wasn't fair to denigrate Jennifer behind her back, especially as she was going to stay with them for a visit. There was always the possibility that William would be right and she and Celine would take to one another and become friends. If that were true, it would be a pity if she were to spoil it.

"Niceness is rather dull," she said instead. "It would be rather fun to be a *femme fatale* for a week, or a day, and see what it felt like!"

Celine fluttered her lashes, a superior look on her face. "You should know if anyone does! William doesn't hover round you because you're nice! I don't know how you did it, Georgie, but I'm awfully glad you did. He feels better about all women since you came along. He's much nicer to me even. I used to think he found me a drag all the time and, after a while, I couldn't say anything sensible to him at all."

"Miss Campbell didn't help—"

"No," Celine agreed, "but someone like you would have coped with Miss Campbell long ago. You may wish you were beautiful, but you can't wish it half as much as I wish I were more forceful and determined. I admire you for that!"

Georgina was astonished. "Nobody else does! I've had to live with the fact that I'm a bully for years now!"

"Since William labelled you as one?"

Georgina nodded. "He still thinks I need watching. I don't mind as much as I did, but when Jennifer comes— *She* never lays down the law! She suggests things to people and, of course, they do whatever she wants them to."

"Even William?"

"Especially William!"

William came out on to the verandah to join them, his chest bared to the sun. He was already the colour of mahogany, which made his eyes seem lighter and the golden lights in them more obvious.

"There's a letter for you," he said to Georgina, and dropped it casually into her lap. "From Jennifer." He watched her pick it up and examine the envelope for herself. "You don't have to check, it's just as it left her fair hand. I haven't steamed it open to find out what secrets you and she are keeping from me!"

"Good," said Georgina. "You're learning—though Jennifer never shares any of her secrets with me." She waved the letter in the air, unread. "Do you want to see for yourself?"

"If I want to read it, you won't keep it from me," he smiled at her. He sat down on a chair and waited. "Tell me what she says," he commanded.

Georgina's eyes slid over her sister's large, spidery writing. Jennifer thought large writing denoted a generous nature and she made no effort to confine herself to more than a couple of words on every line. It meant that what Georgina could have written on a single page was spread over half a dozen, the lines tip-tilted and running into one another. It was large, but it was by no means easy to read.

"She's coming up from Colombo in her own chauffeur-driven car, which Duncan has insisted on paying for. Naturally, he wants her to have the best because he's still very fond of her. She hopes she hasn't broken his heart as she knows what it's like to be parted from the one person in the world for her. Only Duncan is luckier than she, because she hasn't been stolen from him by another. It's doubly hard when someone one has loved and trusted all one's life stabs one in the back. Didn't Caesar say, '*Et tu, Brute?*' to his friend Brutus as he did the dirty deed? She knows just how he felt."

William didn't move a muscle. Georgina looked at him over the top of the letter, wondering what he was thinking.

"She doesn't say exactly when she's arriving," she went on, a nervous tremor in her voice that refused to be dismissed.

"I've never had much time for Caesar myself," William said suddenly.

All Georgina's worst suspicions were aroused. He had to be trying to tell her something and she was too obtuse to know what it was! She thought hard about Julius Caesar, but all she knew about him didn't make him particularly lovable in her eyes either.

"Why not?" she asked.

"He played both ends against the middle. His wife had to be above suspicion to keep the Romans quiet at home while he went off and conquered Cleopatra to make himself master of Egypt."

"He was a great man!" Georgina protested. "One can't judge them by ordinary everyday standards!"

"What other standards would one use?" he asked reasonably. "And, more to the point, when does the individual decide he's great enough to use these other standards!"

Georgina gave him a helpless look. "I suppose he just knows. Besides, I've always heard it that he couldn't resist Cleopatra's exquisite beauty. He probably couldn't help himself!"

"How very convenient," William drawled. "Would you allow such an excuse from me, Georgie Porgie?"

She might have to, she thought, when Jennifer arrived. "I'd try to understand," she said aloud.

He opened his eyes and her own widened at the

gold flash she saw in their depths. "Don't expect me to be so broad-minded if you take off! I've got used to having you at my beck and call and that's the way I like it."

Her heart jerked within her. "But it might not always be enough," she forced herself to say. "I wasn't your first choice—I may not be your last. *She* may be somebody else!"

William smiled a self-satisfied grin. "If she is, don't expect to know anything about her. You won't get away from me as easily as that! You, I shall have and hold till death do us part, no matter what pleasant diversions crop up along the way!"

But Jennifer would make sure she knew! Jennifer would enjoy telling her the details of her conquest and, whatever William might say now, Georgina was as sure as her sister was that it would be Jennifer who would win.

William sat forward suddenly, making Georgina jump. "What mischief are you thinking up now, my sweet? I make my own decisions, Georgie Porgie, and I reserve the right to make most of yours for you too, so don't get carried away by your own sense of importance! I won't be bullied by you, and the only force of arms I recognise from you takes place in bed—and very nice too!" He stood up, pushing an errant lock of hair away from her face. "Won't you ever be content to allow that in me you've met your master?"

If only it were as simple as that! "I may still escape you," she warned him.

The prospect didn't seem to worry him. "Do you want to?" he challenged her.

Sometimes she did. Sometimes she wanted passionately to get away from him, but she hadn't wanted to in the last few days, and she was ashamed that he should know it too.

"I'm an ordinary healthy female," she began. "Most women like to be mastered in bed."

His smile looked to her eyes to be wolfish and not very kind. "We're not in bed now, Georgina, and I'm still your master!"

Celine blinked at them both and eased herself out of her chair, mumbling something about taking a walk across the tea gardens towards the bungalow where Stuart lived. "Atta girl, Georgina!" she added over her shoulder, giving the clenched fist salute as she went. "Give him all you've got!"

The colour swept up Georgina's face. "*Celine!*" she pleaded. "Don't go!"

"I've already gone," Celine answered. "I may be a bit lacking, but at least I know when I'm not wanted. See you later!"

Georgina retired into a sulky silence, but when she saw that it was going to take much more than that to remove William from the strategic position he had chosen, standing over her and, at the same time, preventing her from leaving her chair, she rushed into speech.

"Now look what you've done!" she attacked him. "If she's going to visit Stuart, I ought to go with her. She's quite capable of allowing him all sorts of liberties— in fact, she'll probably demand that he does—" She broke off, not quite knowing how to finish the sentence.

"Make love to her?" William ended it for her. "Stuart will look after her better than you can, Georgie. Your place is here with me."

"Until Jennifer comes—"

"If you feel like that, why didn't you write and tell her she couldn't come?"

She shrugged her shoulders. "She'd have come anyway. She wants you back!"

"And are you going to give me back?"

She shrugged again. "Why not? You were never mine anyway."

"But you are mine, Georgie Porgie. What are you going to do about that?"

Tears pricked at the back of her eyes. "What would you have me do? Bully the life out of her until she turns round and goes away? Jennifer never goes away. She's always there. She always has been!"

"I see. I hadn't realised you felt like that about her—"

"You've always told me I was jealous of her and, you see, you're quite right! She even has Duncan paying for her car!"

William's lips curved into a mocking smile. "Do you want him to pay for one for you too?"

Her indignation knew no bounds. "*Duncan*? That creep? I wouldn't give him the time of day!"

"Then why the jealousy?" he pressed her. "Aren't you satisfied yet that I want you quite as much as you want me? Has our life together lacked anything for you these last few days?"

She refused to answer directly. "That isn't everything," she said darkly. "With Jennifer it wouldn't count at all!"

A distinct twinkle stirred the depths of William's golden eyes. "We're talking about you, little Georgie. I got the impression it counted with you quite a lot."

Incensed, she made a move to get past him, but he had her trapped. "You didn't *ask* me, if you remember. I didn't have any choice in the matter. With you, I never do."

"Exactly!" he encouraged her, just as if he were talking to a recalcitrant child, "Between us, I'll always call the tune—in or out of bed! If you want me to turn my back on Jennifer, you'll have to be specially nice to me, my love." He took her hands in his, unclenching her fists with fingers of steel. "You wouldn't really try and black my eye again, would you?"

"Yes, I would!"

"No wonder Jennifer always gets there before you. She would scorn to use such tactics! I doubt she's ever made a boy cry in her life!"

Georgina's temper was stretched beyond endurance. "What about Duncan?" she demanded crossly. "Haven't you any sympathy for him?"

"Should I have?"

She sniffed. "I'd have said you had a great deal in common! He's behaving better than you did, though. Next time Jennifer spurns you, William Ayres, don't expect me to mop your blood off the floor! I'll be busy elsewhere!"

"Not you, Georgie Porgie—"

"And don't call me that! When I'm free of you, I'll change my name to something different and forget all about your horrid nursery rhymes!"

He pulled her up into the circle of his arms, amused. "You won't forget. It used to be Rowley-Powley before it was Georgie Porgie, and that could apply to any name. Besides, I like your brand of kisses and I like your name, my dear, and I like having you by my side. You'll never be free of me, Mrs. Ayres!"

He had some reason to be confident, she reflected dully, for she too, doubted she would ever leave him until he decided to send her away. And Jennifer would see to that! She would never share any man she thought of as hers, not even with his wife!

His arms closed round her in a most satisfactory way. "Be as tough as you like with anyone else, Georgie, but I know you better than that! You were never reluctant for me to have my way with you, and you're not reluctant to have me make love to you now."

"You can't be sure of that!" she protested. She sounded breathless and pathetically eager. It was *his* fault! His hand searched out her curves and her heart turned over in anticipation of what would come next.

"Can't I? *Can't I*, Georgina?"

"It isn't love!"she burst out.

"Isn't it?" He laughed out loud. "What do you call it? I won't believe you're still pretending to hate me. Are you, my sweet?"

"No." She choked over the word, her hands covering his in a mute protest against their probing. "William, we can't! Not here!"

His lips met hers, exploring her mouth with a thoroughness that deprived her of all further speech. She uttered a sob of pleasure and abandoned the attempt of trying to reason him into being more sensible. She felt herself lifted high up against his chest and wondered at his strength of arm. How dreadful that she should like being coerced by him! She ought to be made of sterner stuff, but she wasn't. She felt very feminine and deliciously weak, and it was the most marvellous sensation in the world.

He deposited her on the bed and stood back from her. "What, no more arguments, Mrs. Ayres?"

She spluttered with laughter, making no effort to move, not even when he knelt on the bed beside her and began to undress her. Only her eyes darkened with the strength of her emotions. "I wish I were more beautiful for you," she murmured against his hand, trying to impede its progress against her naked flesh. She shivered with pleasure as he defeated her ruse. "Oh, William!" she breathed.

"Oh, Georgina!" he mocked her, his lips returning to her mouth. "Confess now, my sweet, that you like it when I have my way with you. You do, don't you?"

"*Yes!*"

He paused in what he was doing, his eyes narrowing as he surveyed her. Then his lips met hers again in a kiss as soft as a butterfly's wings and she could feel his laughter against her breasts.

"How are the mighty fallen!" he taunted her. "But it's not enough. Before I'm through with you, my darling, you'll weep with love for me, and then I'll have you just where I want you!"

William went to work the next day, and time hung heavy on Georgina's hands. She had wanted to go with him, to see how he went about the gigantic task of harnessing a whole river and deflecting its course away from the sea so that not a single drop of its precious fluid was lost to the land.

"Your job is to stay with Celine," William had told her with a touch of severity. "You can come to the site some other time."

"I've got used to having you about," Georgina had tried to persuade him. "What are Celine and I to do all day?"

"You could get Stuart to show you over the tea factory," he had suggested.

"There'll still be tomorrow!"

He had given her an odd look then. "I'm flattered," he had said. "I never thought you'd admit you could miss my company for a few hours."

She had blushed scarlet, cross with herself for being so foolish as to betray her feelings to him. "It's my pugnacious nature," she had defended herself. "I can't fight with Celine—it wouldn't do!"

The glint in his tawny eyes had discomfited her still further. "I'll be back tonight," he had said, and he had kissed her hard on the mouth, scattering her wits to the four winds. "I'll see you then," he had added, and she had been sure that it hadn't been entirely her imagination that he had been as much moved by the embrace as she, and she had been fiercely glad that he found as much pleasure in her body as she did in his.

Celine was in a bad mood too. She claimed she had a headache and retired to her bedroom, refusing to come out. At lunchtime, she looked tired and drawn, and Georgina began to worry in earnest about her.

"What's the matter?" she asked her bluntly. "Is it Stuart?"

"I don't want to talk about it!" Celine retorted. For the first time since Miss Campbell's departure the blank look was back in her eyes and she made no effort to converse or eat, but sat in a withdrawn world of her own, refusing all Georgina's blandishments to make her pull out of it.

"I wish you'd tell me about it," Georgina pleaded with her. "I'm not feeling on the top of the world myself."

A fleeting smile crossed Celine's face. "Missing William already?"

Georgina nodded. "I only fight with him when he's here, but I can't settle to anything with him gone. Silly, isn't it?"

"You're in love with him," Celine sighed. "You're lucky!"

"Lucky!" Georgina stared at her. The tears came rushing into her eyes. "He doesn't love me. He never will. He married me because he thought my sister Jennifer preferred someone else. He wanted to protect her from me!"

"Why?"

"He thinks I bully her into doing things she doesn't want to—that I broke up her romance with him. She wrote him a letter, you see, saying she'd changed her mind and wanted him after all. She gave it to me to give him on the plane, only inside it was written as if she'd wanted him to receive it before the wedding. If he'd had it then he wouldn't have married me."

Celine shrugged. "He doesn't seem to hold it against you. Anyway, why should you care? I wouldn't if I were married to Stuart. I wouldn't care about anything else."

"Not with Jennifer on her way here?" Georgina said dryly.

Celine looked muddled and frowned. Georgina, looking up at that moment, caught her breath afresh at the younger girl's shining beauty, a beauty which was enhanced rather than otherwise by her supreme indifference to the effect it had on those about her.

"I always thought," Celine began in puzzled tones, "that everyone loved the people who are close to them. Everyone else, that is. I didn't love my mother, I hardly ever saw her. She was always out with some man or other. I loved Miss Campbell even less. I'm not sure about my father. I think I did love him—I liked him a lot when he had time for me. I've always felt guilty that I didn't love my mother and she died. But you don't love Jennifer, do you?"

Georgina had always pretended to herself that she did. "I'm sure I do! I don't like her, but I'm sure I must love her!"

"Because she's your sister?"

"Well, yes," Georgina admitted. "I've never thought of doing anything else."

Celine struggled within herself to find the words to explain something else she didn't understand. "Stuart says I don't know how I feel about him either!" she blurted out. "He's going to give me time to find my feet. Oh, Georgie, how can I all by myself? I've been alone so long!"

Georgina felt as helpless as her charge. "Perhaps he's worried that you need someone, but not him in particular," she suggested hopefully. "You don't know many other men, after all."

"I don't have to!" Celine maintained stubbornly. "I want Stuart now. He says we both have to be free in case we find we prefer someone else, just as if his saying that makes any difference to how I feel about him. I'll never be free—even if I wanted to be! But he doesn't need me in the same way. He might find someone else and I think I'd die if he did!"

"Have you told him that?"

Celine shook her head. "He may be afraid because I'm not—not *normal*. He wouldn't tell me so, though, would he? He wouldn't want to hurt my feelings. There must be hundreds of ordinary girls he could marry. I'm frightened he doesn't want me. That's why you're lucky to be married to William. You'll always be a part of him even if he does prefer your sister. I'd rather share Stuart than not have him at all."

Georgina wondered if she could ever be as self-sacrificing, but she already knew that she couldn't. She wanted the whole loaf! For others half a loaf might be better than no bread at all, but it wasn't for her, not if Jennifer had the other half. Not if Jennifer had a single slice, come to that!

"I think you're completely normal," she said aloud. "And you have a much nicer nature than I have. I want what I want, much more than I want what William wants!"

For once Celine looked the older of the two. "Because they're the same thing, Georgie. Otherwise you wouldn't. He can't want Jennifer very badly or he wouldn't have married you. I daresay he doesn't really love either of you, but he's married to you. I'd give anything to be married to Stuart!" And she began to look so miserable again that Georgina felt quite cheerful about her own chances with William by comparison.

William would be coming home to her that evening and she could hardly wait. All would be well, she thought, just as long as William went on coming home. While he did that, they were a team, and the longer a team stayed in harness the more difficult it was to destroy the partnership.

The two girls decided to make Georgina a new dress after lunch. Celine had supplied the material, a beautiful *batik* cotton which she had bought for herself in Nuwara Eliya, but which she had afterwards had thought was too definite a colour for her fair beauty.

"I like it," she said indifferently when Georgina said she should keep it for herself, "but I'll never wear it. Not that shade of green with my hair!"

"Perhaps not," Georgina decided. She couldn't help fingering the thick cotton to examine the pattern more closely. The amount of work that had gone into dyeing the pattern was frightening. She could imagine how long it had taken waxing the area that was not to be dyed any particular colour, and then waxing it again for the next colour, and so on until the whole design was complete. "I'll get you another dress length when I go with William to the site. We learned to do this sort of thing in college, but I can't say my efforts were as fine as this."

"You should see some of the wall-hangings!" Celine enthused. "They're real works of art! I wanted to buy one, but Miss Campbell wouldn't let me. She doesn't like beautiful things."

Georgina laughed. "She's so terribly ugly herself, isn't she? I mean not just ugly in a bearable way, but she's made herself ugly. Poor thing, one has to feel sorry for her for having to live with herself!"

Celine averted her face so that Georgina couldn't see her expression. "I had to live with her for years. I still can't believe she's gone." She hesitated. "I don't believe she started the fire herself, you know, though William thinks she might have done. I think she made that man come and dance outside the window to frighten Mother, though. Afterwards she made him come again and frighten me. She'll never let me go if she can help it."

Georgina felt a strange disquiet settle over her own spirits. "William won't allow her to have anything more to do with you."

"No," Celine agreed. "Not if he can help it. But if I were married to Stuart no one would have to keep her away, would they? I feel safe with Stuart."

Georgina put out an impulsive hand, grasping the other girl's arm. "She won't come back here, darling. William is a dangerous man when he's crossed—as I have reason to know! She wouldn't risk another brush with him."

Celine shrugged off her hand, spreading the material on the floor of the sitting-room. "She would, you know," she said quietly. "She has great faith in her own powers—and so have I!"

"Her powers?"

Celine twisted her lips into the semblance of a smile. "She found out about them when she was a child. They work too. That's why she kept me alive, because one day I'd add to her powers. She was always telling me so. Otherwise I could have died with my mother and welcome!"

"But that's horrible!" Georgina protested, wondering if she or William would ever know what Celine had suffered at that terrible woman's hands.

"That's Miss Campbell," said Celine.

The light was fading from the sky when the sound of a car coming up the drive made Georgina dash to the front door. She didn't care if William did laugh at her, she had to welcome him home in person and, besides, she wanted to tell him about Miss Campbell. But it was not the jeep that William was using that edged its way forward through the trees. This was a saloon car and it hooted at every bend in the way of every Sinhalese driver. A stunning disappointment welled up inside her. She had been so sure it would be William at last, and it wasn't. On the contrary, there was nobody else it could be but Jennifer.

The car drew up beside the front door and Georgina went out to meet her, forcing a smile of welcome on to her lips. Jennifer, elegant and imperious, emerged from the car and smoothed down her skirt with a much-ringed hand. She held up the rings beneath Georgina's nose and laughed.

"I bought them on the way here. Sapphires are two a penny out here and I never could resist them!"

Georgina felt at a loss. Her eyes gravitated to the car again just in time to see another figure getting out of the back on the far side.

"You're not alone?"

"No. Isn't it a giggle?" Jennifer giggled charmingly. "Miss Campbell is my travelling companion while I'm in Sri Lanka. I found her all alone in Kandy and we decided to go on together."

"I know Miss Campbell," Georgina said huskily.

"That's right, she does," Miss Campbell agreed complacently. "I'm back, just like the proverbial bad penny! You can't keep a good man down, can you? And how are we getting on with my poor little Celine, Georgie Porgie—no, I have to say Mrs. Ayres, don't I? Managed nicely without me, have you?"

Jennifer's tinkling laugh ran through the dusk of the evening. "Oh, Georgie! Has that unfortunate rhyme followed you out here too? Shall I speak to William about it on your behalf?"

CHAPTER ELEVEN

Georgina's heart ached in sympathy when she saw William's weary, resigned face. "I was hoping you'd be home earlier," she said.

He pushed the curl off her forehead with an impatient hand. "Don't start on me now, Georgie, there's a dear. It's been one hell of a day! I should have gone down there earlier and seen how things were going—"

"It hasn't been much of a day here either," she interrupted him. "Oh, William, Miss Campbell is here! Jennifer arrived too. Miss Campbell is her new travelling companion."

"Is she, though? I can't say I admire her taste."

"No," she muttered darkly. "And that isn't all! Jennifer *likes* her!"

William gave her a look of exasperated amusement. "If she didn't, she wouldn't have brought her with her. Oh well, I don't suppose it matters really, and quite honestly, at the moment I'm too tired to care about who we have in the house! I'll have something to eat and go straight to bed. Don't worry about disturbing me, my dear. I'll sleep in the other room."

He couldn't have hurt her more if he had struck her. "Must you?" she asked tremulously. "I—I—"

"You don't have to pretend, Georgina. You'll be glad to have your bed to yourself for a night, won't you? It'd be different if we were going to make love, but I'm pooped. I could sleep for a week!"

Georgina threaded her fingers together in a nervous gesture. "Is it always going to be like this?"

"I hope not!"

"It isn't because Jennifer is here?"

His eyes narrowed. "How could it be? I haven't seen her yet. Come on, out with it! What's niggling you about Jennie now?"

Georgina gulped. "I just thought—" he took a deep breath to give herself courage. "She's here now. I just thought you might not want me because she's under the same roof."

"Georgie dear, I'm tired! Haven't I given you sufficient proof this last week that I want you? Jennifer won't make any difference to that! But not tonight, sweetheart. Okay?"

She nodded, unconvinced. "What am I to do about Miss Campbell?"

His irritation surfaced again. "Does it matter? She won't be able to do much harm in a few hours, will she? I'll have a word with her before I leave for work tomorrow."

Georgina's gaze caught and held him. "I'm frightened of her," she confessed. "Celine says she has powers and that she'll never let her go because of them. I think I believe her."

"Rubbish, sweetheart. What powers can she possibly have?"

"I don't know. But she said she'd be back and here she is!"

"Thanks to Jennifer!"

"Yes, but she managed to persuade her to bring her. Jennifer isn't very biddable about that sort of thing. She hasn't much time for her own sex at the best of times, but someone as ugly and unpleasant as Miss Campbell? How did she manage it?"

"Not by witchcraft! I expect Jennifer took pity on

her *because* she's ugly and unfortunate in her manner. She always had a kind heart."

Georgina compressed her lips into a straight line, telling herself it would be folly to pursue the matter further. Besides, what did she expect William to do? He looked more tired than she had ever seen him, and her conscience smote her. He had his own worries, couldn't she cope with the ones that Miss Campbell's presence had brought them? What kind of a wife was she, anyhow, to badger him now when she could see for herself how exhausted he was?

"William—" He looked an enquiry. "I'd rather you slept in my room with me. I won't bother you—"

But he shook his head. "Nothing doing, my sweet. I know you better than that! Of course you'd bother me!" He laughed without any amusement. "Get someone to bring me some sandwiches, will you? And keep Jennifer out of my hair until tomorrow. Can you do that?"

She looked down, veiling her eyes with her lashes. "I'll bring you the sandwiches myself. Sleep well, William."

He tipped up her face and kissed her on the lips. "Thank you, Georgie. Could you believe they were using the wrong core to pack the base of that dam? It will all have to come out again. That'll teach me for allowing you to distract me from the task in hand!" He kissed her again. "If you think it's hot up here, you should try a day out in the sun down there. No, on second thoughts, you'd better not. I like you cool and fresh and sweet-smelling! I must smell like a Turkish bath!"

She rubbed her hand against his chest, smiling. "I don't mind," she said. "You could smell like a pig for all I care!"

He smiled genuinely then and delivered a slap on her

behind. "Who'd have thought you'd turn out to be such a sexy piece?" he teased her. "See that you only show that side of yourself to me, Georgie Porgie, or it'll be you who sports the next black eye!"

"I'm not afraid!" she sang out, dancing out of his reach. "Last time it was I who got through your defences! You never know when I might do so again!"

"Oh, Georgina!" He shook his head at her. "What an appetite for doing battle you have! Don't you ever give up? You must know by now that I'm the natural victor between us."

She looked up at him, her eyes sparkling. "Prove it," she challenged him.

He took a step towards her. "With pleasure! But not now, Georgie! You have our guests to consider, and I have some sleep to catch up on. But one day soon I'll make you cry uncle, and I'll enjoy every minute of it!"

She thought she would too, but not with Jennifer, the true love of his life, in the same house. Her pleasure in the cut and thrust between them fell away from her and thoughts of her sister and Miss Campbell came crowding back into her mind.

"I wish they hadn't come!" she said out loud.

His eyes were kind, but very, very tired. "Cheer up, they won't stay for ever." He turned away from her, going through the bathroom to his own bedroom. Halfway there, he turned and spoke again: "Keep Celine out of Miss Campbell's way, won't you, Georgie? I couldn't stand her screaming her head off in the middle of the night tonight—"

"Then you do think she might get at her?" Georgina demanded.

"I think she may try if it's made easy enough for her. It's up to you to keep them apart. Jennifer will help you, if you explain things to her properly. She brought her here, after all!"

It was strange how obtuse the most intelligent of men could be, Georgina thought to herself, trying not to wince physically as he shut the door behind him. It did hurt, though. She had been looking forward to his homecoming all day, longing for his company, and now to be deprived of it made her want to cry. Nor were Jennifer and Miss Campbell the substitutes she would have chosen to sit opposite her at the dinner table. And what about Celine? Could she be persuaded to have her meal in her room? Georgina sighed, deciding that wouldn't do either. She had to see Miss Campbell some time if she was staying in the same house; it might as well be in company, when Jennifer and she were there to protect her.

When she went in search of the younger girl, however, she was nowhere to be found. Only Jennifer was in the sitting-room, smoking a cigarette in one of the longest holders Georgina had ever seen. This was a new affectation and one that wouldn't last long, judging by the ham-fisted way Jennifer chose to wield it, swirling it about her head.

"Aren't I to be allowed to see William?" she greeted Georgina in her usual sarcastic style. She seldom bothered to charm her own family unless she wanted something from them.

"Not tonight. He started work today and things haven't been going well without him. He's very tired and he's gone straight to bed."

"How boring!"

Georgina kept a stern check on her temper. "He came out here to work," she said mildly. "He likes these Commonwealth projects and he wants it to be a success."

"More likely it's a good excuse to get away from you, Georgie. All men get tired of fighting with you sooner or later, don't they? I could name quite a few

who turned from you to me with obvious relief. You
never learn, do you, my pet?"

"You were welcome to all of them," Georgina replied mildly.

"And William?"

"I'm married to William."

"But for how long? You don't flatter yourself that
you'll be able to keep him, do you?" She looked smug.
"Didn't you guess that I came out here to retrieve my
property from your ungentle hands? I want William, and
I'm going to have him. I made a mistake sending you to
tell him about Duncan. I thought he'd give you beans for
your trouble, not marry you instead of me! Why didn't
he? Not that it matters! He won't stay with you for a
moment longer than he has to, not when he knows that
I'm available. He's in love with *me*, remember?"

Georgina tried to keep calm. "I wonder if he is," she
observed. "He doesn't seem overjoyed by your arrival,
does he?"

"Only because he's afraid of what will happen when
we meet," Jennifer claimed with such certainty that
Georgina could feel herself being pushed into believing
her. She wished she had a similar confidence in herself
to sustain her.

She changed the subject. "Did you know Miss
Campbell used to look after William's ward, Celine?"
she asked.

"Oh yes. She told me at once. You weren't very
clever there, my dear Georgie. She considers you an
enemy, and the Miss Campbells of this world know
how to deal with their enemies."

"Nonsense!"

"What about Celine's mother? I wouldn't be in your
shoes for anything! You put an end to her nice comfortable job with Celine, didn't you? And she needed that
girl—"

"Did she say as much?" Georgina was startled into asking.

"More or less. She came over to me in the hotel at Kandy and asked if I was any relation of yours. I can't say I was flattered at the likeness she thought she could see between us, but she has uncanny ways and she said she could see some kind of thread running between us. I thought it would be amusing to watch her at work on you—she's a very determined lady!—and I owed you a bad turn for taking William away from me. Poor Georgie! Life is going to be very unpleasant for you in the next few days, Miss Campbell and I will see to that!"

"It's not me I'm worrying about, it's Celine," Georgina told her. "That woman—"

"How noble you are! But then you always were. Did you marry William in order to protect me from his wrath over Duncan? It would be just like you! You never would have made Duncan cry if he hadn't been pinching my arm. I suppose William's black eye was like inspired! What have you found to quarrel with him about when I wasn't here to provoke you both? How dull you must have been!"

"We managed."

Jennifer's eyebrows rose in disdain. "In separate bedrooms? *Not* my idea of managing a marriage, I must say!"

Georgina swallowed down her anger. Her sister must have been very busy to have found out so much about the geography of the bungalow so quickly.

"Think what you like," she said. "William has old-fashioned ideas about marriage and I don't see yours appealing to him much. You'll have to settle for something less, Jennie, if you can."

Jennifer was languidly amused. "Become his mistress? Would you hate that very much? Yes, I can see you would. Have you fallen in love with William,

Georgie? Was all that hatred just a pretence because
he so so obviously preferred me? He'll never love you,
my dear. He loves me and he always has! I'll see to it he
doesn't change his mind at this point in your favour,
you can be sure of that. I always have been able to twist
your men round my little finger. It's laughable that you
still have lingering hopes of winning against me—and
with William too! William will come to heel when I
whistle to him, just like all the others, and you'll be left
on the sidelines, which is where you belong! God, how
I hate that holier-than-thou expression of yours! In
fact, I don't like anything about you much. Nor does
Mother. She dutifully sent her love, by the way, and
said she hoped you were going to be sensible and not
thwart your little sister's wishes—"

"And Father?" Georgina interrupted her.

Jennifer's smile was both malicious and contemptuous. "Who cares what Father thinks? He didn't even
send his love to you. He thinks fools ought to be made
to suffer for their folly, and he thinks you a fool for
inviting me to visit you. I do too."

Georgina had never thought she would be glad to see
Miss Campbell come into the room, but on this occasion she was. She patted one of the chairs, inviting the
woman to sit down and asked her if she would like to
have a drink before dinner.

"It's still arrack or nothing," she told her, "but the
passion fruit juice is strong and cold."

"I hope you haven't been allowing Celine to imbibe
alcoholic drinks," Miss Campbell reproved her. "It
won't do her any good. Little girls should be seen and
not heard!"

Georgina eyed her thoughtfully. "Celine has been
very well this last week," she said. "She's all right now
that she's remembered what happened when her mother died. It won't be easy to make a child of her again,

I'm glad to say. She's not a little girl any longer, but a beautiful young woman."

Miss Campbell turned a mottled red, her jowls shaking with anger. "How clever we think we are! But pride goes before a fall, Georgie Porgie, and I for one won't lift a finger to save you when you topple over!"

"Nor I!" Jennifer drawled. "For once, being right won't do you any good," she gloated. "I'll have William and I'll make sure you know all about it! You've always thought you were above being jealous of me, haven't you? You'll learn better!"

Georgina bit her lip, trying to strengthen her resolution to pay no attention to her sister's barbs. But she couldn't hide the pain in her eyes as the door opened again. She expected to see Celine, and she admitted to a certain curiosity as to what would be her sister's reaction to anyone as beautiful as she was, but it was not Celine who walked through the door: it was William.

"Hullo, Jennifer," he said easily. "Miss Campbell."

Jennifer looked up at him through her lashes. "Is that the best you can do, my Billy boy? Don't you dare kiss me with your wife looking on?" She giggled. "Are you afraid she'll beat you up?"

"No to all that," he answered shortly. He turned to Georgina, putting a hand on her shoulder. "Have you seen Celine?"

"No, not since tea-time. Do you want her for something?"

"It doesn't matter. I rang through to Stuart—to tell him about things here—and he wanted to come over. I said I thought it better that Celine should go over there. She isn't in her room."

Georgina rose to her feet. "I'll go and look for her. Go back to bed, William. She'll be all right."

A smile twisted his lips. "Will you be all right too?"

"Of course."

His hand closed over the nape of her neck. "I'll come with you. Stuart is waiting for us by the factory."

"What a fuss!" Jennifer chimed in. "Who cares what's happened to her? We can manage very well without her—"

"No, I can't!" Georgina cut her off, her voice gruff with the effort of keeping her temper. "She's the most beautiful creature imaginable and I'd never forgive myself if anything happened to her."

"Of course not," Jennifer mocked her. "Let's hope she appreciates your efforts to keep her tied to your apron strings more than I did!" She became aware of William's incredulous gaze and blushed becomingly. "Well, you know what Georgie is! She never thought anyone was good enough for her darling sister, who always had to be whiter than white. She bullied me shamefully! She probably bullies the unfortunate Celine too."

Miss Campbell laughed. The sound of it echoed round the room, freezing Georgina's blood. "So you've lost my pretty Celine, have you? Am I invited to come and look for her too?"

Georgina saw her sister flash some kind of message to the older woman, but Miss Campbell was not looking at either of them. Her eyes were on William, cold and staring. "You thought you could stop me seeing her, didn't you? But you're too late! You're much too late! Jennifer and I saw to that!"

"*Jennifer!*" Georgina didn't recognise her own voice as she reiterated her sister's name. "What have you done? Where is she?"

"I didn't do anything," Jennifer protested, pouting sulkily in William's direction. "We did run into someone on the way here, but I had nothing to do with it. Miss Campbell took her away somewhere. *I was glad she did!* Georgina might not care about other people being lovelier than she is, but I do! What a fuss about nothing! She won't come to any harm where she is."

Georgina ran forward in her agitation, but William was before her. He slapped Jennifer lightly first on one cheek and then on the other. "Hysterical female!" he muttered. "Where is she, Jennifer? Or do you want some more of the same?"

"She's *not* hysterical!" Georgina flung at him. "William, if you hit her again, I'll—I'll—"

He took a firm hold on Jennifer's hair, holding up his arm to fend Georgina away from them both. As she straightened her back, determined to make him loose his grasp, she saw that he was laughing at her and tried the harder to get a good blow in before he should take her challenge seriously and, inevitably, would defeat her intention.

"Yes? What will you do?" He took the full force of her fist on his open palm. "I'm only doing what you should have done a long time ago! You don't have to fight *me* on her behalf, Georgie Porgie, not any more. You can settle with me afterwards when we have Celine back safe and sound."

"But, William, Jennifer came here to be with you, and if you're in love with her—"

"I thought she'd be good for Celine!" He released his hold on Jennifer, staring at his wife. "Georgie, I thought you *knew*—"

"Georgie never knows anything to her own advantage," Jennifer said nastily. "I don't know where your beastly Sleeping Beauty is, and I don't care!"

"Sleeping Beauty is my name for her," Miss Campbell said quietly. "Such a good name, don't you think? You won't find her, Mr. Ayres. You're not the right Prince for her, being a married man, and Mr. Duffield doesn't understand her. Nobody understands her as well as her Miss Campbell does! She'll sleep for a hundred years and give her youth to me—"

"My God! What have you done to her?"

"Nothing as yet. But you won't find her. Not even your clever little wife will find her now."

Georgina turned to face her, catching a flicker of uncertainty in the pale, bloodshot eyes. For an instant she couldn't believe it to be true, but she knew that Miss Campbell feared her in some extraordinary way, and she pressed home her advantage with a ruthlessness she hadn't known she possessed.

"Oh yes, I'll find her. Your power is broken, Miss Campbell. Celine is mine!"

"We'll see!" Miss Campbell said grandly, but her fear was obvious now and they could all see it written clearly on her mottled, angry face.

Georgina took one look and shut her eyes to close out the sight. She felt William's arm close about her and shivered against him.

"We'd better go and get her," she said.

"The villagers won't let you in."

Georgina opened her eyes again. "You think not? Rabahindre will talk to them for me." Her fingers clutched at William's shirt-sleeves. "I know where she is," she breathed. "She's in that shed where all the masks are kept."

Miss Campbell crumpled before them. "I must get away!" she shrieked. "I must go now!"

"That seems a very good idea," William agreed. "I'm sure Jennifer will lend you her car and chauffeur to take you back to Kandy, and this time, Miss Campbell, I suggest you don't come back."

"Her father owed me the girl's life! With his wife gone, why didn't he marry me as he promised to do? But no, he gave me Celine instead—and now *she* has taken her away from me!" She broke into laboured sobs, making little rushes towards the door.

"Shall I see her off?" Jennifer asked of no one in particular. "I suppose I ought to offer to go with her? Well, Georgina?"

Georgina chewed on her lip. "Wh-what?" she stammered.

Jennifer sighed dramatically. "You know why I brought her here. You know why I came myself. Are you going to let me stay, knowing all that, or are you going to behave like anyone else would do and chase me away, never to darken your door again?"

Georgina stared at her, and then she looked at William, silently pleading for his help. It seemed she only wanted what he wanted after all.

"Georgina is more gallant than either of us," he stated at last, smiling wryly at his wife and sister-in-law. "No doubt she'll face up to your presence with her usual courage, but not until I've had something of my own to say on the subject. Is Celine in that shed, Jennifer?"

Jennifer shrugged. "I don't know. All I know is this girl came walking down the drive towards us and I wondered who she was. I mean, you don't see anyone as lovely as she is every day of your life, do you? Well, Miss Campbell saw her too, and she got out of the car and spoke to her. The girl seemed to go into a trance. Miss Campbell told me to wait in the car until she got back and I did. She was only gone a few minutes. Then she got back into the car and we came on here." She gave William a shaken look. "What is she? Some kind of witch?"

"She thinks she is. I don't believe it myself, but Georgie thinks she might be one, don't you, darling?"

Georgina swallowed, bemused. "It doesn't matter now her power is broken. She's a sad person, isn't she?"

Jennifer cast her eyes up to heaven. "It isn't true! Georgie, you can't feel responsible for her too! No wonder I've disliked you for years! You never give up on anyone, do you?"

"In your case, I'd say just as well," William put in dryly. "You wouldn't have got very far without her. How did your mother put it? You have so few friends of your own and Georgie's never come to the house when she's away. I've learned a lot about Georgie in the last few days—and a lot about you too!"

Jennifer decided to make the best of a bad job. She smiled winningly at them both, and shrugged her shoulders. "Win a few, lose a few," she drawled. "What are we going to do now?"

William was very much in command of the situation. "You're going to stay here," he ordered Jennifer. "Georgie and I will go and fetch Celine home. And, Jennie, if you want to stay, don't make more of a nuisance of yourself than you can help. Okay?"

"Okay," Jennifer shrugged, accepting this dictate with a complacent smile. Georgina, who had constantly been astounded by her thick skin in the past, envied her her ability to make the best of things no matter how they turned out, and began to wonder what the morrow would bring for herself. William hadn't sounded at all lover-like when he had been addressing Jennifer just now.

"Are you coming or not?"

Georgina started, realising that he must have spoken before but she had been too busy dreaming to listen to him. "Of course I'm coming! Celine will need me— imagine being shut into that shed for hours. William, you don't think—"

"No, I don't," he said with comfortable certainty. "Celine is used to Miss Campbell's ways. She's had to cope too often in the past not to do so now."

"It wasn't much of a life," Georgina mourned. "I hope Stuart realises that!"

William's face relaxed into an indulgent smile. "I'm sure you'll tell him if he doesn't, my little Amazon. He won't dare treat her badly with you around to put him right."

Georgina's gaze swept upwards over his face. His eyes were amused and shone like liquid amber with some other emotion as well. Her heart went into some swooping acrobatics that made it difficult for her to breathe.

"You ought to be in bed," she told him. He looked completely exhausted. "I thought you wanted a good night's sleep."

"So I shall, once we've got Celine back safe and sound. If she's at all nervous, she can share your bed tonight, and then neither of you will feel lonely."

"But, William—"

"Come on, love. Tomorrow is another day!"

And he would be working! She checked the rising hope within her that he might have other plans of his own—plans that would include her!—and tried to concentrate on the matter in hand.

It was easier to do that once they were outside and there was only the light of the waning moon to guide them along the narrow path towards the village. They had to go past the factory to get there and Georgina went running ahead, calling Stuart's name as she went.

"We're here!" Celine's voice answered her. "Georgie, is that you? Oh, Georgie, I knew you would come! And Stuart too! He fetched Rabahindre with the key of the shed and let me out. I don't know when I've been so happy!"

The two girls flung their arms round each other. "She's gone, Celine, and this time she won't be back. You'll never see her again!"

Celine choked with emotion. "I'm *glad* she came! It doesn't matter what she did in the past, this time it all came right! William said it would, but I didn't believe him then. I do now! Stuart won't let anyone look after me now except himself, not even you—isn't that wonderful? Oh, and Georgie, he doesn't *care* that I'm not very bright and all that. He thinks I'm beautiful!" She paused to allow this remarkable fact to sink in, quite unconscious of her listeners' united reaction.

"But Celine, we all know you're beautiful," Georgina said at last, almost humbly.

"Oh yes, *that*!" Celine dismissed her loveliness without interest. "But Stuart thinks I'm a beautiful woman, not a thing to be looked at. That makes all the difference, you see. Oh, Georgie, I'm so happy I could burst!"

Stuart retrieved her from Georgina's embrace, making no more than a half-hearted attempt to put everything on a more normal footing. "She's trying to tell you that we intend to get married," he muttered to William. "With or without your permission," he added with a grin. "I was going to wait until she'd seen a bit more of life, but this last incident has convinced me she's seen more than enough! What she needs is a loving, stable background."

William shook his extended hand with vigour. "I couldn't agree with you more! Do what you like with her. I'm going back to bed!"

CHAPTER TWELVE

"I thought it might be a good time to take you over the tea factory," Stuart suggested.

Georgina tried to look enthusiastic. "Why not?" Why not, indeed? she added to herself. It would be hours and hours before William would be home. He could have looked in and wished her good morning before he had gone, but he hadn't, and by the time she had decided he was not coming and had hurried into her clothes in case she might be in time to have breakfast with him, he was already long gone.

"Jennifer might enjoy it," Georgina forced herself to add. "She ought to see as much as she can while she's here."

Stuart's eyes flickered. "How long is she staying?"

"Until she decides to go, I suppose."

Georgina sounded so dispirited that Celine was concerned for her. "Surely she won't stay now?" she exclaimed.

It was unfortunate that Jennifer should choose that moment to saunter out into the garden to join them. It was the first time she had seen Celine in the full light of day and the look in her eyes was far from being one of unmixed admiration.

"You must be Celine. Well, you don't have to worry, I wouldn't stay anywhere with you around! Very bad for the morale! And, since you're all too shy to ask me, my morale is sagging badly at the moment without having to listen to you telling me how *de trop* I am to *dear* Georgina's perfect marriage! I'll go as soon as my car gets back." She smiled wryly at Celine's bewildered stare. "You have to admit I was useful there! How else would you have got rid of the old harridan?"

"She wouldn't have been here," Celine answered with a logic Jennifer was far from appreciating. Her usual sunny smile broke across her perfect features. "I'm glad she was, though. Stuart says we can get married at once now."

"Stuart?" Jennifer's whole aspect changed at the prospect of meeting a man and not having to make do only with members of her own sex. "Were you here last night?"

Stuart smiled briefly. "I was outside."

Jennifer took a step nearer to him, her whole being concentrated on his lightest word. "How wonderful!" she breathed. "I hope Celine knows how lucky she was to have you rescue her? I quite thought that that little enterprise was going to be left to Georgie. My sister, you know, thrives on manipulating people in and out of incidents of her creation. She has a chronic need to look after everyone all round her. Only there's a snag. There always is a snag, isn't there? Everything has to be done in the way she thinks will be best for you! Take care she doesn't make you out to Celine to be some kind of medicine she has to take three times a day to keep her nerves under control. Romance and nasty medicine don't go well together—and I can see you're romantic just by looking at you! One romantic can always spot another, can't they?"

Celine's lovely smile changed to stony displeasure. "It isn't my nerves, there's nothing wrong with my nerves! I'm not very clever and I have bad dreams, but if Stuart doesn't mind, why should you?"

Georgina thought it was time she took a hand in the conversation herself, dragging herself away from her own attack of the miseries to deal with her sister. How

Jennifer loved stirring things up with her little wooden spoon! But she wasn't going to spoil Celine's happiness, not if she, Georgina, could prevent it.

"Jennifer, don't!" she rapped out.

Her sister turned innocent eyes in her direction. "Don't what?"

But it was Stuart who answered. "I've heard a lot about you, Miss Perry," he said quietly, "*not* from Georgina, but from William. He always said you had soft, gentle manners and a nice nature. Pity he was mistaken."

Jennifer gasped. "What do you mean?"

"I mean Georgina has had a lot to put up with from you in the past, but you won't have her around in the future to smooth your path for you. Shall I hand you a good laugh, Jennifer? Georgie gave your letter to William on the plane as you told her to. Anyone else would have torn it up unread, but not Georgina Ayres! William was furious, as you hoped he would be, but after a while he began to think there was more to it than Georgina hanging on to it until it was too late for him to do anything about it. He decided Georgie was the one who was telling the truth."

"He never said so to me!" Georgina blurted out.

"He will, when he gets around to it," Stuart said comfortably. "Meanwhile, shall we go across to the factory?"

It was a subdued party that made its way along the path towards the factory. Stuart ignored their sulky faces and insisted they paid attention as he plucked a twig from one of the tea bushes and showed them how the white flowers grew underneath the leaves, facing down towards the ground.

"This is the bit which is picked," he went on. "Two leaves and a bud, never more than that. That's what those women are doing over there."

He led them on into the factory, ignoring Jennifer's cries that she didn't want to go up the rickety steps that led to the upper storey of the factory.

"This is where the leaves are put to dry," he explained, pointing to the long racks that stretched their way across the room. "There's a complicated system of air vents that help desiccate them. One of my jobs is to see that they're not left here too long, or for too short a time. After that, the leaves are passed through these rollers—" he pointed out the giant, electrically operated machines—"and a chemical change begins to take place. Oxygen combines with the aromatic juices which are released and fermentation begins. The leaves change colour from green to copper and it takes judgment to know exactly when they are 'done'. The final stage is the firing, which arrests any further oxidization by baking the tea evenly. It depends where the tea is to be marketed as to how much firing we do in the factory. If it has to travel through the Red Sea, for example, it would get a further baking there, and that has to be allowed for."

He rushed them round the building, going rapidly from one process to another, until they came to the place where he did the most difficult part of his work, the tasting area.

"Teas have such lovely names!" he enthused, putting the kettle on to boil. "Pekoe, Orange Pekoe, Pekoe Souchong, Tippy and Flowery, among others. When you taste them you should be able to tell the major differences between them for yourselves."

Georgina took the cup of tea he handed her and sipped it carefully. "Is this a good tea?" she asked him.

"One of the best. Try this and you'll see the difference."

She did and, even to her indifferent palate, it tasted rougher and more bitter than the first tea. "Are there many different grades?'' she pressed him, her interest now thoroughly caught.

He grinned. ''How about pungent, malty, pointy, bakey, thick, coppery, dull or bright? We tasters have our own jargon to describe every kind of tea. How would you like the job?''

He looked over her head as the sound of shod feet came through one of the open doors. ''At last!'' he exclaimed. His smile widened as William joined them. ''I thought you were never coming! Pity, though, you're going to remove my star talent from our tea-tasting competition. I suppose you won't wait for her to finish the course?''

''Not today,'' said William. ''She'll have to come back some other time.''

Georgina clasped her hands together. ''Shouldn't you be working?'' she squeaked. She cleared her throat, and her voice came down a whole octave. ''I didn't expect you for ages!''

''I've been working! Good God, woman, I've been working since dawn to hurry things on and get back to you, and you don't even look pleased to see me!''

Georgina's eyes fell before his. ''I am—of course I am. Only you couldn't even be bothered to wish me good morning, so how am I expected to greet you now?''

William sighed. ''That's my Georgina! How about with a kiss?''

But Georgina couldn't, not with Jennifer standing there watching her, ready to pick holes in her performance. ''Not now!'' she said urgently.

He appeared to find that riotously funny and her anger against him kindled into a steady blaze. ''*Very* funny!'' she jeered at him. ''But you've yet to prove to me that you want my kisses!''

His laughter fell away from him. ''That's true.'' His

tawny eyes challenged hers, making her feel quite dizzy with their impact. "But if you think I'm going to do that in front of witnesses, you have another think coming. Some things are better done in privacy—"

"Because you're ashamed of me!" Georgina flung at him.

His lips twitched. "I want to spare your blushes—"

"You could have fooled me!"

"—but that isn't the same thing at all," he went on calmly. "That's because I don't want others to think I married anyone as stupid as you seem determined to be." He shook his head at her. "Really, Georgina, don't you ever think things out before you come rushing out of your corner, ready to do battle with all and sundry? Well, you're not fighting with me, my girl! Not today! Today you're going to learn what it means to be a wife—"

She panicked. "I won't come with you!"

The golden flecks shone bright in his eyes. "Won't you, Georgie? Why not?"

"Because—" she floundered. "Because I don't want to!"

The gold flecks changed to warm laughter. "You have a lot to learn, little Georgie, and I'm the man to teach it to you. Give in gracefully and come along, my love, because you're coming whether you want it or not, and you know it!"

If she ran, she thought, if she ran hard enough, she could still make her escape through the open door. But what would she do then? She eyed him with all the nervousness of a trapped animal and saw the purpose with which he in turn was regarding her.

"You can't carry me the whole way back to the house!" she declared with a lift to her chin.

"I won't have to!"

Georgina cast a proud, angry look about her, but

there was no help to be gained from either Celine or
Stuart, who were intent only on each other, and from
Jennifer she would scorn to ask so much as the time of
day!

"Where are we going, then?" she asked abruptly,
knowing herself to be defeated.

"On a picnic," he answered without hesitation. "I
have all the food in the jeep, waiting for you. Are you
coming?"

She put her hand in the one he held out to her and
bent her head. "But I haven't forgiven you yet, William Ayres, not for anything!"

"Ah!" His fingers closed about hers with a painful
intensity. "It isn't your forgiveness I'm seeking," he
mocked her. "I've never fancied the role of penitential
sinner much and I won't grovel at your feet, because
neither of us would care for that. I have another proposition to put to you—"

"And I suppose if I don't accept it at once, you'll
coerce me into it just the same!" she interrupted him
shortly. "Why can't you be nice to me, just for once,
just until—until—?" Her eyes widened and she stood
stock still, refusing to budge another inch. "William,
what kind of proposition?"

"Why don't you come and find out?"

She blinked nervously. "Will I like it?" she probed.

"You will, if you don't strain my patience too far
before we get started! Look, sweetheart, I want you to
myself for a few hours and I've spent a sleepless night
and a great many hours of hard work to achieve it.
Don't you think it's time we had a talk, just the two of
us, without any interruptions, and got certain things
straight between us?"

She nodded slowly. "Didn't you go back to bed last
night?"

"For a few hours."

"Was that enough for you?"

His smile was wry. "Lack of sleep doesn't help my temper any. You have been warned, my sweet Georgina! I need you on my side for the rest of today!"

"Oh yes!" she exclaimed. "Why didn't you say so? I thought—" She broke off, wondering exactly what it was that she had thought. A proposition in her experience was the first step on the road to ruin, but as she was already married to William he couldn't possibly have meant the temporary liaison that his words had conjured up. Indeed, it had to be something else, and that something set her nerves jangling and the blood racing through her veins.

She ignored his look of enquiry, a smile of sheer delight hovering at the corners of her mouth. "William, I wish you'd come earlier! It was such a long morning without you! Why didn't you come in to wish me good morning?"

"How do you know I didn't? You were fast asleep when I left the house this morning."

"I wouldn't have minded if you had woken me," she protested. "I thought it was because you preferred to have breakfast with Jennifer."

He cast a quick look in her direction, giving her a push towards his waiting jeep. "Jennifer is essentially an evening person, don't you think?" he returned.

"I'd much rather you didn't think of her as any sort of person," she said in a small voice. "I know you thought you were in love with her—"

"That was a misunderstanding, Georgina. That's one of the things I want to talk to you about. I've treated you very badly, dear heart, but a little bit of it was your own fault. You're going to have to give up fighting me in the future and try a spot of loving instead. Think you can stand it?"

She sat on the canvas-covered seat, her knees together and her hands clasped lightly in her lap. The colour edged up her face as she strove to find a credible answer that would not commit her to more than he wanted from her. None occurred to her.

"Never mind, Georgie Porgie, I can wait." He got into the driving seat beside her, lifting a hand in salute to the others who had come out from the factory to see them off. He grinned happily to himself. "Atta girl, Georgie! At least Celine knows what she wants from Stuart!"

The tea gardens looked particularly lovely that morning. The atmosphere was thin and clear and it was possible to look across miles and miles of tea-planted hillsides and up into the heights where even the tea came to an end, to be replaced by some scrawny laurels, rhododendrons, pipal, balsams and pitcher plants. The land was well watered too, a multitude of waterfalls giving life to some of the rockier gorges.

Georgina was beginning to relax and enjoy herself. She knew what she wanted too. She wanted William, but she wanted him all to herself and, for today at least, that was what it seemed she was going to get.

"This must be the most beautiful place on earth!" she said, increasingly certain that this was going to be the most wonderful day in her life.

"It must be the company you're keeping," he teased her.

She sat up very straight. "Could be." She would have said something more, something a great deal more enthusiastic, but there didn't seem to be any words to express what she was feeling.

William drove on in silence, only speaking again when he told her they were approaching their destination. "Stuart claims this spot is as near paradise as one is likely to get. He'd better be right!"

"He probably is," she encouraged him. "Not that it

matters. It's such a lovely day that I wouldn't care if we were in the middle of Piccadilly Circus!''

He looked at her, his thoughts hidden behind a mask of indifference. "I should," he said.

She clasped her hands tighter together. "Why?"

He smiled ruefully. "Because, my Georgie Porgie, today I'm going to be very gentle with you and you're going to respond in kind. Shouting above the roar of the traffic wouldn't be conducive to the kind of atmosphere I want to achieve." He glanced across at her. "How does the programme appeal so far?"

"I don't mind when you're not gentle," she blurted out. "I l-like being with you, you see."

"Do you, darling? I think you're more generous than I deserve, because in the past I've bruised your spirit more than a little, haven't I?"

Surprisingly, she was amused by that. "I shall enjoy having you apply a little balm," she told him. "William, you fool! You know it will be just the same tomorrow when you want something from me! And I'm just as big a fool. I think I must like the masterful touch!"

"The iron hand in the velvet glove? That's all very well, love, but not without love, and not without the glove. It'll be different from now on, I promise you. I've been obtuse as far as you're concerned, but my eyes are wide open now."

"It doesn't matter," she said uncomfortably.

"Because you're used to being misjudged?" His foot slipped on the accelerator and they shot forward, coming to rest under a group of trees close beside one of the prettiest silver waterfalls that Georgina had ever seen. "It's going to be different from now on!"

She didn't know what to say to that. She was glad to be able to busy herself helping to spread the rug on the ground just short of the spray from the waterfall, and to carry the packages of food and drink from the jeep to the rug.

"Oh, do look!" she whispered, awed. "That bird, over there!"

He glanced where she was pointing. "A blue-tailed bee-eater."

"And that?"

"A blackheaded oriole. It has a pretty mustard-coloured body which you can see better in flight. That one over there is a kingfisher."

"But it's quite black and dull," she complained.

"Wait until it takes off. See it?"

It flew across the water in a blaze of greeny-blue, settling on the other side of the water, its right-angled beak turning busily from side to side as the bird inspected the possibilities of his territory.

Georgina turned impulsively to William. "Thank you for bringing me here! You looked so tired last night, and then to get up as early as you did—it was kind of you, because I didn't think I'd see you before this evening."

"And that mattered to you?"

She nodded, embarrassed. "It was nice having a whole week together before you started work. It spoilt me for having to entertain myself, I expect. I've never had nothing in particular to do before."

"Enjoy it while you can," he advised her. "You'll be busy enough when the children make their appearance."

"Children?" She sounded as if she had never heard the word before.

"The fruit of the marriage-bed," he reminded her dryly.

"Oh." She coloured and turned away, saying again, "*Oh!*"

He sat down on the rug, spreading his long legs out

in front of him and patting the place beside him. "Don't sound so surprised, Georgie. Celine seems to expect it of us, even if you don't!"

"I hadn't thought—"

"What had you thought about?"

She sat down quickly, feeling suddenly weak at the knees. "I don't know. I was busy taking each day as it came." She paused, gathering up her courage. "William, about Jennifer—"

"What about her?"

"She doesn't mean half what she says. I think she is—fond of you, if that's what's worrying you."

His eyes narrowed, the amber of his eyes looking very yellow against the black of his lashes. "It's not. I heard all I wanted to from Jennifer last night. Not that it changed anything. You'd already wrought havoc with my feelings, long before Jennie made her appearance. You're such an innocent, Georgie! Didn't you guess how I felt?"

She bit her lip, trying not to allow the burgeoning excitement within her to get away from her rapidly diminishing control over it. "I still don't know," she said.

But it seemed he wasn't going to tell her—not yet. He lay back, pillowing his head on his hands, and changed the subject.

"Tell me about Jennifer," he coaxed her. "Tell me the truth, and make it as short as you can. She's a dull subject on such a day as this!"

"Dull?" The word exploded out of her. "Aren't you in love with her after all? If you've changed your mind, you shouldn't have allowed her to come all this way to be with you. She'll be furious!"

"I'd say Duncan is more entitled to feel ill-used. I wonder how she persuaded him to pay for her to visit us. It's a damned sight more than I'd do for you, Georgie! Nobody else is ever going to have you but me!"

Georgina traced the pattern of the rug with her finger, waiting for the thunder of her heart to subside a little. "She may go back to him," she volunteered at last. "It's the sort of thing she would do. Perhaps he knows that. He might have been prepared to take a gamble on her, don't you think?"

"Possibly."

"She's a bit spoilt," Georgina continued, picking her words with care. "Our parents have always given her her own way—"

"*And so have you!*"

"She's younger than I am. I could always look after myself, but she's such a delicate little thing—"

"So I thought too! But not for long. I soon discovered which one of you needed protecting from the wolves of this world—*and it wasn't her!*"

Georgina looked at him then. "You mean me?" she asked, astonished.

He smiled slowly at her puzzled expression. "I daresay you'd manage well enough in a fair fight," he consoled her, "but wolves in sheep's clothing seldom fight fair. Like Jennifer!"

She accepted that, but she wasn't going to let him get away with his own deeds so lightly. "Do you fight fair?" she challenged him.

His eyes met hers. "Are you lodging a complaint?"

She shook her head. "I don't want you to think badly of Jennie, that's all."

He propped himself up on to his elbow, unbalancing her as he did so and triumphantly imprisoning her against the long length of his body.

"Jennifer can live with my opinion of her. I doubt it will so much as dent her self-conceit. But last night was the last time she takes you apart in my hearing. There's no comparison between the two of you, and I was lucky enough to get the best of the bargain when I pushed you into marriage with me. I knew it almost at once, and I thought you knew how I felt too. I forgot women have to have everything put into words before they'll allow themselves to believe a man's fallen in love with them—and you more than most, because you still think everyone is going to prefer Jennifer to yourself, don't you? Well, it isn't true. You didn't only black my eye darling; you hit me hard where it hurts most, and I couldn't believe my good fortune that I'd made my bed with you and had every right to make love to you as often as I could persuade you to co-operate!"

She veiled her eyes with her long lashes. "I love you," she said.

He ran his fingers round the collar of her dress, finding the top of the zip. "I know that, sweetheart."

Her eyes opened wide. "How could you know?"

His lips found the hollow between her breasts. "You told me so."

"When?" His closeness disturbed her breathing and she put up a hand to prevent his from exploring any further. "I'm sure I didn't!"

"Not in words perhaps, but I knew. You might have known how I felt about you too, if you'd thought about it. You must have known how much I wanted you!"

"That isn't quite the same thing," she said primly.

His eyes lit with laughter as he kissed her. "With you, I think it is, my lovely wife. You have a rare talent for love."

"Mmm," she murmured, distracted by the increasing passion of his kisses. "I've loved you ever since I was ten years old, only I wasn't going to admit it! You wouldn't have made me marry you otherwise, William Ayres! I might not have known it was love exactly, but

I knew I was going to marry you as soon as you kissed me when I came to tell you about Jennifer and Duncan."

"Hush," he commanded her. "You talk too much. Be quiet and let me kiss you some more!"

But, laughing a little, she wriggled away from him to the far edge of the rug, turning her back on him. "I thought this was going to be my time," she reminded him, her voice not quite steady. "I thought you were going to be gentle and loving—"

He plucked a leaf and tickled the back of her neck with it. For a moment he considered hauling her back into his arms whether she would or not, but then he acknowledged the justice of her complaint.

"Okay, little Georgina, what is it you want to know?"

She turned over to face him, her expression very serious. "I want to know when you began to love me. You didn't at first. You were much too involved with Jennifer to notice me at all."

He bent forward and kissed the tip of her nose. "Not nearly as involved as you thought. I was attracted, that's all, and she seemed a very suitable person to deal with Celine. *Not* my most intelligent move, I know, but fortunately you came along and with great energy put an end to that arrangement for me." His smile deepened, but the glint in his tawny eyes had nothing to do with amusement. "I started falling for you when you claimed you were better stacked than Jennie. You are too!"

"Oh, William, I didn't! I might have indicated that I am—well, better endowed—"

His delighted laughter effectively silenced her. "It amounts to the same thing," he teased her. "Is that all you want to know?"

There had to be a hundred other questions she

wanted to ask him, but she couldn't think of one of them. She edged a few inches to him, overcome by the gush of warm excitement she felt as his arms closed about her.

"William, please love me!" she begged him.

She put her hands against his chest and discovered that his heart was beating as fast as hers. "William?" she murmured, opening her lips to the pressure of his.

"I'm waiting to do so," he said.

The Hungry Tide
Lucy Gillen

"Do you wish to work for me or not, Miss Carson?" he had demanded. His voice was quiet but hinted at menace, so that Rachel gazed at him anxiously while she tried to nod agreement.

"Yes. Yes, of course I do," she had insisted. At the same time she wondered if she had completely taken leave of her senses in wanting to work for such a man as Neil Brett.

She had grown happily attached to the small orphaned boy, Nicholas, put in her charge. But she was dismayed to find that somehow she had grown equally attached to his Uncle Neil....

CHAPTER ONE

RACHEL paid the taxi driver, then stood and watched the taxi out of sight down the long winding drive before she turned back to look at the house again. Seaways was impressive by any standards, a typical monument to Victorian solidity but hardly welcoming. It had a secret, closed look that was somehow discouraging, especially to someone like Rachel who was not at all certain that she should not have gone round to a servants' entrance, if there was one.

Hastily dismissing a moment of panic, she mentally shook herself and went up the three steps to a massive door made from dark timber planks studded over with black iron bolts. Huge bay windows reflected the darkness of a winter's day and faced on to a garden that consisted mostly of rather tired-looking shrubs as far as Rachel could see, although it must have been quite pretty in spring and summer when the rhododendrons were in flower and the willowy bareness of the forsythia was clothed in yellow and pale green.

A hesitant pull on the bell knob brought an almost immediate response in the person of a middle-aged woman with greying hair who smiled and indicated that she should come inside. The way the woman nodded her head seemed to indicate that she recognized her name, and for that small relief Rachel thanked heaven.

"Will you come with me?" the woman said, and led the way across a hall that in no way matched the Victorian appearance of the outside of the house.

It was light and airy and there was no sign of the dark
walls and furniture Rachel had expected to see in such
a house. Deep red carpet deadened their footsteps and
the gloomy grey daylight admitted by one of the
smaller windows showed everything to be white and
gold.

Even the ornately carved staircase was white-painted
and its intricate balustrades gilded. Several water-
colours displayed their misty pastels against white walls
and a delightful Capo di Monte figure of an old man
had pride of place on a small spindle-legged table
against one wall.

The woman, presumably a housekeeper, opened a
door to one side of the hall and stepped just inside to
announce her arrival, almost as if she was a visitor instead of a prospective employee. "Miss Carson's here,
sir," she told the occupant of the room, then stood
aside to let Rachel in, smiling encouragement as she
closed the door behind her.

The room she found herself in surprised Rachel less
than it might have done if she had not already seen the
hall outside, for the same taste was reflected in the decor here. It was a big room with an open fire burning in
the wide fireplace, but it was evident from the warmth
that the fire served merely as a boost to a central heating system that was not at once evident.

Here too the furniture was light and elegant and in
perfect taste, more Georgian than Victorian in period
and obviously none of it copied. Whatever else Mr.
Neil Brett's property betrayed about him it stressed that
he was not a poor man or he could not have indulged
such tastes.

The man himself when he turned towards her was
almost as much of a surprise as the interior of his house
had been, and Rachel wondered if she had ever seen a
man so definitely blond before. He was tall, over six

feet, she guessed, and rakishly lean with hair that was thick and pale as corn-silk and light blue eyes that regarded her steadily as she hesitated to come across the room.

She thought he looked rather surprised, as if something about her was not exactly what he expected, but her own reaction to him startled her most of all. His presence seemed to fill the big room and the force of his personality was such that it was almost overpowering.

He did not come forward to meet her, but waited instead for her to join him by the massive grey marble mantel, saying nothing but conveying his wishes by merely standing there and looking across at her. Her own rather petite stature made long steps impossible and it seemed to take her an interminable time to cross the big room, while all the time he studied her with a frank appraisal that was embarrassing in its intensity.

Her long dark hair curled softly about a small oval face and complemented huge grey eyes and a mouth that trembled rather nervously at the moment, but she doubted if an appreciation of her looks was the reason for that steady scrutiny. Mr. Neil Brett would not be so easily impressed.

"Miss Carson?" He inclined his head but did not offer to shake her hand. With a similar gesture he indicated a chair immediately behind her, but remained standing himself, putting his hands behind his back and drawing back his shoulders. "Please sit down!"

It was a command rather than an invitation, and Rachel obeyed it automatically. She could not have said just why she had expected him to be dressed in a formal suit and a tie and looking like a typical business man, but she could not have been more wrong. He looked rather more like a farmer than a business man and he had obviously made no special effort to appear formal for the interview.

Serviceable denims were tucked into short brown boots and revealed long muscular legs whose length was emphasised by the stance of his booted feet—set slightly apart and planted firmly on the dark green carpet. The sleeves of a faded brown denim shirt were rolled up above the elbows and showed strong brown arms and a column of tanned neck and throat with broad shoulders pulling the shirt tight across the front as he drew back his arms.

A dark golden tan was in such contrast to his blondness that Rachel found herself wondering what ancestry could have produced such colouring. It was particularly noticeable in the strong rugged face where the brown skin was quite startling when it contrasted with such light blue eyes. He suggested power and a certain ruthlessness that was oddly disturbing, and Rachel's flesh tingled warningly.

"You're a trained children's nurse?" he asked, and she nodded, hastily bringing herself back to earth again.

"Yes, Mr. Brett," she said. "I qualified this year."

"I see!"

Again she was subjected to that steady scrutiny and found it equally distrubing. He moved suddenly, a swift movement that at first startled her, and stood with both hands in his pockets, his shoulders resting against the tall mantel behind him. It was probably as near as he ever came to relaxing, Rachel thought, and again experienced that urgent warning tingle when she briefly met his eyes.

"You're younger than I would have expected," he said bluntly. "I presume you have the necessary certificates to prove your qualifications?"

"Naturally!" Colour warmed her cheeks although the request was reasonable enough in the circumstances. No one, least of all a man as thorough as Neil

Brett suggested, would be prepared to hand over the care of his child to just anyone who applied. She opened her handbag. "I have them here if you want to see them," she told him, and passed him the envelope containing her certificates.

He nodded his thanks and scrutinised the papers carefully before handing them back to her. "I see that you qualified only two months ago," he observed. "Is this the first post you've applied for?"

The interview was not going quite as Rachel had imagined it and she felt dismayingly uneasy in this man's presence, more uneasy than she would have believed possible. "I've been interviewed for one other place," she admitted, wondering just how honest she could afford to be.

A raised brow made it obvious that she would have to be more specific than that. "And?" he prompted shortly, and Rachel flushed, lifting her chin in an unconscious gesture of defiance.

"I was unsuitable for the job," she told him, and saw the light blue eyes narrow swiftly when she made the admission.

"In what way unsuitable, Miss Carson?"

Rachel hesitated before she answered. It would be difficult trying to explain that the busy blonde society hostess who had interviewed her last had taken no more than five seconds to decide that Rachel was not what she was looking for at all. "I wasn't given any specific reason," she admitted. "I was simply told that I wasn't right for the post, that's all."

"Hmm!" One brow flicked upwards again and the blue eyes slid in swift appraisal over her small neat figure and the flushed prettiness of her face. "Was the objection to your youth or your prettiness?" he asked, and Rachel's cheeks burned with embarrassment at his frankness.

"I—I wasn't told," she insisted a little huskily. "I was just told that I wasn't suitable and sent away."

"Hmm!" Once again he made that short, non-committal comment and regarded her with a steady, disconcerting gaze for several seconds. "In short, you've had no practical experience at all?" he observed, and Rachel frowned, wondering what he considered working with a dozen small children to be, if not practical.

"I've had quite a bit of practical experience," she told him. "Part of my training consisted of working in a children's home."

One arched brow doubted the practicality of that in regard to the post he had in mind and his mouth curved derisively. "This isn't a children's home," he reminded her quietly. "Have you had experience in private work—as a nurse to a child in a private home?"

Rachel reluctantly honest, shook her head. "Not yet, Mr. Brett." She looked up at him briefly, irritated by the hopelessness of gaining the experience he set such score by if she could not first find someone willing to employ her. "And it's difficult to see how I'm going to gain experience without being employed first!" she added with a hint of challenge.

"So you think I should pay you to gain experience?"

Rachel looked away again hastily, unable to quite hold that steady blue gaze with as much bravado as she would like. "I *am* qualified," she reminded him. "You wouldn't be paying me for nothing, or for anything I'm not perfectly capable of doing! It's really not much of a gamble!"

Neil Brett stiffened, she was aware of it from the corner of her eye, and her hand curled anxiously in her lap while she waited for his objection to her argument. "Are you also trained to be impudent to your employer?" he asked coldly. "Or is that part of your natural character, Miss Carson?"

Rachel hesitated. A natural pertness urged her to answer him with a retort that she was not prepared to suppress her own opinions completely, but she had a feeling that a lot depended on her answer. Perhaps even the fact of whether or not she got the post, and she was strangely anxious to have this job. Not simply because she had not yet found anything to suit her since she qualified, but because something about Neil Brett held a curious fascination for her and she wanted to work for him.

"I'm sorry if you think I was impudent," she said, deceptively humble in her apology, "but I *am* good at my job, Mr. Brett, and I want to gain experience—working for someone like you is the only way I can do that."

He regarded her steadily for a moment longer, than nodded his head as if he had suddenly made up his mind about it. "Very well, I'll give you a month's trial," he decided shortly.

"Thank you!" It was strange the sense of relief she felt when he said that, and she wondered why on earth she should be so anxious to work for him when their first encounter had scarcely been encouraging.

"Are you accustomed to small boys?" he asked, and Rachel nodded, hardly daring to speak in case she said the wrong thing and he changed his mind again.

"I'm quite used to them," she told him a little breathlessly. "I was in charge of six or seven at a time during my training."

He considered for a moment longer, his dark face shadowed and etched with the flickering light of the fire in the darkening room. Standing now with one arm along the marble mantel he looked down at the licking flames and Rachel thought he was far away mentally, if not physically.

One leg was bent, the foot resting on the wrought

iron Victorian fender that guarded the fire, and she found it hard not to notice the tautness of fawn denim against the muscular curve of his leg. Neil Brett was a disturbing man and she would perhaps regret having tried so hard to work for him, but she found the prospect irresistible at the moment.

"Nicholas is four years old," he told her suddenly, and brought her swiftly back to reality. "He's quite a well behaved child, but you might have a little trouble managing him at first."

He sounded, Rachel thought a little dizzily, as if he was talking about an animal rather than his own small son, and her sympathies were already with the child, Nicholas, however much of a problem he might prove to be.

She smiled in a way that left him in no doubt that she was perfectly capable of dealing with any tantrums the child might produce, whoever he was. "One small boy isn't *so* difficult to cope with, Mr. Brett," she observed, perhaps with rather more contempt for his opinion than she realised, for Neil Brett was frowning again, his ice-blue eyes looking at her coolly.

"Your assurance will have more authority when you've met Nicholas and know him," he told her firmly. "Until then allow me to know best, Miss Carson!"

Rachel swallowed hard, trying to stem the retort that sprang to her lips. Then she inclined her head briefly and bowed to the inevitable—even on such short acquaintance it was easy to recognise that very few people would come unscathed from an encounter with Neil Brett. "Yes, of course," she said quietly. "Am I to see Nicholas now?"

"No!"

The reply was prompt and adamant and Rachel frowned over it. One of the things her training had impressed upon her was the need for a certain rapport with her young charge, and a meeting before being committed to taking the post was preferable if not absolutely essential.

Rachel hesitated, uncertain how to proceed. With some employers it would probably have been possible to insist, or at least to stress the importance of that first meeting; but in the case of Neil Brett she doubted if any amount of insistence would do any good.

Because she had no intention of letting her dislike of the situation go unremarked, however, she sighed deeply in resignation and shook her head. "Very well, Mr. Brett," she said, "but it is *quite* important that the right relationship is established as soon as possible. It's most important that your son likes me and that we get on well together—a preliminary meeting can establish from the outset whether or not we suit one another."

Her reasons were of no interest to him at all, she realised, but there was a bright glitter in his light blue eyes as he stood there looking down at her steadily. "My son?" he asked quietly, almost gently, and Rachel felt the colour flood into her cheeks when she realised the awful gaffe she had made.

Too stunned to speak for a moment, she shook her head slowly, not daring to look at him, her cheeks flaming as she sought for explanations, although heaven knew there were grounds enough for her assumption that the child was his son.

"I—I'm sorry, Mr. Brett," she said, after several awful seconds, "but I thought—"

"I suppose it was a natural assumption," Neil Brett allowed coolly, without giving her time to finish her explanation. "Nicholas is my nephew, Miss Carson, he is also my legal ward—do you know what that means?"

"Of course!" She flushed when she detected a hint of patronage in his voice. "I assume that the little boy has no parents and the courts have appointed you his guardian.''

"More or less," he allowed. "Nicky's mother was my sister—there is no one else sufficiently interested in him to give him a home, so he's with me." The light blue eyes looked at her from between thick brown lashes and a hint of what could have been a smile just touched the corners of his wide mouth. "I may not be your conception of the perfect father, Miss Carson, but I'm all he has and so far he's made no complaint!"

"Oh no, I'm sure he hasn't!' She hastened to assure him on that point, for without doubt whatever other failings Neil Brett might have it was plain, to Rachel at least, that he was genuinely fond of his nephew.

He moved away from the fireplace suddenly, a swift restless movement that took him just out of Rachel's sight, and she wondered if she dared turn round in her chair to look at him. There was something about the man that she found irresistibly fascinating, despite the fact that he had scarcely gone out of his way to be charming.

He strode across to the window and stood for a moment there with his hands behind his back, his blonde head held high on that strong brown column of neck. "You need only know that Nicky's mother died last year," he told her in a cool, flat voice that obviously disguised some deep emotion he refused to display. "She drowned in the sea only a mile from here."

"Oh, I'm sorry!"

Her sympathy seemed to surprise him, for he turned round again suddenly and faced her, his eyes carefully concealed by half-lowered lids, his face shadowed because his back was to the grey daylight outside the window behind him.

"I've told you this only because you must understand the need to handle Nicholas with care," he told her quietly. "He has what might appear to be an unreasonable fear of the sea, and I have forbidden anyone to take him near it until he's recovered from his fear."

By anyone Rachel could only assume that he referred to the housekeeper and perhaps other servants who were given charge of the little boy until a nanny could be found for him. Her heart went out to Nicholas in his loneliness, for she felt sure that a small boy in a house full of grown-ups and consigned to the care of servants must be an incredibly lonely child.

"It is something he can be coaxed out of in time," she said gently, and was startled when he immediately strode forward and stood over her, his light eyes glittering bright below drawn brows.

"He will be allowed to grow out of it in his own time, Miss Carson!" he told her forcefully. "You will not attempt to work miracles, no matter what your training has led you to believe you're capable of! Do you understand?"

He stood close enough for her to be disturbingly aware of him in a way she had never experienced before. There was a stunning aura of maleness about him, of sheer masculine vigour that seared her senses like fire and left her breathless with its unexpectedness. Neil Brett was not a man to be taken lightly and she would have to learn to control her reactions if she was to work for him.

Warily she ventured an upward glance at him and saw that a fierce frown drew his fair brows together above the glitter of light blue eyes. In anger he was not only impressive but frankly overawing, and she nodded automatically.

"Yes, of course I understand, Mr. Brett," she said as coolly as she was able, "but I—"

"I sincerely hope you aren't one of those women who think they know everything there is to know about children, Miss Carson," he declared forcefully. "Are you?"

Rachel flushed indignantly, but her heart was racing, triggered by some inexplicable chemistry he aroused in her, and she found it difficult to answer him as calmly and matter-of-factly as she would normally have done. "I've been trained to deal with almost every aspect of children, Mr. Brett," Rachel told him, and tried hard to steady a voice that quivered dismayingly and give quite the wrong impression. "Of course, I don't claim to know everything about children, but I *do* know my job and—"

She almost gasped aloud when a harsh snort of impatience cut her explanation short. He dismissed her claim with a broad, contemptuous sweep of one large hand and it so suggested an impending blow that Rachel instinctively leaned backwards away from it, her head jerked up, holding the gaze of those glittering blue eyes for several seconds before she blinked in realisation.

"Do you wish to work for me or not, Miss Carson?" he demanded. His voice was quiet, but hinted at menace so that Rachel gazed at him anxiously while she tried to nod agreement.

"Yes, yes, of course I do," she insisted, and at the same time wondered if she had completely taken leave of her senses in wanting to work for such a man.

"Then you won't try making rule-book experiments at Nicky's expense!" he told her harshly. "Is that quite clear?"

"Quite clear, Mr. Brett!" Rachel hastily ran her tongue over her lips before chancing another upward glance at that stern implacable face. "I—you have quite the wrong impression of my intent," she ventured. "I wouldn't attempt anything without your consent, of course, and—"

"Good! Then there'll be no problems!"

Rachel stared at him, unsure which caused her more disturbance—his violent insistence on being obeyed implicitly, or the prospect of being in daily contact with a man who promised to be much more of a problem than any employer she had envisaged during her training years.

There was simply no reason that she could see why she did not simply get up and walk out of the house here and now, leaving Mr. Neil Brett to deal with his own problems as best he could. But she was still influenced by that strange desire to stay and work for him and instead of walking out she waited.

For a moment Neil Brett stood looking down at her as she sat with her hands clasped over the handle of her bag, her cheeks flushed with the urgency of her heartbeat. It was quite ridiculous to allow a stranger to have such an effect on her and she was unsure whether she relished the idea or not of being emotionally assaulted.

After a moment or two he moved away, going over to stand beside the mantel again, and she was uneasily aware that he was watching her. The flickering flames of the fire cast deep shadows on his strong tanned features, lending them even more character. An arrogant and disturbing man—too forceful to make him easy to work for, but too irresistible to simply walk away from.

The immediate necessity of finding someone to care for little Nicholas Browlett meant that Rachel was expected to take up her duties right away, and Neil Brett had straight away sent one of his staff with her to fetch her luggage. Her own plans and desires did not enter into it, apparently, for she was not consulted as to whether or not it was convenient for her to move in at once—it was taken for granted.

Despite the autocratic way she was enrolled into the

household, however, she had no complaints about her accommodation, nor about the way she was treated. Mrs. Handley, the housekeeper, was delegated to supervise her moving in and she was allocated a room at the front of the house that was far better than anything she had expected.

It was large and airy and, despite the old-fashioned windows, admitted quite a lot of the grey winter light from outside. The furnishings again reflected Neil Brett's impeccable taste, so that she was always to be conscious of the man even in the privacy of her own room. No matter how brusque and earthily masculine he might be in person, it was evident that he had a collector's taste for fine things and furnished his house with them rather than locked them away for his own pleasure only.

The two windows gave her a magnificent view over rolling Kentish farmland, and beyond it, in the distance, a tell-tale luminosity in the sky betrayed the nearness of the sea. The sea that she was forbidden to visit with her little charge because his mother had been drowned in it.

She stood for a while at one of the windows looking out over the ploughed fields at the curlews and seagulls who gleaned a harvest of their own from the curling brown furrows, and wondered just how Nicholas' mother had died and why. Mrs. Handley probably knew, but she was not yet long enough established in the household to ask questions about the family.

"It's a wonderful view," she said, and turned and smiled at the housekeeper.

Mrs. Handley's pleasant face responded with a smile. "It's nicely placed," she agreed in her quiet country voice. "You'll like it here, I'm sure."

Rachel opened a suitcase and began to take out some of her things while Mrs. Handley smoothed out invisible creases in the smooth perfection of a Victorian patchwork quilt. A whole string of questions were pressing for answers and unless she was mistaken the housekeeper was still with her for a reason. She could have left minutes ago, but she had not, instead she stood by the old-fashioned double bed and, without saying anything, gave the impression that she had something to say.

"I'm anxious to meet Nicholas," Rachel told her, laying a dress carefully across the foot of the bed as she spoke. "You know him quite well, of course, Mrs. Handley?"

"Ever since he was born, you might say," the housekeeper agreed, and shook her head sadly.

"He's an orphan, I gather," Rachel guessed, having heard nothing about Nicholas' father, and Mrs. Handley neither confirmed nor denied it.

"Poor little love," she sympathised. "It seems like everything's been against him, right from the beginning. Mind you," she added hastily as if to rectify a wrong impression, "he's happy enough here with his uncle, and he'll be better still now there's someone to care for him full time."

It was a delicate position to be in and Rachel trembled at the prospect of saying the wrong thing, but she was near to the reason for Neil Brett's guardianship of his nephew, and to ask just one question was irresistible.

"I know about his mother being drowned last year," she said, and saw the immediate change that came over Mrs. Handley's friendly face.

"Sad," was all she said, and shook her head.

"And presumably he doesn't have a father, since Mr. Brett is his guardian," Rachel ventured, only partially discouraged.

Mrs. Handley tightened her mouth and her round

face took on a curiously closed look as she gave one last smoothing pat to the patchwork bedspread before walking towards the door. Turning in the doorway, she looked back at Rachel with a smile that was belied by the strange glittery look in her eyes. "If there is anything more you need, Miss Carson," she told her, "just ask—either Betty or I will get it for you."

Rachel blinked at her for minute, taking time to grasp the fact that her attempt to probe into her charge's family affairs had been firmly and adamantly rebuffed. Whether Nicholas' father was alive or dead was obviously a matter Mrs. Handley refused to discuss.

"Thank you, Mrs. Handley," she said after a moment, and the housekeeper closed the door quietly behind her.

CHAPTER TWO

NICHOLAS BROWLETT proved to be an easy child to get to know, and he had a charmingly old-fashioned manner that made one think he was older than in fact he was. Despite his uncle's warning that he might be difficult to handle initially, he seemed quite well adjusted and quite different from the nervous and unhappy child that Rachel had expected.

He was rather small for his four and a half years, but he looked robust enough, even though he was lacking the same healthy tan that made his uncle's looks so striking. There was a little family resemblance, in fact, apart from their blue eyes, and Nicholas was altogether more typically English with his brown hair, round face and fair skin.

After two weeks they were beginning to get to know one another quite well and it was evident they were going to get along. On the whole Rachel found him obedient and quite amenable, although he had showed swift resentment when she tried to make him refer to his uncle by his title instead of simply calling him Neil. He could be stubborn, Rachel thought ruefully, and would probably grow up to be as autocratic as Neil Brett if he was to spend the rest of his formative years in his charge.

Nicholas now sat on the long box seat that ran the whole width of the big bay window in the sitting-room, his feet curled up under him and a book that had failed to interest him abandoned beside him while he gazed out of the window. "Don't you like your book?" Rachel asked, and he looked at her for a moment with a hint of impatience in his eyes.

"I don't like books," he told her frankly, and she frowned.

"Oh, but you should enjoy them, Nicky," she said. "Shall I read that one to you? Would you like that?"

Nicky's head shook decidedly and he again looked out of the window. "No, thank you," he said firmly but politely. "When Lars comes I can go riding every day."

"Lars?" Rachel looked at him curiously. She had heard nothing about an expected visitor, but apparently whoever was coming was popular with Nicky, for his blue eyes glowed with the pleasure of anticipation.

"You don't know Lars," he informed her, rather superfluously.

"No, I don't." Rachel refused to question him about the identity of Lars, whoever it might be. The name sounded odd to her ears, but Nicky was probably not pronouncing it properly.

"Don't you want to know about him?" Nicky asked after a few seconds of meaningful silence, and Rachel could not restrain a smile.

It was obvious that he laid great store by the expected visitor, and he was only waiting to be asked before he launched into a spate of information about him. She ruffled his thatch of brown hair with her fingers and laughed softly. "All right," she conceded, "you tell me about Lars—I presume he has another name too?"

Nicky was nodding his head eagerly. "Lars Bergen," he informed her with meticulous clarity. "He's my—my sort of cousin."

"Your cousin? Oh, I see!"

Rachel made a rapid mental adjustment to her pic-

ture of Lars Bergen, although she really had no idea
why she had automatically assumed that the eagerly
awaited visitor was a grown man and not another little
boy, except that Nicky's world seemed bounded by
grown-ups.

Of course he would look forward to the arrival of
another child, although it raised the question in Rachel's mind whether she would be expected to take
charge of both children while Lars Bergen was visiting.

The name of the visitor also made it fairly plain that
the cousin was almost certainly of Scandinavian origin,
and she thought that at last she saw a possible explanation for Neil Brett's blond looks.

"Can we go for a walk?" Nicky asked, and Rachel
hastily blinked herself back to earth, nodding her head
in agreement.

"Yes, of course we can," she said, "if that's what
you'd like to do."

She was nothing loath to go walking herself, for she
was fond of the exercise and it would do Nicky good to
have a spell in the fresh air. It was not even necessary
to leave the grounds to enjoy quite a long walk, for they
extended to several acres, apart from one or two farms
and cottages that belonged to the estate.

So much she had learned from Mrs. Handley, who was
willing enough to talk about the estate, though far less
forthcoming about the family who owned it. It seemed to
Rachel pretty certain that there was some kind of mystery somewhere in the family background, and she suspected it concerned her charge. Mrs. Handley did not
seem a naturally secretive woman, but whenever the
question of Nicky's parents arose she immediately became uncommunicative and changed the subject. Perhaps when she had been there a little longer—but that
remained to be seen.

Rachel wrapped Nicky up well in a coat and scarf and

insisted he wore gloves against the cold east wind that blew in off the not too distant sea, then she put on boots and a short thick jacket herself before they set off. A walk as far as the spinney at the bottom of the extensive gardens would give them both an appetite for lunch.

Tall, wide-spreading oaks sheltered the house from the worst of the winds and formed a protective screen between it and the rest of the estate. On an earlier walk Rachel had been delighted to discover that primroses and violets grew along the banks that bordered the ditches, although they were little more than clumps of bedraggled leaves at the moment, huddling below the bare arms of hazel and blackthorn.

Beyond the trees and hedges, the other side of the ditch, was rolling farmland enclosing a tall grey farm-house in the midst and tall, conical oasthouses that stood like sentinels against the grey sky, awaiting the next September harvest of hops.

A few beef cattle scavenged for the last of the grass, eked out by substitute fodder from the yards, and it all looked so dismal at this time of year. But Rachel could imagine it much different in the summer when the fields were lush and green and the now barren hop gardens were strung with their green vines. A warm, contented countryside that changed little and somehow offered the kind of peace it was difficult to find else-where.

Without quite realising she was doing it, Rachel smiled to herself, and Nicky, running back to join her, looked up at her curiously. "Do you like it here, Miss Carson?" he asked, and Rachel nodded.

"I always liked Kent, Nicky," she told him. "I used to spend holidays here when I was a little girl."

"Here?" Taking her literally, he looked puzzled, and she shook her head.

"Not actually here at Seaways," she explained. "But not too far from here—by the seaside."

She had for the moment genuinely forgotten about his aversion to the sea and the reason for it, for she would never have mentioned it if she had stopped to consider. It was a sudden strange look of withdrawal on his face that reminded her, and the droop of his mouth made her wish she had been more careful.

"I don't like the sea," he told her in a flat little voice that touched a chord in her heart and made her want to drop down beside him and hug him close.

Instead she put a hand on his head and ran her fingers gently through the thick slightly curly hair on top of his head. "I know, Nicky," she said quietly, "and I'm sorry I mentioned it."

"It doesn't matter." He sounded so resigned and so adult that the effect was to tug even harder at her emotions.

His huge blue eyes looked up at her for a moment, and she would have reached down and cuddled him, but he was off suddenly across the muddy grass, making sounds that were presumably meant to represent an aeroplane, since his arms were spread wide and he dipped and turned as he ran, his cheeks bright with exertion and the keen coldness of the wind.

He played like that for some time, always just out of reach, so that Rachel began to wonder if he was doing it deliberately, and his course took them more towards the front of the house instead of the back as Rachel had intended. Then suddenly he turned and looked across to where, in the distance, the driveway up to the house wound between its secretive guard of oak trees.

"Lars is coming!" he cried in a shrill excited voice, and dashed off across the parkland before Rachel could do anything to stop him.

"Nicky!" She followed as quickly as she could, but she could not quite match his helter-skelter speed because she was much more wary of slipping and falling on the muddy grass. "Nicky, wait!"

Nicky paid her no heed but ran on, his little legs easily covering the ground, his arms pumping energetically at his sides as he ran, heedless of anything but getting to the visitor as quickly as possible, and Rachel, panting for breath, saw a long silver grey car sweep past the trees on the drive and felt her heart lurch wildly in fear.

If he got to the drive before she did herself he might so easily run straight out into the car. He was such a small figure for a driver to see if he suddenly appeared from between the trees, and she put an extra effort into catching up with him.

"Nicky, stop at once!" Despite her attempts to sound authoritative her voice sounded flat and breathlessly cracked as she ran after him. "Nicky!"

He gained the border of trees some yards ahead of her and she gave one last desperate shout, then closed her eyes in relief when the car stopped suddenly just short of him. In closing her eyes she momentarily lost her balance and missed her footing on the treacherous surface of wet grass, and before she had time to recover she tripped and fell to her knees.

She was not hurt, the ground was too soft to do any damage, but her tights were laddered and a great patch of wet mud adhered to each of her knees and to the palms of her hands when she put them down to save herself from sprawling full length. Her dignity was far more hurt than her body and she felt the colour flood hotly into her face when the car door opened and the driver stepped out to come hurrying towards her.

"Are you hurt?" Strong hands helped her to her feet and Rachel shook her head instinctively, startled to find that an arm was around her waist and a pair of anxious blue eyes were looking down at her.

"No, no, I'm all right, thank you." She brushed ineffectually at the mud on her knees and hands and shook her head, looking across at Nicky, who now stood beside the newcomer with a broad smile of satisfaction on his face. "Nicky—" she began.

"He ran to meet me," the man told her hastily. "I'm sorry, but he always comes looking for me when he knows I'm due to arrive."

There was the faintest hint of an accent of some kind on the pleasantly light voice and Rachel looked at him curiously. There was a distinct likeness to Neil Brett too, although this man was better looking and his skin was fair and much more appropriate with that blond hair and blue eyes.

"You're—"

"Lars Bergen," he said, and inclined his head briefly in a suggestion of a bow, a wide smile revealing excellent teeth. "I don't think I've had the pleasure of seeing you before, have I?"

"Oh no, I'm new here!" Rachel responded to the smile automatically, but she was rapidly having to rethink yet again on the person of Lars Bergen. He was, after all, a grown man and not a little boy, and he was quite an attractive one too. She held out a hand which he took without hesitation and held for as long as she allowed it. "My name's Rachel Carson, Mr. Bergen, I'm Nicky's—I look after Nicky."

"Ah!" The blue eyes appreciated her looks but with a less embarrassing frankness than Neil Brett had displayed, and he again inclined his head briefly in that almost bow. "So Neil has at last found someone to care for Nicky—I am so glad!"

"Lars!"

Nicky tugged at the newcomer's sleeve, tired of being ignored, and Lars Bergen looked down at him for a moment before he bent and lifted the little boy into the air, swinging him round on to his shoulders with little regard for the effect of muddy shoes on a light grey suit.

"You should not run away from your pretty nurse, little one," he told Nicky. "Have you no more sense?"

Nicky giggled, looking down at Rachel with his blue eyes bright and glistening so that she had no heart to scold him for running off as he had. "I was afraid that you might not see him," she explained. "If he'd run out in front of you—"

Lars Bergen smiled, glancing up at the little boy on his shoulders. "I'm used to him running to meet me," he told her. "He always does." He looked at Rachel curiously for a moment. "Did he not tell you he was coming to meet me?" he asked, and Rachel shook her head.

"No," she admitted. "Though he did say that Lars was coming, but of course it meant nothing to me at the time and I didn't know he meant now."

Lars Bergen laughed. "Children!" he declared tolerantly, and started back towards the big silver grey car parked on the drive.

Rachel followed him because she felt there was little else she could do, but she felt horribly conspicuous with her mudstained knees and hands. It seemed she was likely to drive back to the house with them, but she would much rather have walked and crept in unseen until she was more presentable. Although her employer would no doubt expect her to stay with her charge no matter what the circumstances.

Lars Bergen opened the passenger seat door and dumped Nicky unceremoniously on the front side, but it left plenty of room for Rachel beside him, and the man stood by with the obvious intention of seeing her into the car too.

"Oh, I'd much better walk," she objected hastily, and looked down at her muddy hands. "I'm in such a mess!"

"It doesn't matter," Lars Bergen assured her earnestly. "Please come with us, Miss Carson, won't you?"

He was quite a bit shorter than Neil Brett, she discovered when she stood beside him, and much less disturbing at close quarters, but he was undeniably a very attractive man and quite disturbing enough in his own way. His blue eyes were steady and urged her to take the offer of a lift without further argument, and one hand was already under her elbow, persuasive in its own right as he stood waiting to help her into the car.

"Thank you!" She slid on to the seat beside Nicky and he looked up at her and grinned in an oddly suggestive way that struck her as strange in a young child. Another smile from Lars Bergen brought a swift flush to her cheeks as he got into the car on the opposite side and slammed the door.

"Ready?" he asked, and Nicky nodded.

No one could have missed their arrival, for the long silver grey car anounced its progress with an aggressive roar that Nicky found irresistible and copied as they drove towards the house. The distance was short, but it gave Rachel time to study the profile of the man who drove them, and she wondered if he really was Nicky's cousin or if he was more closely related to Neil Brett.

Nicky's mother, she remembered, had been Neil's sister, so it was possible that Lars Bergen was related to both of them through the distaff side of the family. As if he suspected her curiosity he turned his head as they approached the house and smiled.

"I should perhaps have explained," he told her. "I am Neil's cousin—our mothers were sisters, hence the likeness, yes?"

Rachel smiled. It was so easy to respond to Lars Bergen's open friendliness and she liked him instinctively, also she found him very attractive, though perhaps in a less blatant and earthy way than his cousin. "You are alike," she agreed. "Though Nicky told me you were *his* cousin."

For a moment he looked puzzled, then he laughed and nodded his head. "Ah, you were expecting another little boy, hmm?" She nodded and he laughed again, his blue eyes gleaming warmly across at her above Nicky's head. "I hope you are not disappointed, Miss Carson."

"No, of course not," she denied hastily, and he smiled.

"And since Nicky usually spends a good deal of time with me when I am here," Lars Bergen told her, "you will also, I presume, Miss Carson."

The prospect was unexpected but far from unpleasant, and Rachel smiled. "That might not be very easy," she told him. "Nicky said something about going riding together and—"

"Neil likes him to ride," Lars Bergen explained as he stopped the car and came round to open her door. "But he does not have much time to take him himself, so Nicky looks forward to my visits." The blue eyes looked down at her, briefly speculative, and he raised a questioning brow. "Do you ride, Miss Carson?"

Rachel shook her head. "No, I'm afraid I don't."

"A pity!" He led the way up the steps to the house and from the way he simply walked in it was evident that he was a frequent and welcome visitor. "Ah, Mrs. Handley!" He greeted the housekeeper with a smile and indicated his parked car with one hand. "Will you ask Handley to take up my luggage and put away the car for me, please?"

"Of course, sir."

It was difficult to be sure, but Rachel had the feeling that for some reason Mrs. Handley did not like Lars Bergen very much, and she could not help wondering why that was. She was not given long to speculate, however, for Lars Bergen went striding across the hall with Nicky clinging to his coat and Rachel saw little option at the moment but to follow them.

They walked into the sitting-room, Nicky clinging to Lars' coat and Rachel bring up the rear, rather apprehensive when she realised her employer was in occupation. So far, in the two weeks she had been there, he had been missing at lunchtime, and she and Nicky had eaten alone, a situation she found more to her liking, for sharing a meal with Neil Brett and having those icy blue eyes on her every move was disturbing, to say the least.

He got up and greeted Lars Bergen with a firm handshake, but even so there was a certain reserve in the welcome he extended his cousin, Rachel thought. As far her own appearance, he swept a swift and entirely disapproving glance over her mudstained hands and knees and raised one brow.

"Have you had an accident, Miss Carson?" he asked in a cool voice that suggested if she had it was most likely her own fault, and Rachel shook her head.

"Not exactly an accident, Mr. Brett," she explained, and was conscious of Lars Bergen's eyes on her, curious and slightly narrowed. "I fell in the mud," she went on. "I should have gone straight upstairs to change—I'm sorry."

"Did you hurt yourself?" The question was so unexpected that Rachel stared at him for a moment and saw the hint of impatience in his eyes when she did not immediately answer.

"No," she told him hastily. "No, I'm not hurt, but I'm very dirty and I must go and clean up before

lunch." She half turned away, unable to face that
steady scrutiny any longer. "If you'll excuse me," she
said a little breathlessly.

"Take Nicky with you!"

She turned back swiftly, her eyes wide and, for the
moment, uncomprehending. "Take—"

"Take him with you," Neil repeated the instruction
with a certain slow precision, as if she was too stupid to
understand his meaning, and she nodded, her face
flushed with resentment at his tone.

"Yes, of course, Mr. Brett!"

Nicky, not unnaturally, was unwilling to leave his
hero so soon and protested, clinging tightly to Lars'
jacket. "I want to stay," he insisted loudly. "I want to
stay with Lars!"

"You'll go with Miss Carson now and come back
when you have less mud on your shoes and your hair
has been brushed," Neil told him firmly. "Now come
along, Nicky, don't keep Miss Carson waiting!"

"Neil—"

"Do as you're told," Neil insisted quietly but firmly,
"or you'll have lunch in the nursery!" He looked at
Rachel as if he expected her to support him, as of
course she was bound to do. "Miss Carson!"

She took Nicky's hand in hers, pulling him with her
across the room, anxious not to have him make a
scene. "Come on, Nicky," she urged softly. "Let's go
and clean up ready for lunch." Nicky's bottom lip promised by its quiver to turn into a pout and his eyes had
a bright and glistening look as if tears were not far off,
but it took only a brief glance at his uncle to see that the
order was unlikely to be repealed and Rachel's voice
was gentle as she sought to console him. "Come on,
boy," she urged quietly, "come with me."

She was far too occupied with getting Nicky out of
the room with a minimum of fuss to notice the swift,

sharp gleam that came into Neil Brett's eyes as he
strode across the room after them and she looked up,
startled, when he suddenly appeared beside her.

"Go on upstairs, Nicky," he told the boy quietly,
and Nicky, after a brief speculative glance at that set,
stern face, went with only a minimum of complaint.
When Rachel went to follow him, however, she was
brought to a halt by a large firm hand curled about her
arm tightly. "Miss Carson," he said in that cool hard
voice as Nicky went out of hearing, "you will please
not use that—that name for Nicky."

Rachel, too stunned for the moment to follow his
meaning, scarcely remembered just what she had called
the little boy and she shook her head slowly as she
stared at him. "I—I don't understand," she told him,
and he frowned impatiently.

"You called him boy," he reminded her shortly. "I'd
rather you didn't do so again!"

Rachel flushed, her eyes looking up at him bright
with indignation. To make such a fuss about a perfectly
ordinary endearment seemed quite ridiculous in the
circumstances and she was not going to sit down under
such bigoted domination.

"That's quite unreasonable," she objected in as
steady a voice as she could manage. "Surely a simple
endearment used to a child—"

"It happened to be his mother's name for him,"
Neil Brett interrupted harshly. "You won't use it again,
Miss Carson—do I make myself plain?"

Rachel was aware of Lars Bergen watching them
from the other side of the room, although it was doubtful if he could hear much of the exchange, and she
sought hastily for words to explain. Nicky himself had
not been noticeably affected by her use of his mother's
name for him, but apparently his uncle was, and once
again she wondered what there was about his mother's

death that made everyone so touchy about mentioning
her or anything to do with her.

Rachel shook her head, seeking the right words, and
briefly chanced an upward glance. "I'm—I'm sorry,"
she said, "but I didn't know, of course, and—"

"You know now," Neil interrupted shortly. "I trust
you won't forget again, Miss Carson!"

Rachel felt that the rebuke has been unfairly harsh
considering she had done nothing so very terrible and
Nicky had not been upset by it, and she challenged the
instruction in this instance, whereas she would probably not have done in other circumstances.

"Nicky didn't seem very disturbed by my calling him
boy," she pointed out. "Perhaps if—"

"Nicky isn't the only one concerned!" she was informed coldly, and there was a glitter of anger in the
watching blue eyes. "And I do not expect to have you
debate whether or not my decisions suit you, Miss Carson—I expect you to do as you're told!"

"Like Nicky does?" she countered swiftly, and immediately realised how rash she had been.

Even through the thick sleeve of her jacket his
fingers had a steely strength that made her wince and
she fully expected to hear him say she could go and
pack her things and leave immediately. Instead, after a
second or two of shiveringly angry silence, he released
her arm and waved a hand in dismissal. "You'd better
go and clean up for lunch," he told her harshly, and
turned swiftly to stride back across the room, leaving
her standing there.

For a few seconds Rachel stared after him, unable to
believe he had simply allowed the matter to drop, then,
catching Lars Bergen's curious and rather anxious gaze
on her, she turned and hurried across the hall and upstairs.

She must have been out of her mind to have challenged Neil Brett as she had, but somehow it had been irresistible, and the most astonishing part of the whole thing was that he had allowed her to get away with it.

Taking off her jacket in her room a few moments later, she curled her own fingers over the still aching muscle he had gripped so tightly, and shook her head. Neil Brett was just one more mystery in a curiously secretive household, and she had an almost irresistible urge to try and get close enough to understand him better.

CHAPTER THREE

NICKY was so anxious to reach the stable that he broke away from Rachel well before they got there and ran on ahead. He looked so tiny in a sweater and long trousers that were tucked into short riding boots that Rachel felt she would never have allowed him to ride if the decision had been left to her. The chances of falling seemed much too likely and as she was completely unfamiliar with horse riding herself it had always struck her as rather a dangerous pastime.

A hard-topped hat eliminated some of the risk, of course, but even so it was quite a distance to the ground even from the back of a pony as small as Nicky's. The fact that Neil Brett was quite happy about letting him go, indeed he encouraged it, and that Lars would be in charge of him did little to make her change her opinion, although in the two days she had known Lars he had struck her as completely responsible.

The way down to the stable was a tree-lined bridle path from the back of the house. Bare-armed elms spread their huge gaunt skeletons against the cold winter sky and the narrow bridle path was wet and muddy after a night's rain, but the air smelled fresh and was tangily scented with loam from the shrubbery beside the path and the scent of wet leaves underfoot. The wind was a little less cutting this morning, but it still whipped a bright colour into Rachel's cheeks as she followed Nicky along the path and she was glad of a thick jacket over her woollen dress and the long boots that protected her slim legs.

There were three stalls in the stable, all of them occupied. A pair of handsome bay geldings were lodged in two of them and Nicky's sturdy little Welsh pony occupied the one nearest the door. Both Neil Brett and his cousin rode, though Neil's outings were restricted to the limited time he had free from running the estate and he had taken Nicky only once in the two weeks before Lars's arrival, but Rachel wondered if they ever rode together.

The tangy smell of the stable made her wrinkle her nose when she came to within a few feet of the yard and she could hear Nicky's excited voice chattering to Lars inside the building, anxious to be off. She had been down there only twice before, once when Neil took Nicky and yesterday when Lars had taken him, but she hesitated only briefly before going to the door.

Standing in the opening, she watched Nicky hovering anxiously round his cousin, chattering incessantly, and wondered at Lars' patience with him. Both men, in fact, were amazingly tolerant of his chattering and seldom lost patience with him, though the fact surprised her more in the case of Neil Brett than his cousin.

Lars looked up when she appeared and his blue eyes warmed as he smiled at her, a smile that brought her sudden sense of well-being, as if the sun had suddenly come out. They had met briefly at breakfast, but there had been little time to do more than exchange good mornings because Nicky took all her time and attention at breakfast time.

"Hello again, Miss Carson," Lars said. "It's such a pity you can't come with us."

He helped Nicky into the saddle, checking his hold on the reins and the length of his stirrups while Rachel watched a little anxiously as Nicky wriggled himself into a comfortable position. "I don't really mind not coming," she confessed, and instinctively called out a warning when Nicky dug his heels into the pony's plump sides and urged him through the doorway, making her step hastily out of the way.

"He's quite safe," Lars told her with a smile that nevertheless acknowledged her cause for anxiety. "He's very good for his age. Neil taught him well from the beginning."

Rachel, who had imagined Lars as Nicky's instructor, looked at him with her surprise obvious on her face. "Neil—his uncle taught him?" she asked, and Lars nodded.

"Yes—he would never have learned if he had to depend on my spasmodic visits." He watched Nicky through the open door, much less anxious than she was about him, one arm resting along the top of the dividing panel between the stalls, good-looking, confident and completely at ease. "Don't you really want to join us?" he asked, and smiled when she shook her head. "But we'd—*I'd* love to have you along. I don't like leaving you behind."

Rachel concentrated on the confident little figure of Nicky riding round the yard, content for the moment to go no further afield, and did not look at Lars Bergen who stood so disturbingly close. She knew well enough what he was trying to convey, not so much by the words he used as by the low, quiet tone of his voice.

"Nicky's quite safe with you, Mr. Bergen, I'm sure," she told him. "If Mr. Brett trusts you to take care of him then I see no reason why I shouldn't."

He was close enough to reach out with one hand and touch her hair lightly with one finger, a gesture that sent a small shiver of anticipation through her and made her curl her fingers involuntarily into a ball. "But I would much rather have your company," he insisted, and lowered his voice still further, although there was little chance of Nicky overhearing him. "And will you please call me Lars so that I may call you—Rachel, yes?"

Rachel nodded, her heart thudding hard at her ribs as she studiously avoided looking at him. He was a very attractive man and, although she had known him only two days, she already felt irresistibly drawn to him. Perhaps in part because he treated her with so much more gallantry than Neil Brett did.

What her employer would think about their rapidly developing relationship was another matter, however, and she was not prepared to risk Neil Brett's wrath if there was the slightest likelihood of his objecting. So instead of looking at him and giving Lars Bergen the encouragement he sought she kept her eyes fixed firmly on the little figure on the pony and tried to make her voice sound light and matter-of-fact.

"I've no objections at all, if you think Mr. Brett wouldn't mind," she told him. "In fact I'd like it, but if you think—"

"Neil?" She knew he was looking puzzled even without looking at him, and she saw from the corner of her eye the way his shoulders shrugged, as if he failed to follow her meaning. "How can it concern Neil that I call you by your Christian name?"

Rachel laughed a little uneasily. "Well for one thing, because I've only known you a couple of days," she reminded him, "and you *are* my employer's family. Mr. Brett might think that I—"

"Rachel!" He put a hand on her arm, not forcing her to turn, but persuading her with a light touch to look at him, and she saw that the blue eyes were warm and teasing, so that she wondered if he considered her slightly snobbish. "What I do doesn't concern Neil," he told her quietly. "He leads his own life and I lead mine. Sometimes we do not see eye to eye, but mostly we get on well enough, and if I wish to be—friendly with a pretty girl then what right has he to object?''

"None, I suppose," Rachel admitted, and smiled when she met his eyes. He had hesitated before describing his intentions towards her as friendly, but she accepted the fact that he had something rather more intimate in mind, and the idea was not at all distasteful to her.

The stroking finger on her hair touched her neck and she shivered involuntarily. "There is no other reason for you being here than that of taking care of Nicky, is there, Rachel?" he asked, and Rachel looked up at him hastily, her face flushed warmly as she followed the implication all too easily, though for the moment it stunned her.

"No, of course there isn't!" she denied indignantly, and Lars smiled, shaking his head.

"Don't be angry," he said soothingly. "You do not surely imagine that my cousin is a monk, do you, Rachel?"

Quite inexplicably Rachel's heart was thudding anxiously at her ribs and she could think of little to say on the subject of Neil Brett's taste for women. "I—I hadn't even thought about it," she told him, "and certainly not in connection with myself!"

"I'm sorry." He was obviously anxious not to give offence and there was a hint of anxiety in his eyes as he looked at her. "But you are a very lovely girl, Rachel, and you were troubled in case Neil should object to my—getting to know you better." Again that delicate hesitation conveyed his meaning, and Rachel flushed as she shook her head.

"That was simply because I don't want to do anything to cause trouble," she told him, "in case Mr. Brett decides I'm not suitable to look after Nicky." She glanced again at Nicky riding round the yard and rapidly growing impatient at the delay. "I rather like it here."

Lars put out his hand, just a thumb and forefinger holding her chin. "But of course you like it here," he agreed. "And you'll go on being Nicky's nurse for a long time yet. Also," he added in a low voice, "you make this dull place so much more beautiful and interesting, lovely Rachel, be sure I shall do nothing to jeopardise that."

Rachel's heart was beating rapidly and she trembled when his hand settled on her shoulder, the back of it strokingly gentle against her face. "I think Seaways is lovely," she told him in a light, almost breathless, voice. "It isn't dull at all, certainly the interior isn't."

"It isn't now you're here," Lars agreed in the same quiet voice, and bent his head over her as if he meant to kiss her.

Rachel was not sure what she would have done if he had, but before he could accomplish anything a shadow fell across the stable doorway and the light was blocked by a tall, lean figure that stood for a moment, quite still, as if taking in the scene just inside the shadowy stable. Then Neil Brett brushed past them impatiently, a cold icy light in his blue eyes that sent a shiver running along Rachel's spine and made her catch her breath.

He did not look at them again, but lifted down a saddle from the wall and walked along to the end stall where the second gelding awaited a rider. Rachel watched him, her eyes anxious and almost unconscious of pushing aside Lars's hand from her chin.

"You'd better join Nicky," she told Lars half under her breath. "He's getting impatient."

Nicky, in fact, was turning his pony to come back and see if his uncle was going to join the ride too, and he sat outside calling to him in his shrill small voice. For once his cries were ignored, however, and instead Neil turned swiftly and looked at Rachel, his eyes narrowed.

"It isn't necessary for you to whisper, Miss Carson," he told her in a cool voice, and Rachel flushed.

"I—I didn't realise I was," she said, inexplicably breathless. "I was merely suggesting that Mr. Bergen joined Nicky before he grew too impatient."

The blue gaze was immediately transferred to Lars, who hastily looked away while Rachel looked from one to the other uneasily. "If you'd rather I took Nicky," Neil said, "I can, Lars. If you have something you'd rather be doing."

The implication was too obvious to be ignored and Rachel noticed the bright flush on Lars's face as he glanced at her uneasily before answering. "There's no need, I'll take him," he said shortly. "I was merely having a few words with Rachel before we left."

As if to establish his right to do so he again put his arm along the top of the dividing panel behind her in a suggestively intimate posture. That and the use of her Christian name sent one brow arching swiftly upwards to the sweep of blond hair across Neil's forehead, and he spared her a brief look before he again spoke to his cousin.

"I see," he said quietly, and again Rachel detected far more meaning than the actual words conveyed.

It was evident that Lars too made a similar deduction, for his fair skin was still stained with that bright flush and there was a gleam in his eyes that resented it. "I see no reason why I shouldn't talk to Rachel if I wish to," he declared harshly, and Neil looked at him for a moment with raised brows before he answered.

"By all means speak to her," he told him, "but must

you have your meetings in the stable, Lars—with Nicky looking on?"

Whatever was conveyed by the seemingly simple statement that it found a mark, for Lars's good-looking face betrayed not only anger but sudden realisation as well and his mouth was drawn tightly into a straight line. As if drawn by the tension between them Nicky rode his pony into the stable and sat for a moment looking from one to the other, then he looked at Rachel standing in the seemingly protective curve of Lars's right arm and blinked.

It was almost as if he had suddenly recognised a familiar scene and did not want to become involved in it, for he shook his head firmly as he turned the pony again and urged him back across the open yard, his voice shrill as he rode off, shouting out childish exhortations to the pony.

Lars's eyes followed him uneasily, a small upright figure confident but suddenly very vulnerable somehow, and he licked his lips anxiously. "You surely don't think he remembers," he suggested, and a short, harsh snort of derision cut him short.

"Yes, of course he remembers," Neil told him. "Didn't you *see* him remember?"

"But—" Lars shook his head, a whole gamut of expressions flitting across his good-looking features as he watched Nicky circle the yard again. Then he shrugged, a half defiant gesture that made Neil frown. "I didn't think," he said.

"Obviously," Neil said quietly. "But I'd rather you met Miss Carson elsewhere in the circumstances—at least when Nicky's around—I'm sure you see my reasons."

For a moment Rachel thought Lars would simply agree and the matter would be closed, but his eyes had a bright defiant glitter and he glared at his cousin resentfully. "You can't forget about Lynn, can you?" he asked in a harsh voice, and Neil looked at him steadily for a moment, his blue eyes narrowed.

"Can you?" he challenged.

For a moment Lars simply stood silent, staring at him, as if he knew for certain that every argument that came to mind was doomed to frustration. Then he shook his head as if to clear it, his mouth still tight and angry-looking, and without another word to Rachel he led the bay gelding he had saddled out into the yard and swung himself up into the saddle.

"Nicky!"

She heard him call to the little boy brusquely and impatiently, and a second later the two of them rode out of the yard, Nicky's voice coming back faintly on the cold autumn air, asking why his uncle was not coming too, and he turned as they went down the bridle path and waved. His uncle acknowledged the gesture casually before he returned to the task of saddling his own mount, taking no notice whatever of Rachel standing there.

It was not so much anger that gave the rugged features that cold, closed look, she thought as she looked at him through her lashes, but some other, much deeper emotion that she could not even guess at. The name Lynn had aroused such an intensity of feeling that it was clear she had made a very deep impression on both men, whoever she was, and Rachel's curiosity was aroused.

Lars had remarked that his cousin was not a monk, and one implication, as Rachel saw it, was that the mysterious Lynn had at some time been a bone of contention between the two men, although the thought of Neil Brett as a jealous lover was somehow oddly disturbing. It presented possibilities that had not, until now, seriously entered into the scheme of things and she eyed him again through the thickness of her lashes.

If Lars Bergen was good-looking and attractive in a more conventional way then Neil Brett presented a much more serious challenge. His was a more mature and rugged sensuality that would be more difficult to cope with, should she ever allow herself to become involved, and she glanced at him briefly once more before deciding to leave him and walk back to the house. It was unlikely he would even notice her going, for he had completely ignored her once Lars and Nicky had departed.

Before she had taken more than a couple of steps towards the door, however, he called out her name and she spun round swiftly, startled by the unexpectedness of it. Having called her back he said nothing for several seconds but simply stood and looked at her from the end of the stall, his gaze steady and unfathomable so that it was impossible for her to tell what was in his mind.

"You find Lars attractive?" he suggested suddenly, and Rachel flushed.

Her heart was hammering wildly at her ribs and she would have declared it no concern of his if she had followed her first instincts, but at the back of her mind she felt that he had some definite reason in mind for for asking such a question, and instead she merely nodded and endeavoured to put her opinion into words that would not mislead.

"I—I think Mr. Bergen's very attractive and very charming," she said slowly, and once again an expressive brow arched swiftly upwards.

He left the stall and came and stood in almost the same place that Lars had occupied a few minutes earlier, with his right arm along the dividing panel into the next stall. His light blue eyes were cool and steady as they looked down at her and he was much too close for Rachel's comfort, although she did her best to ignore the steady but violent beat of her heart that his proximity invoked.

"But you won't meet him again in the stable, as you did today," he told her firmly, as if he had no thought of being contradicted, and Rachel blinked.

"I—I gather from your remarks to Mr. Bergen that you—you have some special reason for asking that," she said, and would have gone on, but he interrupted her, his blue eyes gleaming in the shadowy dimness of the stable.

"I'm *telling* you, Miss Carson," he informed her, "not asking you. You will not make your—assignations with my cousin here, and especially not when Nicky is with you, do I make myself plain?"

Mingled with the smells peculiar to a stable and horses was that tangy aura of maleness that seemed to envelop her, making her fingers curl tightly as she fought to still the the emotional havoc he wrought. His blue shirt was open at the neck, despite the cold, and the strong brown length of his throat throbbed with life in a small pulse at its base.

"I—I was merely going to explain," she said huskily, after a moment or two, "that I was simply exchanging a few words with Mr. Bergen, as he told you. There was no arranged meeting and nor is there likely to be, especially as you seem to object so—so vehemently!" She looked at him briefly through her lashes, prompted by some sudden impulsive instinct she was unable to resist. "I told Lars you would," she added.

The blue eyes narrowed, looking at her steadily for a moment before he spoke, and she wondered if her defiance took him by surprise. "You told Lars I'd object?" he asked quietly, and Rachel swallowed hard as she nodded.

"I—I told him you'd probably dislike the idea of my becoming too—too friendly with a member of your family," she went on, and started visibly when he removed his arm suddenly for the supporting panel and thrust the hand into a pocket.

He looked quite menacing, somehow, with his feet planted firmly apart on the straw scattered floor and that bright glitter in his blue eyes that she could not yet identify for sure as anger. "So you think I'm a snob," he said, and Rachel shook her head vaguely. Almost certainly if she annoyed him to the point of losing his temper, she would be out of a job, and she disliked the idea of that for several reasons.

"I—I didn't say you were a snob," she denied hastily. "I just mean that you—well that you probably don't see things in quite the same light as Lars does."

"That's quite possible!" To her sensitive ears his voice seemed to have a harsh timbre and she hesitated to meet the glittering blue gaze head on. "Please don't misunderstand my interest," he went on before she could say anything. "I don't care how or when Lars conducts his affairs, just as long as he doesn't involve Nicky—that I will *not* allow!"

"There's no question of it being—of there being an affair," Rachel denied in a small husky voice. "And you have no right to imply otherwise!"

She felt appallingly close to tears and she could think of nothing more guaranteed to arouse Neil Brett's scorn than the weakness of tears. There was something unyielding about him that was new to her, and she found herself wanting to make him understand that there was nothing more than a mild flirtation between her and his cousin—at least so far.

"It doesn't concern me one way or the other," he declared coolly. "My only concern is for Nicky."

"So is mine!"

Neil looked at her steadily for a moment, then he shook his head. "I doubt it very much," he argued confidently. "No young girl as pretty as you can give her whole attention to a small boy when there's a man like Lars around to distract her."

"That isn't true!" Rachel denied it breathlessly, but even to her own ears the denial sounded unconvincing. So far she had not allowed Lars Bergen to distract her at the expense of Nicky, but it was a possibility there was no denying, no matter how reluctant she was to admit it.

Neil swept a bold blue gaze over her slowly until her face burned with colour and it was plain he paid little heed to her denials. His wide straight mouth twitched for a moment in a hint of smile. "Of course knowing that Lars could be coming here sooner or later," he said, "I should probably have taken a leaf out of your first interviewer's book and told you that you weren't suitable."

Rachel's eyes glowed indignantly. Lars had said plainly that his cousin was no monk and here he was making remarks that implied her only distraction was likely to be Lars. It was too much to let it simply pass without comment and she allowed her need to hit back to override discretion as she curled her hands tightly and glared at him.

"Isn't that rather like the pot calling the kettle black?" she suggested rashly, and caught her breath when she saw the bright glitter in his eyes.

Her head swam with a chaos of speculation and her pulses were racing wildly as he stood and looked at her in a way that brought unfamiliar emotions into being. His tall, virile leanness was close enough to emanate a warmth that almost touched her own body and there seemed to be a curious hint of menace in the way he stood so that she shivered involuntarily.

"And what exactly does that imply?" he asked, and Rachel shook her head, unable and unwilling to say anything to make matters worse. The blue eyes quizzed her narrowly. "Have you any complaints about the way I've behaved?" he asked, and once more Rachel shook her head.

"No," she whispered. "No, of course not!"

"Then I can only assume your remark was prompted by something that Lars had said," he told her, and fixed her again with a steady gaze. "Is that right?"

"No!" Rachel denied hastily, then bit her lip anxiously when he raised a doubting brow. "He—Lars simply said that—that you weren't a monk," she told him.

Neil half smiled. "Did you think I was?" he asked, and Rachel realised suddenly that she was shaking her head.

"Good," he said dryly, "I'd hate to have you labour under a delusion!"

"Mr. Brett—"

"Do you want me to prove it?" he suggested, a bright glitter of challenge in his blue eyes, then he laughed shortly when the sudden shifting of his booted feet in the stable straw startled her into gasping aloud. "You'd better go back to the house," he said, shaking his head, and Rachel stared after him when he turned and walked back to the end stall, her eyes wide and slightly dazed.

His response to her jibe had been both unexpected and unnerving and she could feel herself trembling like a leaf, her legs almost too unsteady to do as he said and go back to the house. Instead she followed the broad back as he walked away from her and shook her head slowly.

"I'm—I'm sorry," she ventured. "I—I didn't mean to be—to be—"

"Provocative?" he suggested, turning to look at her over one shoulder, and Rachel shook her head hastily.

"I'm sorry."

His face was shadowed in the dimly lit stall, his forehead half concealed by that swath of blond hair, and Rachel thought she had never seen anyone who looked more virile and masculine. Then he half smiled and it glittered and gleamed in his eyes as he looked at her.

"You might well be," he said quietly, "if you don't do as I say and go back to the house."

He turned away again and once more Rachel looked at the broad, strong back presented to her. She looked at it for several seconds, half hoping he would look around again, then she turned without another word and went out of the stable, her heart still thudding heavily at her ribs as she went.

When she looked back, a few moments later he was riding out of the stable yard, following the same direction that Lars and Nicky had taken. A tall, lean, autocratic figure that stirred her pulses into response again so that she sighed resignedly as she made her way back to the house.

CHAPTER FOUR

Lars had taken Nicky riding with him and consequently Rachel found herself at rather a loose end. Several times during the past week while Lars had been there, she had wished she could ride so that she could have gone with him too, but it was unlikely that Neil would look very kindly on any attempt of Lars' to teach her to ride when she was doing so in his time and on one of his horses.

More by instinct than deliberation Rachel had walked in the direction of the sea, something which she assumed was permissible when Nicky was not with her. Round by the road the distance was a little over two miles but by walking over the fields as she had done it was rather less than a mile and Rachel felt a thrill of pleasure when she climbed over a wooden fence and found herself suddenly and almost unexpectedly on the top of some cliffs, bleak and cold at this time of year, but with a refreshing tang of salt in the air and the gulls screeching and swooping over the grey water its impact was exciting.

Being forbidden to bring Nicky anywhere near the sea she had so far not been herself, although there had been opportunities when she could have come. But the pleasure of it was all the more intense for having been delayed and she stood for a moment and enjoyed the sense of freedom it gave her.

There was a cold wind, but she was warmly clad and the brisk freshness of it whipped bright colour into her

face and blew her dark hair back from her face where
it was not confined to the red woollen hat she wore.
Her thick woollen jacket had a high fur-fronted collar
and she pulled it up around her ears as she started to
walk.

The sea was rough too, churned into a white foam
where it broke on the sandy beach, hissing and roaring
noisily even at that distance, grey and menacing. But
there was something irresistible about it too that never
failed to stir her blood and seeing it in winter was a new
experience for her. It looked grey and cold but much
more exciting than the bright calm of summer, and she
felt drawn to it as never before.

The cliffs were steep and chalky, topped by the short
springy turf that characterises chalk downs, but further
along she could see a place where the face of the cliff
sloped sharply downwards, a break perhaps brought
about by a past fall of chalk, and she considered the
possibility of making use of it. She had plenty of time
before she need get back and she knew from experience that Lars would have no objection to extending
his baby-sitting duties even if she was a little later than
expected.

After several hours of rain the day before the broken
chalk on the downward climb was slippery where it had
grown over with turf and Rachel had to pause several
times to make certain of her next step before she went
on. Perhaps she had been a little reckless to climb down
to the beach when conditions were so far from perfect,
but the sight and sound of the sea so close made the
effort worthwhile and she went on. It seemed so long
since she had visited the coast, and the certain knowledge that Nicky was in good hands gave her the freedom of mind to enjoy herself.

Once down on the beach she found there was less
room for walking than she had anticipated, but a strip

of several yards was enough to enjoy a brisk walk before climbing back to the top of the cliff again, and she thrust her gloved hands into her jacket pockets and went on happily. She would go only as far as the place where the cliffs curved outwards to form a natural bay, that would be well within her scope.

There was no sound but the roar of the wind-lashed water and the wind itself whistling across the narrow beach, and Rachel could imagine she was in another world. A world inhabited only by the screaming gulls and her own solitary figure walking along the strip of damp sand with the towering white chalk cliffs beside her, completely hiding any sign of civilisation and throwing back the sound of the sea like a defiant answer to its roar.

Only briefly did she remember that Nicky's mother had been drowned somewhere along this same rugged coastline, for she had no intention of putting herself into a position where the same thing could happen to her. Soon warm and glowing from her walk, she glanced suddenly at her watch, and realised it was time she started back. Nicky and Lars were probably already back from their ride and although she had no fears of Lars objecting, she preferred to be there to take charge of Nicky and get him ready for lunch in good time.

Turning back brought the wind slightly more in her favour and the return journey should be both quicker and less of a battle. She had gone several yards on her way back, watching the waves breaking on the shore only a few feet from where she was walking, when she noticed that the tide had turned.

In places her outward footprints which had been safely above the waterline were now being washed over by the incoming tide and erased, and it was only then, when she realised the significance of it, that she looked

direction ahead at the way back to her point of access to
the beach. With incredulous dismay she saw that her
way was already blocked and only a few feet ahead of
her the water was even now foaming right to the foot of
the cliffs.

Not quite believing at first that it could actually have
happened, she walked on, staring at the encroaching
tide that every minute lapped more determinedly at the
foot of the chalky cliffs. The beach was slightly wider in
the spot she stood at the moment, but it lessened with
every step she took and a hasty look back revealed no
hope of access from it by any other means than the way
she had come down.

Her situation, as far as she could see it, was not only
hopeless but dangerous too, for being immersed in the
sea with the temperature at its present level could guarantee severe exposure at the least and probably worse if
no one saw her struggles. It was then that she once
more remembered Nicky's mother and her blood ran
cold when she thought of herself suffering the same
fate because she had been careless enough to take
chances with a strange environment.

Determinedly stifling a rising panic, she hurried
along the remaining stretch of sand left to her and
stopped only when she reached the swirling edge of the
water that cut off any further advance. So far the tide
only just covered the way through, but she had no way
of knowing how long it would be before it became deep
enough to sweep her off her feet, and she could not
possibly attempt to swim dressed in boots and a heavy
wool jacket.

To dispense with them in the blustering east wind
would be just as rash and eventually she decided to take
what appeared to be the less uncomfortable and dangerous course. It was only a matter of about a hundred
yards to where the broken cliff gave access to safety

and she felt she had no option but to try and get there before the water got any deeper.

Gritting her teeth, Rachel walked on into the swirling tide, gasping anxiously when the receding waves dragged at the sand under her feet and almost made her fall. She used the cold slippery surface of the soft chalk to help support her, but it was of little use a moment later when the sea came on again and this time threw a foam-edged wall of water at her with such force that she staggered and fell, panting for breath.

The sheer icy coldness of it made recovery difficult and Rachel simply clung to the chalk as best she could while the receding water dragged at her, trying to break her hold and draw her under. "Help!" She heard her own voice as if from a distance and knew she had almost no hope of being heard, but the need to cry out, however vainly, was undeniable. Added to the coldness of salt water that lashed into her face was the briefer warm saltiness of her own tears and she closed her eyes briefly in a silent prayer.

After what seemed like an eternity she opened her eyes again, blinking the clinging salt water from her lashes, and saw that a little way above her head was at least part of the answer to her prayer. The cliff face was not as completely smooth as it at first appeared, and about two feet or more above her a small, pitifully narrow ledge was cut into the white chalk.

Hardly daring to believe it at first, Rachel stared up at it, then pulling herself round to face the cliff she gazed up for several seconds while the sea again flung cold, angry waves at her to try and break her hold. She shook her head, her hands clinging determinedly, then with enormous effort reached up for the edge of the ledge.

Her gloved hands groped in vain the first time, but a

second determined effort had her almost there until a huge wave flowed swiftly along from behind her and flung her off her feet, lifting her into the air and hurling her against the cliff.

Her scream of terror was drowned in the roar of the water, but when the terror subsided and she lay gasping for breath she realised that what she had believed to be the frustration of her efforts had in fact been her salvation. Her lack of inches had made it nearly impossible for her to reach the ledge with her hands, but being lifted into the air by that huge wave had given her the extra reach she needed and her hands had instinctively reached for the ledge.

She lay for a moment, too frightened to move, then gradually the truth dawned on her and she ventured to look down where she had stood only seconds before, shivering and hopeless in a danger of being swept away by the sea. Now she lay with her legs curled up under her on the cold but blessedly firm surface of the chalk ledge, and she closed her eyes, letting the warmth of tears run down her cheeks and turn chill in the blustering wind.

She dared not yet face the fact that she was very little better off than she had been before, but at least she was safe for the time being and she could only hope that the tide did not come up high enough to make even her present place of safety hazardous.

It was barely credible that her watch was still working, but a glance at it revealed that it was indeed still going and she realised for the first time that soon she would be missed. Someone, probably Lars, would realise that she would not have stayed out without saying so beforehand, and some effort would be made to find her. Whether or not they would think of looking for her on a small ledge above the sea remained to be seen, but the thought of someone missing her was comfort enough at the moment, and she sat back briefly and savoured her moment of relief.

The wind was bitter and Rachel shivered in her soaking wet clothes. An hour on the chalk ledge had seemed like twice as long and she had given up hope of anyone finding her. Instead she sat with her arms folded across her chest and her frozen hands tucked under her arms, shivering uncontrollably.

The wind whistled fiercely and the shrill cries of the gulls mocked her shattered nerves until she felt she hated them. She had cried for a while, but it had done nothing except briefly relieve her sense of hopelessness, and now she simply huddled against the wet chalk cliff and endured the shuddering cold and the relentless sound of the wind and the gulls while the hungry tide licked around her narrow refuge, spraying her with its chilling spindrift.

In a half stupor Rachel opened her eyes suddenly when she caught another sound above those she had endured for so long, a sound that made her heart jolt into violent activity as she strained her ears to listen. It was difficult to be sure, for even her own heart-beat contributed to the defeating jumble of sounds that deafened her to anything as faint as a human voice.

"Rachel!"

She stumbled clumsily to her feet, almost toppling over into the sea as she coped with a voice that sounded pathetically inadequate against the wind and the sea. "Here!" she called, her voice shaking. "I'm down here!"

As yet she could not identify the owner of the voice, but it mattered little as long as she was found and she stood up, stretching as far as she was able with safety to call to whoever it was on the cliff top. It seemed incredible that anyone could have thought of looking for her in such a place, but that did not matter either, she simply wanted to be heard.

"Please, please don't go away!" she cried, her voice shrill with panic. "I'm down here—on the cliff face!"

"Rachel?"

The hint of query made it obvious that she had been heard and she spared a second to close her eyes in relief before shouting again. "Down here—on the cliff!"

The blond head could have belonged to either Lars or Neil, but those rugged brown features could belong only to Neil, and Rachel felt a warm and oddly elated sense of relief when she looked up at him. Obviously lying full length on the cliff top, he looked down at her for a second before he said anything, then his strong voice came down to her, surprisingly audible on the blustering wind.

"Sit back and wait," he instructed with characteristic brevity. "I'll be back for you!"

"Neil!"

Her cry echoed the panic she felt when his head vanished from her view and he immediately appeared again, his hands and shoulders visible this time too, bulky in a thick sheepskin jacket that looked blessedly warm.

"I'm going for a boat!" The words that reached her were distorted by the wind, almost snatched away before they were formed, but they were comforting in their certainty. "Don't panic, just sit back and wait—I'll be back for you!"

Dumbly Rachel nodded but her heart lurched alarmingly when he once again disappeared from view and she stared for along time at the yawn of grey winter sky above the grass edge of the cliff where he had been. Then, shivering and soaked to the skin, she sat down on the ledge again, huddling against the wet chalk and wondering at the unexpected glow of warmth that ran over her chilled body suddenly.

Never in the month she had been at Seaways, no matter how often Lars used her Christian name, had Neil Brett addressed her as anything less formal than Miss Carson, not even when it was not necessary to impress Nicky with a sense of propriety. It might almost be worthwhile being half-drowned and flung on to a cold wet ledge of rock to freeze if it achieved a less formal approach on the part of her employer, and unbelievably she found herself smiling.

More than half an hour—Rachel looked again at her wristwatch in despair and hugged herself tightly to try and get more warmth into her chilled bones. She had never felt more wretched in her life and she had begun to doubt if Neil Brett meant to come back for her, although she knew at the back of her mind that the idea of his simply leaving her there was ridiculous. The wind had already snapped what little bit of optimism the promised rescue had brought her and she was again steeped in self-pity when she caught the first sound of an outboard motor. It was coming from her left, at least she thought it was; with so many other sounds around her it was difficult to tell.

Then suddenly it came into view—a small motor launch, its outboard chugging healthily and a wave of white foam parting before it as it skimmed across the choppy grey water towards her. It took her only seconds to spot Neil's blond head in the cockpit beside a shorter, darker man and she once more felt the uncontrollable saltiness of tears rolling down her cheeks as she watched the approach with hazy eyes.

It was only now, as she watched the little boat coming rapidly nearer, that Rachel realised the possibility of Neil being angry about the trouble he had been put to.

She had been rash, she was prepared to admit that much, but nothing more, and she wondered whether he would be willing to make allowances. Wondering about his reaction momentarily took some of the joy out of her rescue and she watched the approaching boat anxiously.

Neil looked a big and over-awing figure with the sheepskin jacket flying open over a thick sweater and he stood in the small boat in an attitude that somehow suggested aggressiveness. The other man was a stranger to her, presumably the owner of the boat, but she was glad of his presence as a deterrent to any outburst of anger on her employer's part, for even as much as she could see of him so far made her certain he was angry.

The boat, bobbing on the churning tide, looked in danger of being smashed against the chalky cliffs but skilful handling kept it a safe distance and at the same time brought it close enough for Neil to reach up his hand for her.

"Jump!" he instructed, but Rachel, now that it came to the point, hesitated.

It looked a dismayingly long way down to the boat and the sea was rocking it so wildly that she had a sudden terror of being plunged again into that icy water. She shook her head, shrinking back against the cliff face, her eyes wide and frightened, too numb even to accept the assurance of those large and helpful hands outstretched to her.

"For God's sake, Rachel, jump!" Neil told her shortly. "I can't climb up there for you, there isn't room, you'll have to jump!"

Rachel licked her lips nervously. "I—I can't."

"Yes, you can, now come on!" He reached up again and his hands slid beneath her arms as she bent towards him, a sudden blessed warmth flowing into her.

She closed her eyes and tears tricked from between her long lashes as she jumped blindly, instinctively, not knowing if the rocking boat would receive her sudden unsteady weight or not.

The boat rocked wildly, spray hurling in over the side while the boatman did his best to steady it, and Neil's hands still held her firmly, safely, as she fought to keep her balance. "O.K., miss?" The strange voice made her turn swiftly and she looked at the short dark figure of the boatman blankly for a moment, then nodded, still not daring to speak. "Good!" the man said cheerfully. "We'll soon have you back home now!"

Rachel simply nodded again. Her brain, like her body, was too numbed with cold and the stark reaction of fear to respond more fully and she simply stood there in the cockpit of the little boat like a small, bedraggled urchin. Then suddenly, without realising she was doing it, she swayed against the solid warmth of Neil, her hands clutching him tightly.

His arms took her hesitantly at first, then after a few seconds he suddenly hugged her close and Rachel felt herself trembling, shivering with a reaction that was both relief and response to the firm masculine body that seemed to envelop her completely as she pressed her face to the softness of his sweater. The open front of his jacket enfolded her like warm wings and she closed her eyes in the exquisite pleasure of emotional satisfaction.

He said nothing, but a few seconds later he gently put her away from him and she noticed a little dazedly that he did not look at her directly but rather concentrated on the task of removing his thick jacket. "Take off that wet coat and put this on," he instructed quietly, but Rachel instinctively shook her head.

"Oh no, I can't—what about—"

"Will you just for once do as I say without arguing?"

he asked impatiently, and Rachel was aware of the dark man looking at her with a curiously speculative glint in his eyes and he guided the speeding boat back along the coast.

She caught her breath a moment later when Neil began to unbutton her wet jacket, stripping it from her without a word, then pushing her arms into the deliciously warm sheepskin, his mouth set tightly in determination. The boatman, Rachel noticed uneasily from the corner of her eye, was smiling, and as she hunched her shoulders gratefully into the thick, snug depth of the sheepskin, she wondered what he was thinking.

Glancing up at the tanned and rugged face of her employer, she blinked the last of the tears from her eyes, feeling suddenly and strangely elated despite the aching coldness of her body. "Thank you," she said huskily.

Neil said nothing, but she thought she caught a hint of a smile in the light blue eyes before he looked away again, and Rachel wondered if he had ever been as angry as she had supposed. He was watching the approaching shoreline and there was a curious air of satisfaction about him that puzzled her for the moment.

His car was parked on the quay not far from where the boat landed them and he spared only a few seconds thanking the boatman, then hurried across the cobbled surface of the quay towards the car, but Rachel's legs felt too unsteady and weak to match his step and she hung back against the hand under her arm.

Frowning, he looked down at her and she felt ashamed of the weakness of tears, but there was nothing she could do about them and they coursed down her cold cheeks unchecked. "I—I can't walk so fast," she said in a small apologetic voice. "My legs feel—feel wobbly and I—"

"Of course, I should have thought of that," he interrupted hastily. "It's reaction, naturally!" He did not hesitate a second longer, but lifted her up into his arms with an ease that startled her so that she instinctively put an arm round his neck and hung on tightly while he strode across the quay to the car.

Rachel was too stunned to say anything and he deposited her on the front seat as easily as Lars had done with Nicky, closing the door quickly and striding round to his own seat. There were so many things she wanted to ask about—like how on earth he had found her, but when he slid into the seat beside her and the warmth of his thigh pressed against her she could only stare ahead at the road and try to do something about the rapid and disturbing beat of her heart and the sensations he aroused in her.

She had no idea where they were, but it was obvious that he must have driven to somewhere along the coast where he knew he could borrow a boat and she realised just how much trouble she had put him to. So far she had not even thanked him for coming to find her, but at the moment she felt oddly shy and she simply sat there beside him with her hands drawn back into the warmth of his jacket sleeves, saying nothing as he drove out of the town and sped along a country road that she could only assume led them back to Seaways.

He looked warm enough in a thick blue sweater and even his hands, gloveless and strong on the steering wheel, looked capable of warming her own chilled ones and for a while the notion occupied her mind to the exclusion of all else. Realising how she was daydreaming suddenly, she shook herself back to reality and looked at him through the thickness of her lashes.

They were already turning into the drive at Seaways and she had still not expressed her thanks for rescuing her. "I—I haven't thanked you for finding me," she

ventured in a voice that betrayed her uncertainty, and
Neil turned his head briefly and looked at her.

There could have been a hint of smile on his wide,
straight mouth, but she was not sure, and he turned
away again before she could confirm it. "I was the one
who found you," he told her in a quiet voice, "because
no one else considered you crazy enough to have gone
near the sea in this weather."

Unsure just how to take the bluntness of his confes-
sion, Rachel blinked for a moment before answering.
"I see," she said, and to her surprise he smiled.

"I'm sure you do," he said calmly.

"You haven't a very high opinion of my intelligence,
have you, Mr. Brett?" She asked the question in a
small unsteady voice that somehow sounded more hurt
than she had intended it to, and he turned his head
again briefly and looked over his shoulder to her.

"Your intelligence isn't in question," he told her.
"But I happen to see you as impulsive and—rash, if
you like; walking along the beach in the middle of
winter would appeal to you, but it wouldn't even occur
to you to check things like high water marks. I know
you like the sea because you implied as much by wanting to take Nicky there, and when you were missing for
so long it stood to reason that something had happened
to you. Lars searched inland, I chose to look along the
cliffs first—as it happened I was right."

Rachel shivered, chilled again suddenly by the memory of her near disaster. If he had not thought her rash
and impulsive enough to walk along the cliffs she
might well have suffered the same fate as his sister had,
and for the first time it occurred to her how much it
must have meant to him to rescue her from that particular situation.

She looked at him through her lashes for a second,
struggling to find the right words to tell him how sorry

she was. "I—I know how you must have felt," she ventured. "I mean, about having to rescue me from the—from where I was." She was making a sorry mess of explaining, she realised, when she saw how set and withdrawn his expression was. "What I mean is," she went on hurriedly, "I know that your sister was—" She swallowed hard, her hands shaking as she held them tightly together on her lap. "I'm sorry you had to be reminded," she finished huskily.

Neil braked the big car gently to a halt in front of the steps, then turned slightly in his seat to face her. There was a cool distant look in his blue eyes that made her shiver and Rachel curled her fingers anxiously as she hastily avoided his gaze. "There was nothing I or anyone else could do about that," he told her in a flat voice, "and you have no need to feel guilty about anything—if that's what you're trying to say."

"But I wouldn't have—I mean, I hate reminding you of something that must be—painful," Rachel explained a little breathlessly, not sure that she was doing anything to help matters by trying to explain.

"I don't imagine you deliberately got yourself half drowned," Neil told her in a cool voice, "So you have no need to explain either. What you *do* need to do is to get into a hot bath and then into bed. Mrs. Handley will make you a hot drink and then we'll see if Doctor Corder need be called."

He strode round the car and opened her door and Rachel let out a cry of surprise when he bent and lifted her into his arms. "I can walk!" she told him, despite the fact that her arm was already encircling his neck, and he looked down at her with one brow raised. "I can, honestly," she insisted. "And I don't need a doctor."

Neil said nothing for the moment, but instead of

standing her down he took the stone steps up to the front door with very little effort, putting her down on her feet only when they stood in the hall. Rachel slid her arm from his neck, reluctant to lose the warm, strong contact of his body, and for a second he stood looking down at her with a deep, unfathomable look in his eyes.

"After you've bathed and Mrs. Handley's put you to bed with something to warm you," he told her quietly, "then I'll decide whether or not you need a doctor."

"But, Mr. Brett—"

He practically dragged her to the bottom of the stairs, then once more stood looking at her with that challenging gleam in his blue eyes, his hands turned backwards on his hips. "If you feel you can't manage the stairs," he told her, "I can carry you."

"Oh no, no!" Rachel urged her trembling legs forward and took the first step. "I can manage easily, thank you!"

Neil nodded as if he was satisfied she was telling the truth, but he still stood watching her. "Then I'll send Mrs. Handley up to you, and try and find Lars and tell him you're safe and sound." he told her, and Rachel nodded resignedly as she started upstairs again. "Oh, and Rachel!"

She turned, looking at him warily, finding his use of her Christian name strangely affecting in more familiar surroundings. "Yes, Mr. Brett?"

"I'd like to be afforded the same privileges as my cousin," he said in a quiet voice, "so try and find Neil as palatable as Lars, will you?"

Rachel looked at him for a moment blankly, until she remembered her plaintive cry to him when she had seen him disappear from the top of the cliff. She nodded, her unsteady legs shaking with weakness but wary of being carried again because she did not know just how far she could trust her own reactions to him in the present situation.

"I'll try," she whispered, and caught a glimpse of his smile as she turned away.

CHAPTER FIVE

ONE day's complete rest was long enough to effect a recovery and although the housekeeper expressed some doubt about her fitness Rachel insisted on getting up and returning to her normal routine. She had had nearly thirty-six hours of lying in bed and being waited on by a willing Mrs. Handley and she was tired of the inactivity, apart from feeling something of a fraud because she felt better after even a few hours and would have got up sooner if Neil had not issued instructions that she was not to be allowed to.

Nicky, she understood, had been told only that she was suffering from a slight cold, and Rachel could see the reason in that, for telling Nicky that she had been close to drowning would probably have had a much more dramatic effect on him that it had on Rachel herself. She was far too emotionally stable for there to have been any lasting effect on her nerves.

She went in to Nicky the following morning as usual and he showed a touching concern for her when she went in. His solemn blue eyes looked at her with an almost adult concern and he asked how she was without any prompting from the attendant Mrs. Handley, who had insisted on helping.

"I'm fine now, Nicky, thank you," Rachel told him, and gave him a close hug for his concern, realising for the first time just how fond she had grown of her small charge in the weeks she had been there. He was a fairly self-possessed child, but that curiously adult manner was somehow oddly endearing in so young a child.

"You got lost," Nicky said, as if he knew all about it and, after a hasty glance at Mrs. Handley who nodded reassuringly, Rachel smiled in agreement.

"Yes, I got lost," she said, "but fortunately Neil— your uncle guessed where I'd be and found me."

"Neil said you was mad," Nicky added with stunning frankness, and despite her effort to do something about it, Rachel felt her cheeks flush warmly with colour.

"Did he say that?" she asked casually, as if her heart was not racing so fast it made her breathless. "Then I expect he's right, don't you?" she added, well able to believe Neil had expressed just those sentiments.

"He always is," Nicky remarked matter-of-factly, and Rachel thought there was simply no answer to that.

When she came down to breakfast with Nicky, Lars expressed his concern more anxiously although he was careful to omit any mention of the circumstances of the incident. His good-looking features were drawn into an anxious frown as he looked across the breakfast table at her, and he shook his head over her pallor.

"You don't look very well at all," he told her. "Are you sure you're all right, Rachel?"

Suspecting that Neil was more interested in her answer than he appeared to be Rachel nodded. "Yes, of course, Lars, I'm fine."

His eyes were a darker blue than Neil's and much less capable of concealing his feelings and he looked at her anxiously. "You look so pale," he insisted. "Perhaps you should rest for another day or two, or at least take things easy." He glanced at Neil. "I'm sure Neil wouldn't mind in the circumstances."

Neil looked up from his breakfast and Rachel hastily

avoided his eyes, her heart beating rapidly at her ribs. "The decision was Rachel's own," he said quietly, "not mine."

"But you see how pale she is," Lars urged, and Neil's blue eyes studied her for a moment, noting the pale softness of her skin and the darkness around her grey eyes.

"What about it, Rachel?" he asked. "Do you feel you need more time to recover?"

His use of her Christian name surprised Lars, and it did not please him either, if his slight frown was any indication, so that once again Rachel was driven to speculate. No matter what veneer of tolerance and politeness they put on their general behaviour, she thought, there was always that current of emotion between them, only barely concealed; passions she could only guess at and wonder what caused them. Almost certainly the mysterious Lynn whom Lars had referred to had something to do with it, and once again Rachel speculated on what kind of a woman could affect two such strong-minded men so dramatically.

Rachel blinked herself hastily back to reality when she realised that Neil was still watching her with a faintly curious glint in his blue eyes as he waited for an answer. "Oh, I'm fine—really," she assured him hurriedly. "I don't need any more rest, I've already spent far too much time in bed as it is!"

After a brief, narrow-eyed scrutiny Neil nodded, apparently satisfied, but Lars was less easily convinced and was obviously bent on stressing her need for longer recovery. He reached over and took her hand, his fingers gently caressing, arousing her tingling sense to a response that startled her.

"But why not let me drive you into Mergeton, just for the ride?" he urged persuasively, and from the pitch of his voice it was safe to assume that he hoped to be inaudible to Nicky. "It would be good for you to have a complete change of scene, Rachel," he insisted, "and I'd love to take you."

It was obvious that Lars saw the opportunity as too good to overlook and meant to persuade her into going with him whether or not she was fit enough to resume her care of Nicky, and Rachel wondered whether Neil Brett saw through the plan as easily as she had herself— almost certainly he would. Whether Lars meant to include Nicky in the invitation she was not at all sure, but she doubted it in the circumstances. Before she had the opportunity to ask him, however, Nicky raised the question.

"Me too, Lars?" he asked. "Me too, eh?"

From his initial frown it was obvious that Lars had not intended to include him, but he did his best to smooth over the fact by smiling at Nicky and winking one yes. "You wish to play gooseberry, little one?" he asked, and Nicky laughed uncertainly, glancing from Lars to his uncle and back as he tried to puzzle the meaning of the question.

Neil said nothing, but he looked up and caught Rachel's gaze, holding it steadily as he looked at her over the rim of his coffee cup. It was a challenge, Rachel realised that, and one she could scarcely fail to recognise. Almost certainly he would not object to her going with Lars, but he was waiting to see if she took advantage of the opportunity to be alone with Lars or if she would stand by her declaration that she was quite fit enough to care for Nicky again.

"Lars is only teasing you, Nicky," she told the boy quietly. "We'll both drive into Mergeton with him." She looked across at Neil, her chin unconsciously angled in a gesture that was as much defensive as defiant. "Unless your uncle objects to us going, of course," she added.

"Not at all." The expression in his eyes was unfathomable, but it disturbed her vaguely and she hastily avoided it, giving her attention to Nicky while he disposed of the last of his breakfast.

"You run along and start getting ready, Nicky," she told the boy a few seconds later. "I'll be up to help you in a few minutes, as soon as I've finished my coffee."

Only too anxious to be away, Nicky got down from the table and hurried out of the room, banging the door behind him, a gesture that made his uncle frown. When Rachel turned back to the table Neil's eyes were on her again, their expression still cool and unfathomable, although a faint hint of smile touched his wide mouth.

"You need not take Nicky if you prefer to go with Lars alone," he told her, and for some inexplicable reason Rachel felt her face flush warmly as she put down her empty cup.

It was as if he still challenged her willingness to take the boy and she resented it. Privately she was prepared to acknowledge the fact that she would have enjoyed a morning in Lars' company without the encumbrance of her young charge, but she had said she was ready to take Nicky and Neil had no cause to question her sincerity.

"Of course I'll take him," she said. "It's my job to look after Nicky, and I've said I'm perfectly fit again, Mr. Brett."

"Mmm?"

"If you'll excuse me, I have to go and help Nicky!" She sounded breathless, she knew, but a raised brow had reminded her of her promise to be less formal and something in the depth of those blue eyes questioned her reasons for changing her mind.

"Rachel!" He offered no reason for calling her back as she got to the door, and she knew that Lars was watching, puzzled by something he could not understand.

She shook her head, instinct providing her with an answer, her grey eyes holding his briefly while she stood in the open doorway, looking over her shoulder. "I'm sorry, Neil," she said huskily, and hurried out into the hall after Nicky.

She could hear his childish voice prattling to Mrs. Handley somewhere along the landing, so she had no fears that he would get into any immediate mischief and she took her time. The strange, indefinable air of unrest that characterised Seaways, she felt, was gradually involving her in its mystery and the thought of it was disturbing.

It was almost as if a restless spirit roamed the beautiful old house and the tension that existed between Lars and Neil served its unrest. Seaways must surely once have been a happy house, Rachel thought, it was inconceivable that it had not been at some time in its long history, perhaps even as recently as when Nicky's mother was alive, before she died so tragically last year. It was curious, she reflected, that no one so far had made any mention of Nicky's father, unless perhaps the explanation was the obvious and all too common one.

What was so strange was that an air of weariness and mistrust still disturbed the tranquillity of the old house and she could think of no reason for it. Nicky was a delightful and endearing child and not so far given to showing symptoms of the nervous stress that his uncle had warned her about, so there should have been little to cause the atmosphere that she daily became more aware of. Shrugging uneasily, Rachel carried on towards the tireless sound of Nicky's voice, resigned to the inexplicable at the moment.

To reach her own room and Nicky's she had to pass

Lars' room which was on the same side of the landing,
and as she passed it she noticed that the door was open.
Most likely Mrs. Handley had been along, changing
bed linen or checking on the progress of the daily
woman who came in from the village, and she had accidentally left it open.

The temptation to glance in was irresistible and she
did so almost automatically. Only a wardrobe and an
armchair were visible through the opening, and a small
bedside table on which Lars' gold wristwatch had been
left carelessly abandoned beside a large framed photograph of a young woman.

It was probably wrong of her, but Rachel came to a
halt by the open door almost without conscious effort
and stood looking across at the photograph, a sudden
and quite inexplicable urgency in her heartbeat.

The photograph showed a girl of about twenty-two or
three, pretty in a rather childish way, with light brown
hair and huge eyes. Her mouth half smiled and it
looked both sultry and faintly sulky, and there was a
look about her that was in some curious way familiar.

Seeing the portrait so prominently displayed by Lars'
bed, Rachel was unable to resist lingering long enough
to read the message that was scrawled in thick black ink
across the bottom of it. *"Lars—forever, my darling,
Lynn."*

The outing had for the most part been enjoyable, although Rachel found herself unable to forget for very
long the portrait she had seen beside Lars' bed, of the
mysterious Lynn. She wanted so much to ask about
her, to discover just who she was, and mostly, she admitted to herself, because the girl had obviously meant
something at some time to Neil Brett.

The girl had without doubt figured quite largely in
the lives of both Neil and Lars, but it was her connec-

tion with Neil that interested Rachel most. She could not bring herself to ask about her and yet in one way she felt she almost had the right to, for Neil had compared her own situation with that of Lynn, whoever she might be, when he had ordered Lars not to meet Rachel again in the stable while she was with Nicky. Where Nicky fitted into the situation she had no idea, but that was just one more puzzle she must one day solve.

At the moment Nicky was playing on the gravel paths that wound through Mergeton's public park, darting between the bordering shrubs and shouting with glee when he emerged at some point further along. As far as Nicky was concerned the day had been an unqualified success and he was enjoying himself enormously.

It was cold but quite fine and a watery sun shone occasionally from behind the thick grey winter cloud, so that even the weather appeared to be on their side. They had lunched at a very expensive restaurant but abandoned the idea of going for a drive in favour of a walk in the park, mostly to please Nicky who got restless when he was confined to the car too long.

There was something pleasantly intimate about sitting beside Lars on the green park seat watching Nicky chasing the birds who came to feed, but complete pleasure in the situation was denied Rachel because she could not erase those sultry but curiously childish features from her mind.

She studied Lars' fair good looks while he was engrossed in Nicky's antics and she tried not to think of herself becoming too serious about him. Not that she had inclinations that way at the moment, but if the sexily attractive Lynn had declared her love to be for ever then there was the possibility that he was not as free as he appeared. It might well be why Neil had more or less issued a warning, and she blinked in the sudden realisation that she did not even know if Lars was married or not!

As if he sensed her sudden tension Lars turned and smiled enquiringly. "You're not cold?" he asked, and Rachel shook her head. Lars studied her for a second, then turned and faced her, taking her hands and looking just a little anxious, Rachel thought. "Then what's wrong, Rachel?" he asked. "I know there's something, you've been so quiet all day, and it's not like you at all to be so—so solemn."

"I'm all right, Lars, honestly." She had to admit he had cause for comment, for she had been pre-occupied and she supposed he was entitled to an explanation, but at the moment she found it hard to put her feelings into words.

"You don't still feel—unwell?"

Rachel shook her head. "No, honestly, I'm fine!"

"Then smile, hmm?" He leaned towards her and it seemed almost inevitable that he was going to kiss her so that she instinctively drew back. Whether it was because Nicky was close enough at the moment to see what they were doing and she had Neil's warning still in mind, she was not sure, but her reaction brought a frown of dislike to Lars' good-looking face. "You do not want me to kiss you?" he asked, and for only the second time since he arrived she noticed that he had an accent.

Her brain was spinning, confused by a chaos of emotions and doubts, and she shook her head without even realising it. "Lars, who is Lynn?"

"Lynn?" She felt the strong hands that held hers unconsciously tighten their grip and Lars' blue eyes looked at her uncertainly for a moment before he answered. When he did she thought his accent was stronger than she had ever noticed it, as if he chose his words with infinite care. "Why do you ask about Lynn now?" he asked, and Rachel shrugged uneasily.

"I—I remember you mentioned her when you and Neil were talking in the stable one day," she reminded him, and thought for a moment that for some curious reason he seemed relieved by her answer, although she could not imagine why.

He bent his head and studied his own figures for a moment, twining them into Rachel's hair where it curled on to her shoulders. "Lynn is dead," he stated suddenly and with painful frankness. "She was Nicky's mother."

Rachel stared at him and her heart was rapping anxiously at her ribs, bereft of words for the moment. Not for anything now could she let him know she had seen the portrait in his room, nor that dramatic declaration of undying love. There was something much more complicated about the household at Seaways even then she had imagined, and she shook her head, wondering if Lars could possibly be as unaffected by Lynn's death as he appeared to be. It seemed impossible that he was, and yet he had made the statement quite baldly and with no sign of emotion.

"She was your cousin," Rachel said, but he did not reply.

It was not difficult to imagine the additional complications involved with Lars and Lynn being first cousins, nor to imagine Neil's disapproval of the affair, so that she wondered if Neil had broken up the romance or whether Lynn's premature death had brought it about.

It also raised the question of whether Lars had been responsible for a break between Nicky's parents, but if that was so then surely it would have been Lars who was never mentioned in conversation, not Nicky's father, and Lars was still a welcome visitor at Seaways, despite that air of reserve between him and his cousin.

She sighed inwardly at the many unanswered questions that seemed to grow more all the time, and still Lars did not look up. Looking at his bent head Rachel felt suddenly sorry for him. He was good-looking and charming and it was quite possible that he had genuinely loved his pretty cousin.

It was no more than a year since the tragedy of Lynn's death and probably neither he nor Neil had sufficiently recovered from the shock of her death to look at past indiscretions dispassionately. It would explain their edgy and brittle politeness towards one another too, with both men mourning her, but for different reasons.

Lars raised his head at last and looked at her for a moment before he spoke. "Would you like to go back?" he asked, and glanced at the overcast sky. "It's going to rain, I think, and you must be cold sitting on this bench for so long, Rachel."

She smiled, although it was quite true that the sky looked very threatening and she had become rather cold despite her thick clothes. "It is turning chilly," she agreed. "I suppose we'd better think about going back."

Lars pulled a face, grimacing at the gathering clouds. "I dare not let you run the risk of getting wet again and catching pneumonia," he told her with a short laugh, "or Neil would never forgive me!"

Without warning Rachel's cheeks flushed warmly and she shook her head to deny any likelihood of his being blamed for whatever happened to her. "It's very unlikely that you'd get the blame if I do catch pneumonia," she told him. "It's far more likely that Neil would say it was all my own doing for being such a fool, like he did when he rescued me from my last drenching!"

"Neil," Lars echoed softly. "I noticed the new air of familiarity at breakfast this morning!" He glanced over his shoulder to make sure that Nicky was safely out of earshot, then turned to her again. "What exactly happened during that dramatic rescue, Rachel, that put you and Neil on such—intimate terms so suddenly?"

Rachel did not immediately answer him, but she got to her feet and called Nicky to her, her cheeks still warm with colour, although she refused to become indignant about the implications he was making as he probably expected her to. "Nothing at all happened except that Neil saved my life," she told him quietly. "And after all, Lars, I have in fact known Neil for a lot longer than I have you and I already call you by your Christian name!"

Lars got lazily to his feet and stood facing her, one gloved hand under her chin. It was hard to make herself remember that it was only a year since Lynn Browlett had died and that everything pointed to Lars having been her lover. He was so close that his mouth almost brushed hers and his breath was warm on her lips when he spoke.

"But with me it's different, surely, isn't it, Rachel?" he said.

Her heart was hammering hard at her ribs and the cold wind might have been a warm summer breeze for the glow that she felt, but Rachel was aware suddenly that Nicky was tugging at her coat and she looked down at him.

She saw the same anxious, vaguely uneasy look that he had worn when he had seen her with Lars in the stable that day, in a position that suggested intimacy. He must have witnessed his mother in the same situation with Lars more than once, if Neil's hint was to be believed, and the familiarity of it troubled him as Neil had said it would.

Rachel put a protective hand on Nicky's head and half smiled. Heaven knew what would happen if she should ever become more serious about Lars, but at the moment she was more concerned with not letting Nicky see her as a painful reminder of his mother.

"We'll go home now," she said.

Rachel had spent a restless night, in part because Nicky had gone to bed much later than usual and the excitement of a day out had made him restless. She should, she knew, have tried to quieten him before she put him to bed, but she had been rather preoccupied and so gave him less attention than usual.

She smiled at him now as she brushed his thick mop of brown hair back from his forehead. He was a good-looking boy and very much like his mother, which was why the portrait of Lynn had struck Rachel as familiar.

With her mind brought back involuntarily to Lynn, she sighed inwardly. If there was a restless spirit at Seaways there was little doubt that it was the uneasy memory of Lynn, and her love for her cousin must in some way contribute to it. There was no way of knowing what would have happened if she had lived, but Lars seemed already recovered sufficiently to see Rachel as her successor. If Lynn had loved him as deeply as that message on the photograph suggested, it was no wonder her memory hovered like an unhappy shade over the old house.

"Can I go and see Taffy?" Nicky's question brought Rachel hastily back to reality and she smiled instinctively.

Taffy was his little Welsh pony and he sometimes liked to go down and see him before he had his breakfast, although it was a practice that Neil frowned on. Rachel sighed and pulled a face at his reflection, shaking her head. "You know your uncle doesn't like you visiting the stable before you've had breakfast," she reminded him, but Nicky thrust out his lip in a way that again reminded Rachel of the portrait of his mother.

"I won't be long," he promised. "And Handley's there, he doesn't let me get dirty, Miss Carson."

Her hesitation was only brief, then Rachel nodded, smiling resignedly as she gave a last brush to his smart grey trousers. "Just see that you *don't* get dirty," she warned him, "or your uncle will be angry with me as well!"

Nicky was out of the bedroom door in a moment and she heard him scampering down the stairs, so quickly that she held her breath until he reached the bottom for fear he missed his footing. She would have to take Neil's initial disapproval on her own shoulders, but the prospect did not worry her unduly.

Rachel went downstairs only seconds behind Nicky and as he went towards the breakfast-room door she heard voices raised—men's voices, easily identifiable even at some distance. Whatever they were arguing about Lars at least was making little effort not to be overheard.

Rachel hesitated, anxiously uncertain whether to go in and pretend she had heard nothing or to go back to her room until such time as the quarrel had burned itself out. It was the first time she had known them to quarrel openly and it was Neil who gave her the first inkling of what it was all about, speaking in his cool, firm voice and only just audible to her.

"Just stop and think before you get Rachel involved," he told Lars. "She's the kind of girl who'll take you seriously and she's—vulnerable."

"Oh, nonsense!"

Rachel, her face burning with embarrassment, could well imagine Neil's expression at being so abruptly ridiculed and she bit her lip anxiously as she hovered by

the door, seeking enough courage to go in. "I'm warning you, Lars," Neil's voice reached her again, as quiet
as ever but with an icy edge to it. "If you—"

"For God's sake, she's not Lynn!" Lars interrupted
harshly, and Neil's response was angry and violent.

No longer caring whether or not it was ethical to in-
terrupt their quarrel, Rachel was anxious only to put an
end to the exchange before it became physical as well
as verbal, and she opened the door suddenly and
walked in. A heavy silence fell on the little room when
she appeared, but the atmosphere was so charged with
violence that she shivered.

As she looked from one to the other her heart thudded anxiously and there was a bright, anxious gleam in
her eyes as the tip of her tongue briefly relieved the
dryness of her lips. "Good morning!" she ventured,
but her voice trembled so much that it was doubtful if
Neil, from where he stood, even heard it, and neither
of them answered.

Lars stood by the long sideboard, his fair good-
looking face flushed and his eyes dark with resentment.
A hint of sulkiness pursed his mouth in much the same
way she had seen Nicky do on occasions when he was
denied his own way. It stunned her for a moment to
detect anything so distinctly childish in Lars, and she
hardly believed it.

Neil stood over by the window with his back to the
light so that his expression was less easily judged, his
rugged, tanned face half in darkness. His blond head
was outlined by the winter sunshine behind him and its
posture suggested a savage arrogance that would yield
to no one. There was nothing even remotely childish
about Neil and Rachel felt an involuntary shiver when
she looked at him, her limbs weak and trembling with
anticipation.

It was Neil, of course, who recovered first and he

came striding across the room suddenly with an icy
glint in his eyes and his features set like golden granite
above the high collar of a grey sweater. For a second he
said nothing, but his eyes moved swiftly over her
flushed face and his mouth had a tight, firm look that
betrayed his anger.

"Rachel?"

He had no need to put into words the question that
was plain enough in his eyes, and Rachel nodded her
head in a kind of breathless acknowledgement. "I—I
couldn't help overhearing," she told him, "but I've
only just this minute come downstairs, Neil."

"Nicky?"

She shook her head. "He's gone down to the stable
to see Taffy. I know—"

He waved a hand to dismiss the unimportance of
such minor disobedience. "How much did you overhear?" he asked, and she glanced warily at Lars, seeing
him as the less violent one, though scarcely more reassuring.

Such intense passion as charged the atmosphere of
the little room was something new to her and it disturbed her strangely, though not in quite the way she
expected. There was a certain excitement about the situation that set her pulses racing and stirred strange and
unfamiliar sensations into being.

Lars met her gaze briefly, but his dark blue eyes
were wary as well as angry and resentful and Rachel
wondered what had been said to provoke the quarrel,
whether the blame had been his or Neil's. Then she
flicked an uneasy glance at Neil's shadowed face before
hastily looking down at her hands as she replied.

"I—I heard you warn Lars," she admitted. "That's
all."

"That's all!"

"Well, I could scarcely help overhearing some of it!"

Rachel objected. Her eyes were bright and shining, defiance as well as heaven knew what other strange and disturbing emotions shone in their depths. He had, after all, been angry in her defence, if the brief exchange she had overheard was any guide, and that knowledge gave her an unfamiliar glow of awareness as she faced him.

"No doubt!" He sounded as cool and self-possessed as always, and already, she guessed some of the tension was going from him. Then he shook his head, his eyes icy cool. "You'd better forget you heard anything at all," he advised quietly. "You don't need to become involved in private quarrels, Rachel."

"But I heard you mention my name," Rachel told him, and sought to steady her voice when she looked at him. "I think that involves me whether I want to be or not. You really don't have to concern yourself, Neil," she went on hastily, before he could say anything. "I'm quite capable of taking care of myself."

Neil's light blue eyes held hers for a moment, then slowly moved over her flushed face, coming to rest on the tremulous softness of her mouth. "Are you?" he asked. "That remains to be seen, doesn't it?"

"I—I appreciate your concern for me," she went on, wishing her voice did not sound quite so small and unsteady, "but I do know what I'm doing and—"

"I hope to God you do!" Neil interrupted harshly, then turned abruptly and strode past her to the door.

A tall, lean and infinitely disturbing figure—Rachel watched him leave the room with her heart thudding hard in her breast. It was intriguing to speculate why Neil Brett should take sufficient interest in her affairs to issue what amounted to a warning to Lars—intriguing and quite inexplicably exciting too.

CHAPTER SIX

It was a little over a week since Lars had returned home to Sweden, although it hardly seemed that long. The day after he had quarrelled with Neil he had announced that he thought it was time that he went home for a while, although according to Mrs. Handley he came and went frequently, so the quarrel could have been quite incidental.

Lars had promised Rachel before she left that he would be back before too long, and she had no reason to doubt it. It was a curious thing, but she was convinced that, despite their differences and the suggestion of tension between them on occasion, the two cousins were genuinely attached to one another.

Even the tragedy of Lynn's premature death was a common bond and Rachel had wondered more than once if it was the ever-present shade of Lynn that brought Lars back so often. He was very fond of Nicky, of course, and that could be his prime reason for returning so often, also he was a confessed Anglophile.

So far Rachel had learned nothing about Lars' affair with Lynn, and the matter still intrigued her, the more so because Lars and Neil seemed to compare her with Lynn, a somtimes discomfiting comparison.

It would be scarcely politic to ask Mrs. Handley about anything so personal to members of the family, although it was certain she knew, but she was very loyal and very attached to Nicky and her employer. Possibly less so to Lars, but even so she was unlikely to gossip about any of them, and Rachel was obliged to remain in ignorance with the pretty, petulant face of Lynn constantly recurring in her thoughts.

Nicky missed Lars, although he was content enough in his uncle's company and Rachel felt sure that his love of Neil was much more deep and enduring than the somewhat lighthearted affection he had for Lars. Lars amused him, made him laugh and was tolerant to the point of over-indulgence, but with Neil he would sit in the evening before he went to bed, reading a book or chattering about the things he had done during the day. Their closeness during these evening sessions sometimes gave Rachel a curiously protective feeling as she watched them, a feeling she could not quite explain.

Her own sensibility concerning her employer and his cousin were less easy to define. Lars was amusing and charming and he made her feel very young and lighthearted so that she missed his company if only for those reasons. Neil, on the other hand, affected her in quite a different way.

Whenever she was in the same room with him she was tinglingly aware of his presence, of that aura of earthy virile masculinity that was impossible to ignore, and sometimes her reaction to him startled her. Whether Neil would have noticed her absence was debatable, she thought, but she was quite certain that Seaways would have seemed much less attractive without him.

She hastily brought herself back to earth suddenly when she realised that Nicky was running across the grass towards her, his childish voice calling her name and his face anxiously uncertain as he spread his arms and encircled her legs, hugging close to her.

Seeking a cause for his sudden flight, Rachel looked

beyond him to where the tall bare oak trees lined the winding driveway up to the house and at first saw nothing. A second later, however, a man emerged from their shelter and started across the grass towards them, and Rachel took Nicky's hand firmly in hers, watching the man curiously, a faint flutter of suspicion making her eye him narrowly.

He was probably only a passing motorist seeking direction, but she had for a second felt a distinct sensation of doubt and she could not understand why. When the man came closer she could see that he was quite good-looking, although not outstandingly so.

"I suppose I'm trespassing?" he said before Rachel could speak, and she felt herself relax slightly at the sound of his voice.

It was cultured and pleasantly deep and had only faint overtone of some north country dialect; as if he had spent some time in the south and almost obliterated his original vernacular with its softer tones. Rachel nodded, half smiling as she held on to Nicky's hand, aware that the little boy was now peering at the stranger, made bolder by her presence.

"I'm afraid you're trespassing," she said. "Are you lost? Perhaps I can help you."

"Oh no, I'm not lost, thanks!" The man smiled and shook his head, then he looked across to where the leafless trees and shrubs allowed a partial view of Seaways. "I saw the name on the gates and caught a glimpse of the house from the road," he explained. "It's pretty old, isn't it?"

Rachel smiled, understanding at last. "I believe it's Victorian," she told him. "More than that I can't tell you, I'm afraid. Are you interested in old houses?"

"Some!" He had eyes whose actual colour eluded her, but they seemed to be somewhere between grey and blue and they narrowed slightly when he looked down at the house again. "Do you own it?" he asked, and Rachel laughingly denied it.

"I wish I did!" she told him. "But I only live and work here—looking after Nicky."

She glanced down at Nicky still standing close beside her and for the first time the stranger appeared to notice the boy. "Hello," he said bending slightly at the waist to speak to him. "So you're Nicky, are you?" Nicky nodded agreement, though somewhat hesitantly, and his hand clung even more tightly to Rachel's. "Cat got your tongue?" the man teased and Nicky looked up at her anxiously.

"He's just a little shy," Rachel explained. "We don't see many strangers here."

"No, I suppose not." The man was still looking at Nicky, a glistening curiosity in his eyes. "Aren't you at school yet?" he asked him, and Nicky shook his head. It was Rachel who answered for him.

"He isn't quite old enough yet," she said, anxious for there to be no doubt about Nicky's intelligence even if he was a little unresponsible. "He's five next June, aren't you, Nicky?"

"June, eh?" For some reason the man seemed to find the information interesting, unless he was simply being politely curious. He squatted on his heels and looked at Nicky with a persuasive smile, shrugging goodnaturedly when Nicky avoided his hand. "And your mamma has a nanny to look after you, hmm?"

It was a bombshell Rachel told herself she could not possibly have anticipated and she drew Nicky close to her, a protective hand about his head as she looked at the man, knowing she could not blame him, but unable to keep a hint of reproach out of her voice. "Nicky— lost his mother last year," she told him in a hushed voice. "His uncle takes care of him."

"I'm sorry!" He looked again at Nicky, but Rachel

felt that there was as much speculation as pity in his expression and she was puzzled by it.

"Why don't you run around and play again, Nicky?" she suggested gently. "But stay where I can see you, won't you, dear?"

After a brief hesitation Nicky nodded his head, then he ran off quickly, almost as if he was anxious to escape, and only seconds later he was making those noisy imitation engine sounds that were his favourite form of play. The man watched him for a second, then pulled a face as he looked down at her.

"I'm afraid I said the wrong thing," he said, but oddly enough did not sound as apologetic as he might have done so that once again Rachel was puzzled by his manner.

"You weren't to know," she told him. "But Nicky's very sensitive about it still."

"Of course." He looked across at the house again as if he had lost interest in the child. "I'll bet there's plenty of room for kids to run around in a place like that," he remarked.

"It's beautiful inside," Rachel said without commenting on its size. "The outside doesn't really do it justice."

For a moment the man's eyes settled on her, curious and almost speculative. "You sound as if you like it here," he suggested, and Rachel nodded.

"I do," she agreed. "I love it here!"

Again his eyes looked at her narrowly, speculating on her reasons for being so enthusiastic. "Good boss?" he enquired, and Rachel saw no reason to deny it.

"Yes," she said without hesitation, "he's very good."

"And rich too, obviously," the man guessed with a hint of malice in his voice. "The nearest I ever get to a place like this is by paying fifty pence to look around it."

"Oh, I'm afraid Seaways isn't open to the public," Rachel put in hastily, and the man laughed shortly, a sound in startling contrast to his pleasant voice.

"No, I can't see Neil Brett opening up his house to sightseers!" he declared, and for a moment Rachel stared at him, for she was quite certain she had never yet mentioned Neil by name.

"Do—do you know Mr. Brett?" she asked, and once again the man laughed—that harsh, humourless sound that Rachel found oddly disturbing without quite knowing why.

"I suppose you could say I do—in a way," he told her, and she frowned.

"I don't understand—" she began, then stopped when the man shook his head impatiently.

"I don't suppose you do," he told her shortly, "but it doesn't matter—forget it!"

"If you called to see—"

Again she was cut short by that harsh laughter and blinked uneasily. "I haven't called to see anybody," he told her. "I—well, I suppose you could say I was just curious."

"About Seaways?" Rachel found it hard to simply walk away and end this rather discomfiting conversation, and somehow the man intrigued her and she tried to imagine what had brought him to Seaways if he had not called to see Neil or one of the staff.

He looked down at her briefly, then smiled and shrugged. "Curiosity's my failing, love," he said, and laughed again for no apparent reason.

"If you—"

Conscious suddenly of a dramatic change in his manner, Rachel stopped short and turned her head curiously, following the direction of his gaze. Nicky still played alone just off to their left, but it was not Nicky who had his attention, for while she still puzzled over it

Neil's blond head appeared suddenly, plainly visible above the dark-leafed rhododendrons.

The stranger said nothing, but he watched steadily while Neil made his way round to the corner of the house, and once again Rachel felt strangely uneasy. The man had denied any knowledge of him, but it was fairly certain that he at least guessed who Neil was, and she felt more convinced than ever that she had not mentioned his name.

Neil himself obviously had no inkling that he was under observation, for he did not even turn his head in their direction and after a few seconds the man beside her turned, a curiously glittering look about him. "That's your boss?" he asked, and Rachel nodded, horribly uncertain about answering so many questions.

"Yes," she said, "that's Mr. Brett."

"He's the one who's looking after the boy?"

Rachel's heart was pounding urgently and she looked at him for a moment warily. "Did—did you wish to see Mr. Brett?" she asked, and from the man's expression it was plain that he recognised the fact that he was being politely but firmly snubbed.

She felt badly out of her depth, dealing with this itinerant stranger, and she wished Neil would see them, for he was much more capable of dealing with him, whoever he might be. Having watched Neil out of sight the man turned again and looked at her. There was a hint of smile about his mouth, but it did not reach his eyes and she shivered involuntarily.

"No, thanks, love," he said, "I don't want to see him—it wouldn't serve any useful purpose at the moment." He inclined his head briefly. "Thanks for the chat—it's been nice meeting you!"

Too stunned to reply, Rachel merely nodded. Then the man was looking past her, narrow-eyed as he watched Nicky running around with his arms out-

stretched, dipping and weaving his mouth puckered
and emitting imaginary engine noises, oblivious of
everything but his game. Shaking his head, the man
shrugged and walked off, back towards the trees along
the driveway. It was only seconds after he disappeared
that Rachel heard a car engine start up and she stood
for a moment staring at the ribbon of bare-armed oaks.

"Nicky!" Suddenly anxious, she called him to her
and they made their way back to the house, but the face
of the curious stranger still lingered uneasily in her
mind.

It was Nicky who first mentioned the man at dinner
that same evening, and Rachel wished she had spoken
of it herself, for Neil eyed her suspiciously, almost as if
he suspected she had deliberately kept the meeting
quiet. Not that Nicky said very much, but the brief fact
that Rachel had been talking to a strange man in the
grounds was evidently enough to arouse Neil's interest
and his blue eyes regarded her steadily.

"You met someone in the grounds?" he asked, and
Rachel instinctively shook her head.

"Not by design, if that's what you mean," she denied. "He suddenly appeared from among the trees
along the drive—presumably he had a car parked somewhere nearby, because I heard one start up just after he
left."

"You didn't know him?"

Rachel shook her head. She resented the suggestion
of suspicion more than she cared to show at the moment. "I thought at first he might be a motorist looking
for directions," she explained, and Neil looked at her,
struck by her choice of words.

"It's unlikely," he observed, "we don't get many
stray motorists out this way."

Rachel was tempted to tell him that the man seemingly knew Neil's name without her mentioning it, but on second thoughts she wondered if it was a good idea. She knew little about his past life and the man could well be someone he would prefer not to meet again. The man's whole attitude and his mode of reference to Neil had hardly suggested an amicable relationship.

"Maybe he *was* simply lost and he didn't like to admit it," she ventured, but Neil frowned as if nothing so simple satisfied him.

"You said you thought *at first* he might have been someone looking for directions," he reminded her. "What changed your mind, Rachel?"

It was difficult being as frank as she would like to have been in front of Nicky and she glanced at him before shaking her head at Neil. He said no more on the subject, but a brief glance at him was enough to realise that the matter was only temporarily suspended.

It was after she had put Nicky to bed and came downstairs again that Neil met her in the hall. "I'd like you to join me," he said without preliminary, and Rachel nodded, although with some misgiving, for heaven knew what he expected her to be able to tell him.

Usually in the evenings when Nicky was safely in bed she sat with Mr. and Mrs. Handley in their cosy little room, or else she used the smaller sitting-room at the back of the house and either read or caught up on her letter writing. Only very occasionally did she join Neil in the big sitting-room, for she found him disturbing company at any time and more especially so when there were only the two of them.

The wind outside swished the branches of a tree angrily against the window and sharp scatters of rain beat noisily on the panes, but inside the big room was warm and comfortable—a cosy, inviting scene with a fire in the hearth flickering brightly and big, round oak logs sputtering into showers of sparks.

The only illumination came from a couple of table lamps and they gave a soft subdued glow that concentrated light only into one small section of the big room. Neil saw her seated in one of the deceptively frail-looking armchairs the room was furnished with, then he seated himself opposite to her on the other side of the fireplace.

The soft light from one of the lamps cast dark shadows over his rugged features and gave him a curiously graven look, as if he had been hewn from bronze, an illusion that was fostered by the strong tanned hands and forearms emerging from the sleeves of a light blue sweater.

The whole setting was so warm and suggestive of intimacy and the man opposite her so affected her senses that Rachel felt her pulses responding to thoughts that came unbidden into her mind and stirred emotions in her that she barely recognised. There was something so utterly familiar about Neil Brett and yet he was still virtually a stranger to her, a stranger that her instincts clamoured to know better. To get closer to the man she suspected he could be behind that icy façade.

Even in the few seconds she had sat there by the fire she had become so immersed in her own thoughts that she started almost guiltily when he spoke. "You know what I want to talk to you about?" he asked, and for a moment Rachel sought wildly for his meaning. The very existence of the man she had met in the grounds had been forgotten in her preoccupation with Neil.

Then she nodded, bringing herself hastily back to earth. "I—I think so," she said. "It's about the man—the one I spoke to this morning."

He nodded briefly. "Was today the first time you'd seen him?"

Rachel blinked. "Oh yes, of course it was!" she said, but Neil looked at her narrowly.

"You're sure?"

Uncertain just what he was getting at, she frowned. "Of course I'm sure, Neil," she told him. "If you think—"

"I don't know what to think," Neil interrupted shortly. The blue eyes held hers for a moment and she thought there was anxiety as well as a hint of suspicion in them, a suspicion that brought as much hurt as resentment. "I don't know you well enough, Rachel," he went on after a second or two. "I don't know whether it's possible that someone—a lover, perhaps, could have found where you are and followed you here."

Rachel stared at him for a moment, her cheeks flushed and a bright, dark look in her eyes as she struggled to see his point of view. A lover, he had suggested, and she almost laughed when she recalled that Lars had once tentatively suggested Neil himself for that role.

"A lover?" she said huskily. "Would you expect me to have a lover follow me down here?"

For a moment the light blue eyes swept over her face and figure, then he nodded, apparently quite serious about it. "Yes," he said softly, "I would."

Hastily Rachel looked away, her heart thudding wildly. "I haven't a lover," she told him in the same small husky voice. "Nor is it anyone else to do with me, Neil."

"Then who?"

He spoke softly, almost as if he spoke to himself, and Rachel shook her head slowly. It was obvious that now he had excluded anyone of her acquaintance he shared her own initial suspicion about the stranger, although heaven knew why. A passing motorist should surely not cause such a furore, but the man himself had aroused her suspicions and she in turn had communicated them to Neil.

"Neil." She hesitated and he looked across at her, his blue eyes darkened by the firelight. "I did wonder about him," she explained rather vaguely, and Neil frowned.

"You wondered?" he echoed, and Rachel shrugged, warily confiding.

"I asked him if he wanted to see you," she explained, "but he—he said it would serve no useful purpose."

Neil looked at her for a second or two, his eyes narrowed as if he was trying to follow her exact meaning. "You asked him if he wanted to see me?" he said. "Why?"

It was difficult to explain to him exactly how she had felt when the stranger had so glibly used his name and she shrugged uneasily under that discomfiting scrutiny. "I don't really know," she confessed, "except that— oh, I don't know, there was just something about him! He spoke about the house and I thought at first that he was lost and he'd stopped to ask directions, but then he said he was interested in old houses."

"And?" He sounded impatient and Rachel shook her head hastily.

"I told him that Seaways wasn't open to the public," she explained, but he knew that already. Also—" She hesitated, but went on hastily when she saw Neil's impatient frown. "He knew your name," she said, and Neil's eyes narrowed sharply.

"You didn't tell me that at first," he said shortly. "Why not?"

Rachel shrugged. "I—I don't know—it bothered me, but—"

"I think you'd better tell me all of it," Neil interrupted harshly. "Where exactly was he?"

"He came out of the trees alongside the drive," she told him. "Nicky came run—"

"Nicky?" He barked the name at her so sharply that Rachel blinked. "He spoke to Nicky?"

"Well, yes," she said. "Nicky ran back when he saw him coming.

There was a definite air of tension about him, a certainty that had only been hinted at before, and Rachel felt her heart thudding anxiously when she looked across at him. His big hands were clasped together as he leaned forward in his chair, his elbows resting on his knees, and there was a taut, dark look on his face that aroused uneasy responses in her.

"Neil," she began, "do you—"

"Describe him," Neil told her shortly. "What did he look like, Rachel?"

"He was good-looking." She searched her mind for details of the man's appearance, wondering at his sense of urgency. "Not as tall as you are, more Lars' height— brown hair, quite dark brown and—I'm not sure about his eyes, they were either blue or grey."

Neil sat with one hand running through the thick blond hair at the back of his head and there was a tight, drawn look about his mouth, a glitter in his eyes that sent a shiver down her spine like ice water. "Browlett!" he said in a harsh whisper, and Rachel stared at him. "Michael Browlett!"

Her heart was racing so hard she was quite breathless with it and she looked across at Neil's shadowed and unfathomable features in stunned disbelief. "Browlett," she echoed in a daze. "That's—"

"Nicky's father!" Neil confirmed harshly, and Rachel still stared at him unbelievingly.

She took a moment to wonder why, with all the possibilities that had passed through her mind about why the strange man was there, it had never once occurred to her that he might be Nicky's father. Why Neil and not his father was Nicky's legal guardian had several possible explanations, but what puzzled her was why Neil was so disturbed at the idea of the man seeing his son.

"I—I had no idea," Rachel said. "If only he'd said who he was I'd have—"

"You did exactly right to come back to the house," Neil told her shortly. "I hope you'll have as much sense again if the situation arises."

Rachel looked at him uneasily, not at all sure if she either followed his reasoning or approved of his apparent determination to forbid a further meeting. "Is he likely to come back?" she asked, and Neil shrugged heavily.

"It's likely," he said. "Until I can make some enquiries, Rachel, I'd rather you kept Nicky close to the house unless either Handley or myself is with you, is that clear?"

"It's clear enough," Rachel agreed, beginning to see things in a slightly different light now that she knew the man's identity. "But surely if he *is* Nicky's father—"

She stopped short when she caught the glittering look in Neil's eyes. "I suppose," he said in a flat, hard voice, "it's too much to ask that you do as you're told for once without question?"

Rachel curled her hands tightly, not at all sure that to deprive a man of the sight of his son was ethical. "You won't—you wouldn't let him see Nicky?" she asked, and Neil frowned warningly.

"Rachel! Don't interfere in things that you know nothing about!"

"But do you have the *right?*" Rachel insisted earnestly. "He's the boy's father, Neil, surely you can't—"

Neil got to his feet in a sudden, swift movement that made Rachel gasp. It seemed to her to constitute a threat so that she got up herself and stood facing him on the other side of the fireplace, a small uneasy figure with bright anxious eyes that watched him warily.

"You know nothing about the circumstances," he told her. His voice was hard and flat and in chilling contrast to the anger that glittered in his eyes. "Just do as I say, Rachel, and don't try to change things when you don't know what the results could be!"

"You're telling me I mustn't take Nicky out into the gardens again?" she ventured, and he shook his head impatiently.

"I'm telling you to stay near the house unless either Handley or myself is within call," he said. "He can play in the gardens, of course, just as long as someone is within call."

"I see." Rachel tried to sound matter-of-fact, but in the circumstances it was difficult. "It isn't going to be easy trying to explain to him," she said. "What reason do I give him?"

Neil's mouth tightened, as if he suspected she was looking for arguments. "You simply tell him that he mustn't go running off alone the way he does," he told her. "He's obedient enough to do as he's told, surely!"

"Yes, of course he is," Rachel agreed, "but—"

She drew in her breath sharply when a strong hand reached across and curled itself round her slim wrist, the fingers cruelly tight on her soft skin. Drawn nearer to him by the irresistible strength of his grip she stood in front of the bright fire, looking up at him with huge eyes made dark by the shadows that surrounded them.

"You have a choice, Rachel," he told her very quietly and speaking slowly as if he chose his words with care. "Either you do as I say and stay close to the house unless someone else is with you both, or you go—right now! The choice is yours and, much as I know Nicky would miss you, if you can't bring yourself to follow instructions then the solution is in your own hands!"

To Rachel the ultimatum came as a cold shock and
she found it hard to put anything into words. She simply stared at her own captive wrist, her eyes suspiciously bright with threatened tears, for she knew he
meant every word of it. He would see her go with no
regrets at all and it was that realisation, perhaps more
than any other, that stung most.

"Is that what you'd rather I did?" she asked in a
small unsteady voice, and for a moment Neil said nothing.

Then he shook his head slowly and she realised that
the anger in his eyes was already less evident. "I think
you know that's nonsense," he said. "You're very
good with Nicky and he likes you. Also I hate having to
get used to new staff."

They were all very good reasons, Rachel recognised,
but they were so severely practical that for a moment
she felt the coldness of disappointment. If only he
could have made his reasons more personal, more
gentle. He looked so tall and almost frighteningly
earthy standing there in the flickering firelight that she
felt her heart pounding like a hammer at her ribs when
she looked at him.

Lars, she reflected ruefully, would have expressed
his reluctance to see her go in quite different terms,
and almost as if he guessed what was in her mind, Neil
shook his head suddenly, a hint of smile on his wide
mouth. "Also," he added, "I should have to face Lars
when he comes back and I'd find it rather awkward if
you weren't here."

"Of course!"

Rachel felt her pulses flutter erratically when the ball
of his thumb began to move slowly and gently on the
soft skin of her inner arm. It was an incredibly sensual
caress and she scarcely believed it could be Neil who
held her like that, although Lars had once implied that

there was more to his cousin than she had so far experienced.

"Of course!" he echoed softly.

Rachel coped with another flutter of uncertainty when he smiled and suddenly shook his head. Almost convinced that she was the cause of his amusement, she snatched her arm out of his grasp and looked up at him with bright, reproachful eyes. "I have things to do," she told him in a small, unsteady voice. "If you'll excuse me."

He said nothing until she opened the door into the hall, then he called her back, though she came only hesitantly, her eyes wary. "You haven't told me," he said, "whether you're willing to stay and do as I say, or if you've decided to leave. Which is it to be, Rachel?"

Briefly Rachel met his eyes and the challenge in them was unmistakable so that she instinctively lifted her chin in defiance of it. "I'll stay," she said, "for Nicky's sake!"

She gasped aloud when he bent his head suddenly and without warning brushed his firm mouth against her lips in a warm, gentle pressure that ran through her like fire. "Good!" he said softly, and watched with glittering eyes as she hurried from the room.

CHAPTER SEVEN

"If Mr. Brett thinks it's best, then most likely it is,"
Mrs. Handley said in her quiet country voice, and Rachel sighed inwardly at the inevitability of it. Mrs.
Handley's loyalty to her employer was firm and uncom-
promising and Rachel wondered if Neil realised what a
gem she was.

Rachel had been complaining, with no real malice,
about having to stay close to the house all the time. It
irritated her at times to have her movements restricted,
and Nicky did not understand it either, although he was
easily enough mollified when his interest was taken
with something else.

"I'll be glad when Nicky and I can go where we like
again," Rachel said, and Mrs. Handley nodded sympa-
thetically.

"I expect so, my dear," she said. "Perhaps it won't
be too long now."

Nothing so far had been mentioned about Rachel's
meeting with Michael Browlett, but she had little doubt
that Mrs. Handley knew all about it. She and her husband had never done other than work at Seaways and
there was little that was likely to remain unknown to
them.

In the time Rachel had been there she had become
quite friendly with the Handleys, but never so far had
anything made them change their reticent manner
where the family was concerned. Rachel sat now in
their little sitting-room next to the kitchen, talking to

Mrs. Handley while Handley worked in the kitchen garden and at the same time entertained Nicky.

Watching them from the window and listening to Nicky's chatter Rachel recalled again the features of Michael Browlett, and she had no doubt at all that Neil had been right in his identification of the man, for there was a similarity between him and Nicky that was unmistakable in hindsight. It seemed such a pity, she thought, that they could not meet, just once, and recognise one another.

Of course Mrs. Handley would know all about Michael Browlett too, although it was unlikely she would be any more forthcoming about him than about anything else concerning the family. If she mentioned anything, however harmless it appeared, the housekeeper would revert to those monosyllabic answers she always did.

Unable to resist passing comment, for all it was useless, Rachel looked at Nicky and smiled. "Nicky's like his father," she ventured, but once again, as she expected, that invisible barrier was raised.

"Handsome little boy," Mrs. Handley agreed, and Rachel almost laughed at such determined evasion.

With having her personal freedom restricted to some extent because of her meeting with Michael Browlett, however, Rachel felt she was now more closely involved and that she had a right to some answer at least, so she pressed on where at one time she would have fallen silent. "I don't quite see why Neil—Mr. Brett objects so strongly to his father seeing him," she observed, but realised her mistake immediately when Mrs. Handley took up arms in her employer's defence.

"Mr. Brett does his very best for the boy," she declared sternly. "It's not every unmarried gentleman would take on the upbringing of a little boy the way Mr. Brett has!"

"Oh, I agree," Rachel agreed hastily. "I think he's wonderful with Nicky, but—I don't know, it doesn't seem right not to let his natural father see him sometimes."

Mrs. Handley's round homely face was flushed and her eyes showed an unmistakable glint of anger as she pulled back her thin shoulders and bridled indignantly. "No natural father would 'ave gone off the way he did!" she declared firmly. "That mite wouldn't have had no father at all if it hadn't been for Mr. Brett! Better than that feckless creature who was responsible for his being born, and who's to say he hasn't got the right to keep the other one away after all this time?"

Rachel was stunned momentarily by the fierceness of the tirade and she blinked at Mrs. Handley a little uncertainly. "But even so," she said, "isn't Mr. Browlett allowed access to his son?"

"Why should he have?" Mrs. Handley demanded with a disparaging sniff. "Nobody even knew if he was alive or dead until now, since he careered off before the mite was born and no one's heard of him since—it's not likely he cares much for him anyway."

Rachel shook her head, stunned by yet another revelation about Nicky's background and wondering how much more there was still hidden. "Do you mean he'd—he'd never seen his father before the other day?" she asked, and Mrs. Handley shook her head.

"That's right," she said, tight-mouthed. "And I reckon he never will again if Mr. Brett has his way. It could upset the little lad seeing him and learning who he is, after all this time."

"He might be pleased to have his own father," Rachel ventured, and once more Mrs. Handley gave a snort of derision.

"Best thing for that little mite it to let him stay just as he is," she opined. "He's had enough things happen to him in his little lifetime, bless him, he's best left alone with his uncle. There's nothing unstable about Mr. Brett, and the boy's not likely to have any more shocks while he has him."

"Shocks?" Rachel looked puzzled, but she knew she was not destined to learn any more when she saw the tight, closed look on the housekeeper's face again.

"Talking's no good," Mrs. Handley said. "He's safe enough here with his uncle."

It seemed to Rachel that past events at Seaways must have been even more disturbing than she had realised and she felt quite inextricably involved in them, even though she knew so little. Nicky's background was more unstable too than she had first feared and since her conversation with Mrs. Handley she felt a strong sense of protectiveness towards him.

It was three weeks since Lars had returned to Sweden and she was a little surprised to discover that she missed him rather less than she expected to. She missed his gallantry and his charm, of course, and it was always good for her morale that he was so obviously smitten, but Neil had spent much more time around the house during the past fortnight and he more than made up for his cousin's absence, though in a quite different way.

Neil spent more time with Nicky now, something that delighted Nicky and also threw Rachel into close and more frequent contact with him. Since the appearance of Michael Browlett he seemed unwilling to let Nicky out of his sight for long and he had taken him riding several times. It was curious, but whenever she saw them together Rachel felt almost tearful, for their genuine affection for one another was quite touching and Nicky obviously enjoyed the extra attention he was receiving.

Rachel watched them approaching now, with Neil mounted on one of the geldings and toweringly tall beside Nicky perched astride the squat sturdiness of Taffy. Smiling to herself, she wondered at Neil's infinite patience with the boy's endless chatter as he urged Taffy to keep pace with his uncle's bigger mount.

She was much less nervous of the horses now that she had become more used to them and after she had helped Nicky down she stood watching while his uncle made sure he took proper care of his mount. Young as he was Neil considered he was old enough to learn the correct way of doing things, and Rachel was bound to agree in principle. Neil, she thought, would make a strict but loving father and it was a pity he had no children of his own.

Hastily she pulled herself out of that realm of speculation and tried to concentrate on the activity that was going on in front of her. Thinking of Neil in that way was a fairly frequent occurence lately, and the fact both disturbed and intrigued her. There was something about seeing him with Nicky that made him appear in quite a different light from the stern and autocratic landowner, and somehow she never tired of watching him or of being in his company.

With unsaddling and grooming completed Nicky raced off to offer Handley his help in unloading some newly arrived hay, and Rachel could hear him, chattering as always, giving the patient Handley his advice. She was about to follow Nicky across the yard to the feed-shed when Neil called out to her from the other end of the building.

"Rachel!"

She turned, her heart fluttering wildly as she looked at him. He was in the end stall completing the grooming of his own mount, and for a while she wondered if she had been mistaken in thinking she had heard him call her back, for he ceased his task only when she had walked the length of the stable and stood near him.

Then he straightened up, running one hand through the swath of blond hair across his brow, his light blue eyes shadowed in the darkness of the stable, and her pulses stirred again when he looked at her. Fawn trousers fitted close to the strong muscular calves and his booted feet were planted firmly on the straw-covered floor. A thick cream wool sweater lent added darkness to his tanned and craggy features and he looked not only slightly aggressive but disturbingly and inescapably masculine.

As always Rachel's senses responded to him urgently and she did her best to still the deafening thud of her heart as she looked at him. "You called me back," she reminded him, and despaired to notice how unsteady her voice sounded.

A brief smile warmed Neil's blue eyes as he looked at her. "I wondered if you knew that Lars was coming back in about ten days' time," he said. "I heard from him this morning."

Rachel shook her head. "No, I didn't," she admitted, and wondered why he had taken the trouble to call her back when it would have been just as easy to mention it at lunch time. "Nicky will be delighted," she added, and Neil raised a brow curiously.

"I thought you would be," he remarked, "that's why I told you." He half turned away for a moment, running a casual hand over the bay's glossy coat, not looking at her. "Haven't you heard from him too?" he asked. "I thought he would have told *you* he was coming."

Rachel preferred not to think there was sarcasm intended and she shook her head slowly. "I don't really see why he would," she told him. "Why should he keep me informed of his plans?"

Again Neil turned and looked at her directly, his blue eyes steady and glinting with challenge. "Oh, don't be naïve, Rachel," he said sharply. "You know perfectly well why he'd let you know he was coming back—you're not so simple that you have to ask me that!"

His manner was both hurtful and unexpected, for during the past two weeks their former animosity had dwindled to almost nothing and she hated to see it return. "And neither am I—whatever it is you think I am to Lars!" she told him in a voice that must have betrayed how she felt, and for a moment Neil simply looked at her steadily without saying anything.

The he shook his head and there was a hint of smile on his lips as he half turned again, so that she could only see him in profile. "You make it sound as if I accused you of something," he told her, "and nothing is further from the truth, Rachel. You know I have no interest at all in what you and Lars do, as long as it doesn't affect Nicky."

"Of course—you've made that quite clear!" Rachel agreed shortly. It was hard to accept the fact of his disinterest without showing some resentment of it, and it was plain that her tone surprised him, for he raised a brow over it.

"I'd have to be quite blind, however," he went on coolly, "not to realise that you—like him. Whenever you were together it was pretty obvious how you felt."

Rachel had no idea why he had decided to stage this scene, but it was obvious that he meant to provoke her and she looked at him with bright, reproachful eyes, trying to see his reasons. She had never given him any cause to suppose that she took Lars' lighthearted romancing seriously and the present situation both puzzled and disturbed her.

"It—it would be silly to deny that I like Lars," she told him in an unsteady voice. "In fact I find him very attractive, any woman would, but I've known him for far too short a time for anyone to suggest there's anything serious about it, Neil! It's quite—quite ridiculous to suggest anything like that!"

His eyes were watching her again with an unnerving steadiness, focused on her mouth, as if it fascinated him, and Rachel could feel the rapid and uneven beat of her heart as it pounded uncontrollably. "I merely suggested that you liked one another," he reminded her gently, but Rachel shook her head.

"You only *said* that," she insisted, "but you implied a whole lot more, Neil, and it simply isn't true!"

Rachel's hands curled tightly into themselves when he shook his head slowly, his eyes shadowed and unfathomable. "Shakespeare—I think it was Shakespeare," he said quietly, "who said—methinks the lady doth protest too much!"

"Neil!" There was no mistaking his meaning and she glared at him, both hurt and angry. "You don't believe me!" she accused. "Well, I—I don't care whether you do or not!"

"Why *should* you care?" Neil asked, and Rachel frowned.

She was trembling like a leaf, her eyes bright and glistening with what felt suspiciously like tears because she did not want to quarrel with Neil and he seemed bent on doing just that, though for what reason she could not imagine. She was alarmingly aware, as never before, of that powerful whipcord body standing so near, and the effect on her senses of a tangy combination of aftershave and leather, and there was nothing she could do about the tangle of sensations that made her head spin.

"Neil—" She hesitated, her eyes searching that strong rugged face for some clue to his reason for starting this. "What are you trying to do?" she said in a small uncertain voice, and unbelievably he laughed and shook his head.

It was a soft deep sound that had the effect of making her heart beat so fast she instinctively put a hand to her breast. "I'm not quite sure," he confessed. "But I know that Lars thinks he has only to raise his finger to you and you'll go to him—would you, Rachel?"

Rachel's heart clamoured so wildly that she had difficulty breathing other than in short, uneven snatches, as if she had run a long way. "No," she whispered.

Somehow Neil's left hand was at her waist, its broad palm spanning her slimness under her jacket, the fingers strong and irresistible as he drew her towards him. Then his right hand slid too beneath the thick wool jacket, bringing its strong persuasion to bear, pressing hard to the middle of her back until she was conscious of nothing but the powerful force of those steely arms, and the glittering brightness in his light blue eyes.

There was a sense of excitement in contact with his strong, hard and infinitely masculine body that shivered through her like fire and ice and she tried to say something, to murmur his name. But her voice came as no more than a faint whisper of sound which he smothered with his mouth before it became words.

Her arms reached up, encircling his neck, her hands in the thick blond hair above his ears, and her body was pressed so close to him that she was aware of every muscle straining her even closer. It was like nothing she had ever known before and she yielded to her own new and urgent needs with only a faint tremor of doubt.

Only once before had she been in his arms, when he had rescued her from the icy ledge above the sea, and she found comfort there then. Now there was a sensuous, irresistible excitement that demanded a response from her—a response that she gave willingly enough.

"Neil! Miss Carson!"

The childish treble penetrated Rachel's mind only dimly at first, but then Neil released her, reluctantly she felt, and stood looking down at her. His hands were still at her waist, hard and warm through her sweater, and his eyes, shadowed in the semi-darkness, gleamed as warmly as ever.

There was a hint of smile on his mouth, a smile that somehow disturbed her, and he inclined his head towards the open door into the yard where Nicky's insistent shrill voice was calling to them again. "I think someone had better go and rescue Handley," he said, and for a moment Rachel looked up at him uncertainly.

"Neil! Miss Carson!"

Nicky's voice came nearer as he ran across the yard, and Rachel stepped back suddenly, turning towards the door, her eyes slightly dazed still. Her heart was beating with such violence that it was difficult to think clearly, but it was obvious that Neil was perfectly controlled and somehow that troubled her.

The faint smile still crooked one corner of his mouth and his eyes seemed, to Rachel's sensitive gaze, to hold a hint of mockery for those few heart-stopping seconds that had affected her so deeply. She looked at him steadily, almost appealingly, for several seconds and she thought she saw a change in his expression, but then Nicky came hurtling in at the door, his voice shrilly indignant.

"You didn't answer me!" he accused. "Why didn't you answer me?" He stopped for a moment, standing in front of them, and there was a small frown between his brows, then he took Rachel's hand and tugged at it. "I'm hungry," he declared. "I'm hungry, Miss Carson!"

It was Neil who answered him, pulling off his riding cap and ruffling his thick hair into tumbled untidiness. "You're always hungry," he told him with a smile. "And it's no use worrying Miss Carson about it, because it isn't time for your lunch yet."

"But she promised me chocolate," Nicky declared indignantly, and Neil glanced at her curiously.

"Did you do that?" he asked.

Rachel nodded. "Yes, I'm afraid I did."

There was a curious glint in Neil's eyes as he looked at her for a moment without speaking, his hand still on Nicky's untidy head. "Do you often indulge him with chocolate?" he asked.

Still trembling from his kiss, Rachel found it hard to give her mind to more mundane things, but she glanced down at Nicky's anxious and faintly indignant face before she replied. "I—I do sometimes," she said. "Not very often." She felt that the glitter in his eyes betrayed disapproval and almost unconsciously her chin thrust out in a brief gesture of defiance. "I *thought* you wouldn't approve!" she said.

"But you still did it?"

The softness of his voice shivered over her like ice and she clung to Nicky's small hand tightly. "Only occasionally," she insisted. Somehow his easy transition to stern guardian angered her because he could so easily shrug off that soul-stirring incident of a moment ago when she still trembled from its effect. Looking down at Nicky, she pulled a rueful face. "You'd better not have your chocolate, Nicky," she told him. "Your uncle doesn't want you to have it—I'm sorry."

Nicky looked up at his uncle with his lower lip quivering suspiciously, almost ready to cry, and his huge eyes were wide and accusing. "But, Neil—" he began.

"Of course you can have it," Neil told him quietly.

"You were promised it and I don't believe in breaking promises." Without a word Rachel reached into her jacket pocket and handed Nicky the promised chocolate, her cheeks flushed as she suffered Neil's steady gaze. He gave the boy time to remove the wrappings then ruffled his hair encouragingly. "You go and watch Handley for a minute," he told him. "Miss Carson won't be long."

Nicky, munching happily on his treat, went out into the yard again and the sound of his voice when he called out to Handley in the feed-shed came back to them clearly on the cold air. Uncertain why she was being detained, Rachel made a tentative move to follow him, but a large hand thudded firmly on to the wooden partition beside her and startled her into pressing herself back against it.

An arm barred her way, a strong muscular arm that she knew from experience would be quite capable of stopping her by force if necessary, and she felt trapped. The vigorous arrogance of his stance set her pulses racing and she turned her head away swiftly when he leaned on his hand, a movement that brought his face close to hers and the sensual warmth of his body into contact with her own trembling form.

"Now," Neil said firmly, "perhaps you'll be good enough to explain the reason for that little scene just now. Why you told Nicky I wouldn't let him have his chocolate."

"I didn't," Rachel denied breathlessly. "I only—"

"I'm not an idiot and neither am I deaf, Rachel!" He leaned closer, pressing her lightly against the partition, and his other hand gripped her chin suddenly, turning her to face him and making her gasp at the strength of his fingers. "I don't like being made to appear the ogre you made me," he told her, "and especially not to Nicky!"

"Neil, please, I didn't *mean* anything by it," she insisted. "I—I just said it because—because I was angry."

"Angry?" The relentless fingers kept her facing him and she bit her lip anxiously, shivering when his breath warmed her mouth. "Why?" he asked softly. "Why were you angry? Was it because I kissed you?"

Her heart racing wildly she shook her head. "How could it be that?" she whispered huskily. "That wasn't anything important, was it, Neil?"

"Rachel!"

Her legs felt so weak that she could barely stand and the rapid throb of the pulse in her temple almost stifled her as she stood there, her body just touched by the vigorous, masculine warmth of his. It was the heavy clump of Handley's boots on the yard outside that snatched her back from a kind of haze of unreality.

"Nicky," she said breathlessly. "I can't hear him, Neil, he—he must have gone!"

"It doesn't matter, he won't go far!" The strong firm arm still blocked her way and his eyes gleamed with determination despite Handley's nearness.

"But I must go after him!" Rachel insisted, and ducked swiftly under his arm. The move caught him by surprise and she managed to run the length of the stable before he caught up with her. His fingers curled round her arm, stopping her short, and he would have swung her round again to face him, but Handley's curious gaze was on them and Rachel took advantage of Neil's hesitation to shake herself free. "It was *your* instructions that Nicky mustn't be left alone," she reminded him in a husky whisper. "He's on his way back to the house, but I can catch up with him if I hurry!"

For a moment she thought he was going to argue with her despite Handley's interested proximity, but then he let her go suddenly and shrugged his shoulders resignedly. Rachel turned and ran after Nicky and her heart was thudding hard in her breast as she caught up with him. She had an almost irresistible urge to turn round and see if Neil was watching, but instead she put a hand on Nicky's head and smiled as they walked down the bridle path to the house.

With Lars being back it meant that both Rachel and Nicky would inevitably see less of Neil, for Lars was almost sure to take over some of what Rachel referred to as the bodyguard duties. She was unsure just how she felt about having Lars taking Neil's place, but it was a fact that she found Lars a much less disturbing companion.

There had been snow during the day and now, as the evening drew on, there was a crispness in the air that promised frost by morning, and the stars were clear and bright around the fat yellow winter moon. Nicky was in bed and Rachel had succumbed to Lars' persuasion to come for a stroll as far as the gates, looking up at the stars where they appeared between the tangle of skeleton branches overhead.

It was vaguely creepy walking down the drive at night with their own shadows drifting silently beside them and, quite involuntarily, she shivered. "Are you cold?" Lars was immediately concerned for her, putting an arm round her shoulders, his fingers strong and comforting on her arm. "Is that better?" he asked, and Rachel smiled.

There was something disarmingly frank about Lars that was almost irresistible. "I'm not really cold," she told him. "It was just someone walking over my grave, that's all."

They walked in silence for a while and somewhere an owl wooed the full moon with its soft call, the bare trees shivering in the wind that brought colour to Rachel's cheeks and made her glad of Lars' additional warmth about her shoulders. The thin layer of snow on the drive already crackled faintly when they trod on it and confirmed the early signs of frost. In a way there was a strange, gaunt beauty about winter that Rachel had never discovered in town and, once she had walked long enough to stimulate her circulation, she felt quite glowingly warm.

"What have you been doing with yourself while I've been away?" Lars asked, and she smiled up at him, shaking her head.

"Nothing out of the ordinary," she told him. "Of course it's made a difference not being allowed to take Nicky very far afield, but—" she paused, wondering if he yet knew about Michael Browlett's unexpected appearance. There had been little enough time to mention it since his arrival that after noon, but it was possible that Neil saw the incident as important enough to mention. "Do—did Neil tell you about Nicky's father?" she ventured, and Lars nodded.

"He told me," he said, "but I can't help feeling that he's taking the whole thing too seriously."

"Perhaps." She was unwilling to pass judgment on Neil because she had no doubt at all that he cared deeply for his little nephew and would never consider anything that concerned his well-being as too much trouble to take seriously. "I didn't realise who the man was," Rachel told him. "Not until Neil told me, he recognised his description. It's odd," she mused, frowning curiously, "but he asked me to identify Neil— doesn't he know him? And how could Neil recognise *him*?"

"Lynn had a photograph, I believe," Lars told her, "but I never saw it, and he never came to Seaways, of course."

"Of course?" She echoed his words curiously. "Why was that, Lars? Didn't the family accept him?"

Lars shrugged, the moonlight revealing a new ruggedness in his good-looking features that gave him the same suggestion of strength his cousin had. "No one saw him," he told her. "Lynn eloped with him, and when she was expecting Nicky—he left her. I doubt if Lynn herself knew him for more than a few months."

It was not at all as Rachel had imagined it, despite Mrs. Handley's moment of confidence, and she said nothing for a few moments, trying yet again to find some kind of stability in Nicky's earlier background. The wonder was that he was as normal and friendly a child as he was with the bad start he had had in life.

"But why?" she asked, and went on to explain when she saw Lars' puzzled frown. "I mean, Lynn came from a wealthy family, if he was a—a fortune-hunter, which I assume is what the family think, surely it made little difference to his position whether they had a child or not—his wife was still rich."

"Oh, Lynn was wealthy," Lars agreed, "but Mrs. Fran Munger was—still is—even wealthier, and Michael Browlett caught her eye. He was working in the States, only playing small parts, but not so small he was overlooked by one of the richest women in the world."

"He's an actor?" Rachel asked. "I didn't know that."

"He hasn't needed to do much for the past five years," Lars told her dryly. "He's been living the life of Riley in America."

"And now he's back in England," Rachel mused. "I wonder why."

Lars' arm tightened around her shoulders and he laughed shortly, his face half-buried in her hair. "You don't keep up with the international gossip columns, it's obvious, Rachel," he said. "Mrs. Fran Munger married another husband last month, another millionaire, of course—Michael Browlett's lost his meal ticket!"

CHAPTER EIGHT

IT was a fairly warm day with a promise of sun behind the thick damp mist that presently hung over the countryside and gave only glimpses of distance, making Rachel feel that Seaways was isolated in a soft grey cloud, miles from anywhere. It was a curious feeling and she shivered a little as she dressed, again reminded of that hint of mystery that seemed always to be present in the old house.

While she stood brushing her hair in front of the mirror her mind again returned to Michael Browlett, Nicky's father, and she wondered if he really would try to gain control of his son now that he needed him for the fortune he would bring with him. Surely, she thought, no court would uphold the claim of a father who had never seen nor attempted to see his son until his own financial straits made him realise what a desirable acquisition he would be.

And Neil—what of Neil, if his brother-in-law's claim were to be successful? Losing Nicky would break his heart, and she could not bear to think of it happening. While she was supervising Nicky's toilet she realised, too, how much a change of guardianship would affect her. Not only because she had become very attached to Nicky over the past couple of months, but because if Nicky was no longer at Seaways she would no longer be needed there herself, and that was a prospect she faced very unwillingly, even though it was bound to happen sooner or later when Nicky got older.

Ready at last, she walked down the stairs behind Nicky's small hurrying figure, and wondered for the first time just what she would do when her time at Seaways was finished. Her training had taught her that it was inadvisable to become too attached either to her charge or her environment, but somehow she felt so inextricably part of Seaways and the family who lived there that the idea of leaving dismayed her. Not the least disturbing part was the prospect of never seeing Neil again once she had outlived her usefulness to him.

Nicky burst into the breakfast room with his usual bright good morning for his uncle, and he had wriggled himself up on to his chair before Rachel even had time to enter the room. It was a surprise to find Neil alone, for usually by the time she and Nicky came down for their breakfasts Neil and Lars had almost finished theirs, but this morning Lars had barely begun.

Raising a brow, Neil looked first at his wristwatch and then at the clock on the mantel, as if he doubted their accuracy. "Good morning," he said, and a faint smile tugged at one corner of his wide mouth when he looked at her. "You've beaten Lars to it today, you're early."

Rachel finished tucking a serviette under Nicky's chin before she looked at her own wristwatch and then she too glanced at the mantel clock and frowned. "My watch is very fast," she mused, "I'd no idea we were so early." She looked across at Neil and half smiled. "I hope we shan't disturb your peace too much if we join you."

He shook his head and she caught a bright quizzical look in the blue eyes that regarded her from below the thick sweep of blond hair across his brow. "Not at all," he told her, "as long as you're not disappointed because Lars isn't here too."

Rachel, suspecting his motives, looked across at him

and frowned. "Of course not," she denied quietly. "Why should we be? Lars will be down soon enough, I expect."

"Sure to be," Neil agreed. "He'll be taking Nicky riding, won't he?" He ate in silence for a moment while Rachel saw to it that Nicky had a bowl of cereal to appease his appetite. "I'm surprised Lars hasn't taught you to ride," Neil observed after a few seconds. "Then you could go with him and Nicky."

As it was something that had crossed her own mind more than once as a possibility Rachel looked across at him briefly and shook her head. "I had thought about it," she confessed, "but then I remembered that you wouldn't agree to it."

Neil flicked one light brow swiftly upwards and the blue eyes held hers steadily for as long as she could bear the scrutiny. "Oh?" he queried. "What gave you that idea?"

"For one thing," Rachel told him a little uncertainly, "because they're your horses and you'd be paying me while I was learning."

Neil ate in silence for several seconds, then he looked directly across at her in the same moment that she glanced up, and colour flooded warmly into her cheeks when she met his eyes, her heart thudding hard at her ribs. "You still have a bad opinion of me, don't you, Rachel?" he asked in a soft voice. "Do you really see me as such an ogre that I'd forbid you to learn to ride just because you work for me? Is that how you see me—as some kind of martinet?"

"Oh no, of course I don't!" She was uncomfortably aware that Nicky was beginning to take an interest in what they were saying and it almost changed her mind about reminding Neil about her first meeting with him. Then glancing at Nicky from the corner of her eye she looked directly at Neil. "But you did say before I started work for you," she reminded him, "that you didn't see why you should pay me to learn!"

It was touch and go, she realised breathlessly, whether or not he lost his temper, and she could feel her heart hammering with such violence at her ribs that it made her head spin. Then he smiled, a tight, bitter smile that showed in his eyes as an icy glitter. "I asked you, if I remember," he said coolly, "if you expected me to pay you to gain experience." Briefly the blue eyes held hers determinedly and she shivered involuntarily. "I should have known you'd remember that," he said, and Rachel flushed.

"I'm—I'm sorry." She half whispered the words and was aware that not only Neil's blue eyes were watching her but Nicky's too, and she shook her head anxiously as she took up her own cereal spoon and began to eat. "I shouldn't have mentioned it," she admitted, and Neil laughed shortly.

"But you couldn't resist it!" He eyed her quizzically for a second or two, then leaned forward on one elbow. "I suppose Lars knows your reason for not learning to ride?" he suggested, and she shook her head. "Didn't you tell him it was because of what I'd say that you couldn't learn?"

"The question of my learning to ride has never arisen," Rachel informed him a little breathlessly. "Lars has never mentioned it and I'm not sure whether I'd like it or not, although it would be nice to be able to go out with Nicky and Lars."

"And with me?" Neil suggested quietly.

Rachel could feel the hand holding her spoon trembling like a leaf and she hastily put down the spoon and clasped her two hands together while she looked across at him warily. "If you asked me to," she told him in a small breathless voice, and he half smiled, his eyes searching her face, lingering on her mouth in that disturbing, intense way that set her pulses racing.

"I'm driving into Mergeton this morning," he said quietly. "If you—" He stopped in mid-sentence when the door of the breakfast room opened and Lars came in.

Nicky shouted a greeting and started immediately asking about their ride after breakfast, and Rachel murmured a greeting as she hastily picked up her spoon again, conscious that Lars was frowning over the bright flush in her cheeks. It was several seconds before quiet descended again and Rachel suddenly realised that Neil had already finished his breakfast and was drinking down the last of his coffee without bothering with toast and marmalade.

He got to his feet murmuring an apology and ruffling one big hand in Nicky's thick brown hair as he passed him. "Be good," he admonished him, and strode towards the door. He did not, Rachel noticed, even glance again in her direction and she felt strangely bereft as the door closed behind him and his tall, lean shape disappeared into the hall.

She would have given much to know what he had started to say to her when Lars appeared. From the little she had heard she felt almost sure it had been an invitation to drive into Mergeton with him and she knew she would have accepted without question if Lars had not interrupted. What she found harder to face was the apparently easy way he had given up the idea when his cousin appeared, and she wondered if he still believed her to be more than half in love with Lars.

It was pleasant having Lars back again at Seaways, but after the past weeks Rachel was ready to admit that she missed Neil's company much more even than she had expected to. Sometimes it was difficult to understand her own feelings where Neil was concerned and she had long since accepted the fact that he could affect her emotionally much more deeply than Lars or anyone else ever could.

As for the strange love-hate relationship that Lars and Neil had, it was past her understanding, although it possibly had something to do with the fact that blood was thicker than water, and they reminded her more of brothers sometimes than cousins. They could disagree as violently as Rachel had heard them do and yet there was no suggestion that Lars should stay away from Seaways for good. Even his affair with Lynn had not brought that about.

During the past few days, since Lars returned, the weather had taken a definite turn for the better and it almost seemed there was a touch of spring in the air, although early morning saw wet, chill mists rolling in from the sea over the farmlands.

Things were more or less as before, with Nicky riding every day with Lars and the three of them taking a walk sometimes. Rachel said nothing about Neil's near-invitation to drive with him into Mergeton, if that was what he had intended, and she hoped Nicky would have forgotten about it too, for Lars would find it too much not to comment on it and she felt oddly shy about it.

Obviously Nicky would have gone with them and yet, somewhere in the back of her mind, was the odd feeling of certainty that he had meant the invitation for her alone, and she could not shake off the sense of excitement it gave her. More difficult to understand and to accept was the way he had suddenly cut short the invitation.

"We could drive into Mergeton again," Lars suggested, and Rachel nodded agreement without really hearing what he said.

"But not today," Lars qualified hastily when Nicky showed signs of demanding immediate departure. "I'd like to make it a whole day's outing, and we've already lost half of today."

"Tomorrow?" Nicky demanded, anxious to have the matter settled as soon as possible, and Lars smiled down at him tolerantly.

"Maybe, little one," he told him. "If Rachel would like to."

He ostensibly gave an answer to Nicky, but he looked at Rachel as he made it and it was obvious that her preoccupation puzzled him to some extent. Neil would have no objection, of course, to them going into Mergeton with Lars and all of them would enjoy the change. Although it had almost certainly not been Neil's intention to confine them, his edict that they should not go far afield without either himself or Handley in attendance had done just that in effect. Reluctant to trouble them very often, when both men had work to do, their movements had been restricted whether Neil meant it so or not, by her unwillingness to ask.

"I'd like that," she told Lars. "It'll make a change to go out for the day."

Lars' blue eyes glistened with laughter, not altogether without malice, Rachel thought, and he looked down at her with one fair brow raised. "Hasn't Neil taken you anywhere?" he asked, and Rachel shook her head.

"It isn't any part of Neil's job to take me out," she told Lars defensively, perhaps more defensively than she realised, for she saw Lars' good-looking face register surprise at her tone. "He's very busy always and I'm quite capable of going into Mergeton alone in my time off. If I'd wanted to take Nicky anywhere I'm sure he'd have taken us if I'd asked him, but as it happened we were quite happy here."

Lars once more flicked a brow into the thick fair hair over his forehead and his blue eyes regarded her speculatively. "So you're Neil's champion now," he remarked. "I find that rather a surprise, Rachel, I always thought you and Neil were—" One expressive hand conveyed with remarkable explicitness her initial antagonism towards Neil and she found herself unable to resist a smile, although her cheeks burned pinkly under that speculating scrutiny. Nicky was running ahead of them and she was thankful he was not near enough to overhear them.

"I'm no one's champion, Lars," she told him in a quiet and studiously controlled voice. "I merely stated a fact—Neil's under no obligation at all to take *me* out, and if I want to take Nicky anywhere it's up to me to ask him to take us."

Lars' blue eyes teased her and he slid an arm around her shoulders, drawing her close to him so that she was conscious of the warm vibrance of his body. "Nor am I under any obligation," he told her, "but I want to take you out for my own pleasure—I would have thought Neil was capable of appreciating that fact as much as I do!"

"Neil's my employer," Rachel reminded him, looking up at him and smiling, "you're not!"

"And therefore better placed for taking advantage of you," Lars pointed out with embarrassing frankness, and smiled at her broadly. "As I would do!"

With the memory of Neil's kiss all too easily brought to mind, Rachel shrugged uneasily. "Maybe," she said.

"For instance," Lars went on undeterred, "in his place I'd have taken you with me into Mergeton today, even if it is on business and even if it meant taking Nicky along too."

It was tempting to tell him how close she had come to being asked to go with Neil, but Rachel resisted it, for she was not yet ready to face Lars' speculation once he knew about it. "I'd hardly expect him to take passengers when he's on a business trip," she told him, and Lars laughed and hugged her to him again.

"Oh well," he said, "his loss is my gain!" He dropped a light kiss on her cheek. "While Neil sorts out Nicky's financial affairs, I go walking with you—I think I have the advantage of him!"

"*Nicky's* financial affairs?"

Rachel looked at him curiously. It had never occured to her that Nicky might be wealthy in his own right and she had to do some rapid readjustment. She had seen him only as a poor orphan, and assumed that he had nothing of his own, whereas a child in his position, of course, was quite likely to have money of his own.

His mother had in all probability been as wealthy as his uncle was and almost certainly Nicky would have been her heir. Neil, naturally, being his guardian, would assume responsibility for his financial affairs as well, so his business trip was quite understandable.

Lars was looking at her curiously, as if he half suspected her innocence in the matter was assumed. "Didn't you realise how rich Nicky is in his own right?" he asked, and Rachel shook her head.

"It hadn't even occurred to me," she confessed. "I simply thought that Neil took care of him because no one else would. It never occurred to me that he was a—a poor little rich boy."

"I suppose that's what he is," Lars agreed thoughtfully. "Although he's likely to be even richer, the way Neil handles his investments, and he's much happier now that Neil has sole charge of him than he ever was with his mother."

Another fragment, Rachel thought musingly, another indication that neither Nicky nor his mother had led very happy or secure lives. "I see," was all she said, and asked no more questions. Neil seemed to loom so large in everyone's life that she wondered what they would all have done without him.

She walked beside Lars, thoughtfully quiet, for some time, and the fresh wind whipped colour into her cheeks and blew the soft wisps of dark hair back from her forehead where it peeped from beneath the woollen hat she wore. Watching Nicky playing just ahead of them she pondered on how much else there was to learn about Nicky and his mother. Lynn became more of a mystery all the time and she was more than ever convinced that the worst was yet to come.

Nicky was happy—happier than he had ever been, if Lars and Mrs. Handley were to be believed,and she wondered if Lars would ever have had the courage or the inclination to care for him as Neil did. She thought not. She was aware suddenly that Lars was looking down at her and he smiled when she looked up at him enquiringly.

"Shall we?" he asked, and indicated a low brick wall that flanked the steps up to the front door. When she nodded he drew her across to it and sat himself down, pulling her down beside him and placing an arm around her waist. "Why do you think Michael Browlett is suddenly taking an interest in his son?" he asked, and Rachel shook her head.

They sat looking across at the damp, untidy shrubbery with its cheerless winter tangle given a brief beauty by the pale sun shining on wet leaves and bare branches. Somewhere near Nicky was making his favourite engine noises as he ran in and out of the trees and shrubs, much too energetic to sit down.

"You mean—" Rachel looked up at Lars uneasily. It was hard to attribute such callousness to anyone connected with Nicky, but the fact had to be faced.

"He has to find a way of earning a living again now,"

Lars reminded her bluntly, and Rachel shook her head slowly.

"That—that simply hadn't occurred to me," she said after a moment or two. "But I suppose it's possible that he would do something like that. If he could get custody of Nicky—"

"He'd be in charge of a goldmine," Lars assured her wryly. "Neil's done well investing Nicky's money."

"But only for Nicky's sake!" Rachel insisted hastily. "He wouldn't do anything wrong, not with Nicky's money, not Neil!"

"Not Neil," Lars echoed, and turned her until she was half facing him, his blue eyes searching her face, a dark speculative look in their depths. Sooner or later, she knew, Lars would again remark about her frequent defence of Neil, but her reactions were purely instinctive and there seemed little she could do about it.

Her heart was thudding hard at her ribs and she could feel its urgency even through the thick jacket she wore, where her hands pressed together in the pockets in front of her. There was a bright flush in her cheeks too that was not entirely due to the brisk wind and Lars' blue gaze missed nothing of it.

It was strange, but being so close to Lars was much less exciting than the same proximity would have been with Neil, and she dared not stop to wonder why. Lars was young and good-looking and she was definitely attracted to him, but somehow he simply did not have the same profound effect on her senses that Neil did.

He put a finger under her chin and gently lifted her face to him and his eyes were fixed on her mouth. His voice, much too soft for Nicky to hear even if he had been nearer, was warm and persuasive and so very faintly accented that it was barely discernible. "You're very lovely, Rachel," he said. "Much too lovely to be buried here at Seaways."

"But I'm not buried," Rachel denied hastily. "I love it here, Lars, you know that."

"And I love you!" He made the statement firmly and confidently, despite the softness of his voice, but it was scarcely credible that he meant it and Rachel stared at him unbelievingly.

His breath was warm on her lips and she felt her heart beating urgently as she tried to turn her head away, to avoid that steady gaze that fixed itself on her mouth so unwaveringly. But Lars was not to be denied and he substituted a large but gentle hand for the one finger that supported her chin and made movement impossible.

"Lars." She tried to keep her voice steady, but it trembled in spite of her efforts and she licked her lips anxiously. "You've—it's only a little over three weeks that you've known me, Lars," she pointed out. "It—it isn't very long."

"But it's long enough," Lars assured her close to her mouth. "You mustn't expect me to waste time as Neil does, sweetheart. He had you to himself for several weeks, but he has not taken advantage of his opportunities—I will!"

"No, Lars!" She managed at last to free herself of that persistent hand on her chin and looked at him with bright, anxious eyes. "I—I like you," she admitted. "In fact I find you very attractive, if you prefer me to be frank, but I'm—I can't let myself be swept along like this as if I have no say in the matter."

"Oh, but of course you do," Lars assured her earnestly. "I am hoping that you love me too—that would make everything right."

"I—I don't." She looked at him in dismay, so afraid of being swept up into something she could not control. "I've said I—I like you, but that's all, Lars. I don't love you."

Lars' blue eyes were warm and persuasive and he held her in the curve of his arm, hugged close to him, his mouth only inches away. "I could persuade you," he said softly. "I want you to come back to Sweden with me when I go next time. Will you do that, Rachel?"

Rachel stared at him, shaking her head slowly when she recalled her conversation with Neil in the stable. "Lars thinks he has only to raise his finger and you'll go," Neil had told her, and she had denied it. Now she was faced with an invitation that it was obvious Lars fully expected her to accept, unless she had taken it all more seriously than he intended.

"Don't be silly," she said in a small husky voice, "of course I can't come to Sweden with you!"

"I see nothing to stop you," Lars insisted coolly. "You will surely not be expected to work for a whole year without a holiday, and once I have you to myself I can persuade you to feel differently about me! Let me try, hmm?"

"Oh, Lars, please be sensible!" She looked at him wide-eyed, not sure, even yet, that he could be completely serious. "I haven't known you nearly long enough to—to just go traipsing off to Sweden with you!"

"You'd rather stay with Neil?"

He asked the question quietly, but Rachel detected the edge of steel in his voice and shook her head slowly. The innuendo was unmistakable and it touched on a very delicate nerve, but she was not prepared to admit to Lars that she would prefer to stay with Neil, if it came to a choice.

"I'd rather stay in a very good job," she told him, and hoped she sounded as firm and cool as she tried to. "I've no one to compare him with, I know, because this is my first post, but Neil's a very good employer and I'm very happy at Seaways."

"But even Neil cannot dictate where you spend your holidays," Lars insisted. "And I'm sure I could persuade you round to my way once I had you to myself."

Rachel looked up at him for a moment steadily. This, she thought must be what Neil had been warning him about when she had heard them quarrelling so bitterly that morning. He had warned Lars not to involve her and Lars had retorted that she, Rachel, was not Lynn. For the first time she wondered if he had ever put the same proposition to Lynn and if Lynn had been easier to persuade into going off to Sweden than she was herself.

"I couldn't do it, Lars," she said. "For one thing Neil would know it wasn't simply a—a holiday." She shook her head firmly. "No, Lars, I couldn't."

"I don't see how it concerns Neil," Lars insisted, his blue eyes resenting her refusal, while one hand stroked the side of her face that was turned to him. "You'd know it was something more than a holiday, and so would I, but whether Neil knew or not isn't important. If you want to come there's nothing he could do about it!"

Rachel eased away from the caressing hand that stroked her cheek and shook her head, brushing back the wisps of hair from her face. "He wouldn't care one way or the other what I did," she told Lars, and looked up sharply when he laughed, her brows drawn into a frown.

"Oh, he'd care," Lars said confidently. "He'd certainly care!"

For a moment Rachel looked at him, her eyes searching his good-looking face for a clue as to his meaning, and her heart was thudding anxiously as she sat huddled on the low wall her hands in her pockets, curled tightly. "Enough to decide I wasn't fit to look after Nicky any longer maybe," she said, far more matter-of-factly than she felt. "And I couldn't blame him for that, Lars."

"Rachel!" He reached out and stroked her cheek again, his eyes glowing warmly as he looked down at her, so persuasive and confident he was hard to resist.

She pushed aside his hand, quite gently, and held his gaze for as long as she was able, then looked down at the firm, confident smile on his mouth and shook her head. "I won't be persuaded, Lars," she told him, and looked down at her wristwatch, "and I think it's time we went in now, it's getting colder and Nicky—"

It was quiet, she realised suddenly, much too quiet if Nicky was still pretending to be an aircraft and making those noisy engine sounds he was so fond of. The only thing she could hear was the soft rustle of the wind in the shrubbery and somewhere in the distance the sound of a car, gradually disappearing along the road.

"Nicky!" She got to her feet, her hands and legs trembling, straining to hear the slightest sound of the mock aeroplane. He never ignored a call, not more than once, and she called again. "Nicky!" It was quiet—too quiet.

Lars, jerked into action by the edge of panic on her voice, got to his feet and strode across to where the wet, sad-looking shrubs huddled under the bare trees, and there was a note of anxiety in his voice too when he called, "Nicky!"

CHAPTER NINE

It was little more than an hour and a half since it happened, but to Rachel it seemed like hours since she had suddenly decided to call Nicky to her and go inside. Since she had got up from her seat on the wall to call him and received no reply. Her eyes were dark with anxiety and hazy with unshed tears as she stared blankly in a kind of stunned disbelief at Lars.

Lars too showed the effects of shock on his good-looking face as he stood facing her in the hall, neither of them daring to suggest what had really happened. He looked pale and drawn and it was difficult to believe he was the same man she had sat with only a short time ago, a man so full of self-confidence and brimming with ideas for taking her to Sweden with him.

The laughter and the air of confidence were gone and he ran one hand through his thick blond hair in a gesture of despair—that reminded her of Neil. It was the reminder of Neil that made Rachel sick with apprehension, for the thought of having to break the news to him dismayed her almost more than the actual fact of Nicky's disappearance.

It was a fact now that had to be faced—Nicky *had* disappeared and no amount of self-delusion would make any difference. It had seemed like no more than a few minutes that she and Lars had sat on the wall beside the steps discussing the rights and wrongs of her going back to Sweden with him and whether or not Rachel could ever love him, but in that short time they were preoccupied with their own affairs they had not even noticed that Nicky's familiar engine noises were no longer audible.

It was only when they called to him and he did not reply that the awful truth began to dawn on them—he was no longer within calling distance, he was no longer anywhere at all that she could see, and Rachel's heart had almost stopped when she realised what had happened.

The worst part was realising that she had done exactly what Neil had been so insistent on avoiding. She had become so involved in her conversation with Lars that Nicky had been left to play alone and out of sight. Neil would never forgive her, and that would be the hardest fact to face—the knowledge that she had betrayed his trust in her.

At first she and Lars had searched for him, only half believing he was actually missing and still hoping that he was hiding somewhere, that even if he had gone off alone he could not have gone very far. But eventually they had been forced to face the fact that it was not simply a game and Mr. and Mrs. Handley had been enlisted to help look for him, though with no more success. It was clearly that wherever Nicky was he was nowhere at Seaways, and someone was going to have to break it to Neil when he came home.

The sound of his car on the drive immediately put her into a state of near-panic and Rachel looked up at Lars with anxious grey eyes, her mouth trembling. he was going to be not only angry but hurt and she could see only herself as the culprit at the moment.

"I—I can't," she whispered huskily. "I—I don't know how I'm going to tell him, Lars!"

Suddenly it seemed Lars looked much older and there were lines that ran from his mouth and betrayed an anxiety at least as great as her own, but he put a firm and comforting hand on her shoulder when he spoke. "Leave it to me," he told her. "I'll tell him, Rachel." His accent, she noticed absently, was much more pronounced than ever before, and she wondered if he too felt panic at the idea of breaking the news to his cousin.

She shook her head, still seeing herself as the culprit, and tears trembled on her lashes as she stood listening to Neil's confident tread on the steps. She put up her hands to her mouth to check the anguish that caught in her throat and threatened to choke her. "No," she whispered. "I—I have to, Lars; it's—Nicky was my responsibility!"

There was no time for Lars to argue whose responsibility it was, because Neil was already coming in through the door, a tall forceful figure in the more formal dress he had put on for his visit to town—dark grey tweed that somehow made him look even bigger than usual and a cream shirt that showed off the tanned ruggedness of his features.

He glanced only briefly at Lars, then swept immediately round to Rachel's pale tearful face, his eyes narrowed. "What's happened?" he asked in a flat, almost resigned voice that was somehow more affecting than an outburst of anger would have been. "In God's name, Rachel, what's happened?"

"Nicky—" Her voice choked in her throat and the tears she had tried so hard to contain flooded down her cheeks when she saw the blank stunned look in his eyes. "It—it's Nicky," she tried again, "he—" Again her voice and her courage failed her and she simply shook her head.

"Tell me!" Strong hands gripped her shoulders so hard that she cried out and her head spun dizzily when he shook her. "Where's Nicky?" he rasped harshly. "Where is he, Rachel? What's happened to him?"

"He's gone—he's missing, Neil!" It was Lars who answered for her and Neil swung round on him, his blue eyes hard and icy and his mouth set relentlessly while strong fingers still dug hard into Rachel's shoulders.

"How?" he demanded. "How could he go missing when you and Rachel were with him?" Lars cast a brief, telling glance at Rachel, saying no word but telling Neil all he needed to know, and his eyes narrowed until they were little more than icy slits. "Yes, of course," he said, his voice steely hard, "you had other things on your mind, didn't you?"

"Neil, please!" Rachel cried in despair. "It—it wasn't how you make it sound at all, please—"

"It doesn't matter a damn *how* it sounds!" Neil interrupted harshly. "The only thing that matters to me is finding Nicky. I presume you've searched the grounds and the house thoroughly; have you informed the police?"

Rachel stared at him, too stunned to reply, and it was Lars who once again answered for her, following the meaning all too easily, apparently, for he looked at Neil warily. "Do you think we should?" he asked. "If Nicky's only—"

"Do you think he's only?" Neil asked coldly, and Lars shook his head. "It's obvious who Nicky's with, and the sooner we can have him stopped the better."

"Oh, no!"

Rachel put her hands to her mouth and stared at him over trembling fingers, her eyes wide and unbelieving. Neil looked at her for a moment with that same steady, ice-cold gaze that made her shiver miserably, and his mouth betrayed the derision he felt for her reaction. "You don't approve of having the police informed?" he asked harshly. "Perhaps you have a better idea of how to get Nicky back?"

"I—I don't have an idea at all," Rachel admitted miserably. "But if he's with—"

"Oh, he's with his father," Neil assured her in a cold, flat voice, "I've no doubt about that at all. Is that what you wanted, Rachel? Has your training taught you that there's no substitute for the natural parent, no matter how callous or uncaring he might be? Is that what they taught you?"

It was almost as if he had struck her a physical blow and Rachel closed her eyes for a second on the hard and pitiless look in his eyes. She was shivering as if she was chilled through to her very bones and there was a sickening sense of hopelessness in her heart that offered no glimmer of relief.

"You know I wouldn't—I wouldn't have done this deliberately," she whispered huskily. "You can't believe that, Neil!"

"I have to believe what I see," Neil rasped sharply. "Nicky's gone, and that's proof enough that I was right to suspect something like this would happen. Michael Browlett gave enough warning when he turned up here that day and you saw him. He's probably been around ever since waiting for his chance—a chance you presented to him on a plate this afternoon!"

"But—" Rachel bit her lip in anguish. "If he has Nicky—how can he hope to keep him? The courts wouldn't let him have custody after all these years, surely they wouldn't, Neil!"

Neil's stern, rock-like features cracked briefly into a travesty of a smile as he looked down at her. "Oh, he doesn't want Nicky," he told her harshly. "He just hopes to persuade me to pay for the privilege of keeping him. It isn't kidnapping, of course, he is Nicky's father, so they wouldn't call it that, but he knows that I'd sign over Nicky's inheritance, every last halfpenny of it, to have him back and to avoid putting Nicky through the agony of a court case over who has custody of him!'' He looked as if he was about to say more, but after a second he made a short, sharp sound that dismissed her as a complete fool and strode across the hall to the telephone.

Rachel did nothing while he gave the basic story to the police over the telephone, and Lars did not even put a hand on her in an attempt to console her. It was not the moment for Lars to offer consolation, not with Neil's tall, vengeful figure only a few feet away, and anyway Rachel was inconsolable.

It was her fault, she could not deny that, even though Lars must inevitably share some of the blame; she had been entrusted with the care of Nicky completely. It was something that Neil prophesied could happen and now it had.

Neil put down the telephone and stood for a few seconds, quite still, his hands gripping the edge of the table and Rachel could see that his knuckles were white-boned in the strong brown fingers. Then he turned and faced them again, his eyes still cold, but darkened with the realisation that Nicky really was gone, and Rachel's heart yearned to comfort him.

"Neil—" She ventured a step towards him, but stopped short when he looked at her.

"Where were you when he—disappeared?" he asked in a cold flat voice, and Rachel instinctively glanced at Lars before she answered.

"Out there, in the front garden," she said huskily, and anxiously ran her tongue over her dry lips. "We were sitting on the low wall by the steps to the front door and Nicky was running around in and out of the shrubbery. We—we were talking and—"

"Talking!" His scorn hurt much more than he could ever know and Rachel flinched from it, but she held his gaze determinedly.

"We were talking," she repeated in a small flat voice, "and we didn't notice that Nicky—that we couldn't hear him any longer. Those engine noises he likes making when he's playing," she explained when he looked briefly puzzled. "It was when I went to call him to come in that—" She bit her lip hastily rather than let the tears cause a sob in her voice as they threatened to, but Neil's eyes were harshly unforgiving as he looked down at her.

"When you eventually remembered that you were responsible for him," he said, and Rachel put a hand to her mouth, her eyes dark with anguish.

"It was as much my fault as Rachel's," Lars intervened, and his voice shook with emotion.

Neil looked at him with narrowed eyes for a moment. "I know that quite well," he told him coldly, "but neither of you could be trusted when it came to the point, could you? I thought Rachel was safe to leave in charge when you were around, I had her assurance on that and I believed her—it seems I was wrong after all!"

"Neil, for God's sake!" Lars curled his hands into tight hard fists and for a moment it looked as if he might strike out so that Rachel caught her breath and prayed that they would not take the quarrel any further. Lars drew in a deep audible breath and shook his head. "Don't punish Rachel any more, Neil," he said more quietly, "she didn't let Nicky go deliberately, your own sense must tell you that!"

"Punish her?" Neil's blue eyes looked at Rachel for a moment, so cold and blank that she shivered under their scrutiny, her heart drumming hopelessly at her ribs. It was obvious that he had no idea how much he could hurt her, but Lars had seen and tried to help. "What have I done to punish her?" Neil asked.

"Can't you see?" Lars asked. "The fault was as much mine as Rachel's, and you can't go on—" He shrugged, his eyes on Rachel and so filled with compassion that she could not bear it.

She shook her head slowly, looking at Lars with her huge grey eyes dark with hurt. "Don't, Lars," she whispered. "I—it doesn't matter." She looked up at Neil, seeking some glimmer of compassion, but found none, only that cold blankness that refused to feel anything but the loss of Nicky. Then turning away hastily before she broke down and cried, she walked across the hall to the stairs—nothing anyone said now would make any difference.

The police had been polite and kind, and Rachel had gone through the motions of telling them what Nicky had been wearing, where and when she had last seen him and how long she and Lars had been before they noticed he was missing. It was an ordeal she suffered in a kind of trance, for she still found it hard to believe that Nicky could really be gone.

Lars too had talked to them, given them much the same information she had herself, and all the time Neil had sat and listened, saying nothing, his ice blue eyes watching them, impatient when they answered vaguely and never once giving Rachel the glimpse of warmth and understanding she sought so anxiously from him.

Mrs. Handley came in when the police had gone at last and asked if they wanted dinner at the usual time. Her eyes, Rachel noticed, were swollen with crying and she looked at Rachel only once and with such reproach that Rachel was close to tears again herself.

She instinctively shook her head at the idea of sitting down to a meal, but both Neil and Lars presumably found some kind of comfort in following the customary routine, so she was obliged to join them, a small silent figure with Nicky's empty chair beside her to remind her.

Once or twice Lars looked across at her, but she had refused to meet his eyes, and the two men had gone over the last few minutes before Nicky's disappearance again and again until she could have screamed. "He can't hope to get him out of the country with him," Lars said, trying to sound more confident than he was, and for the first time Rachel realised the full possibilities of what had happened.

"He won't try to get him out of the country," Neil argued in that same cold, flat voice he had used all along. "Not until he's issued the ultimatum—told me what price I have to pay for getting Nicky back."

Lars had smoked incessantly ever since Neil came back and he lit another cigarette now, his long hands not quite steady when he applied the flame to its tip. "The money!" he said bitterly. "It all boils down to Lynn's money, doesn't it? If only Nicky hadn't been willed all that money this would never have happened, there would have been no chance of it happening!"

Neil's blue eyes narrowed sharply and he too took another cigarette and lit it—both men, it was obvious, were far more nervously tense than their outward appearances first suggested. "Who else could you expect Lynn to leave her money to?" he asked harshly. "You surely didn't expect her to leave it to Browlett, did you?"

"No, of course not!" Lars shook his head. Resting his elbows on the table, he clasped his long hands together and frowned. "The question is whether Michael Browlett will claim she was—well, not quite in her right mind when she made the will," he suggested, and Neil again looked at him in sharp disagreement.

"Because of what happened last year?" he demanded in a voice that sent chills down Rachel's spine as she listened to it. Somehow she felt she should say something, break in and remind them that she was there, for they seemed to have forgotten her existence for the moment. They were like two antagonists in a ring, circling each other, finding each other's vulnerable spots, waiting to strike, and Rachel shivered at the prospect. "You know better than anyone why that happened," Neil said flatly, and Lars' good-looking face flushed as he ground out the barely touched cigarette with a fierceness that betrayed his anger.

"You'll never let me forget that, will you?" he asked in a voice little more than a whisper. He sat with his empty hands on the table in front of him for a long moment, then, as if he could stand their inactivity no longer, he reached for another cigarette and lit it. "I can't believe that Lynn—did what she did because of a—lighthearted love affair," he said. "I did nothing to suggest it was anything else but lighthearted, and—"

"It wasn't lighthearted to Lynn!" Neil argued harshly, and despite her reluctance to be a witness to what must surely be a very private argument, Rachel found herself undeniably involved. Whatever had happened to Lynn Browlett a year ago, she was about to find out, and her heart was thudding so hard at her breast that she held her breath as she waited for Neil to go on. "She loved you," Neil said, "and you didn't even realise it!"

"How could I?" Lars' voice had the sound of despair and, despite the fact that he appeared to be emerging as some kind of heartless philanderer, Rachel felt sorry for him. "How could I know she'd try and take Nicky with her?"

Rachel felt cold and still suddenly, and the haunting shade of Lynn Browlett seemed stronger than ever it had as the three of them sat there round the table. Anger, resentment and her own cold realisation mingled in an atmosphere that hung over them like a tangible threat.

The truth about Lynn had proved to be far more awful than Rachel could ever have imagined, and for a few chilling moments she actually wondered if she could be having a nightmare and that none of it was true. She could, with little effort, visualise that pretty, petulant creature in the photograph being driven by despair to attempt her own life, but to try and take Nicky with her—

It was no wonder that Nicky was afraid of the sea and that Neil had forbidden her to take him anywhere near it; the wonder was that he was so well adjusted after all he had been through, and she felt her heart contract at the mere thought of him being with a man who, although he was his father, was in reality a stranger interested only in how much he was worth to him.

It was some time before Neil replied to Lars' anguished question, and Rachel found herself waiting as anxiously as Lars did. A spiral of blue smoke hid Neil's strong, rugged features and his eyes had the darkness of despair as he gazed down at his empty plate, his hands clasped in front of his face. There was an air of dejection about him that Rachel found hard to bear, and she longed to offer consolation—but how could she when she was the indirect cause of his misery?

Then he shook his head slowly, as if he was very tired. "How could you know?" he echoed quietly. "You never really knew Lynn at all, did you, Lars?" He looked up at last and straight at Lars, studying the good-looking face almost as if he was seeing it for the first time. "But you keep coming back," he said, and his voice implied a question, so that Lars looked at him curiously.

"You know why," he told him. "I care for Nicky as much as you do, Neil, I've never denied that."

"But you wouldn't have married Lynn and given him a proper family and a home," Neil said quietly. "You *do* love him, I know that, that's why I've never suggested that you stay away from Seaways, and because I felt that somewhere inside you, you really did feel more for Lynn than a—a lighthearted affection. Lately, however—"

For the first time his eyes came to rest on Rachel and she shivered when she saw from their expression that he really had forgotten she was there. Lars too looked across at her as if he only now realised that he was not alone with his cousin, and his eyes took in the paleness of her face and the soft, hurt look about her mouth as she looked at Neil.

"I don't really think you have any more perception than I had with Lynn," he told Neil, and Rachel saw the swift frown that drew Neil's fair brows together.

Lars, more perceptive where her feelings were concerned, had recognised her hurt and the reason for it before she had done so herself. It was only now when she looked at Neil and felt a great surge of pity and longing for him that she knew how much she loved him, and the realisation was, in the circumstances, almost unbearable.

She pushed back her chair and got to her feet in one swift nervous movement, avoiding Lars' expressive blue eyes that watched her with a kind of curious pity. Her main anxiety at the moment was to escape from the room before Neil too realised what she had only now learned about herself, and she did not stop to make formal excuses, but simply murmured a few almost inaudible words, and hurried out of the room.

She could not leave Seaways until she knew Nicky was safely back with Neil, but as soon as she knew that there was no alternative for her but to go. To suppose he could feel anything but scorn for her after what had happened would be hopelessly optimistic, and she could not bear to stay, even if he allowed her to, knowing he despised her.

CHAPTER TEN

THE night had seemed endless to Rachel and she had lain in the darkness, her brain as well as her body refusing the sleep she ached for. Even the moon denied her the comfort of its light; hidden by clouds, it left her room as black as pitch while she lay and listened to the dreary rattle of rain on her window.

Even when the first chill light began to creep across the grey winter sky it found her still awake, haunted by things she had no power to change now. Neil's face was before her every time she closed her eyes—cold, angry and unrelenting. His harsh words still pricked her conscience.

Neither could she forget Nicky, alone somewhere, probably crying because there was nothing familiar and he could not understand whyRachel had not come to take him home by now. The stranger who was his father, he had disliked on sight, and she remembered how he had come running back to her that day in the grounds when Michael Browlett had appeared so unexpectedly.

Nicky had trusted her to protect him from the unknown as Neil had trusted her, and her heart thudded in despair when she realised how she had failed them both. Hidden away somewhere Nicky would be confused and frightened, and heaven knew what tortures Neil was going through, thinking about him. Turning suddenly, she buried her face in the pillows, smothering the despairing cry that rose to her lips, her only relief in tears.

There seemed to be no sound in the house when she lifted her head again, although something, she thought, had roused her from the misery of half-consciousness. Beyond the uncurtained window the light was a little stronger, though still grey and chill and darkened by clouds that scudded before an east wind that would cut like a knife. Her eyes felt swollen and tired with weeping and she could find no comfort in the dishevelled bed that she had tossed and turned in all night long—it was as well to leave it as to lie there any longer.

Moving almost unconsciously, she bathed and dressed, not caring what time it was and whether or not it was too early for anyone else to be about. There was no one at Seaways she could face in her present state. She carefully avoided looking into Nicky's room as she usually did in the morning, for he would not be in there and she could not bear the sight of his small bed bereft of its occupant.

She went downstairs, dazed from lack of sleep, and it was only when she got down into the hall that she realised she had put on a topcoat over her indoor clothes. It seemed as if some instinct had prompted her to dress for going out, to take a walk as a means of avoiding the ordeal of breakfasting with Neil and Lars and also to inject some activity into her weary limbs. There was no one about when she opened the front door, and she closed it behind her, quite unaware that she was being observed from the doorway of the kitchen.

Rachel took the longer road to the sea, for even in her present fuddled state she could realise the impracticability of trying to walk across the heavy clay of ploughed fields after last night's rain, and her appearance drew more than one curious look from early rising farmworkers as she made her way along the narrow, winding lanes to the sea.

The day was scarcely begun yet, but already she fore-saw little promise of anything but more unhappiness, and she impatiently brushed a hand across her eyes when the haze of tears briefly obscured her vision. She felt so helpless and yet there was little she could do personally about finding Nicky—the people with the experience and best qualified to search for him were already doing all they could.

Seeking some small consolation, she told herself that both Nicky and his father were good-looking enough to draw second glances, and if Nicky was as unhappy as she knew he would be his tears would almost certainly attract attention too. The prospect of him not being found did not bear thinking about, but at the moment her own misery occupied her almost as much as Nicky's did.

She must face the future without Neil, that much was certain, and even thinking about never seeing him again once she left Seaways brought the tears flooding into her eyes again. If only she could have realised sooner how much she loved him, then she could have acted differently. She could see now that Neil had offered her something very precious during those few weeks Lars had been away and she had been too blind to see it.

She shook her head, again using an impatient hand to brush away the tears, dismissing the what might have been as beyond recall—there was nothing to be done about it now. There was a slight break in the scudding clouds suddenly and for a moment she caught a glimpse of a pale ice blue sky above the grey—if only her own outlook offered as much hope she could have been happier.

Nearer the sea the wind took on an even harsher chill and she shivered as she looked across at the thick dark soil turned into neat furls by the plough. Overhead a cloud of screaming seagulls swept down, squabbling among themselves, their noise frightening off the quieter lapwings who also gleaned a harvest from the bare clods, the wind carrying their high plaintive cries to her above the chatter of the gulls.

Heaven knew why she had chosen to come this way, unless it was because Lynn Browlett was so recently in her thoughts, but somehow she felt that the grey turbulent mood of the winter sea would fit in with her own melancholy. The wind was much colder even than she had expected and she shivered as she made her way along the cliff top, her long hair whipping back from her face and her cheeks stinging with the salt-laden dampness.

Below was the narrow strip of beach where she had walked, and she shuddered when she remembered that icy drenching and how she had clung so desperately to the narrow ledge above the water until Neil came and rescued her. She had not realised then how much more painful it must have been for him than she suspected to pluck her from the same hungry tide that had killed his sister.

Poor Neil, he had had so much to face during the past few years, and now she had by her carelessness delivered him yet another blow. She had learned from Lars that Neil's father had died only a short time after Lynn ran off with Michael Browlett, and then, when her husband deserted her, Neil had given Lynn and her baby a home with him.

He had seen her through that only to have her enter into a romance with their cousin that was bound to end with someone getting hurt. And when Lynn took her dramatic way out it was Neil once again who picked up the pieces and made a home with him for Nicky. It was no wonder that he had judged her in that cold, hurt anger when she had lost him the one person in the world he really cared about.

Because she loved him she suddenly felt every hurt as if it was her own, and now that there was no one else about to see, she let the tears roll down her cheeks unchecked, but even that brought no relief. Neil would never trust her again, and she did not see how she was going to bear the hurt of leaving him.

She clenched her hands tightly in the pockets of her coat and looked down at the restless grey surface of the sea, shaking her head as the cold wind whipped her hair back and stung her cheeks like ice. At last she could identify with Lynn; she knew exactly how she had come up here to the cliff top in despair because she loved Lars too much to face life without him.

Those angry grey waters crashing against the cliff face offered an end to the agony of a life without Neil— to the bitter anguish that held her body stiff and cold against the icy wind.

Rachel was so cold that her limbs felt numb and immovable and she stirred at last, drawing a deep shuddering breath and brushing one hand across her cold cheeks where the tears had dried into her soft skin and left it stiff and dry. She had no watch with her, but she could see from the state of the tide below that she had been there for some time, just standing there on the cliff, staring down at the angry, grey cold sea and thinking about Neil.

Her feet were chill and ached with cold and her hands too, despite the comparative warmth of the coat pockets, were still and unresponsive when she tried to pull up her coat collar closer round her face. If anyone had missed her at Seaways it would be presumed she was still sleeping, and she almost wished she was. She would have given almost anything to arouse enough feeling in Neil to make him come out and look for her as he had done before.

Taking a last shuddering look at the sea crashing on to the rocks in white-foamed fury, she turned and made her way back along the cliff. The wind was now partly behind her, blowing her hair up and over her face as she walked, and she needed one hand to brush it away every few seconds so that she could see where she was walking.

It was when she cleared its long strands from her eyes that she suddenly realised that someone was coming towards her, braving the wind in the opposite direction, and for a moment her heart almost stood still when she recognised him.

There was no mistaking those long anxious strides that brought him closer with every second, or the thick blond hair blown into confusion as her own was, the features carved in golden granite above the collar of a sheepskin jacket that swung open as it almost always did. A big, awesome yet comforting figure that was coming straight for her as she stopped dead, her eyes wide and anxious in the pale oval of her face.

She tried to judge if it was anger that lent such urgency to his stride, but at a distance it was impossible to tell, and at the moment she would have welcomed even his anger as long as he was there. Trembling, she watched as he came closer and saw the drawn cold look on his face mellowed into a sudden warmth.

He said nothing at first, but she was snatched into his arms and held closely against that warm, powerful body, closing her eyes on the sheer ecstasy of it. His hands, strong and gentle, were soothing, comforting and unbelievably exciting as he slid them beneath her coat and the warm wings of his jacket enfolded her as they had done once before when they stood in that small bobbing boat below the cliffs.

He buried his face in the wind-tossed tangle of her dark hair and his voice spoke softly against her ear. "He's back, Rachel!" and for a moment she even had to stop and remember that it was Nicky he referred to.

She raised her face at last, her eyes wide and doubtful, wanting to believe she had heard him aright but scarcely daring to. She licked her parched lips and they tasted dry and salty. "Nicky?" she whispered. "Nicky's back?"

Neil nodded and the look in his blue eyes was enough to convince her that it was true. "They were found last night in a hotel in London," he told her. "The police brought him home this morning and he's already asleep."

"Oh, thank God!" She closed her eyes and for a moment she seemed to sway, even in the firm closeness of his arms., The relief she felt left her feeling incredibly weak and suddenly nothing was impossible.

Neil drew her close again, burying his face in her hair, his voice muffled when he spoke again. "And no sooner have I recovered from one shock than you give me another," he said huskily. "I wanted to tell you that they'd brought Nicky home, I couldn't wait for you to come down, and—" He laughed, and it was a short and oddly shaky sound as if he had been close to tears, "Mrs. Handley said you weren't there!"

"Oh, Neil!"

He pressed his mouth to her cheek, that short, anxious laugh fluttering against her hair again as he hugged her close. "You weren't there, Rachel—how could you *do* that to me?"

Rachel said nothing, but her fingers, stiff and cold as they were, conveyed her contrition as plainly as if she had spoken it. The softness of his sweater was warm on her palms and her fingers explored the suggestion of smooth skin beneath it, a warm sensual excitement running through her whole being as she stood enfolded in his arms.

"Mrs. Handley saw you leave the house," he told her, still in that strangely muffled voice that suggested a panic only just abated, "and I couldn't believe it at first—I thought you were still sleeping!"

"I didn't sleep," She looked up at him, the dark rings of weariness evident about her grey eyes and he bent his head and gently kissed her lowered lids. "I didn't hear Nicky come back either," she said, frowning curiously. "How could I not hear him, Neil, when he's in the next room?"

"Because he was afraid of being alone," Neil told her softly. "I put him into my bed and stayed with him until he went to sleep—I thought you were asleep too, but I would have woken you to tell you he was home. When Mrs. Handley said she'd seen you go out—"

"You knew where to find me!" Rachel guessed, but he shook his head and the arms around her held her even more tightly.

"She had misgivings, seeing you go out so early," he said huskily, "and she went upstairs to see which way you went, but she hadn't the sense to tell me, to tell somebody that you'd taken the sea road—I could have hit her!"

"Neil!"

She whispered his name, her face still pressing to the broad comfort of his chest, and Neil kissed the softness of her neck with infinite gentleness. "I was so afraid," he confessed in a whisper. "I was so afraid of what I'd find, my love!"

My love! Rachel lifted her head again and her eyes were bright and warm between the fringe of dark lashes that still looked spiky with tears. "I didn't think," she confessed. "I suppose—I suppose I thought you wouldn't care one way or the other, after what I did."

Neil looked down at her, his blue eyes never less icy-looking than now, and there was a half smile on his wide mouth that gave Rachel the urgent desire to be kissed. Instead he studied her for a long moment, his eyes searching every feature of her flushed face, lingering on her mouth in the way that sent a shiver through her.

"I could more easily have made allowances for what happened," Neil said quietly, "if only you hadn't been with Lars. That hurt more than you'll ever know!"

Rachel shook her head and her fingers stroked the soft wool of his sweater, lingering on the spot where the steady beat of his heart pulsed with life. "You just wouldn't believe I wasn't in love with Lars," she reproached him, and Neil kissed her mouth lightly before he answered.

"I didn't know what to believe, Rachel," he said gently. "I'd seen it all before and—" He stopped and shook his head. "I was so unsure. I know how—potent Lars can be be, and you admitted that you found him attractive."

Rachel traced a pattern on the thick wool seater with a fingertip and lowered lids hid her eyes from him. "He—he wanted me to go to Sweden with him," she said, and raised her eyes suddenly to look at him, her eyes bright with a hint of challenge. "*He* knew why I wouldn't go!" she told him in a small breathless voice, and Neil bent his head swiftly, his mouth hard and urgent on hers, making her catch her breath and curl her hands against the broad warmth of his chest.

Elatedly certain at last, Rachel yielded to the demands he made on her, every nerve of her body responding to the strong, gentle persuasiveness of his. The wind could have been as cold as ice, she had never felt more flowingly warm, and her heart beat wildly, uncontrollably in response to new sensations that aroused desire in her she had never thought herself capable of.

Holding her close, Neil looked down at her, saying nothing for a few seconds, his eyes once again searching her face, as if he would never tire of looking at it. "I could only think of you last night," he told her in a deep, soft voice that did incredible things to her emotions.

"Your pale little face and big eyes—I must have been blind and insane to treat you the way I did and to let you go like that. I should have comforted you and instead I was angry, angry and hurt because I knew you'd been with Lars when Nicky was taken. I didn't expect to sleep last night, but it wasn't Nicky who haunted me, it was you, and this morning when you were gone—" He shuddered and the force of it touched her own body, making her tremble. "Can you forgive me, Rachel?"

"Forgive you?" She reached up and touched his strong, rugged jaw gently with a fingertip. "I love you, and the fact that you're here now makes anything else unimportant." She lifted her face and kissed him lightly on his mouth. "I hurt you," she said softly, "but I didn't mean to. I'd never hurt you the way your sister did, Neil, you must know that."

"I know that now," he echoed. "You'd never be as foolish as poor little Lynn."

It was easier now to mention Lynn, now that Neil had spoken about her, and she looked up at him for a moment, her eyes seeking some likeness to the photograph she had seen on Lars' bedside table. "I—I saw a picture of her in Lars' room when the door was open one day," she told him. "She—you weren't very much alike, were you?"

He said nothing for a moment, then he turned her in his arms and hugged her close to him as they started to walk back along the cliff. "Lynn was only my half-sister," he said, and his voice was quiet and steady, confiding at last the way she had always hoped he would.

"She was a silly, pretty little creature, but I loved her, perhaps because of what she was rather than in spite of it. She was only seventeen when she ran off with Browlett and I suppose we could have stopped them, but—" he spread one large hand in a gesture of helplessness. "My father doted on her and it was always difficult to be angry with Lynn. Nicky's very much like her."

"I thought so," Rachel agreed quietly, and Neil looked down at her for a moment with a curiously unfathomable look in his eyes.

"You know about her and Lars?" he asked, and it was plain that even now he did not find it easy to talk about it.

Rachel nodded, hugging herself more close to him as she spoke, anxious to let him know she understood. "I know," she said. "In part you told me yourself, when you and Lars were arguing in the stable one day and you mentioned her again the day you and Lars—"

"When I warned him not to hurt you the way he had Lynn!" he said shortly, and for a moment there was a trace of that cold anger in his voice. "If he had, I'd never have forgiven him!"

"And yet you forgave him for Lynn," she suggested gently, and Neil looked at her for a moment steadily, his blue eyes dark with something that touched a response in every nerve of Rachel's body.

"I forgave him for Lynn," he agreed quietly, "but what happened was, in part, Lynn's own fault. I warned her, but she wouldn't listen, any more than she would when my father warned her about Michael Browlett. Lynn was young and very easily swept into an affair, but she wasn't as—as vulnerable as you are, my darling."

"Neil!" She turned and faced him again, drawn into the warmth of his arms again, enfolded in the strong, masculine force that shivered through her own body like fire and ice.

His blue eyes held a glistening warmth she had never seen there before and she reached up her arms and circled his neck, her fingers gently stroking the thick blond hair that curled above the collar of his jacket. "I love you," he said softly. "If I *had* lost you to Lars or to—" He glanced briefly at the cold grey tide below the cliff and shook his head. "I couldn't have faced it, Rachel, even with Nicky back I couldn't have faced losing you!"

Rachel leaned back against his arms, her grey eyes more bright than ever when she looked at him. That dear, familiar face with its deceptively stern mouth and ice blue eyes was something she would never grow tired of looking at, and she smiled suddenly. "I don't think I could have gone," she confessed. "Somehow or other I'd have found a way to stay near you—and you still need someone to take care of Nicky."

"From now on I'll take care of both of you," Neil told her, and pulled her close into his arms again, his mouth seeking hers just as that little patch of blue winter sky appeared from behind the clouds again.

Wild Inheritance
Margaret Pargeter

When a distant cousin died, leaving her his croft in Scotland, Alexa Lewis made up her mind to put her past behind her and live life to the full.

The only thing she knew for sure about her Highland property was that it was managed by a man named Fergus, whom she imagined to be an elderly transient.

Imagine Alexa's surprise when she found a proud, vital man in place of the one she'd expected, and found herself falling in love...only to discover who he really was and the sad truth of what it was he really wanted from her!

CHAPTER ONE

THE Midlands, Alexa decided with a wry grimace as she reached the definite conclusion, was a dull place to live. There was nothing to cheer one, not even the weather. March had been capricious with more dull days than fine; a regrettable state, which, if the darkness of the sky was anything to go by, did not look like improving.

She sat quite still, curled idly in her chair like a small lazy cat, contemplating it moodily from the high window of her cousin's study. Down below, on the wide playing fields, not yet brightened by the fresh greens of a bursting spring, some of the junior girls were playing netball. The P.E. teacher's piercing whistle merged and came shrilly with the sound of distant traffic.

There was a note on her cousin's desk explaining briefly that she had gone to see one of her staff and would be back in a few minutes. Alexa sighed. Her respite would be short. When Edith said a few minutes she meant exactly that! Again her eyes rested on the surging crowd of girls outside, and she knew a sudden nostalgic longing to be among them. It had always given her a curiously sensuous feeling, running against the wind, feeling it ruffle her hair, lifting the thick strands of it from her hot forehead. Down there was freedom. Here was only dull repetition, the daily round providing little cheer. Not that she had noticed so much, she was ready to confess, not until she had received the letter from Inverness! One startling letter!

Abruptly she jerked upright on her seat, her wide

almond green eyes, so often dreamy, now full of decision. This in itself was an achievement. It wasn't easy to be full of decision when one was slightly under average height and too slender to give one's words much weight. Why couldn't she have been more like Edith? Alexa wondered. Edith had such presence. She was tall and well made and the force of her personality could be felt before she even spoke.

Alexa recalled there had been occasions when she'd stood up to Edith; it wasn't impossible if one chose the right moment carefully. Now, because of changing circumstances, the time could be appropriate. There could indeed be more danger from her own uncertainty than from any opposition Edith might supply.

The measured tread of footsteps in the corridor outside warned her of someone approaching. She was not surprised when the door opened and her cousin entered. Edith Graham was a woman of some dignity, as befitted her position. Her face, in repose, was inclined towards severity, but this afternoon she wore a slight smile as if something had pleased her.

The smile faded a little as Alexa jumped to her feet, uncoiling in one swift, graceful movement from her chair, her fluid young body seeming alive with antagonistic challenge.

Inwardly Edith sighed. Sometimes the ability to cope with Alexa seemed a bit beyond her. When the girl had been younger—yes. She had always rebelled against authority, even in the schoolroom, but had not been entirely unbiddable. Amenable, Edith would admit, if she were led, not driven, but there was a reckless streak in her that needed a firm hand. She was too vividly impulsive for her own good! How she was to exercise any control in the future, Edith was at loss to think. Frank, her fiancé, might not be much help. She felt this instinctively.

Again she sighed, this time audibly, reflecting some of the impatience moving within her. Alexa was obviously still overflowing with foolish ideas. Clearly they had accumulated since their discussion yesterday morning, Edith had hoped to have heard the last of it! She was fond of the girl, how otherwise could she have tolerated her over the years? Perhaps if her parents had lived things might have been different.

All that nervous energy, that quicksilver quality, made Alexa impossible to pin down. Yet she was a pretty child, Edith confessed, and could be wholly generous, extremely affectionate. No one would imagine she could be such a handful! She was certainly too much for a dedicated career woman like herself. She would rather deal with a dozen schoolchildren, or any member of her staff.

With a despairing click she closed the door and walked quickly to her desk. No use beating about the bush. Alexa quite clearly had something to say and there would be no peace until she was allowed to get it off her chest. She flicked an inquiring glance over the tense young figure beside the window. "Well... ?" She raised resigned brows.

Alexa hesitated, startled for a few seconds. "You're looking at me rather oddly," she said.

"Stop prevaricating, Alexa," Edith kept a tight rein on her impatience. "I'm a busy woman but not completely unobservant. How can we settle down to work when you're almost choking with whatever it is on your mind?"

Alexa swallowed hard, Edith's tone was not encouraging. Then the afternoon sun, coming through a break in the clouds, lit the small room with a dazzling brilliance. It seemed like a good omen! She felt it warming her back as she squared her taut shoulders and took a deep, bracing breath. "I've made up my mind, Edith," she said defiantly. "Whether you approve or not, I'm going."

"I think I guessed," Edith retorted dryly, "so don't get hysterical about it!" Her eyes were cool on Alexa's flushed cheeks. "I had hoped you would see sense, but even so I do consider it my duty to point out the dangers of this journey you contemplate. You appear to have catalogued the delights without due regard for any of the pitfalls. Haven't I always had to be the brake for your too impulsive nature?"

From habit Alexa found herself nodding obediently. In Edith's voice lay all the authority of the headmistress of a highly respected girls' school, a role which she combined so zealously with that of a guardian and cousin. That the present situation couldn't continue didn't seem to occur to her. Apart from anything else it wouldn't be practical.

"I have appreciated," Alexa said quickly, "all you've done for me, but don't you see, probably the legacy will prove a sort of blessing in disguise. You're about to marry a wonderful man, and Frank doesn't really deserve someone like me around. I'd only get in the way."

"You've always managed to do that, my dear," Edith remarked mildly, not unkindly, "I'm used to it. I've never known anyone with such ability to be in the wrong place at the wrong time, and it scarcely seems fair to turn you loose among a lot of unsuspecting strangers."

"Ouch!" Alexa grinned, adding wryly, "It could be just what I need."

"I doubt it!" Reflectively Edith removed her aggressively large spectacles, waving them with emphasis in the air. Deliberately, it seemed, she shied away from any mention of her future husband. She was over fifty and this would be her first marriage. She didn't find her affections easy to discuss. "Occasionally, Alexa," she continued, "you make it difficult for me to believe you are twenty. You don't always look it, and with your wild ideas, I feel you are rather lacking a proper sense of responsibility."

"Cousin Edith!" It was Alexa's turn to throw up her hands, "you know that's not really on the level, and I'm not in your sixth form now!"

"You expressed yourself better when you were," Edith rejoined sharply.

Alexa ignored this, as she had taught herself to take no notice of the majority of hurtful things Edith said. Edith, after all, had given her a home and looked after her since she was five, which proved she had much more generosity of spirit than was always apparent.

"I'm sorry." From habit, more than anything else, Alexa supplied the expected apology.

"But you're still determined to ignore my advice?" Refusing to be mollified, Edith brushed Alexa's rueful words to one side, gazing at her disapprovingly.

"Not entirely." Her clear voice laced with restraint, Alexa gazed warily back. She must be careful. The situation was difficult to say the least, though on the face of it relatively simple. Yet if she didn't move carefully Edith would, before she was through, have any disadvantages exaggerated out of all proportion. "Won't you look at it this way?" she suggested softly, in her most coaxing tones. "It's very natural I should wish to visit the country where my father came from, and now I receive news that I've inherited a house. A croft, in fact! It's not such an unusual situation. Why, people are being left houses every day."

"Usually," Edith replied coldly, without flickering an eyelid, "those they are already living in, or something in the near vicinity."

"Usually," Alexa agreed, "but not always!"

"Suppose," Edith proposed inflexibly, "we start at the beginning?"

As Alexa blankly nodded her tawny head, knowing it would be useless to try and stop her, she began:

"Over fifteen years ago, my dear, when your parents died, you were but a baby, and what else could I do but take you in—bring you up? All through the long years I've concentrated on this without a thought for myself. And now what happens? A man who has never previously seen fit to look near you dies and leaves you his property; a house so remotely situated as to be, in my opinion, totally unacceptable. How is it that this distant cousin of your father's, this Angus Lewis, has never chosen to make himself known until now? It smacks of a mystery somewhere, I'm convinced, and one which might not be very pleasant and have nothing directly to do with you!"

"Oh, come off it, Edith!" Always forthright, Alexa forgot the need to move diplomatically. "I know this man has never sought me out, but maybe I should have taken the trouble to make myself known to him. To an elderly man who happened also to be a bachelor, a small child must have presented unsolvable problems."

"Not necessarily so!" Edith refused to be impressed. "I did attempt to communicate, but not once did he have the courtesy to reply in person, only through his solicitor. And then he made no bones about the matter—he wanted nothing whatsoever to do with you. He didn't so much as express one single regret, even through his man of law, regarding your dear parents. Nor has he contributed in any way, I might remind you, towards your upbringing."

"Then it must have been his conscience troubling him at the last minute," Alexa suggested, trying to be casual. Hadn't she heard the same tirade many times before, if with slight variations! And since she could hardly remember her parents, and had never once seen this far distant relation, she had long ago been able to squash the odd, niggling twinges of despair. "But," she continued with attempted lightness, "it is only one house."

"One house, my dear, and if we can believe what we're told, a good-sized one at that, can be worth an appreciable sum of money today!"

"But in the Western Highlands?"

"Especially in the Western Highlands."

"You probably think I should sell it?" Alexa asked.

"The idea," Edith declared, "had occurred to me, but of course there may be conditions. A peculiar legacy like this is often smothered in them."

"You make it sound like sauce!"

Edith's lips thinned. "Must you always be so flippant, Alexa? You must see what I mean?"

Alexa sighed, strangely unwilling to agree. "You make it sound like a beautiful cake spoilt by the wrong ingredients!"

"Which could prove extremely disappointing, and it's better to be forewarned."

"It seems," Alexa glanced at her cousin with frank admiration, "that while Angus Lewis decided he was under no obligation, you never stopped to consider such a thing. If I did sell the house," she assured Edith gratefully, "I would want you to accept some of the proceeds as—well, a sort of gift, if you like..."

"A recompense, I think, is the word you're looking for." Edith coloured with annoyance. "Really, Alexa, you would never be be renowned for tact! You know very well that I've never wished for any financial reward. Indeed my salary has always been adequate, and my future husband is not entirely penniless."

"I know..." Alexa floundered helplessly, feeling

completely witless and wondering crossly why Edith
could usually manage to reduce her to this state. If she
hadn't known better she might have suspected Edith
derived a certain pleasure from it. "I'm sorry," she
sighed with some confusion, "I didn't intend to insult
you. I'm old enough to appreciate everything you've
done. But," she went on in a little rush, "if you refuse
to accept anything, then would you really mind if I kept
the house and tried to make a living from paying
guests? I could take in bed and breakfast visitors, perhaps, to start with. Until I was properly organised."

"Good gracious!" For a moment Edith appeared
clearly at loss for words, and a startled silence reigned.

Alexa was quick to follow up her advantage. "After
all, Edith, I should imagine the house will be furnished, and the solicitor did mention an old retainer, a
servant by the name of Fergus. I should think Fergus
will have a wife around somewhere to give a hand
when required. People living in isolated places are usually grateful for employment. This Fergus—so the letter says—looks after the livestock on the croft. There
must be cows, you see, and that sort of thing. I expect
I'll have to do something about the produce. One
couldn't possibly waste gallons of milk!"

Her voice trailed off as Edith interrupted dryly. "I
imagine your average tourist will want something more
than a glass of milk. I'll admit," she nodded, "that you
cook well, but otherwise you're completely inexperienced. Since you finished your studies you've run this
flat and helped with the school secretarial work, but
this can in no way be likened to running a boarding
house."

Alexa insisted with equal dryness, "I should think,
on occasion, it would compare very well."

Recalling the amount of entertaining Edith did, the
general running about to be done, Alexa was more

than convinced that an enterprise such as she had in mind would be simple. "The solicitor in Inverness did ask me for a quick decision. Because of the livestock, maybe, but he did mention that there's someone who is keen to purchase the entire croft."

"Let them wait," Edith muttered abruptly, seemingly referring to the would-be purchaser. "I did read the letter!" Her still smooth brow creased as she leant back to gaze contemplatively at Alexa's eager face. "You could be well advised to sell, but you mustn't hurry. It might even be a good idea to see the property first, yet it would definitely be inadvisable for you to attempt the journey alone."

Edith talked as though the west coast of Scotland was some outpost in Siberia! Before Alexa could protest she continued, "Such a journey could be fraught with difficulties, as I've already pointed out. Your father's mother, your grandmother, was a Maxwell—she died, I believe, before your parents married, but there are bound to be some branches of the family left."

"Distant cousins, you mean?" Alexa asked curiously, not quite following this new line of thought.

"Yes," Edith nodded. "If there are any left I believe they will be distant cousins. I do seem to remember your mother telling me that your father's family, the Lewises, that is, were furious when he married her. Apparently they'd decided that like his father before him, he too should have a Maxwell bride."

"You mean," Alexa felt bewildered, "he was already engaged to this other girl?"

"No—at least," the crease in Edith's brow deepened slightly, "as far as I know there was no formal engagement, but according to your mother it was expected. This is why both families more or less cut him off. Certainly it was the reason why he came to England and never went back."

For a few seconds Alexa digested this in silence. Old half-forgotten, far-off things. Strange how they retained the power to hurt, even those with whom they were only indirectly connected! "You've never been so explicit before," she said at last, her green eyes dwelling somewhat warily on Edith's reflective face.

Edith straightened. "There was never the need to be," she answered shortly, giving the impression that even now to recall such an incident was distasteful to her. "I've never met any of these people myself or even heard from them. It wouldn't have served any useful purpose to have reviewed the matter annually if that's what you had in mind?"

"You don't think—or perhaps you do, that they would make trouble for me after all this time?" Alexa was unable to keep a slight nervousness from her voice. "You don't think they would harm me?"

The corners of Edith's rather thin mouth twisted. "You have a regrettable tendency to enlarge everything, my dear, but for once I'm inclined to be suspicious. The Maxwells, in your father's own opinion, by the way, were not a particularly forgiving lot. Neither was he, come to think of it. Your mother once told me that never in all the six years of their marriage could she persuade him to return."

"Yet this Angus Lewis left me his house?"

"Yes, but don't you understand what I'm trying to explain?" Edith's eyebrows lifted impatiently. "This all happened a long time ago, but old feuds sometimes die hard. Your father's people the Lewises favoured this other marriage as much as the Maxwells, and after all this time there doesn't appear to be any obvious reason for this sudden burst of generosity. It could, I grant you, be a perfectly genuine gesture; a certain quirk in human nature often drives people to do quixotic things, but at this late date I have a feeling that Angus Lewis's magnanimity could be related to something which has little to do with a young cousin whom he has never seen."

Alexa's fingers clenched in sharp dismay. What Edith said startled her. "You sound as though you're issuing a warning." She spoke tonelessly.

"I'm definitely advising you to be careful!" Edith agreed.

Several days later Edith's wedding went off without a hitch. Frank Benson, a lecturer at the nearby university, was a man of considerable private means. He was a widower with a grown-up son and daughter. The daughter was married and lived only a few miles away, but his son, Clive, a young man in his twenties, worked and lived in London.

Frank had a large house which stood in its own grounds on the edge of the town, and Edith would be very comfortable. Even so, she wasn't giving up her teaching post immediately, and insisted that Alexa could go on living in the school flat, and carry on as usual when Frank and she returned from Greece where they would be spending their honeymoon.

Alexa was undecided. She liked Frank, who was kindly and middle-aged and disposed to be fatherly, but she could think of no good reason why he should be saddled with a sort of step-cousin-in-law during the first weeks of his new marriage. And even if she was living at the flat there would be the ineitable comings and goings.

It might be easier for everyone if she went ahead with her half-formed plans to go to Invercraig. That such a chance to escape might never come again, she refused to admit had ever crossed her mind! If she did go to Scotland it must be chiefly, if indirectly, for Edith's benefit, but it would be quite wrong, Alexa felt, if she used such a motive as an excuse to further her own ends.

It was the beginning of April; Easter was early that year. The sun shone and the wedding was an undoubted success, if one could judge by the lightness of the atmosphere and the amount of champagne drunk by dozens of gaily talkative guests. All the town's best-known people were there; mostly the older set, influential and affluent. Alexa would have been deaf and blind if she hadn't been subtly aware that she herself aroused quite a bit of conjecture. They didn't ask outright, but their curiosity came over quite clearly. The poor child whom dear Edith had so kindly reared at no small sacrifice to herself—what did she intend doing with her now? It could be quite a problem!

Alexa circled in their ranks and smiled carefully, the smile becoming rather fixed as the afternoon wore on. She might have told anyone who cared to ask her directly that she had ideas of her own, but as no one did ask she never had the satisfaction of declaring she was going to Scotland. That she would refuse to be a burden any longer, to Edith or anyone else!

Yet when the time came to wave Edith goodbye, Alexa was suddenly glad such thoughts had remained unsaid. Edith looked radiant. Alexa could never remember seeing her radiant before, and wouldn't have wished for anything to spoil her happiness. A letter that she could leave, which Edith would receive later, would be more tactful. This would prevent her from worrying about anything until she and Frank returned from Greece, and by then she would probably be so involved with her marriage she would forget to be cross.

Alexa went ahead with plans for her journey very methodically. First she wrote and told Angus Lewis's solicitor she was coming. Her intention was to call at Inverness and collect the keys for the house if he had

them, which she thought he might; and he might also
have other bits of information, apart from that which
she already knew. This might be useful, and even if he
didn't have all the answers there was no harm in asking. He might just know if the Maxwells were still in
existence, and if so, were they disposed to be friendly?
If her grandmother had been a Maxwell, she had a
good excuse for inquiring! She had come to the conclusion that she must be the only Lewis left, otherwise
Angus would never have left her his property.

After much deliberation, she decided to take Edith's
car—not that it was Edith's car now, as Edith had presented her with it before she went away. Frank had
given her a brand-new one as a wedding present.

"It's old, my dear," she had patted the shabby bon-
net affectionately. "Frank tells me it would fetch very
little should I try to sell it, so you may as well have it.
You'll at least learn something of the drawbacks of running your own."

Alexa realised that Edith meant expenses. She could
drive, but had rarely been allowed the use of the car,
ancient though it might be. When she had managed to
borrow it she'd always had to put in her own petrol,
which she couldn't really afford as Edith hadn't paid
her very much. This gift, Alexa suspected, would fore-
stall any chance of her using the new model.

Which wasn't, however, a very charitable thought,
and Alexa dismissed it. She would take the old one to
Scotland and hope it would manage the mountainous
roads, the deep valleys, to say nothing of the floods and
inclement weather. She need never worry about trains
and buses if she had her own transport, and it would be
useful for all sorts of things should she decide to stay at
Invercraig.

She packed a lot of luggage; all her clothes and several packages of books, books which she had gathered

and grown fond of over the years. It made sense to take them, she considered. It was unlikely there would be television if the house was isolated, and even a radio might not be possible if reception was poor. She also took some large old pots and pans, cooking utensils which she had found stowed away in the old-fashioned larder at the flat. They would come in handy if she had ever to cater for a lot of visitors, and Edith would never use them, she knew.

When everything was completed and the flat swept and dusted, Alexa asked Clive if he would help her work out a possible route to the Highlands.

Like Edith he was doubtful but, unlike her, his doubt was tinged with a tolerant amusement. "You're sure you're doing the right thing?" he probed, feeling towards this girl whom he scarcely knew an unusual protectiveness.

Alexa smiled; it was nice of him to worry, but she wished he wouldn't. In all probability the question might only be a mere formality, but it did give the impression that she wasn't competent enough to manage on her own, which wasn't terribly reassuring to someone hoping to start up in business. "I hope I'm doing the right thing," she said brightly.

His own grin widened. Already, although he had only met Alexa at the wedding, he liked her a lot. This afternoon he had called at the flat with every intention of cultivating her friendship, and found it quite disappointing to learn that she was about to depart for regions not easily accessible to a man who must work for his living in London.

Lazily outflung in an armchair, he glanced ruefully over her, liking what he saw. She was a slender stem of a girl who seemed rather defenceless and young, younger, he would have said, than her twenty-odd years. At first glance she looked a lot less, with her narrow hips and small enticing breasts, that beautiful tawny hair and silk-like skin which he had a curious desire to touch. Her dreamy, wide-open eyes of a wonderful almond green, fringed with a density of long lashes, were set in a small, almost classically cut face, and her wide, softly curved mouth looked as though it had been painted there by the hand of an artist.

Almost he groaned aloud, knowing the pain of frustration. All that long glossy hair, those slender limbs about to slip from his grasp before he'd even held her. His mouth ached for a moment to feel the responsive pressure of hers, envying any man who would know such sublime pleasure. For all the Porcelain quality there was a wilfulness about her which evoked a positive surge of physical awareness.

"Please..." Alexa stirred a little beneath Clive's scrutiny, fearing the possibility of another lecture. If he was about to chastise her over Invercraig, then she had neither time nor inclination to listen. "I think it would be better," she explained, "if I disappeared for a while. I shouldn't like to feel I was underfoot when Edith and Frank return, and Invercraig will at least serve as an excuse."

Clive made an effort. "What will Edith do without you? I've heard," he remarked, with brutal frankness, "that you're the general dogsbody."

"Not true!" Bright spots of colour lit the pale planes of Alexa's face only to subside as quickly. "Well," she conceded, "in a way I suppose you might almost describe me like that, but my life here has been far from unpleasant."

"And who," asked Clive, not wholly convinced, "will carry on with the good work when you're gone? I expect I shall be gone myself, but I'd hate to get in the way of any repercussions when the happy couple return!"

"Really!" Alexa's wry grin contained little amusement. Clive Benson might be an exceedingly smart executive, but he cut no ice with her. He had no right to express even a veiled criticism of his new stepmother, if he valued Edith's future friendship. However, he was perhaps the type who never meant the half of what he said. "Edith," she hastened to tell him, "was considering cutting down on office staff anyway. She thinks there are too many downstairs. And she won't be relying on me to cook so many meals now that she's married, as she'll be with your father most evenings. I believe that after the summer term she'll resign. She hasn't actually said so, but I have this feeling."

"So you're leaving her in the lurch?"

Alexa laughed vexedly. "Of course not! Haven't I been explaining! I've given the matter careful thought. I owe Edith too much ever to do that, but none of us are indispensable."

"Some are more than others," he retorted enigmatically.

"I must," he said, after spending a lengthy hour poring over road routes and maps, "come and see you when you get settled in. Occasionally I take a break in August. I have a friend in the same area," he tapped the map reflectively, "who has a grouse moor. I might even kill two birds with one stone."

Alexa, who felt she was beginning to know him, was in no way impressed by his naïve wit. "I shan't have time to entertain friends," she hedged, "not my first season."

"Don't worry." Audaciously he bent to kiss her beautiful mouth hard. "I'll pay whatever it is you're charging, willingly!"

The touch of her mouth made him slightly dizzy, allied to the startled flush of anger in her cheeks. What a little innocent the girl was! Again he rebelled that fate was removing her from his immediate clutches. How rewarding it might have been to dally with her a little, to teach her to respond properly in a man's arms. Right now she was like some small, fiery kitten, but he knew instinctively that she had possibilities! "I know you'll forgive me," he grinned unashamedly as she pushed him away.

Alexa got rid of him as fast as she could while trying to hang on to her equilibrium. How dared he seize hold of her and kiss her like that, and without appearing a complete idiot, what could she do about it? Kissing nowadays seemed to be regarded like a mere hand-shake, not to be taken seriously! Yet the knot of fury in her breast was a long time abating. Her route was all marked out and she was grateful to Clive for his help, but she hoped she'd made it clear that if he ever came to Invercraig he wouldn't be welcome.

A long time afterwards Alexa wished she might have seen Invercraig first in daylight, but this was not to be. She was, she supposed, fortunate to get there in any sort of light at all as her car had broken down in Inverness and she had been delayed for almost two days. Those two days had proved agonisingly frustrating, but there had been nothing she could do about it; it didn't help that she had to wait for the most part of the first day before seeing Angus's solicitor, as he'd been called away unexpectedly in the morning, due to an emergency which he didn't explain.

Alexa had spent the morning wandering around Inverness, admiring the old town set so splendidly on the River Ness but unable to concentrate wholly on the scenic beauty. She was taut with impatience, full of apprehension, dazed to think she had actually come so far, and felt that the world was shaking curiously beneath her feet. If this was premonition she might do well to pay heed, she thought, but she refused to allow that it could be of any importance. Every new venture must be a journey of uncertainty, and to learn to accept this need not necessarily mean defeat.

Nevertheless she was glad when the hour of her appointment arrived, even though she was to be disappointed at its outcome! The solicitor had been able to tell her very little, and the useful bits of information she had hoped to glean from him hadn't been forthcoming. She had a faint suspicion that in some matters he had been deliberately obtuse, but as she hadn't exactly known what she was after she hadn't found it easy to complain.

His first expression of ill-concealed surprise when she walked into his office hadn't helped. And for no logical reason she could think of, it struck her as rather peculiar that he had immediately given her the key to Angus's house, almost as if he'd sought right away to be rid of her!

While she momentarily stared at it lying in his hand, he explained, "Naturally I took one when I was there after the funeral."

"Who has the other, then?" Alexa asked, presuming he meant that there were two.

"Fergus," he supplied briefly.

"This man Fergus..." she murmured crossly, because she felt she was starting the wrong way round. "Who is he?"

Robert Kerr rubbed his chin with thoughtful fingers. "Fergus has helped Angus over the years from time to time. He is what I suppose you would call in your part of the country a gentleman of the roads."

"You mean..." Alexa felt startled and didn't bother to hide it, "a tramp!"

"No!" he stated firmly, but without explanation, "Fergus is not a tramp."

Impatient with his deviousness, she left it at that, her mind moving on to something else. "How did my cousin manage otherwise?" she inquired.

"Extremely well," she was told, "for a man in his eighties." All of which seemed to leave her none the wiser!

"I intend to keep the house," she said then, suddenly fretful with half answers and craving something more decisive.

"I'm pleased to hear it, my dear." At this point he actually smiled a little, as if something amused him. "It's a very nice house. Very nice indeed, and there is land. I don't know what you intend doing with the land?"

"How much—land?"

"About fifty acres, but the soil is poor. You could keep the house and sell the land—that would be best."

"Oh, but I couldn't do that!" Alexa squared her slim shoulders. "I want above all things to be self-supporting, so I shall need all the land I have."

His eyes narrowed thoughtfully on her determined face, and the thread of amusement seemed persistent. "Land," he'd declared, "can be something of a burden as well as an asset, unless looked after properly. And as you're without experience, it could scarcely be made to support you."

"But it must have supported my cousin," she retorted sharply. "I believe he had very little actual cash. And I hope to acquire some experience very quickly," she had finished grandly.

"Angus lived off the croft to a certain extent," the man agreed cautiously.

"And I presume," she supposed, "he would have some sort of pension."

Mr. Kerr had nodded unhappily, moving on to other formalities quickly with the slightly harassed air of a

man not quite sure of his ground. Alexa's slender
body, her general appearance of fragility did nothing to
convince him he was acting for the best in not advising
her to go straight back where she came from.

Alexa wasn't kept long, but she arranged to see him
again a month later when there would be more papers
to be signed and further details to be discussed. This
would give her time, he advised, to find out if she
really wished to keep the property, an observation she
hadn't felt able to argue with without seeming rude.

She had come north through Perth, Pitlochry and
Aviemore, and this afternoon, after lunch, she had left
Inverness and travelled west. Clive's route had proved
extremely reliable, but as she progressed deeper into
the Highlands the land had grown wilder. It was a
lonely land with icy-looking streams and rivers, not yet
warmed by a summer's sun, that tumbled through
green and wooded glens backed by high mountains,
and, as she went further westwards, they ran into the
wild sea lochs which bit deeply into the solitary terrain.

Greatly taken by it, she had lingered too long in
some of the more spectacular places. Now, as she came
to Invercraig, which in spite of her good map she found
more by chance than anything else, it was almost dark.
Too dark for her to see more than the faint outline of a
house which appeared to be crouching across the road a
few hundred yards from the sea. Apprehensively she
stumbled from the car to stare at it. Nowhere could she
see a light. Not that this was to be expected, but if this
man Fergus was around she had thought there might
be some sign of him.

It seemed to take a great deal of courage, more than
she had thought possible, to pull herself together, to
nerve herself to walk over the heathery grass towards
the croft.

CHAPTER TWO

ALEXA advanced towards the croft cautiously, pausing
with every other step to gaze around. Not, she told herself firmly, that there was anything to be nervous
about, but it was better to be prepared. Prepared for
what, she wasn't quite sure, but through the gathering
darkness the house with its small, lifeless windows
looked anything but welcoming!

Antagonistic might have been the appropriate word.
As if the spirit of the house resented her. A cat—she
was sure it was a cat—went hunting along the top of the
wall on her right, crouching low on the stone, its fur
blown back, pausing every now and again, head lifted.
What prey was it seeking, or did it search for a mate?
Another cat, any cat—cats were never fussy. Not like
herself, who had never found a man who would do.
Hard to please, Edith had called her, and maybe she
was right, although she would have said this was a peculiar time to think about it.

Panic suddenly gripped Alexa hard, along with the
knowledge that if she was almost shaking with fright it
was entirely her own fault for arriving at this time of
night. Her wits must have deserted her! How much better to have waited and come in the morning.

Such regrets, however, were fleeting. Whatever else
she lacked it was not courage. Turning her head
slightly, her hair streaming behind her in the wind, she
could smell the earthy, musty fragrance of peat blend-

ing smoothly with the salty tang of mist borne from the sea. If she was to stay here she must get used to the darkness, to learn to ignore the strangely fey atmosphere which could distort reality, building upon the imagination until one had little sense left.

She made her way slowly to the entrance and stood outside the solid front door. She had had the sense to come equipped with a large torch, but when she tried to switch it on, to her dismay it wouldn't work. Try as she might, no amount of fiddling would make it work, and as the darkness deepened, she was aware of the rising wind, of the first twinge of real fear.

Her nostrils contracted against the sickly fear of it as it held her in relentless bonds. Robert Kerr had mentioned that there was a generator which produced electric current, and that Fergus would show her where it was, but quite obviously there was no Fergus here. The swift impatience which was one of her faults brought with it a little anger, dispersing some of the quivering apprehension, allowing more normal breath.

Why had nothing gone right? What had she done to deserve any of this? First her car, then the torch, now Fergus! A mere tramp—who had chosen not to be here when he must have had a good idea she was coming! Apart from the fact that Robert Kerr had assured her that Fergus was fully conversant with the terms of Angus's will, she had read that in the Highlands people always knew of these things. So he had no excuse!

Maybe inside she might find a candle and matches— Angus must surely have kept a good supply. Swiftly, cross with herself for not thinking of it sooner, Alexa found the key and inserted it in the lock. Unfortunately it wouldn't move an inch.

"Oh, damn!" she cried aloud, softly furious as she tried unsuccessfully again and again before being finally forced to give up. This key and lock had never been made for each other! Although the lock was rusty this much was obvious. The silly solicitor must have given her the wrong key. His office was probably stuffed with them—the property of his unfortunate clients!

Almost weeping with frustration, she was about to turn away to seek other temporary accommodation, when from one of the buildings behind the house, she saw a light. Astonished, she gazed, feeling herself all the time growing colder. A few minutes ago such a sight might have brought comfort, but now for some reason there was none to be found in the flickering yellow glow. There was only an absolute, terrifying chill, a morbid fear of what she might find should she choose to investigate.

What might be lurking in the barn? Suddenly, as Alexa stared blindly, the humour of the situation struck her and slightly hysterical laughter rose in her throat. It helped a little, although it did not entirely release the tension which seemed momentarily to paralyse her limbs.

Really! It was probably only this man Fergus after all! Very likely he had been sitting there for hours waiting for her as she had been expecting him to. He might have fallen asleep—that light could never be strong enough to read by—but there was only one way to find out!

Yet as she carefully groped a path across the rough yard, Alexa's newly found courage seemed to leave her. It was uncanny, the wayward surge of her devastating imagination, and everywhere was the intensely creeping darkness! The very air seemed sharper, and the wind stung her face as it went about its business. She could hear it moving over the lowering rooftops, searching out the loosened lintel, the creaking hinges, moodily stirring the deep patterns of shadow. Not even

the fleeting breaks in the clouds offered comfort as any
filtering traces of light seemed to increase rather than
detract from the general eeriness of the atmosphere.

Again she felt an instinctive fear which refused to be
banished, a fear that sent small tremors through her
whole body and accelerated her heartbeats until they
seemed to be drumming in her ears. Fine perspiration
broke out on her brow as she thought with swift longing of the relative safety of the flat at school. Placed as
it had been next door to the married caretaker's accommodation, it had never been lonely as this place was
lonely. A croft on some wild Scottish moor, its one
companion the restless, pounding sea!

The light still flickered against the dusty pane and,
entirely it seemed of their own volition, Alexa's feet
were guiding her towards it. Anything was better, she
decided, than just to stand staring at it. Fergus probably
slept in the barn if he didn't have his own cottage—if
he was a tramp this was quite possible.

The barn door creaked when it was pushed open, but
she neither heard it nor was actually aware of what she
was doing. Her hands felt clammy and she could feel
herself trembling from head to foot. As the door
moved she could see nothing at first through the dim,
cobwebby interior. Above her as she crept tentatively
forward were ancient beams, beneath her feet the
brown crunch of old bracken or straw, and overall the
musty, faintly repulsive smell of old, crumbling buildings.

Then, in the feeble flicker of yellow lantern light,
she saw the tall figure of a man. He had his back towards her and appeared to be tending some cattle
which were standing against the opposite wall. To her
angry astonishment it appeared he had known she was
there, as before she could speak he spoke himself,
without having even the courtesy to turn around.

"If you've lost your way," he said curtly, "I'm afraid I can't help you. There's a hotel some twenty miles down the road. At this time of the year no doubt they'll appreciate your custom."

Alexa's voice caught in her throat and for a brief space of time words evaded her. The tremors attacking her limbs accelerated, but there was something else, born from the sight of him, something she didn't understand. There was a sense of inescapable disaster, enough to throw her completely off balance. It was like the finger of fate touching her and she shivered. All of which seemed curiously incomprehensible as she couldn't properly see his face, only the shadowed outline of him, broad and bulky with the loose clothes he wore. His voice smote her deeply with his soft yet crisp overtones which spoke of an alert mind—one which didn't tolerate fools gladly, or girls who wandered in the dark of the night! He wouldn't stop to consider that she might be here by right.

Unexpectedly she felt a saving impatience. "I presume," she cried on a funny little gasp, "that you're Fergus? Didn't you hear my car?"

The effect of her words was gratifying, if slightly confusing. The man turned, not quickly, but there was something in the stiffening of his body that expressed a certain wariness. He hesitated for one breath-stopping moment before sticking the long fork he was holding in a pile of fodder, and came a few steps nearer. Even in the bad light Alexa could see the glitter of his eyes as they focused upon her. He didn't appear to have heard her first question but answered her second.

"In this part of the world, ma'am," he drawled, "cars that stop at night are commonplace. If I ran each time such a thing occurred I would get little else done. I can only repeat—if it's accommodation you're after I'm afraid you'll have to go further. We don't take visitors here."

"But I'm not a visitor!" Wildly her voice rose, even to her own ears slightly hysterical. Why did he pretend not to understand her? His face looked dark and harsh, coldly menacing, oddly frightening. His eyes, fixed on her face, were unfathomable, full of a peculiar aversion. He was sinister—evil—too big! Her thoughts reeled on drunkenly as her mind grappled with the full extent of her predicament. This man was a tramp, and what did anyone know of a tramp? He could be a monster, a wicked unprincipled monster, with a strength far in excess of her own!

In that instant Alexa's nerve broke, and with a little cry she broke away from him. She must flee before he caught her. She could feel his intense dislike, the taut flick of his leashed control. Fine tremors were hitting her again, lending wings to her feet as she stumbled for the door.

Renewed panic struck her when she couldn't find it. Where was it, the door she had entered only a few minutes ago? It couldn't just disappear. Desperately she tried to focus. She was going crazy! There was the window. Frantically she leapt towards it like some small trapped animal.

"What the devil do you think you're doing?"

His shout rang through her tortured head as she tried to reach the window, beating at the glass with her small clenched fists. There was a soft explosion of wrath as he came up behind her, catching her dazed, swaying body from the imminent danger of the broken pane. "Stop it," he said, "or I'll hit you!"

She blamed his words for the pain that struck her together with his exclamation as he grabbed her hand. Imprisoned in his, blood flowed, and there was something which he said beneath his breath, something she didn't quite catch but didn't like the sound of. "I repeat," he added in a low, furious voice, "if you don't stop behaving like a young imbecile I'll hit you. And don't think I'm joking!''

Alexa didn't! She was trapped and she knew it; held tightly in his arms and so terrified she was almost fainting. His arms were hard, too strong to allow any possible escape, and as if to punish her for such inexplicable behaviour they tightened, pressing her to him until they hurt more than her hand did. Every button on his jacket seemed to bite into her skin as he held her against him, lifting her with easy strength as with an expert flick of his fingers he doused the lantern, leaving them completely in darkness.

"Dear God," she prayed silently, "what will happen now?"

Her voice, when it did come, was little more than a whisper but she was scarcely conscious of it. "If you don't put me down," she gasped, "I'll go straight to the nearest police!"

He took not the slightest notice—if he even heard her he made no reply. Certainly he made no attempt to do as she asked. There came the bang of the barn door, the coolness of wind on her burning cheeks, a swift, nightmare journey which she thought might have no end. She continued to struggle, to scream hysterically against his chest, but to no avail. It was like pitting her strength against a mountain, fighting elements beyond her experience in some wild, barren land.

Sheer fright made Alexa imagine she was about to lose her senses, but before she was completely overcome she heard another door opening and was aware of a bright, flooding light. It beat upon her closed eyelids, keeping her momentarily helpless in his arms.

Then she felt herself lowered into a chair none too gently, and heard him speaking to her, this time with a surprising patience in his voice, and not unfriendly.

"If you would care to open your eyes, young lady,

you would see I'm not quite the monster you imagine."

For a moment she did not move or speak, and his hands left her with a shrug of broad shoulders. She sat perfectly still, clinging to the chair, trying to steady her still trembling body, to gather some semblance of composure. She had been terrified when captive in his arms, but now she looked desperately bereft, like a tortured child, overreacting.

"Stop it, girl!" He had left her for a few moments and now he was back, a glass in his hand, and thrust it into hers. "Drink it up," he ordered, as her eyes flew open. "You certainly seem to need it, then we'll have a quick look at the damage."

As her hand clutched the weak drink of whisky and water they looked at each other fully for the first time. Alexa's eyes were enormous, the pupils enlarged by tension, a fluid, iridescent green. Dressed in a thin shirt and flared slacks she sat staring up at him, experiencing a swift moment of breathlessness which she told herself must be the aftermath of panic. "Thank you," she whispered, because there didn't seem to be anything else to say.

He gave her a faint, pitying smile as he surveyed her from his great height, evidently deciding to be tolerant with her. Not, in any case, apparently intent on attacking her person as she had feared. That was, his expression said as if reading her quivering thoughts too plainly, something to be ashamed of. "What would I want," he murmured, "with a child like you?"

The accompanying mockery came over quite clearly as she continued to stare at him without supplying an answer, if indeed, he expected one. She had known he was tall, but hadn't taken in the dark and forceful presence of the man. She had somehow got the impression from Robert Kerr that Fergus was elderly, but this man was fairly young; in his thirties, perhaps, not more. Of course, she remembered, he hadn't actually agreed he was Fergus, although who else could he be? Hadn't he been tending the cattle and carried her in here, obviously having the right key!

She blinked, bright colour staining her cheeks, wanting to ask again but not daring to. How, exactly, was a tramp supposed to look? Her eyes travelled slowly, unconsciously down the length of him. He wore a pair of shabby trousers and an equally shabby jacket, but she recognised his clothes had a cut about them that couldn't be bought off the peg. There was, she supposed, nothing wrong with being a tramp—it could merely be an expression of the freedom sought by many. Those who attempted to explore the world in small boats, people who forsook their homes for caravans, and many like herself who searched for freedom and adventure in the few odd acres. Most must be tramps at heart, if not in reality, searching for ever for an earthly El Dorado.

The man might beg his clothes, only she couldn't imagine him doing this. There was an element of pride in the set of his shoulders, the line of his jaw, the stubborn squareness of his chin. He had an air of authority about him, a dominating power not usually found, she was certain, in a "gentleman of the road".

He turned from her, unhurried in his own close scrutiny, but as he noticed her bright colour fading, his glance dropped to her hand. He went to a cabinet in the corner, taking from it a small roll of bandage and a bottle of disinfectant which he sprinkled in some water in a bowl which he carried back to Alexa's side.

"Better to be safe than sorry," he grunted, regarding the cut on her hand with a scarcely flattering indifference as she glanced at it, frowning.

"It's nothing to make a fuss about," she retorted

stiffly. And, indeed, there didn't appear to be. The cut, when more closely examined, turned out to be little more than a scratch, although it was bleeding slightly.

Again indifferently he sat down beside her, balancing the bowl on his knees while he reached for her hand which he immersed ruthlessly in the water, totally disregarding what she said. "Even a scratch, if neglected, can turn septic, and that window is far from clean."

"Which isn't exactly my fault," she cried, rather foolishly.

"Just about the most stupid remark I've ever heard!" His jaw clamped tight as he threw her hand back in her lap, followed by a clean towel. The bowl he carried back across the room, tipping the contents down the old stone sink in the corner. The angle of his head spoke volumes!

Coping with the towel and bandages with her left hand wasn't easy, especially when the atmosphere seemed steeped in disapproval. "All right," she choked, "I do apologise, but if you cared to use a little imagination you might understand how frightening it is to arrive at a place like this and find everything in darkness. You could at least have left a light burning!"

"I could," he replied, coolly, "if I'd known you were coming, but the houses up the west coast are not expected to act as sort of inland lighthouses for lost tourists."

"You deliberately misunderstand!"

"And you don't choose to be very explicit."

There wasn't much to be gained by staring indignantly into those curiously light grey eyes, but for a moment Alexa attempted to do so, before her own dropped in some confusion to her now stinging fingers. She didn't seem to have the right kind of strength to fight him, and for the time being at any rate, it might be wiser to pretend to be more acquiescent than she was naturally. Undoubtedly, after probably having much of his own way with Angus, he resented her presence, but it was an attitude she didn't care for. However, if she was to stay here she would need to familiarise herself with the place completely before dispensing with his services, and for the meantime it might pay her to restrain her temper, to keep her withering opinions to herself.

She gave a faint sigh, as if the effort of rational thought had exhausted her, and hearing it, his tautened mouth relaxed slightly an he came towards her, a strip of plaster in his hand. "This might be better than that," he said quietly, taking the bandage from her and expertly applying the adhesive. "I didn't see it on the unit when I came in."

There was an unexpected note in his voice and she turned her head, her eyes touching his well-shaped mouth, feeling again a peculiar, unexplainable sensation going through her—she remembered she had felt it first in the barn. And for no explainable reason her lips trembled suddenly and she felt almost ready to cry.

"Cheer up," he said lightly, and as she glanced at him, startled, she saw how the lamp gilded his bold, decisive profile.

Her own smile came rather tremulously as he regarded her neatly finished hand. "Thank you, Fergus, I suppose I was rather silly."

He ignored this. "Leave it," he said. Then, more slowly, "Would you mind telling me how you come to know my name? Just as a matter of interest."

"Robert Kerr told me."

"Robert Kerr!" His light eyes narrowed over her as full comprehension struck. As his eyes roamed her vivid young figure, the loosened hair which floated around her shoulders, the breakable fragility of her bones. "Good God!" he exclaimed, on his feet in a trice, towering over her, "You can't mean you're the new owner—Angus's cousin!"

"I am!" Because of the mocking disbelief in his voice her own rose defensively. "He told me," she went on, knowing an irresistible desire to annoy, "that you work here, when you aren't—er—tramping the roads."

"He did, did he!" His exclamation was abrupt, if not so sharp as before. Somewhere, Alexa felt it instinctively, there was a note of caution, but so fleeting as to be gone before she could really decide if it had in fact existed. Heavy lids instantly hooded his eyes, precluding any clues, and there was nothing to be gleaned from his hard, handsome face. "It sounds," he said, grey eyes glinting, "as though you've discussed me pretty thoroughly. What I can't understand is why he allowed a girl like you to come here alone. Or, indeed, to come here at all?"

Alexa clenched her good hand up into a tight ball and took her time in replying. Really, the man had a nerve! "You don't imagine," she smiled coldly, "that he could stop me? I do happen to own this place now. Perhaps," she rushed on, incurably reckless, "you're disappointed at being left out of his will?"

He seemed to consider this with a hint of inward surprise, and to her astonishment he actually nodded his head. "I was disappointed," he conceded, "but not in the way you're thinking. As for his will—well, I had no idea he'd made one until after he died. It was only then that I learned he had left his entire property to someone called Alexa Lewis, but again I hadn't the slightest notion you would be like this."

His tone suggested a lot of things which were far from flattering and she felt a growing dislike. "I can't see that you have any right to criticise, Fergus," she said impetuously. "After all, it's not as though I intend depriving you of your job. You can stay for as long as you like, or until I'm able to do without you."

"How very magnanimous of you, Miss Lewis," his voice drawled sarcastically. "You'll never be able to do that, so get that straight!"

Her head went back against her seat with a returning flicker of the fear she'd known earlier. "You aren't by any chance threatening me!" she spluttered, with rather a marked lack of dignity.

He considered her flushed face for a brief second. "Let me put it this way, Miss Lewis," he answered suavely. "You could never manage on your own in a place like this. How old are you? Sixteen?"

Her temper rising, Alexa glared at him. Drat all men! Hadn't Clive Benson asked much the same thing? "My age," she replied, "has nothing to do with you, but you can rest assured I am more than sixteen."

"I'm not wholly convinced," he taunted, not waiting for an answer before putting another question. "You surely don't intend staying here by yourself?"

"Why not?"

He came nearer, standing over her, mildly exasperated, with the air of a man attempting to explain something to a deliberately dense child. "Why not, indeed! Apart from the many other considerations, do you know anything at all about running a croft?"

"Not yet," said she.

"Well, then...?"

"My chief preoccupation will be in running this house as a small hotel," she informed him, her chin tilting smugly, "while yours, for the time being, will be to assist in the smooth running of the land. I hope to become almost completely self-supporting. And you can rely on it that I have the wherewithal to pay your wages."

For one heart-stopping moment she thought she had
gone too far. There was a blaze of something in his face
which betrayed a fine fire within, yet when he spoke his
voice sounded almost normal, although his words
seemed to have an uncomfortable depth. "I suppose,"
he shrugged, "you expect me to be grateful?"

Alexa swallowed, finding her high-handed demeanour a little difficult to retain. "I'm glad," she croaked
uncertainly, "you have no objection."

She noticed he didn't answer directly, "I suggest,
Miss Lewis, that it might be better to wait until morning before making any more irrevocable decisions. By
which time you might have reconsidered."

"After spending a night in a strange house? Really,
Fergus, you are transparent! You'll find I don't scare so
easily."

The suspicion that he had a temper wasn't this time
wholly imaginary! Alexa quivered, acknowledging her
unusual bad manners even while she regretted them.
But a girl, she felt, would have to be a little pertinacious
with this man, otherwise she would go under. He was
not a man to take notice of gentler qualities. It would be
better to start as she meant to go on with Fergus.
"What is your other name?" she asked quickly, her
pulse jerking oddly as his face darkened.

He opened his mouth, then his jaw clamped. "Never
mind," he said.

"How do you mean—never mind?" His voice was
quiet and for a moment, imagining she had subdued
him, she felt quite elated.

"I don't have one." His eyes seemed to be challenging her, leading her on. "Maybe," he suggested, "I've
forgotten. Being a tramp, you see, I don't happen to
need one. I'd be much obliged if you'd just content
yourself with Fergus."

Which seemed quite ridiculous, but indisputably his

right if he so wished, although there must be certain legal matters that demanded his full name. Didn't he pay tax?

"I shouldn't worry any more tonight, Miss Lewis," he was saying softly. "Rather than sit here arguing it might be wiser if you went to bed. After a good night's rest you might feel different about a lot of things. I'll see you in the morning."

"Oh—wait a minute," Alexa heard herself crying as to her dismay he turned and made for the door. As he halted, still with his back towards her, she stammered, "There are several things I must know. You can't just walk out on me like this! What, for instance, do I do for a light?"

Still without turning completely he indicated the old-fashioned lamp on the table and the torch which he had switched on when they first came in. "You can make do with these tonight," he said smoothly.

"But," she protested unevenly, "I was led to believe there was a generator?"

"When it works."

The man was infuriating! "You mean—it's not working at the moment?"

"No."

"Why not?" Again she felt her temper rising as she jumped to her feet. "You must have had a good idea that someone would be arriving."

His shoulders tensed, and although she couldn't see his face, she imagined his hard mouth tightened. "You're quite wrong there, Miss Lewis," he replied curtly. "I was led to believe that the new owner was possessed of a little sense and was prepared to sell the place, not to arrive in the middle of the night with her head full of hare-brained notions." As Alexa gasped speechlessly, he continued, "As for the generator, I am not prepared to start at this hour repairing a contraption which should have been pensioned off years ago.''

"Then tell me," Alexa almost shouted, stung to a fine fury by his effrontery, "what I'm to do!"

He laughed—a hard ring of laughter. "Why ask me? I'm afraid, Miss Lewis, that if you choose to come like this then you must be prepared to put up with some inconvenience. But I'm sure, with your agile tongue, you'll be more than able to cope. Now goodnight!''

Indifferently, before she could attempt to stop him again, he left. Was gone, without giving her a chance to ask about the house. Where he might advise her to sleep? She had hoped to learn where he slept himself if he had waited!

Trying to check her indignant thoughts, she sat down again despairingly. She felt suddenly tired and deflated. Far from being able to cope, as Fergus so audaciously suggested, she felt more like bursting into tears. Biting her lip sharply, she tried to pull herself together, and stared around the large, stone-floored kitchen reluctantly. There was something rather frightening at being alone in a strange house at night. In spite of Edith's warnings she hadn't thought the croft would be so lonely. Magazines usually showed several such holdings placed only a few hundred yards apart.

. Of course she could have neighbours. She hadn't asked Robert Kerr or Fergus, and it was too dark to see. Somehow she must manage to conquer her fears and get through this first night. This alone, Alexa was convinced, would be an achievement in itself. If she fled now she might never find the courage to return. Besides, surely Fergus would be sleeping in the barn? Although she didn't like the man, such a thought brought a positive surge of comfort.

Maybe she ought to have requested he slept in the

house? But no...if he had been the elderly servant with a wife as she had expected, then perhaps. But Fergus was not particularly old, and she would have to be extremely insensitive not to guess that he could be very human if he chose! There seemed no point in inviting trouble, even if he considered her a mere child.

So immersed was she in speculative contemplation of the formidable Fergus that she almost jumped out of her skin when she felt something furry brushing against her leg. Rats! was her first panic-stricken reaction as she leapt from her seat.

She looked down, and relief drowned terror, bringing helpless laughter as she saw it was only a cat, possibly the same one she had noticed earlier on the wall. It could have come in when Fergus went out. Whether or not it was the same one she couldn't really tell, but it seemed disposed to be friendly in spite of the abrupt way she had sent it spinning, and it advanced towards her again, purring diligently.

"Poor puss," Alexa said aloud, stooping to pick it up. "Don't you enjoy being here on your own? Perhaps like me you're lonely?" Straightening, she hugged the small grey cat to her. It wasn't exactly an object of beauty, but it probably had a nice nature. Gently she stroked the soft fur and the purring increased in volume until she was sure the small body would never contain it. "Wait a minute," she spoke soothingly, putting the small cat carefully down. "No doubt, like myself, you're hungry? Shall we see what we can find?"

Milk, she decided, glancing around her, would satisfy a cat's needs, but she doubted if Invercraig boasted a daily delivery. Come to think of it, hadn't Robert Kerr mentioned a cow? There was no sign of either a bottle or bowl of milk anywhere in the kitchen units or pantry, nor were there any tins. She had thought Angus might have kept a tin of evaporated milk for emergencies, but there was none to be found.

It was then that she remembered the small bag of provisions which she had dropped by the door of the house before going to investigate the light in the barn. There were only a few things, but enough, she hoped, to make a meagre supper and a cup of tea in the morning, when she would find the nearest shop and purchase more.

It was then that she discovered that the door leading outside from the kitchen was quite different from the one she had tried to open previously, so there was nothing for it but to grab the torch and creep outside. The cat came with her, not seeming to want to let her out of its sight, but Alexa felt uncommonly grateful for its company. The bag was still where she had left it, and clutching it to her she quickly returned to the house, not willing to stay in the windy darkness any longer than was necessary. Her courage had been sadly depleted by her former adventures in the barn.

It seemed hours later before she managed to get a fire going in the kitchen grate, and a kettle boiled. In her search for gas or some other form of heating, she had been no more successful than when she had looked for milk. The fire took time, and the kettle even longer to boil, but while she waited she fed the cat and arranged some crockery on the kitchen table. She had bread and butter and cheese, with an apple and a huge mug of tea made with tinned milk and two tea-bags.

Afterwards, strangely replete, she made up the fire. There was wood which she found in a cupboard and some pieces of peat. In the corner beside the fire there stood an old wooden settle, on which were a few large, soft cushions, and it was here that Alexa decided to spend the night. Somehow she couldn't bring herself to venture through the rest of the house until the next day. She hated to admit she still felt nervous, but this was something she was reluctant to do. It would be awkward with one hand, she told herself, to traverse unfamiliar corridors in the dark clutching a lamp. Fergus's remarks, should she accidentally set the house on fire, would, she imagined, be more scorching than the blaze itself!

So she washed her face as best she could with her good hand and, after running a comb through her long tawny hair, settled down by the now cosy hearth. She covered herself with a large rug which she found in what appeared to be the linen cupboard, as it was full of an assortment of sheets. The rug was old, but warm and thick, and the little cat crept up beside her, again proving curiously comforting.

The wind moaned and blew against the window outside as wearily she half-closed her eyes, watching the flames light up the sooty chimney breast in a galaxy of colours from dull red to bright gold. A piece of wood cracked sharply and she thought of Fergus with a mixture of a dozen muddled emotions. Her heart gave a quick lurch which she didn't fully understand. If he was a tramp he was an odd one! All that sardonic ill-humour—such steely strength. They would never do well together, she was sure of that! He certainly hadn't welcomed her warmly. Indeed, at some unfathomable level she felt she was about to fight a duel—one which she seemed instinctively to know she had little hope of winning.

The small cat stirred on the rug and Alexa felt a wave of irritation sweep over her. Wasn't it foolish to consider a battle lost almost before it had begun? Not that she had any intention of fighting Fergus. As the new owner of the croft it was she who must do the dictating—if she stayed!

"Poor pussy," she whispered to the comical little

cat, rubbing its soft ear with her finger. "You'd like me to stay, wouldn't you, even if Fergus doesn't?"

She giggled a little at her own peculiar joke, yet could feel no answering laughter in her heart. Would she ever feel at home here? she wondered, gazing more soberly around the low-beamed old kitchen as the firelight painted weird shadows on the walls. She doubted it, but in spite of her uneasiness she would have been surprised to learn how quickly she fell asleep.

CHAPTER THREE

THERE was a mouse in the woodpile outside the back door. At least Alexa thought so when she woke next morning and hobbled to the window, her limbs quite sore and stiff from sleeping on the hard wooden bench. The cushions, which had acted as a sort of padding, had apparently fallen to the floor during the night, and she had suffered accordingly. However, there would be other, proper beds upstairs, which would eliminate any necessity to sleep down here another night.

It seemed that her companion the small grey cat had not been very comfortable either, as it was already up, sitting on the heap of logs a short way across the grassy yard. For a few minutes she watched it crouched in sphinx-like silence, its sharp eyes riveted on a tunnel in the wood. Was it searching for its breakfast, she wondered, or merely providing evidence that, as a working cat, it was worth its keep?

Alexa yawned and turned away from the window, having no wish to witness the ultimate outcome, and rubbed her good hand wearily over her eyes. She wasn't usually so tired at this time of the morning.

Then suddenly, as her head cleared, she wondered with startled surprise how the cat happened to be there. The door, she was sure, had been firmly closed and locked, and the key reposed on the kitchen table. It was all very confusing—unless there was a hole in the wall or something which she had yet to discover.

Bewildered, she picked up the key, and made for the door. Then, to add to her confusion, in the small inner passage between the two doors, she found a whole pail of milk. Only then did she realise what must have transpired. Fergus—it could surely be no one else—had another key. Hadn't he used it to get in the previous evening when he'd carried her from the barn? It seemed obvious he had come in with the milk, and perhaps heard the cat crying and let it out. In doing so he must have seen her lying inelegantly on her hard couch! Alexa felt her cheeks growing hot as she thought about it—as she imagined his derisive appraisal, his amusement over a girl who had been too scared to seek a more conventional bed in the dark! He would undoubtedly be full of caustic remarks which she might be forced to listen to soon.

As it happened, it was to be sooner than she expected. Scarcely did she have time to close the door when, without so much as a knock or any kind of warning, it was thrust open again and there he stood! Having but reached the table, Alexa turned and stared, unable immediately to gather her scattered wits. He came in like a cold blast of mountain air, far larger and more calculatingly masculine than she seemed to remember. His darkness, combined with a sort of—presence, took her breath away in an unreasonable fashion, one which she didn't appreciate, not being used to being affected one way or another by a man.

"Good morning," she managed, with commendable poise considering her inner discomfiture. "I didn't," she added, with excessive emphasis, "hear you knock."

He grinned, not apparently much put out by her disapproving tone, or her equally unenthusiastic expression as her eyes slid over his unshaven chin which jutted at an angle more derisive than her own. "You must excuse me," he said dryly. "When I looked in before you were fast asleep. I wasn't aware you were up. Actually I brought a few things and intended cooking myself some breakfast. A man doesn't work well on an empty stomach."

"Neither does a woman," she retorted coolly, making a somewhat belated attempt to do up the buttons of her thin shirt which must have come undone during the night. Only his wandering, speculative scrutiny had drawn her attention to it. "If you'll excuse me," she spluttered, her cool deserting her, "I'm going upstairs to wash!" Had he really intended eating breakfast more or less over her unconscious body? How did one weigh up such a man?

He made no reply as she stumbled from the kitchen, but before she turned she noticed the indifferent quirk at the side of his mouth. As her eyes dwelt momentarily on his mouth her pulses jerked unreasonably and she sought distraction in objectivity. Really, those trousers! They looked as though he might have slept in them. But, as she ran quickly up the shallow flight of stairs, she glanced ruefully down at her own. Perhaps it was a case of the kettle calling the pot black. Her own were just as untidy and creased through wearing them all night, but at least she didn't make a habit of it.

So far as his trousers went, there were sure to be a few old pairs which had belonged to Angus. If the size was all right perhaps she might offer them to Fergus when she knew him better? From the glint in his eye it struck her that he wasn't a man to accept anyone's cast off clothing, but she could always try. At first she must go carefully and try to remember Rome wasn't built in a day. Still, at school she had learnt to exercise a little tact.

It took longer than she had expected to wash, as first she had to find the bathroom, then it was necessary not

to wet her cut hand. Not that it was anything to fuss
about, but this morning it was throbbing uneasily and
might prove to be a nuisance if she didn't take care.

The bathroom, which she found without difficulty as
the door stood open, was a small cubicle at the top of
the stairs. Like the kitchen it seemed old-fashioned and
boasted only cold taps. How on earth did one manage
for a bath, she wondered, glanced with some dismay at
the rather antiquated bath, and made a mental note to
ask Fergus in one of his more approachable moments.

Having finished her toilet as best she could she ran
down again, regretting as she tried to smooth the
creases from her shirt that her luggage was still in the
boot of her car. It seemed incredible that she'd forgotten all about her car last night, let alone the luggage! If
she asked Fergus nicely he might bring it in for her.
This would be a great help—if he agreed. It would give
her time to get settled in, to explore the house properly.

Back in the kitchen she was surprised to find Fergus
frying bacon on the stove. "You must be brighter than
I am," she smiled appreciatively, "I could find no food
last night, nor could I get the cooker to work when I
wanted to boil some water."

He lifted his head to glance consideringly at her now
morning-fresh face, at her long fair hair neatly coiled at
her nape, the tawny colour of it contrasting so beautifully with her soft green eyes. His eyes narrowed
slightly, lingering on her rose-pink lips, parted tentatively in a slightly nervous smile. "The bacon, Miss
Lewis," he explained at last, "was in the second larder
over there, and the cooker is operated by Calor gas
which you probably forgot to switch on."

Alexa flushed as she surveyed the sizzling pan in
which three yellow-yolked eggs were now almost done
to a turn. "I suppose," she said, her impatience return-

ing, "you brought those in with the milk! It seems strange," she added crossly, "that it didn't occur to you to inform me of this last night. With your agile mind I'm sure you wouldn't overlook the fact that I'm not familiar with all these things."

The faintest suspicion of a smile flickered on his lips, although his eyes seemed to taunt her. "If you recall, Miss Lewis, you didn't appear particularly eager to listen to advice. In fact," he mused slowly, "I would only have been wasting my time, as you were much too busy putting me in my place."

His place? What exactly was his place? Her eyes widened as she stared at him frigidly, sensing she would only receive some off-putting answer were she to ask. He moved abruptly and started arranging eggs and bacon on two plates, not noticeably disturbed by the icy silence, nor the absence of her usually swift retort.

Alexa blinked, rapidly. She had had just about enough of his broad back which he was too fond of turning, far from politely. He had a far from tramp-like subservience—acting as though he owned the kitchen! Even the quality of his "Miss Lewis" had a false ring about it.

He said now, not apparently willing to allow her the luxury of uninterrupted reflection, "If you can manage it you'll find some cutlery in that drawer over there. I've already made coffee and brought in the milk."

"Oh, yes, the milk!" Stung by the thread of sarcasm in his voice, she found herself grasping wildly at any means of retaliation. "Just what am I supposed to do with a pailful of milk?"

"Why ask me?"

"Why ask you?" Alexa spluttered on her first sip of coffee. "Well, who else could I ask? You work here, don't you?"

One black brow rose and a tight smile just touched

his wide mouth. When he spoke his tone was deceptively soft. "Perhaps it was the impression I received that you don't welcome advice, as I said before. A wise man learns to bide his time."

Alexa frowned, not caring for the slightly threatening double meaning she seemed to read in his words. He had a nerve! He appeared to think it quite in order that he should sit, without so much as a by-your-leave, and eat breakfast with his employer; and, as if this wasn't quite enough, was not above criticising her motives. Instinctively Alexa's fingers curled tightly around her cup. If only he didn't look so aggressively masculine! Her heart jerked, as disturbed, it seemed, as her balance, and she dragged her eyes away from his hard, sensuous mouth, the strong brown column of his throat.

Again she found her only defence in attack. "You seem bent on emphasising my manners, or rather the lack of them," she cried, "I merely asked a simple question."

He laughed, pouring himself another cup of his excellent coffee.

"It's very good," she complimented him irrationally, passing her own cup, hoping there was some left. Momentarily she forgot their shared antagonism.

"Beans," he murmured dryly as he obliged, "I grind them fresh. There's nothing quite like it. As for the milk, about which we seem at loggerheads, there's a machine through there in the pantry that separates the cream which in turn you put into a churn and make butter."

"Just like that?" She couldn't help but gaze at him uncertainly.

"Almost," he assured her solemnly.

"Well..." For a moment, diverted, her mind groped with gallons of cream and butter, commodities which would surely prove useful, "that doesn't sound too difficult. What about eggs?"

"Eggs?"

"Yes, eggs," she repeated, trying not to sound impertinent as she pointed to the eggs and bacon on her plate with an emphasis not unmixed by impatience. She had an idea he was being deliberately obtuse again. "I expect," she said sweepingly, "I shall have to keep some chickens."

To her surprise, because he seemed so imperturbable, he looked slightly startled. He said shortly, "I'm afraid I can't help you there, Miss Lewis. You'll have to excuse me."

"Oh, but…"

"No buts about it," he cut in curtly, as though reading her mind. "I suggest one step at a time. And quite a lot of sensible thought before you think of taking even the first one."

"I—I don't know what you mean." Alexa felt warm colour flood her cheeks as his eyes flicked over her grimly. Beneath his close scrutiny she felt a sensation that was quite new to her, a sensation that did odd things to her breath.

"Miss Lewis," he said softly, "I'm inclined to suspect you were a little hysterical last night, which was perhaps understandable in the circumstances, but I can't help thinking you weren't really serious when you talked about staying here permanently."

"Of course I was serious. I mean—I am serious. Why shouldn't I be?" Trembling, she tried to hold that glinting gaze but failed. Indignantly she stared down at her toast, her appetite suddenly gone. "I'm not exactly sure," she admitted sullenly, like a small child, "about a hotel, but I do intend to provide bed and breakfast accommodation. After I have a look around the house and assess its possibilities."

"Miss Lewis," he returned, still dangerously soft-voiced, "haven't you seriously considered the risks involved? A young girl like yourself living here alone. It's just plain ridiculous."

He didn't smile when he said it, and Alexa's eyes sparkled angrily with resentment. "You sound just like Edith when you talk like that," she said.

He sighed, with the air of a man prepared for a long hard struggle. "As I have no idea who Edith is I'm afraid I'm unable to comment, but she does sound like a lady of some sense."

"Edith is my mother's cousin," she explained without meaning to, as he was obviously not the sort of man to be interested in odd relations.

He wasn't. He ignored Edith completely and didn't ask about her mother, but he did touch, with ill-concealed impatience on Angus. "I wonder," he said with almost insulting despair, "if Angus had any idea what he was doing when he left the croft to you? I believe he had never actually met you?"

"If it's confirmation you're after, Mr.—er—Fergus, then the answer is no, but I'm sure you're really more conversant with the facts than I am."

For a moment, as his mouth hardened, she knew a flicker of something like fear. Or was it something else that threatened to overwhelm her as his hand reached out to lift her chin with no pretence of gentleness, forcing her to look at him? "One of these days," he prophesied hardily, "your reckless tongue will land you in real trouble! I do know that Angus had a fine contempt for his relatives, which maybe explained why they never bothered with him."

His fingers bit deep and, unable to escape, she bit her lip sharply in an attempt to prevent herself crying out. "If that's implied criticism," she choked, "then you can take it back. I wasn't really sure I had relations in these parts, and never had an opportunity to investigate."

"Never?" he mocked, releasing her suddenly, as if he'd lost interest.

"Not really," she whispered, suddenly finding it impossible to nod her head, blinking hard. Her chin, when her own fingers explored it, felt bruised. "You hurt me," she complained.

His heavy shoulders lifted briefly. "Never mind. If anything let it serve as a sort of warning. Sometimes," his voice deepened ominously, "words have no appreciable significance to a girl like you."

Coldly she tried to out-stare him. Failing dismally, she wondered why she didn't dismiss him immediately. A tempting thought, and peculiar in so much that it had crossed her mind twice in less than twenty-four hours, but one which she realised was quite beyond her capabilities at the moment. It would be wiser, she excused herself, to wait!

Calmed by such rational thought, she decided to ignore what he said. "No doubt," she conceded, her heavy lashes falling demurely, "you don't care for those who ignore your advice."

"Miss Lewis," he said smoothly, ignoring her words as if they were of no more consequence than flies, "have you any idea how isolated we are in this part of the west coast? In many places, nearer to civilisation, what you have in mind could be quite feasible, but not here. Angus, if he were still alive, would be the first person to warn you."

"And as he can't, you consider it your undoubted duty! Or are there other reasons, Mr. Fergus? If you remember," she rushed on, before he could deny such allegations, "I arrived in the dark, and haven't yet had the time to look outside."

"I'm sure," he rejoined disagreeably, "that in your

present frame of mind, whatever you see will not stop you reaching the usual conclusions. Those who travel to these remote areas, Miss Lewis, are apt to be over-awed by the scenery. To such an extent, I'm afraid, as to sometimes allow it to overrule common sense."

"Something which you seem to think I'm extremely short of?" she challenged mutinously.

"I'll allow you probably have your fair share," he conceded magnanimously. "My chief complaint is your lack of local experience, and you're too young. Much too young!" He spoke with emphasis which brooked no denial, his eyes again exploring her face with odd consistency.

Alexa drew in her breath as, beneath his close regard, her pulses fluttered. She wanted to cry out: "Why don't you want me to stay?" but the words remained unspoken. There was just the faint quiver of her lips to suggest they had been there at all. Instead she said abruptly, "I can't help being what I am, no more I suppose than you...if I'm too young then you must protect me. I'm sure you'll be around to ward off the frightful catastrophies you have in mind."

His mouth twitched slightly as he drawled sardonically, "You aren't by any chance appealing to my better nature?"

"If you have one," her eyes flew open wrathfully with a quick change of temper at his tone. "Somehow I doubt it," she declared defiantly.

His brief laugh came to her. "Well, stick around long enough and you may find out."

She stared at him, uncertain of his meaning, struck right off course by what seemed an entirely different tack. "Anyway," she mumbled at last, "I have most of spring and summer to look forward to. This will at least give me a chance to reach some sort of definite conclusion before winter sets in. Besides, I don't think any place is altogether isolated nowadays, and I do have a car.''

He made a small mocking sound, in no way impressed. "Heaven preserve me from irresponsible females," he taunted, coming abruptly to his feet. "I'll leave you then, Miss Lewis, to survey the promised land. If nothing else it will probably provide food for thought. I'll see you this evening."

Swiftly he turned on his heels and was gone, before she realised she had forgotten to ask him about her luggage. There was also the problem of hot water—and the little cat, who was at that very moment entering the kitchen proudly carrying its prey, one small, dead mouse!

Alexa, beset by impatience, ran to the window, but Fergus was nowhere to be seen. Where, she wondered with a grimace, could he be off to? She could have done with his help. Yet it was useless to pretend that his absence didn't bring a sense of release. When he was around there was an undercurrent of tension which she was sure didn't make for a good relationship. It would be better perhaps if she learned to manage without him. It wouldn't do, she decided with a peculiar shudder, to become too dependent on such a man.

It was, she found, difficult to know where to start, and in the end her car took priority. After all, if Invercraig was as isolated as Fergus declared it was, transport must be important. Once the car was safely parked nearer the door, then she could begin going through the house.

For years afterwards that first day at Invercraig seemed to represent a voyage of discovery, and not one that Alexa would care to repeat. She had been aware, as she had approached Invercraig the previous evening, of the road that clung precariously to the side of the mountain, a mountain which had appeared to sweep steeply on into the pounding sea below. For the few

miles she had travelled that particular stretch she had
been almost glad of the encroaching darkness, a swift
failing of light which had happily hidden such frightening heights and depth from clear view. She still remembered her relief on reaching Invercraig, the first break
in the twisting, narrow road.

Now, as she stepped from the house, she saw that it
stood further from the road than she had thought, but
that the track to the door seemed reasonably sound,
something for which she felt grateful. No tourist seeking a night's lodgings would wish to tramp through
miles of heather. Yet on gazing around, Alexa was
quick to realise that even such a useful commodity as a
road failed to make Invercraig a particularly attractive
spot. With some dismay she allowed her eyes to
wander. One could imagine the croft had been dropped
at random into a deep cleft between two mountains.
There wasn't a lot of flat land so far as she could see,
and what there was appeared to take the shape of a narrow pass, rather like a dry river-bed, running away in
front of the buildings to disappear after several hundred yards around the foot of an almost vertical
boulder. In places it seemed no more than a track, with
the ground trampled and dirty.

The mountains towered close, blue-grey and spectacular against the horizon, but because they were so
near, their impact seemed to stun the eye rather than
enchant it. Nor from this point was there any glimpse
of the sea to widen the view, although the sound of it
could be heard clearly. This morning, with dark clouds
framing the sky, the pounding force of it seemed curiously at one with the bleak surroundings. There was
something oddly threatening about it that reminded
her uneasily of Fergus. With a shrug Alexa turned back
to the house. It would serve little purpose to grow morbid.

The house itself, to her amused despair, wasn't entirely pleasing. Or was it her own discordant mood which must find fault with everything? She had expected spectacular beauty. Common sense ought to have told her she wouldn't find it everywhere, but during the last few days, as she had come north, she had been enthralled by it, and it seemed unfair that she didn't find it here.

Invercraig House, she decided as she attempted to regard it fairly, might have looked better if it had stood alone instead of huddled among what seemed to be a collection of rough buildings. It was long and low, its proportions not displeasing, but it had obviously been sadly neglected. Angus had apparently not believed in spending money on paint, and even Alexa's inexperienced glance could tell that some of the woodwork was badly in need of repair. There would be much work to be done before it was ready to receive visitors, but a little time and patience might work wonders. She breathed a sigh of relief that Edith wasn't with her, imagining the scathing remarks such shabbiness would surely have produced.

She stepped back, running her eyes quickly over it, wholly absorbed for the moment. Fergus might—he just might, be persuaded to give her a hand if she asked him nicely. If she tried a little gentle persuasion she might get her own way better than by ordering him around.

Such a course—what it might involve—shocked her strangely, and brought home to her abruptly that she was in no way experienced enough to deal with a man like this. A man who expected her to believe he was merely a tramp, who had experience written all over him. Even she, in her innocence, could see that, and she had no means of assessing where irresponsible behaviour might lead her. He could, if driven too far, walk out! On the other hand... Here Alexa stopped, aware of a warning in the misty recesses of her mind which she would rather not contemplate.

In an attempt to put him swiftly from her thoughts, she went to the car, which was still standing where she had left it. One of the tyres seemed soft, she noticed, and bending down she tried to examine it. If anything more went wrong, repairs were going to cost a fortune! Surveying the flat tyre, she was so unhappily lost in her thoughts she didn't hear another vehicle come up behind her.

"Is it help you'll be needing, miss?" a voice cried lightly. A voice that declared that one flat tyre was nothing to worry about!

Startled, Alexa rose from her knees, confused to be caught in such a position, even if she did have a legitimate excuse. A large delivery van was stationed a short way behind her, and a tall young man, apparently the driver, was standing beside it, surveying her with frank interest.

"Do you want any help?" he repeated, as she blinked at him uncertainly for a second, and he must have decided she hadn't heard his first query.

"Oh no..." Alexa found her tongue at last. "That is, I'm not sure, but thanks anyway for offering."

He grinned, as if her embarrassment amused him, but on his face there was also a glimmer of interest. "I can easily change that wheel for you," he suggested pleasantly, "it will at least prevent you getting dirty and save you time if you have to move on."

"Oh no—that is—" At so much repetition their eyes met and together they laughed, their laughter mingling in the way of the very young. Alexa liked what she saw, a youngish man in his early twenties, who looked every bit as pleasantly spirited as he sounded. "I'm sorry," she smiled. "Perhaps I should explain that I live here.

If you're local you might like to know I'm the new owner. Alexa Lewis is my name."

"Well—you don't say!" There was nothing pretentious about his exclamation. He looked surprised but also delighted as his eyes lingered on her pink cheeks. "You must be the cousin we've been hearing about, but I had no idea you would be like this!"

The pink in her cheeks already deeper, Alexa didn't ask him to explain. When he introduced himself she merely nodded briefly and smiled. Too much of Colin Macdonell might prove overpowering! "News evidently travels fast in these parts," she murmured.

"We knew you were coming," Colin amended blithely. "What we don't know is whether or not you intend to stay."

"I think so. For a while at least," she said slowly.

"I'm glad," he replied, and there was nothing stinted in his admiration. "I'm sure you won't regret it."

"I hope not," she answered, with more emphasis than she was aware of.

"If I can help at all I'll be delighted," Colin continued. "Perhaps, in turn, I should explain that I'm a medical student, so I do have time. That is, I do usually," he went on with a frown. "Right now my old man, who owns the grocer's shop in the village, is ill, and I'm delivering provisions while I'm home for Easter."

"Well, you can't help everyone," Alexa smiled, thinking he was indeed very nice. And it was perhaps providential that he had come this way—she couldn't eat Fergus's bacon and eggs for ever. "You must tell me where your father's store is," she added quickly, "I could do with some things."

"If you make out a list I could deliver it after lunch," he offered.

He was going too fast. Suddenly Invercraig seemed too overflowing with dominant men. "I'd rather," she said carefully, "go down to the village myself, to begin with anyway. It will provide an opportunity to meet my neighbours, that is," she added with another smile, "if you'd be kind enough to change my tyre?"

While Colin worked he talked, and without seeming rude or ungrateful Alexa had no means of stemming the ceaseless flow. She perched on a stone at the side of the road and prepared to listen, although she paid only scant attention as her mind dwelt ruefully on uncompleted tasks in the house. None of which were Colin's fault, she reprimanded herself sternly.

Even now he was saying helpfully, "The village is a mere ten miles down the coast. You probably came through it on your way here, but I'd advise you to be careful. The road can be extremely treacherous—one mistake and you're into the sea!"

"Oh, I'll be careful," she promised indifferently.

He went on, apparently impressed by her cool demeanour, "I'm sure you'll do well here, and I certainly hope you do stay, although I hear you have a good offer for the land."

"Good heavens!" Startled at last from her reverie, Alexa looked up. "How did you know?" she gasped.

Colin, pausing a moment from his self-appointed task, glanced at her bewildered face and laughed. "We could be guessing, Alexa, but it's common knowledge around here that Maxwell would do almost anything to get this little property. It's even said that he expected to receive it through Angus's will when he died. No doubt you'll be hearing from him if you haven't already done so. He's a man very used to having his own way."

"Maxwell?" Alexa murmured, suddenly stunned. "He would be a sort of cousin too?"

"Oh, as for that," Colin declared, going back to the

wheel, "I'm not sure. I believe there was a distant relationship somewhere, but that could apply to a lot of people in the glen. No, my old man reckons Maxwell had a sort of verbal contract with Angus about the track, and an understanding about future ownership after Angus had gone. Actually Angus made it more or less common knowledge himself, but something appears to have gone awry. The joke's certainly on Maxwell now, and they say he doesn't appreciate it one bit."

Alexa felt herself trembling. Robert Kerr had certainly mentioned a would-be buyer, without divulging any facts! He must be a man of little imagination, otherwise how could he have kept such information from her, knowing how badly it could affect her position here? A word of warning could surely have been given in confidence. Why, this Maxwell could easily be a distant connection of her own, and from the way Colin spoke of him, not one whose acquaintance was to be desired.

Painfully she swallowed a lump of self-pity in her throat. "This track you speak of," she gulped, "I'm afraid I don't follow you. Fergus never mentioned any track."

"Fergus wouldn't." Colin gave the slack nuts a last quick twist with the wheel brace. "Fergus, you see, works for Maxwell too, and is something of an opportunist. What he will be doing is commonly known as biding his time, waiting to see what happens. You could be better rid of him."

Alexa choked on a surge of quick anger, not unmixed with despair. So this accounted for Fergus's absence—his treachery! Yet how could she immediately take Colin's advice! She prevaricated, without quite knowing why. It was something she would need time to think about, something to consider carefully, and not

while her mind was churning distractedly in several directions. Besides, for a little while, until she was more
familiar with the place, she might find it difficult to do
without him.

"I wonder," she pleaded, feeling it was somehow
imperative to know, "if you could explain in more detail about this track? You might like to come in and
wash," she added politely, as Colin glanced rather
pointedly at his oil-covered hands.

Once in the house she made him coffee; she could
do no less after he had taken the trouble to change her
wheel. She couldn't find any biscuits, but he didn't
seem to mind. "You're probably in a hurry," she
apologised ruefully, as she asked him to sit down.

Colin said he wasn't—not particularly. "There's
plenty of help at the shop," he grinned. "Dad isn't
very busy at this time of the year and a grocery round
like this is more of a social occasion. I've only one or
two calls left to make."

"All the same," Alexa advised at the risk of sounding inhospitable, "you'd better not stay too long."

"Okay, hint taken," he grinned as he drank his coffee, "I expect you've got heaps to do if you've only just
arrived. I can always come back. But you did want to
know about the track?"

Alexa nodded, biting her lip with a hint of impatience. Colin, it seemed, believed in procrastination!
"Yes, please," she prompted, as he paused.

"You probably haven't noticed it yet," he said, "but
the track runs straight through your land and disappears around the side of the mountain a short distance
from your front door. Well, Maxwell owns several
thousand acres on each side of this holding and this
track through your land is his most convenient link between the two. Otherwise it means he must drive his
stock along four miles of notoriously dangerous road—

the same road you used last night when you came here. For about eight months of the year, during the tourist season, it would be an extremely hazardous journey with one sheep, let alone hundreds! So now you can see why this croft is so important to our friend Maxwell!"

Alexa stared at him blankly, trying desperately to absorb what he told her. "In a way," she admitted, "but not completely. I mean, why should this man place himself in such a position? Couldn't he farm his two pieces of land as separate units, and do away with any necessity to use Invercraig?"

"Not really," Colin shrugged, "although it might be difficult for you to understand wholly if you have no experience of such things. One tract of land is, or has become, I believe, more or less interdependent on the other. Maxwell purchased his second piece of land a few years ago from a chap who used it chiefly for shooting."

"Shouldn't he have thought about this problem then? It seems quite illogical to have left it to providence. After all, what guarantee did he have that Angus would be cooperative? Or would continue to be so?"

"You're asking me, Alexa Lewis!" he grinned. "Angus, it's said, promised him. I suppose one would call it a sort of gentlemen's agreement, and to be quite fair, it's also said that Angus did extremely well out of it."

"In what way?" Alexa asked, adding wryly, "as you seem to know so much..."

"My dear girl," Colin laughed, not in the least disturbed by her tart tone, "very little happens around here which isn't public knowledge. One doesn't have to listen at keyholes. Certainly it's known that Angus received a very handsome remuneration by way of rent."

"Which makes it seem peculiar that his solicitor

didn't mention this," replied Alexa, rather indiscreetly. Robert Kerr hadn't been specific.

"Solicitors," Colin pointed out, "usually deal only with fact. If there was no legally drawn-up document then he couldn't mention one."

"So it would seem," Alexa frowned, forgetting she was talking to an almost complete stranger. "But one might have thought that Maxwell might have suggested more or less the same terms for me—through Angus's solicitor."

"You should probably give him a little time," Colin shrugged. "It would perhaps be much more satisfactory from his point of view if he could buy the croft outright. If you refuse to sell he might come up with something else."

"I'd like to assure him to his face that I have no intention of selling—or giving him a lease," Alexa cried mutinously. "He'll find I'm not so easily bribed!"

"Well, keep your hair on!" Colin grinned, draining the last of his cup, and rose lazily to his feet, deploring the necessity to be gone. "There's just one thing…" he turned as Alexa followed him to the door, his slightly freckled face suddenly anxious. "Maxwell isn't the man to let a mere girl stand in his way. So be warned!"

CHAPTER FOUR

FERGUS didn't return until quite late in the evening, by which time Alexa felt almost too exasperated by his prolonged absence to be civil. Yet when it came to reprimanding him the right words didn't come easily. There was something about him which forestalled normal reactions to such blatant behaviour, so that she found herself murmuring, if somewhat dryly, that she hoped he'd had a good day.

As if in no way aware that a slightly outraged expression belied her polite inquiry, he assured her solemnly that he had, but would appreciate a little light supper. "I'm just going out to milk your cow," he informed her. "If," he added infuriatingly, "you haven't already done so?"

Just one more way of making her realise how indispensable his services were! Alexa's glance was icy as she was forced to shake her head. "But it's not a bit of good your bringing more milk in here," she cried, "until I know how that machine in the larder works! It's all in pieces...I don't even now how to put the beastly thing together!"

"Don't you?" he murmured, with provoking innocence. "When I come back," he promised gravely, "I'll show you—if you have my supper ready."

If—his encompassing look seemed to add—you're a good girl, and nice to me!

It took all sorts, Alexa decided indignantly as she placed some soup in a pan over a low flame on the

cooker and quickly cut a pile of substantial ham sandwiches. Working, as Fergus appeared to do, for two
employers undoubtedly placed him in a strong position—
or so he seemed to think. Strong enough, anyway, to
force her into the unenviable position of having to accept him on his own terms.

Her smooth brow creased with vexation, she set two
places on the scrubbed deal table. She might as well
join him as she had been too busy before he had arrived to think about eating. Besides, if she was only to
see him at mealtimes it might be better to accept the
inevitable and make the most of it. There were things
she must ask him about the animals on the croft. And
maybe, if she refused to let his arbitrary manner disturb her, she might learn something of the mysterious
Mr. Maxwell—something more than what Colin had
divulged.

Not that Colin had been unhelpful, far from it, but
his involvement wasn't personal. In a situation like this
his attitude probably only reflected the general interest
of the glen. No doubt he would sit on a sort of mental
fence with many others, speculating, in the forthcoming battle of the track, on whether she or Maxwell
would win. Nor would it take a very astute brain to
guess who they had their money on!

There was just a grain of comfort to be gleaned from
the notion that while she herself had the disadvantage
of being a stranger, Mr. Maxwell might not be without
his enemies. Once she became familiar with the village
she might find someone who would be willing to help
her fight this man, even if only in an advisory capacity.
There were always, if one looked hard enough, ways
and means!

Apart from Colin, the more Alexa thought about
making a friend in the village, the more she liked the
idea, and regretted not going there after lunch. Colin,

however, had been able to supply her with most of the provisions she needed from those which he normally carried on his van. She had even managed to get some bones with which she had made the soup, now simmering with an extremely appetizing aroma for Fergus's supper.

She had felt quite pleased at the time that she wouldn't need to go to the village until another day, but now she wasn't so sure. The time she had thought saved might have been better spent exploring possibilities other than those of the croft!

However, perhaps it wouldn't be wise to take everything Colin had told her too seriously. While his words had contained a convincing ring of truth, there might also have been an element of exaggeration. Nor did she mean to discuss what Colin had said with Fergus—not the bit relating to her own strategic position between Maxwell's two pieces of land. If Maxwell was paying an excellent wage, there would be little doubt where Fergus's loyalty would lie.

It was probably very silly to give someone like Fergus so much as a second thought, but it was likely he was acquainting Maxwell with her every move. Betraying her to a man who had no compunction it seemed about getting rid of his own relations if, Colin said, they stood in his way. It might pay dividends to keep a close eye on Fergus, and only tell him what she wanted Maxwell to know!

Almost before she had finished laying the table, Fergus returned with another pailful of milk. "All from one cow?" she gasped in dismay, somewhat startled by the quantity of it.

"All from one cow," he repeated suavely, not visibly affected by her dazed expression, as he swept her without further comment into the larder. Here he proceeded to fit together the pieces of machine into which he eventually poured the frothy white milk. Afterwards it occurred to Alexa that in assembling the machine, he didn't work as quickly as usual. Which seemed strange, as he must be very familiar with it.

"The milk," he said, proceeding to demonstrate, "must be dealt with while still warm. It's really quite simple, you just turn the handle."

"Really...?" Alexa felt far from convinced.

"Come here," he commanded, "and try for yourself."

Alexa tried and failed. To her utter chagrin, when she tried to turn the handle it jerked and raced, then ground to a stop, rather like an old gramophone. "Stupid thing!" she cried, patience deserting her immediately.

"Calm down!" Fergus yelled, smothering what seemed suspiciously like a laugh, as he rescued the groaning separator with one hand and grabbed her shaking fingers with his other. "Let me show you," he grinned. "You can't hope to become accomplished in two seconds!"

Wrathfully Alexa tried to step back, only to find her hand imprisoned beneath his on the machine, which was now rhythmically turning. "See how easy it is?" he murmured, his brilliant gaze slanting to her flushed cheek.

Unable to escape, Alexa stood tautly beside him, her fingers subconsciously catching the precise movement of the handle without being fully aware of it. The evening before she had felt unexplainably alarmed by the vivid sensations aroused when he had carried her in from the barn. These, throughout the course of the day, she had managed to dismiss as sheer imagination, but there was nothing imaginary about the flame which seemed to sweep through her again at his touch. Something in her veins seemed to sing, shattering rational thinking, leaving her only with the hazy knowledge that she would do well to be wary.

She could feel her heart beginning to thud, although apart from their hands there was no contact, if one could discount the proximity of his hard, disturbing body. Unhappily she felt the quick sting of tears against her eyelids. There was so much here that spelt danger! Perhaps she ought after all to have listened to Edith and waited until someone older and more experienced had been able to accompany her to this wild and probably barely civilised place.

As if sensing something of her inner agitation and amused by it, the man relented, letting go of her hand. "You appear to be a very rewarding pupil," he said enigmatically, "naïve but quick to learn. I'll finish this while you go and serve my supper. I won't be long."

Minutes later, almost before Alexa's breathing had returned to normal, he followed, placing a small jug of cream on the table as he sat down. "I took the liberty," he said, "of helping myself, but don't worry, there'll still be enough left for your butter if you know how to make it."

Alexa ignored what seemed another of his taunting queries, but as she ladled soup into deep plates she kept her eyes averted. "We can't just have plain cream," she objected, not caring in the least if he chose to put the whole of it in his soup or coffee, but because it seemed somehow imperative she made a stand somewhere. Fergus gave the impression he was about to take over!

He smiled, accepting his soup with a murmur of thanks. "I shouldn't have thought you had dieting problems," he mused, his eye running lightly over her, deliberately misunderstanding. "A little extra weight wouldn't hurt you."

He didn't have to emphasise that he considered her too thin! "You'll find," she retorted, sitting herself down opposite him, "that my weight, or rather lack of it, in no way affects my capabilities. And," she added tartly, "I don't appreciate such personal remarks from a—er—"

"You mean, servant?" he helped her out blandly, without turning a hair.

There was silence. If he expects me to deny it—or to apologise—then he can think again, Alexa thought angrily. But she sought refuge in dignity, refusing to allow him to provoke her into reckless speech. With a too elaborate politeness she asked, "I hope my soup is to your liking?"

He nodded his head, indifferent it seemed to her dry sarcasm. "It's very good." He broke off a piece of new bread. "So good," he went on meditatively, "that I can scarcely believe it came out of a tin."

"It didn't," she said, falling into the trap completely.

His eyebrows raised, he pounced immediately. "There were no suitable ingredients in the larder."

Her expression changed. Would he always be one step ahead? She might as well explain, he would have his own way of finding things out. "Colin Macdonell called. He thought I might need something."

"Did he, indeed?" Alexa imagined a thread of annoyance, a sharper look in the eyes which examined her face. Disparagingly he said, "Young Macdonell's curiosity was likely to get the better of him, but no doubt you appreciated his convenience."

Alexa resisted a strong impulse to throw something. "Put like that," she retorted sweetly, "I suppose I did. He supplied most of what I wanted, which was more," she added irrationally, "than I could say of you!"

"Oh, give me time, Miss Alexa," he drawled with some amusement, his tone changing. "All things come to those who wait," he quoted, "and there are more things to life than groceries."

Alexa's impulses gathered strength, and in restraining herself she found her hands clenching. "Not when one's larder is bare," she said sharply, "and your only means of help has more or less walked out on you!"

His eyes glittered with malice on her hot cheeks. "If you happen to be referring obliquely to me, Alexa, I had other things to do."

"So I believe!" her voice was still sweet with saccharine hostility.

"And so..." she felt his eyes bore into her, "Macdonell has been busy!"

That could mean anything! She would apply her own interpretation. "He had other provisions to deliver when he left here," she said coolly. "He only passed the time of day."

"That," he rejoined, with extreme dryness, "I can well imagine."

With a small jerk that spoke volumes Alexa jumped from her seat to fetch the coffee-pot from the cooker. How dared he sit there and question her motives, or those of her friends! Wouldn't it be more in keeping with his position to apologise for his absence? It was quite obvious that he was wondering if Colin had mentioned Mr. Maxwell. Well, let him guess! A little of that wouldn't do him any harm.

Returning to the table, she changed the subject deliberately. "After Colin went I went through the house. I see there are three good-sized bedrooms which I could use for guests."

"Two," he amended, his eyes narrowed against her level tones. "Unless you intend to continue sleeping in the kitchen, you'll need one for yourself."

"There is something I must ask you." Rather nervously she swallowed. "I found a sort of loft above this kitchen, quite nicely fitted out as a bedroom. Did you sleep there?''

His eyes were suddenly alight with malice, quite out of sympathy with her obvious embarrassment. "I did," he drawled coolly. Just how, his eyes taunted, do you intend to deal with this?

Alexa gulped again, feeling a sudden surge of help- less self-pity. He didn't like her—didn't want her, and didn't believe in hiding the fact! No matter what his station in life was supposed to be, it was clear he was a man who was used to dominating other people. He wouldn't help her out one bit, not having a scrap of consideration for others! "Last night," she faltered, "you didn't?"

"No," he agreed.

"How do you mean—no?" she cried, her courage returning as she stared at him.

"I haven't slept in the house since Angus died," he explained indifferently. "I can always start again if you would like me to?"

"No, no, of course not," Alexa muttered unsteadily, her gaze dropping with some confusion from his. "I expect," she added swiftly, "you've made other ar- rangements." It would never do to share a house with this man. Even she in her innocence knew that!

"Of course." She might have known from the sar- donic quirk of his lips that he was fully conversant with what she was thinking. "What is it, then, that you wish to know about the attic?"

"Nothing. That is," she told him carefully, "I was thinking of sleeping there myself."

For an instant his dark brows knitted. "Don't you care for the other part of the house?" he frowned.

Alexa bit her lip, making a great to-do of pouring out coffee, not prepared to give him the satisfaction of knowing how she felt about the house. Earlier she had thought the outside depressing, but had hoped the interior would prove nicer. After all, her glimpse of it that morning as she ran upstairs to wash hadn't been too awful. Then, to her dismay, her subsequent explorations had revealed much that wasn't desirable. The bedrooms, all three of them, were low and dark, the corridor leading to them equally low and uneven. Downstairs the lounge and the small dining room were not much better, and it seemed obvious that before visitors could even be considered she would need to put in a lot of hard work. While wallpaper at least was in a fairly good condition, the whole looked as if it hadn't had a good clean-up in weeks.

Yet she felt oddly reluctant to speak of any of this to Fergus. Instead she said slowly, "It's not quite what I've been used to."

"What have you been used to?" His question was abrupt, demanding an answer, yet suddenly she received the impression that he really wanted to know.

"A flat," she replied starkly, wishing but failing to make it sound more interesting than it had been.

He accepted this apparently without surprise, his eyes intent. "And what sort of career did you pursue before you came here?" he asked, obviously bent on filling in her background.

Surprisingly, Alexa found herself answering meekly. "I helped Edith with her work. I believe I mentioned her this morning."

She didn't elaborate, recalling his lack of attention, and was startled when he retorted crisply, "That in no way explains the nature of your job!"

Almost, Alexa decided indignantly, as though he suspected she hadn't had one! She enlarged, but briefly. "I worked where and when I was required. In the course of a day I might have a hundred and fifty duties. Edith, you see, is the headmistress of a very large girls' school."

"She reared you?"

His expression spoke of the farmyard! Alexa's thickly-lashed green eyes widened defensively. "If you like to put it that way."

"Your parents died when you were an infant?"

"About five." She stared at him, resenting what seemed like an intrusion. "Why ask me all this when you appear to know all the answers? I suppose Angus talked!"

"He told me so much." His manner now was slightly guarded. "The winters here are long. Since you arrived," he continued enigmatically, "I've formed my own conclusions."

"Based entirely on our brief acquaintance?"

"Long enough," he asserted coolly, "to make me reissue my earlier warning that it wouldn't be a good idea for a girl like you to take paying guests."

"Just how have you weighed me up?" she cried, her cheeks pink, her eyes bright with unwise challenge.

He leant across the table towards her as he had done that morning, but this time his grey eyes were no longer quite so indifferent. "One glance into the nearest mirror might provide a better answer than I could give." At her slightly doubtful, still puzzled expression, he went on dryly, "People are usually extremely decent, but in any society anywhere, there's always the element of risk. It would be an entirely different matter if you had someone living with you. As it is, you'd be wide open to abuse from the first doubtful character to come along."

"The single landlady isn't unknown," she pointed out.

His decisive mouth clamped impatiently. "Not unknown," he agreed, "but unusual in a spot like this. And not at your age."

"I'm not," she defended herself indignantly, "as vulnerable as all that! You exaggerate. Besides, you might be around."

"Not all the time, my dear, Alexa," he assured her, adding with a totally taunting glint in his eye, "Are you suggesting I set myself up as your protector? You could simply be jumping from the frying pan into the fire."

Alexa's breath came out on a sharp note of rejection. "Now you're being ridiculous!"

"Not entirely," he ran the hard eye of an expert right over her, taking in the faded blue Levis, the thin, polo-necked soft green sweater which exactly matched her eyes. "White skin," he said softly, "long golden hair and skinny body. Put like that it adds up to nothing, but taken as a whole, it's more than enough to make any man look twice."

He spoke quietly, with authority in his voice. Instinctively she stiffened. Even in the gloom of a lamp-lit room there was a fine air about him, a beautiful arrogance, something to send a shiver slithering down Alexa's spine. Here, she guessed, was a man with a deeply sensual attraction for women. Beneath his wholly mocking gaze the feeling came back, and her traitorous heart quickened its beat until she feared he might hear it.

Her colour flaming, she jumped to her feet, only to find him around the table in a trice, his hands catching her wrists and jerking her ruthlessly towards him.

"If you touch me I'll kill you!" she cried wildly, emotion surging through her as he pulled her hard against him.

"Try it," he commanded suavely, holding her completely his prisoner.

She did try to escape, but she seemed unable to move. Her limbs, at his touch, went weak, reducing her efforts to an ineffectual tremble as strength seemed to leave them. "Let me go," she gasped, trying desperately to hang on to a modicum of sanity. "You've only known me for hours!"

He took no notice of her small fury, hauling her closer as he grasped and thrust the long, tumbled hair from her face. "Hours or years," he taunted, "have no bearing whatsoever on the emotions. Aren't you even experienced enough to realise that?"

His gaze glittered over her as he continued his unhurried inspection, and wildly she tried to stay the waves of sensation which radiated between them. He was clearly a man in control of himself—surely he could exercise some restraint!

"I don't have to answer any of your impertinent questions!" she choked, almost sobbing as she beat small clenched fists against his chest without visible impression. Tilting her face back, she stared up at him. her eyes sparkling green with bright fury.

As their eyes met, his wholly relentless, Alexa's lashes fluttered and fell, unable to sustain his blatantly mocking glance. Swiftly, without further comment, he bent his strong head and kissed her wide, shaking lips, his own cool and hurting for the space of several taut seconds.

Beneath the searching expertise of his, Alexa's mouth moved helplessly, knowing that where there should only have been loathing, a sudden vivid excitement, a lick of fire like lightning was going through her. There was nothing she could do to stop the sweeping response which thrust her body involuntarily against the man who lightly held her. Undercurrents of what must have been a physical magnetism flowed, and she was lost, clinging to him when by every rule of her restrictive upbringing she should have been pushing himself away.

Then, with a detachment she envied, he was doing

just that with her; thrusting her from him back into her chair in one swift premeditated movement. His gesture was disciplined, faultless, as was his brief laughter. "Now can you imagine what could happen, were I some determined, unprincipled stranger?"

"You're worse!" She spoke blindly, momentarily covering her shocked face with both hands, unwilling for him to know that the touch of his lips had devastated her like a mighty tornado. "I hate you," she cried on a shuddering breath, "I hate you!"

"Never mind," he murmured, with the air of a man giving comfort to a child. "You'll feel better in a few minutes. You only think you hate me. A little demonstration usually proves a point more effectively than words. I'll see you in the morning."

Alexa, her fingers defensively against her bruised mouth, attempted to choose one of the withering comments surging in her head, but immediate speech evaded her, and before she could find her voice again he was gone, the outer door closing decisively behind him.

"See you in the morning—in the evening—later in the day..." Stupidly she found herself staring at the closed door, the words reverberating. That was all she seemed to hear, with no explanation as to what he did in between the short periods he so magnanimously spared her! Well, she'd had just about enough of Mr. Fergus! How dared he kiss her as he had done! A man who was not only a stranger but one with so little responsiblity towards his fellow men that he chose, in spite of his fine words, to live as he did! Now, at least, he had provided her with a legitimate excuse to be rid of him. He could after this devote himself entirely to his friend Maxwell.

It was only later, when she was climbing into bed in the attic, that she remembered she had forgotten to ask him about the animals on the croft—an omission which contrived to fill her with a vast despair, involving as it must the apparent necessity of putting up with Fergus for yet another day.

During the weeks which followed Alexa found that despite her resolutions, she wasn't to get rid of him so easily. Yet while he continued to come and go more or less as he pleased, he kept his distance, giving her no further reason for complaint. If occasionally she thought this new courtesy slightly overdone, she hastened to assure herself that she would rather have it this way than as he had been on the evening when he had shared her supper!

He hadn't asked for an evening meal again, nor had she offered, merely assuming that he managed to find one somewhere, and declining to let him know that she wondered. Often at night she didn't even see him, but found without fail the usual pail of milk on the doorstep, which constituted, she sometimes liked to imagine, a sort of silent apology for his unaccountable behaviour.

At other times she wasn't so sure. At the dead of night, safe in her small bedroom, she was aware of vague longings which she kept hidden even from herself, unwilling to admit that their relationship, after such an explosive start, had declined into something depressing by its very uniformity.

Swallowing a distinct sense of outrage, she asked Fergus about the livestock and learned that she was the proud possessor of one cow, a dozen sheep and a small pony which, as she didn't ride, seemed slightly surplus to her requirements.

"You can always learn," Fergus pointed out obligingly. "You might even come to enjoy it. And if you should get lost while out exploring he would always bring you home quite safely."

Alexa ignored this advice, along with what she considered his sly reference to her short excursion into the hills, about which he could only be guessing as he was never here to see. "I'll think about it," was all the reply she made.

He told her that she also owned several chickens which had unfortunately been allowed to run wild and lay their eggs wherever they fancied. He showed her one nest in the top of the hay loft, a precarious position from which she slithered down almost into his arms. That he set her straight again without so much as a flicker of an eyelid did nothing to stop the suddenly accelerated beat of her heart.

"You could try a little control," he grinned, his fingers lingering before leaving her wrist where he must have felt the quickened pulse. "You might find it a lot easier until you learn how to manage such things."

Instinctively Alexa knew he didn't refer to chickens, but she contrived to let him think she did. It would be his way of revealing his opinion of her too impulsive emotions, and inwardly she squirmed as she jerked away from him. "I'm sure you need have no further worry on that score," she retorted coldly. "You can safely leave the...er...chickens to me."

On another day he advised her not to sleep in the attic. "There's only a narrow skylight in the roof. If there should be a fire in the kitchen you couldn't hope to escape."

"You slept there," she frowned, not looking at him.

"I'm a man," he said grimly.

Alexa, quite aware of this, felt something flare within her. "All right," she agreed, too brightly, "I like the attic because it's cosy and warm, but the small room at the top of the stairs will do."

Later that same day she went to the village to purchase some of the essential supplies Colin hadn't had with him when he had called. There was also the need to collect some paint and cleaning materials, but she doubted if she would find these in a small village shop. Wistfully she thought of Inverness, where she had spent so much time, and where she could have bought everything necessary, had she but known.

Invercraig lay high up on the west coast above Lochinver, in a land of wild, wide acres, dotted by innumerable lochs. It was the land of the golden eagle, the wildcat, pine martens and deer. Seabirds and seals lived along the shore, and over it all the great wild winds blew. The coastline, softened by long sandy beaches, was spectacular, banked as it was by wide stretches of moor and forest.

Driving quickly, Alexa felt almost bemused by it, by the ever-changing sky that threw vivid patterns of shadow and light across the sea and mountains. The mountains made her conscious that by comparison she was small and alone, completely vulnerable and entirely without experience in a land where it must be essential. There was an emptiness within her that suddenly cried out to be filled; a fiercely fundamental longing irrationally tied up with one man.

With a shudder Alexa tried to keep her full attention on the road. No traitorous body should be allowed to dull the brain. This way lay only ultimate despair, the normal outcome of folly.

As on the day she had arrived there was very little traffic, and she saw now just how very narrow were the northern Scottish highways. Little more than wide tracks in places, they swept and curved in front of her in such a grandly majestic manner as to make one completely overlook their limitations. Yet, considering them clearly, she could understand Colin's theory that, hemmed in as they were on this particular stretch by mountains, it would be almost impossible for Maxwell to drive his stock along them in summer.

The village, to her delight, was small, so small that if she hadn't known where to find it she might have missed it altogether. It lay slightly off the coast, sheltered from the more exposed mainland, a straggling yet picturesque row of different sized houses.

In the shop, to her surprise, she found all the necessary paint and equipment she required. She also found Colin.

"I thought of coming along to see you this evening," he said, after she had asked about his father and he had assured her briefly that he was keeping better.

"Don't, unless you can wield a paintbrush," she replied. "I intend to begin right away."

"In that case," he grinned, quite without shame, "I'll come tomorrow."

As if he expected she would be finished! Alexa didn't mention she might be even busier. Let him come! She enjoyed a little lively chatter, and she could rely on him bringing her news of Maxwell's movements as any new ones developed.

Colin left her at the butcher's discussing the relative merits of a joint. Seemingly as curious as Colin, the butcher asked her frankly if she intended staying at Invercraig.

"I think so," she said with a passable show of indifference before inquiring swiftly, "Did you know Angus, then?"

"I did that!" Vigorously the man nodded his head. He continued with the air of a man discussing the weather, "You will know, of course, that Maxwell himself made an offer. He would like your place."

Rather startled by his swift disclosure, Alexa stared. If she had hoped to find someone who didn't care for Maxwell she obviously hadn't found him here! This man appeared to have Maxwell's interests very much at heart. "I haven't met Mr. Maxwell yet," she told him, with emphasis which she hoped might be repeated, "but I'm hoping the pleasure might not be too long delayed. Is he usually a man who conducts his business behind people's backs?" she smiled.

"Excuse me, miss!" The man had been remiss enough to cut his finger, but even if he was surprised by his own negligence, he paid little attention to his hand. "Himself," he assured Alexa, borrowing some of her own emphasis, "isn't a man to go behind any man's back!"

"Possibly not," she agreed soothingly, deliberately pretending to misunderstand, "but many men are rather afraid of women."

Something unheard-of, so far as Maxwell was concerned! Yet it wasn't without possibility. Almost she could see such thoughts flicking through the butcher's mind.

"Do you know, miss," he exclaimed at last, unconsciously scratching his greying head with bloody fingers, comprehension suddenly drawing, "you could be right. Such an idea never occurred to me, but you could be right! After all, he's a man of considerable means, not so young as he was ten years ago, and still unmarried. And there is my wife always making out he's too hard to please!"

Alexa left him rubbing his chin thoughtfully after serving her generously with some especially nice steak and succulent bones, with which she decided to make more soup for Fergus. If nothing else he seemed to enjoy her cooking, having told her more than once that her porridge and mixed grill was something a man might walk miles for.

Her remarks about Maxwell she left the butcher to consider, entirely without conscience. If she had been indiscreet, a man who tried to cheat a girl out of her home deserved little better. If anything it was his conscience that required prodding, not her own!

Colin came as he promised the very next day, and on the following morning Fergus said, "I think you'd be wise not to encourage Macdonell. He's not your type."

"How can you tell?" she asked, placing the toast which she had prepared for their breakfast sharply on the table. "I realise you don't care for him, but how would you know what pleases me?"

He grinned at that. "I'm capable, Alexa, of guessing. Certainly Macdonell would never please you long."

She glanced at him, her feathery brows knitting. It never ceased to surprise her how little he resembled his popular image. He was immensely attractive, something which even the shabbiness of his clothing failed to disguise. She knew a moment of measureless longing, a persistent yearning that might develop into pain unless she took herself in hand. Her face grew remote as she withdrew almost visibly, her eyes like cool pools of green clouded water. "He does provide a little company," she cried, clutching what seemed to be her only weapon, the coffee-pot, firmly. "Otherwise I could finish up by talking to myself."

He shrugged, his heavy shoulders lifting carelessly. "Most of us do that from time to time. Much better than cultivating the wrong friends."

"I can't see," Alexa retorted, "how you could push someone like Colin into that category. He is, after all, a medical student, which must count for something!"

"You tell me." Obviously unimpressed, he slid his cup across the table. "Do I get any coffee this morning, or do you intend to have it all yourself?"

Uncomprehending for a moment, her eyes met his sardonic ones. "Of course," she muttered crossly, regretting his ability to make her forget what she was doing. "Colin did help me with the decorating."

"By holding your hand when your head ached, I imagine."

Alexa stirred an unnecessary amount of brown sugar into her own coffee, her mouth set in mutinous lines. "You don't have to be sarcastic! When I went to the village a few days ago he was helping in his father's shop. Not so many students would do that!"

"Ah yes, the village! Another place where your dexterous tongue has been working overtime."

"What do you mean?" Too late she remembered her conversation with the butcher, and as she spoke hot colour ran beneath her skin, although why it should she couldn't guess, as what she'd said had nothing to do with Fergus. And, although he did help her a little on the croft, Maxwell surely couldn't hold Fergus responsible for the few remarks she chose to make while buying meat!

His mouth tightened as he regarded her slightly tilted chin. "I mean, Miss Alexa," he said hardily, "you would perhaps be wiser not to speak of what doesn't concern you."

So he had heard something? There was a cool glint of anger in his eyes that assured her he had. Yet she still felt unwilling to face any sort of a showdown until, she tried to tell herself, she could be certain of the outcome. Recklessly she pretended to misunderstand him. "You seem intent this morning, Fergus, on instilling a little wisdom into my head. Something which perhaps because of the earliness of the hour, I don't appreciate. If passing the time of day in Colin's shop is to be judged a crime then I have no defence, but I can't remember speaking of anything that might justify your losing your temper!"

"Really!" his voice snapped sardonically, his inflection bringing a deeper flush to her cheeks. For several seconds they stared at each other across the table, her green eyes holding his until she could stand it no longer.

Silkily he suggested, "You would have no idea how small items are repeated in some parts of the world, how news travels quickly."

"So," she said, stumbling to her feet, making a big thing of carrying her breakfast dishes to the sink, "if one felt the need to say something, but had failed to make contact with the recipient personally..."

His brief laughter cut in sharply, "You get the general idea, Miss Innocence. Just whisper it in the nearest ear and it will reach him—fast!"

CHAPTER FIVE

Two weeks later Alexa had a letter from Edith. She and Frank had arrived home and although she didn't say so outright, Alexa gathered they were very happy. About Alexa, Edith was obviously not so content.

"How could you do such a thing?" she wrote. "I fear such behaviour reflects on the way I brought you up! If on occasion I imagined I was too firm, this recent escapade—and I can call it nothing else—convinces me I haven't been strict enough. I do implore you, Alexa, to return home. I really find it most inconvenient to be without you—" And so on...

Most of which, Alexa could see clearly hid the fact that the replacement Edith had talked of so glibly had not come up to expectations. No...! Quickly Alexa squashed such uncharitable thoughts. Maybe Edith quite genuinely missed her and might be anxious. Slowly Alexa refolded the letter, putting it back in its envelope. Edith had enjoyed her honeymoon in Greece, she loved her new home, and, as the summer term had just started, was busy. If she went back she would only be in the way. Edith missed her because she was used to having her around, but Frank would soon help her forget. When she replied, Alexa resolved to tell her she wasn't yet prepared to part with the croft.

Edith's letter, although not entirely unexpected, made Alexa strangely restless, and when Colin Macdonell walked in after lunch she asked if he would like to accompany her on a ramble among the hills.

"I'd like to explore behind the croft," she explained, surprised but rather pleased to see him, yet not keen to stay and talk to him indoors. This walk, which she had intended to take ever since she had come here, seemed to present a reasonable excuse. "I've followed this track which Maxwell is after through the mountains on its southern side, but I've never been north. I suppose this Mr. Maxwell has a house or something through there and I'd like to see it."

"Oh, for heaven's sake!" Colin grumbled, looking more than a little put out. "Why go there? He isn't open to the public, you know."

"No one," she hastened to assure him, "supposes he is! All I want is one quick glance from a distance. I have no wish to speak to the man."

"Actually," Colin warned, "it's more like a castle than a house. In fact if it will save us the journey, I can give you a visual picture of Glenaird, a guaranteed replica of the real thing. It's large, and packs a punch like the man himself."

Alexa laughed. "You could never work for a travel bureau," she teased. "Your description tells me precisely nothing. I've never heard a house described like that."

"You want me to elaborate?" he grinned, running swift fingers through his wire-like hair which he didn't seem able to control.

"You ought to wear it shorter, then you would manage it better," she advised abstractedly, her mind still half on Maxwell's house.

So was Colin's, apparently, as apart from a wry shake of his head he took no notice. "Glenaird," he declared, "is reputed to be luxuriously furnished with carpets a foot deep. There are also satin-lined boudoirs where he's said to entertain his lady friends while he shoots intruders from his bedroom windows."

"Don't be an ass," she giggled. "I thought he was only interested in sheep?"

"Judge for yourself when you meet him," he returned cryptically.

"That," Alexa assured him, "is not what I intend to do. Besides, if I'd felt it necessary to introduce myself I should have called on him formally. As things stand I have nothing to say."

"You might fall for him. I've heard he has quite a way with the fair sex."

"You appear to hear quite a lot!"

"I believe," he retorted lightly, "in keeping my eyes and ears open. By all means—if you must—I'll accompany you to Glenaird, but I can't guarantee what the outcome will be."

"I'll risk it." Alexa belted her raincoat tightly around her narrow waist. "Maxwell," she quipped as they went out, "must have quite a reputation!"

"One which I envy," Colin shrugged. "A couple of weeks ago he had Lola Lorenzo staying for the weekend. What wouldn't I have given," he added frankly, "for even one short half hour!"

Lola Lorenzo, Alexa knew, was a well known star of television and film fame, much renowned for her sultry good looks. "Does he live on his own?" she asked, her curiosity aroused in spite of herself by Colin's last remark.

"There is," Colin supplied as they cut across the level field behind the croft, "an old aunt who comes and goes."

"And when she goes there are others who arrive?" Alexa, while slightly scandalised, was unable to resist asking.

"Well"—Colin laughed smoothly—"you can't really blame him. He's an attractive man and women chase him."

Alexa sighed, hurrying her feet among the heather. "I mustn't listen to any more," she cried. "I must remember, although we've never met, that he's my kinsman—if a hundred times removed."

"He wouldn't allow a little thing like that to stop him." Colin grabbed her arm as he caught her up. "He'll make mincemeat out of you, my girl, once he catches sight of you. I'm surprised he hasn't already been around."

Colin's teasing could get wearisome, but one didn't have to treat it seriously, and on this occasion Alexa had no idea why she went slightly pink and answered soberly, and rather ridiculously: "There's a little matter of property standing between us."

"Something for which you might have cause to be thankful," Colin grinned, pulling her up behind him to the top of the high ridge that overlooked the northern precincts of Glenaird. "How much easier we could have travelled by road!" he panted, more breathless than Alexa, collapsing beside her on the pine-needle-strewn grass beneath the trees.

"We haven't climbed so very high," she pointed out reasonably, gazing thoughtfully to the higher ridges above them, their impressive lines of receding ledges and terraces sweeping ever upwards to end in countless mountains stretching away in the distance with the winding arms of the sea ever curving among them. "It is hot, though," she added ruefully, beginning to remove her coat.

Colin took it from her and pulled her up against him, sliding his hands around her warm body. For a brief moment she tolerated his swift embrace, willing, if reluctantly, to accept it lightly. Then as pressure increased, she pulled decisively away from him. "I'm not," she told him firmly, "that kind of girl."

"I don't believe you!" His few minutes' rest had

done nothing for his breathing. "Not," he said, slanting her a swift look, "with your face and figure. Anyway, I don't see how you can complain—I only gave you a hug!"

"Don't, then," she snapped, remembering with irritation another man saying much the same thing. Colin would be accusing her next of being promiscuous! Surely she didn't give this impression? She sat up straight, taking her eyes from his indignant face, concentrating on the mountains.

They had walked over three miles, and such a distance on rough grass in just over an hour must be good going. Colin deserved a rest, but nothing more, and as he had come of his own free will without being specially invited, Alexa didn't consider she owed him anything. Just about to ask how much further there was to go, she was surprised when he soberly pointed to a break in the enshrouding trees.

"There you are," he lifted his hand, indicating with resigned fingers, "if you won't enjoy a little fun then we'd better stick to business. There in front of you is his lordship's castle."

Startled, Alexa found herself scrambling to her feet, the better to see where he pointed. She hadn't known they were so near. "I wish you wouldn't insist on calling him that," she exclaimed, attempting to hide an unaccountable eagerness.

"Dark like the man...!" Colin's voice behind her quoted, mockingly dramatic, taking not the slightest notice of her sharp rebuke.

Alexa scarcely heard him, or if she did there was only the faintest of quivers to signify she had. Craning through a fine tracery of pine branches, she saw in the distance a house—or was it, as Colin said, a castle? Certainly it was large enough to suggest fortress-like proportions, but from here, hemmed in as she was by the forest, it was difficult to tell. Grey and sprawling, with rugged lines, was how she summed it up. Standing in a clearing among green lawns, it was a setting such as she had longed for at Invercraig, and now she stared almost in envy. A picture-book setting with the moors and mountains at a respectful distance enhanced rather than lessened its beauty as they seemed to do at the croft.

"He doesn't use the half of it now, you know," Colin continued. "He has only one servant in the house, although he doesn't skimp things outside so much."

"He has Fergus!" She spoke too strongly, not thinking.

"I doubt if he'll have him much longer," returned Colin.

"How do you mean?" Wide-eyed she swung around to him, Glenaird strangely forgotten.

"Well, it's pretty obvious, isn't it?" Not paying a great deal of attention, Colin looked back to the house. "Anyway, he sometimes takes to the roads."

"Oh, I see..." Unable to justify a surge of bleak dismay, Alexa put it from her. "Can't we get a little nearer?" she asked, deliberately dragging her thoughts from Fergus.

"I shouldn't like to risk it," Colin grinned. "Maxwell, I believe, doesn't appreciate the uninvited guest, and I have no wish to spend the night in his dungeons."

"You've got to be joking!" Alexa laughed, yet she had no desire to see Maxwell herself, not unless he sought her out in a civilised manner. "Fergus," she said, looking straight ahead, "is forever trying to persuade me to sell Invercraig. He doesn't actually confess he knows who wants it, but I have no intention of selling to that man down there!"

Colin didn't pretend not to understand whom she referred to. "He did expect to buy it very cheaply."

"So you've told me, and I think he has a nerve." Unhappily she realised they had been over this before, but like any grouse the repeating of it brought comfort, even if the discussion of it could also arouse a small sense of unjustifiable guilt. Apart from Fergus, who was naturally prejudiced, there was no one else to talk to. Bitter resentment surged irrationally as she surveyed Maxwell's broad acres. "Owning all this," she cried, "it seems incredible that he should try to cheat a girl out of her inheritance!"

"Some say it's the other way round." Colin, losing interest in such views which had been familiar to him from childhood, sat down again, rolling on his back, and idly contemplated the huge arch of sky above him, finding more entertainment in projecting a little mischief.

"I don't follow you." Startled, Alexa glanced down at him.

"It's common knowledge, as I told you, that Angus promised to leave it to him."

"And I don't know why everyone should continue to take such an interest!" she exploded indignantly. "My father was Angus's second cousin—so I do happen to be a relation."

"So was Maxwell's father, too. A second cousin, but on the other side, which makes it all the more interesting."

Alexa flushed with annoyance. "I wish people would mind their own business," she said.

Later, when they returned to the croft, Colin asked, "Is Fergus around? I have a message from my father."

"He probably won't be here until later," she replied, somehow reluctant to mention he might not be there at all that evening.

Colin merely shrugged. "You might tell him when he does turn up to call at the store next time he's passing. I'm afraid I won't be back."

Colin was returning to his university on the following day, and told Alexa that because of her he was reluctant to leave. "But I'll see you on my first long weekend," he assured her, and seemed disappointed by the lukewarm enthusiasm of her half-hearted smile.

It was the beginning of June before Alexa had her first visitors, by which time she had the place looking quite spick and span, even if she could do little about the general image. The paintwork shone and the windows gleamed, and she had persuaded some small flowers to grow against the front of the house. A few nasturtium seeds which she had sown among them were already clambering up the rough old stonework, promising bright splashes of colour in the weeks to come. Invercraig, she decided ruefully, would never be an object of beauty, but its ugliness, in summer at least, could perhaps be disguised.

It would never be, she confessed to herself, a house she could love. Nothing much about it really appealed to her, and she occasionally did toy with the idea of selling it. Yet some perverse streak in her nature discounted the possibility. This, and the irritating knowledge that Maxwell wanted it, and that even if she didn't care for the house, she seemed to find an increasing affinity with the countryside within her. The coastline was rugged, indented by a dozen bays, all covered in a fine red sand. The mountains were rugged, rather frightening in their awesome silence, and remote, appearing never to have been touched by the hand of man. The eagle soared, ruthless in its search for prey, the fox roamed the lower slopes and sometimes in the night Alexa fancied she heard the tortured cry of some unsuspecting animal. Why, when in everything she sensed hard inflexibility, was she slowly allowing it to bind her inexorably a prisoner? There were some questions which evaded logical answers, so it was better to pretend they didn't exist. Common sense would no doubt prevail in the end, if she was patient.

The visitors who came were two middle-aged people with a teenaged son who was recovering from a minor operation. Alexa had managed herself to erect a sign at the end of the farm road as, knowing Fergus's views on the subject, she couldn't bring herself to ask him to help. When that very first evening brought instant success she felt delighted that her efforts were to be rewarded. The few hundred pounds which Angus had left she knew wouldn't stretch indefinitely. Already she had spent quite a bit on decorating and bedding, and although Fergus still refused to accept any wages she did try to repay him by providing a good breakfast, and making him an occasional meat pie which he took with some cheese for his lunch.

At seven in the morning, with her visitors still asleep, she ran downstairs to prepare breakfast. She had plenty of time. She would give Fergus his first, before she laid the fire in the dining room, then she would see to the guests.

To her surprise she found Fergus already in the kitchen, fuming. It was the first time, apart from odd moments, that she had seen him looking really annoyed and not bothering to hide it. Without so much as one polite word of greeting he began, "You have someone staying?"

Carefully, as she shot past him, she glanced at him from under her lashes and busied herself unnecessarily about the cooker as the bacon was almost done to a turn. "I have," she mumbled, groping clumsily with the percolator, finding his attitude more than a little overbearing. He looked like a positive thundercloud with that expression on his face.

"Paying guests?" His voice flicked sharply.

"Of course." She grabbed the porridge and carried it to the table, still contriving not to look at him, and because of this she felt vexed with herself. What had she to be furtive about? His dominating manner was ridiculous, his autocratic presence something to be ignored.

Fergus sat down with more than a hint of impatience, his glinting eyes taking in her rumpled hair, the shirt tucked tightly into jeans but not yet buttoned down the front. "Do you always," he asked, his gaze lingering derisively on bare flesh, "run around half naked, as well as ignoring the advice of those more able to judge clearly?"

She flushed scarlet as her fingers flew defensively to her throat, hating him. Food, she decided, would choke her! "Haven't we been through all this before?" she spluttered, tersely, "Mr.—er—Fergus..." she hesitated with pointed deliberation on his name... "I have to make a living somehow! If we must be frank, the few pounds my cousin left—along with the few odd bits of livestock I possess—wouldn't keep me for ever! One can live off the land to a certain extent, but the land I own, give or take a few blades of grass, is little more than heather."

For a moment she thought she caught a glint of something like amusement in the quirk at the side of his mouth, but his next words discredited such an impression. "Odd bits of livestock indeed! No one but someone like you would refer to animals as such. As for the croft, haven't you been offered a more than generous price for your land, Miss Lewis? What almost amounts to so much a stalk for your despised heather."

Ah! so it was out at last—into the open. He did

know! At least it was obvious he had heard rumours, if he hadn't had it from Maxwell himself. And, while she might have seen this new line of attack coming, it hurt Alexa strangely that Fergus should consider her stupid not to sell. The hurt went stinging through her veins, making her flinch, making her shout almost wildly, "It's not the heather I despise, it's Maxwell and all he stands for!"

"Which happens to be...?" Fergus's eyes pinned her down, dangerously cool, issuing a challenge.

Recklessly she took it up, past regarding the warning tremor rushing through her, scarcely aware that her mounting temper had driven out discretion. "Egotism— if I must spell it out! He's apparently so familiar with women that he expects to rule the lot of us! Well, I for one am not prepared to be trodden under the ground to make way for his sheep, while he uses the time saved by driving them through my land to entertain his girl-friends!"

There, it was out! Let Fergus put that in his pipe and smoke it! One of the maids at school had been forever using that expression—it had a fine ring about it. She hoped Maxwell could read smoke signals! And it was of no use Fergus, in his apparently self-appointed role of arbitrator, trying to make peace between them. He would only succeed in wearing himself out.

So carried away had she been in expressing her displeasure against the odious Maxwell that she missed the explosive flash of anger on the face of the man sitting opposite, the grim hardening of his mouth, instantly controlled. It was there and gone in a flash, in the few seconds that her glance spun from him, and when she looked again there was only cold indifference in his eyes.

"You appear to be well informed," he said. "You go too much to the village. It doesn't pay to repeat everything you hear, even if you are fool enough to believe it. Gossip can harm the relater of such tales often more than the defenceless victim."

"Wow!" she laughed incautiously. "You couldn't say that Maxwell is defenceless, surely?" Her head went back at such an outlandish suggestion, her eyes, full of renewed courage, taunting. Certainly she sensed that Fergus was angry, but she rushed on heedlessly, filled with a sort of tempestuous desire to get beneath his skin. "He does have you, does he not, to fight his battles? One can't help but admire his choice of weapons."

Fergus's coffee cup hit his saucer sharply, his control only leashed. "Occasionally," he said grimly, as their cool glances met and clashed, "a man can come up against something which is extremely important to him; something which he thinks, mistakenly perhaps, might be better fought for by less conventional methods. But that's not to say there's any doubt as to who, in this case, will be the ultimate victor."

Alexa swallowed the slither of sheer dislike that ran blindingly through her. There was also a flicker of hurt because he was so clearly on the side of Maxwell. She had experienced it before—a hurt that could easily slip over the borderline of pain, a vague longing that seemed to grow irrationally with discouragement. More bitterly than she knew she cried, "He certainly seems to have a rare champion in you, but there are some battles where strength alone won't prevail."

"You speak in riddles, Miss Lewis." His eyes glinted. "I presume you mean when the oppostion happens to be a woman?"

"You could say ... very few men would come out the absolute victor. Even Maxwell, I've heard, has his price!"

Momentarily Fergus's face was savage. As Alexa's

Wild Inheritance

voice faded wildly, his chair went back with a crash. "Far be it from me," he said curtly, "to quarrel with your hysterical statements. I might even warn you, if you were prepared to listen, that you could be playing with fire; such rash eloquence has a habit of rebounding. I shouldn't like to see you, Miss Lewis, caught in a coil of your own making!"

Fergus was insufferable! Why had she never seen it before? Through the heavy thumping of her over-excited heart his words caught her, slamming her sideways, affecting her already choking breath, rendering her face scarlet. "You've been full of warnings and heavy disapproval, ever since I arrived!" she flung at him, her voice coming hoarsely. "Sometimes it seems to me, Fergus, that we have nothing left to say to each other. I wonder why you continue to arrive each morning—surely not even a man like you could be susceptible to the charms of a well-cooked egg?"

There was that in her tone which was thinly insulting, and for a moment, viewing his taut jawline, she imagined she had gone too far. Apprehension surged as she noted his hands about to grab her, violently eager with their strong, well-shaped fingers to shake the life from her quivering body. Murderous was the swift, overall impression, though swiftly under leashed control. He didn't like what she said. Maybe she ought not to have spoken as she had done. Never could she remember speaking to anyone like this before, but what else could he expect, attacking her with such incredible threats, such diabolical tyranny?

She was surprised, though she refused to admit relief, when, as suddenly as it had arisen, his temper seemed to leave him. There was just a hint of steel left in his eyes to suggest things stowed away for later reprisal; he even managed a sarcastic grin, though it went no further than his sensual mouth. "As you yourself have said, Miss Lewis, every man has his price.''

At the shrug of his broad shoulders she felt as murderous as he had looked a few minutes ago, and quite shaken up inside. "If you'll excuse me," she muttered, ignoring what he said, icily polite as she rose with a defiant flourish from the table, "I must start preparing breakfast for my guests. If you've quite finished?" she added, her meaning twofold.

"I'm on my way." Curtly he took the hint, pushing in his chair as he got to his feet. Narrowly his gaze lingered. "If I'd known you were going to be in such a black mood this morning, Alexa, I wouldn't have brought along the present I left tied up in the yard."

"A present—tied up in the yard? Oh..." Pink stained her pale cheeks and her bones unpredictably melted. "Why, Fergus," she said, her veins singing because he had thought of her, all resentment suddenly gone. "How nice of you—and how mysterious. Am I allowed to see?"

"You might. Come along." Surprisingly he took her elbow, thrusting her gently through the door. The morning air, still with a crystalline freshness, was as effective as wine, making her curiously light-headed. Across the mountain tops the sun was rising, filling the world with brilliant colour, catching the early dew and turning it to a million pin-points of sparkling iridescent gems. "Look," Fergus commanded softly, and there, sitting patiently against the fence, was a small dog. "A West Highland terrier," he told her, "whose name is Glen. Nothing, I am sure you'll agree for once, could be more appropriate."

Unpredictable tears stung the back of Alexa's eyes as she stared. "Why me?" she cried, blinking her heavy lashes and holding herself tensely in an effort to conceal from Fergus her too easily swayed emotions.

His dark brows met as his keen eyes noticed her renewed agitation. "Now what is it?" he sighed. "I'm afraid I don't understand you."

"I don't altogether myself," she confessed. "It's obvious you think I need protecting. Is this your way of emphasising your point?"

"In another minute," he said tersely, "I'll choose another way of emphasising my point, as you so graciously put it—and it might hurt! I refuse to argue with you twice on the same morning. A dog does spell protection, but only to a certain extent. The thought uppermost in my mind when I brought him along was company. You can talk to him."

She tried to ignore any kindness in his tone, but could see a sort of cold patience in the grey eyes fixed steadily on her own. Her gaze was the first to falter and for a moment she felt curiously ashamed. Was it so very peculiar that Fergus realised a dog could be talked to? He was sensitive. In a dozen different ways she'd been aware of it. Even when she reduced him to cold fury he could still sense her every change of mood. She might have known this ability didn't merely relate to people!

And the small dog was beautiful—at least, it wasn't so much the dog as its expression. Such a wise little face, cocked knowingly on one side, and Fergus, whatever his reason, had brought it to her! Overwhelmingly confused, she fell on her knees, and was about to throw her arms around it only to find Fergus's cautionary hand on her shoulder.

"Just take your time," he instructed, "and give Glen his. He's an agreeable little chap, but don't rush things. You're far too impulsive."

"Don't spoil things," she exclaimed, although she did modify her headlong approach to gentle pats and small murmurs of immediate affection. "Is he—was he your dog, I mean?'' she asked, suddenly anxious, if he belonged to Fergus, how could she take him?

"In a way," he replied, straightening abruptly from the rough stone wall against which he had been lounging, watching her total absorption with the little terrier. "I haven't really time for him and, until I have, I would be greatly obliged if you would look after him for me."

"I see," said Alexa, although she didn't. How could one not have time for such a fetching little creature? But of course Fergus had a lot on his mind. "Yes, I'll certainly look after him for you," she went on, because put that way, it sounded more as if she were doing him the favour. "You can have him back when you're ready."

"It might not be too easy," he warned, "if you get too fond of him. Then you won't want to part with him. Now I really must go!"

With the now-familiar lift of his hand he was gone, and taking Glen's lead Alexa stared after him. He was the most exasperating man! It was sometimes difficult to know what to make of him, but for some reason he was beginning to affect her strangely. She even found herself looking forward to his coming and hating to see him go away. That he liked to dominate there was no gainsaying, and he could be extremely boorish when he chose. Yet the days were too long when she didn't see him, and the sound of his footsteps brought irrational pleasure surging to her breast. A tremulous feeling of anticipation which she found increasingly difficult to ignore.

Trying vainly to control unsteady heartbeats, she watched until he disappeared around the farm buildings. He didn't turn his head. "Come on," she whispered, gathering up Glen. How churlish could one get—he might have waved! Rather belatedly she remembered her neglected guests. "You can help me get them breakfast, my pet," she said.

Alexa's first guests stayed almost a week, but to her surprise she didn't make a great deal of money. She just about broke even. Totting up her bill for extra provisions, she realised she should have charged more than she had done, or probably ought not to have served such generous meals.

These particular holidaymakers had only been going to stop one night to begin with, but then they had decided they liked Invercraig and the surrounding district and asked if they might remain. Alexa had agreed. She had also agreed to make them an evening meal, and it was here she supposed where she had gone wrong. The air had seemed to produce large appetites, so Alexa had provided second helpings and sandwiches before bedtime, along with extra ones and a flask occasionally for lunch. These quite substantial extras they appeared to disregard as when it came to settling up, they would only pay the first figure quoted, which had merely been for bed and breakfast and tea and biscuits late at night. The woman had, with what she seemed to imagine was a generous gesture, left an extra pound on the hall table as she'd gone out. It really, Alexa decided, didn't make sense. Mostly everyone in the village had nothing but praise for the average tourist. The fault must be her own. Next time she resolved she would be extremely careful.

None of this she dared to mention to Fergus, whom she had only seen once since the morning he had left Glen. She felt bad enough about it without having to endure his derisive remarks and more of his tiresome advice about the dangers of entertaining without a suitable bodyguard! "Your master, at times," she told Glen, "can be a bit overpowering!" But Glen didn't seem one bit impressed. He had settled down nicely, and Alexa remembered he would be used to living at Invercraig. She was more convinced of this when he insisted on curling up each night on the old wooden settle in the kitchen below the loft where, of course, Fergus had slept. The little dog made friends with the small grey cat and she often found them curled up together in front of the warm fire, apparently well satisfied with their lot.

After the first guests had gone there was a lull, then came more who happily paid all she asked and declared themselves delighted with her hospitality, which proved rather a balm for her shattered confidence. Despite this she found herself increasingly restless, and decided she was missing Colin and his light-hearted chatter, although she hadn't seen all that much of him. Resolving to seek a little company, one afternoon after lunch she got out her car, popped Glen into the back and went back down to the village.

At the shop Colin's father was busy but pleased enough to see her. "Did Colin remember," he asked, after they'd exchanged the usual remarks about the weather, "to leave a message for Fergus?" They hadn't seen him for quite a while.

"I haven't seen him myself for a day or two," she answered, assuring him that Colin had left a message and apologised because she had forgotten to pass it on. "I'm terribly sorry," she said, really feeling quite guilty. "Is there anything I can do?"

Mr. Macdonell shrugged. "It's only some tobacco, but it's rather special and difficult to get. He doesn't like to be without it."

Alexa frowned. "No, well, I can easily take that. I haven't seen him smoke."

"Haven't you?" The man looked slightly puzzled, and his assistant who had been listening at the other side of the counter cried, "Why, Fergus smokes like a chimney!"

"Almost," Macdonell smiled.

Unconsciously Alexa wandered to the other side of the shop to examine an array of bottles. She was recalling that when Fergus had been annoyed in the kitchen and held her in his arms, she hadn't been aware of anything to suggest he smoked. Shamefacedly she remembered thinking that, in spite of the peculiar career he followed, he was always so beautifully clean. She had been conscious of nothing but the faint fragrance of a good shaving lotion. However, probably her memory didn't serve her all that well.

The display of bottles, when she realised where she was standing, amazed her. Macdonell must stock everything under the sun! French brandy, whisky, Burgundy, claret, port, sherry, rum, vodka, gin, Madeira, clear white wines, sensuous red ones, ales and beers…

"Mostly for the tourist," Macdonell called soberly.

"You have to blame somebody!" cried his irrepressible assistant, and collected a black look.

Alexa's eyes lighted and lingered on the champagne, gold-topped, black-bottled elegance. Today was her birthday, which indirectly accounted for her depression. Two days ago there had been a card from Edith, together with a small cheque which had been posted early to make sure it arrived on time. In it she again advised Alexa to come home, her impatience coming through the written words quite clearly. She had finished by saying it was entirely Alexa's fault that she was celebrating her birthday alone.

Celebrating was hardly the word, Alexa thought sourly. There had been no other indication at all that anyone else remembered her birthday. When she had collected the mail that morning from the box at the end of the road, there had only been another letter from Inverness, another communiqué from Mr. Maxwell via Robert Kerr, offering this time to take the land, leaving her the house with grazing rights for her horse and cow, should she so wish.

Fury had mingled well with her disappointment over her lack of cards. Without looking at it twice she had thrown Maxwell's offer into the kitchen fire and watched it burn. Which had really been silly, because he could in no way be blamed for friends who had forgotten. She had never had birthday parties at home—it was probably a case of out of sight, out of mind.

Now, thinking of Maxwell's offer, she almost giggled aloud. He must be the greatest! He offered more and more each time. If she was patient she might finish up a very wealthy woman!

Macdonell's glance of sudden suspicion deepened as she grabbed a bottle of champagne from the shelf and paid for it there and then, before she could change her mind.

"Celebrating?" the perky assistant grinned, smothering the bottle in tissue paper with an expert twist at both ends.

"I could be..." Lightly Alexa tried to raise an answering smile. "It's my birthday, you see."

Afterwards she regretted saying anything about it. Certainly there was no one here to bother with her birthday and she'd been foolish to explain. She surely didn't need an excuse before drinking anything she chose! Armed with Fergus's tobacco, a pile of groceries and her champagne, she kept her foot flat on the accelerator almost all the way home.

It was late before she finished her chores. She now milked the cow in the evening when Fergus didn't come—and he wasn't there tonight. She was far from expert; the animal frequently knocked the bucket over, spilling all the milk. It had been a hard struggle, the learning of it, but she had succeeded. Just one more step, she considered, on the road to independence. After this she fed the chickens, fed and brushed down the little pony then took Glen for a long, long walk along the shore.

It was almost eight before she returned, before she started to prepare for her party.

CHAPTER SIX

OF course, Alexa assured herself, it was really ridiculous to even think of having a party, but as she walked along the seashore a few ideas had entered her head. Her old friends had obviously forgotten her, and there were no new ones she knew well enough to ask to join her, but there seemed no reason why she shouldn't wash her face and put on a dress and enjoy a little celebration on her own.

Her depression might be justified. There was a debit side, but on the other hand she did have assets. She had a cake, and there was Glen and the little cat, and a roof above her head that was relatively sound. The stock outside was all well and her bed-and-breakfast venture actually beginning to pay—after its almost disastrous start! In fact she was settling down. She could drink to this if nothing else. It made sense, surely, to count her blessings rather than to dwell on her misfortunes?

The sitting-room fire was already laid and she put a match to it, watching for a few minutes until it was really light. Then she laid the table with a salad and cheese and put the percolator on the cooker before running upstairs to change.

She had only brought three dresses, and two of these were still in a suitcase beneath the bed. The one she had unpacked was a silky chiffon with rather a daring low neckline. Ruefully she held it up in front of her before the mirror, then decided not to wear it. For the house it did seem too elaborate, deserving a better occasion—with an audience, she thought wryly—to admire it. Eventually, instead of a dress she donned a pair of clean blue Levis and, as a slight concession, a fluffy white blouse, buttoned briefly as was the fashion, and with wide, transparent sleeves. Around her neck she strung a gilt chain necklace which glittered against her skin where it caught the light. Her hair she brushed out until it hung heavy and shining, curving silkily into her throat and over her shoulders. It was getting long, too long. When she—if she went back to Inverness she must find a hairdresser and have it cut. Meanwhile it would have to do. The Levis felt slack, as if she had lost some weight, and she tightened the belt a little, studying the effect. Then, suddenly impatient with herself, she turned away from her reflection in the glass. Wasn't it silly to be bothering with details like this when there was no one around to see!

The small sitting room was warm, but not so warm as the kitchen. After a brief half-hour Glen returned to his bed on the old settle, leaving Alexa by herself.

Supper, she found, was not much fun on a festive occasion when eating alone. Unhappily she glanced at the table, disenchanted with the plainness of the setting, her mind lingering dreamily on lace, on sparkling crystal, with gleaming silver and beautiful china, and perhaps masses of flowers in huge goblets. And of course, the lighting from fairy-like chandeliers would be subdued, and there would be someone special sitting opposite, speaking softly, his eyes as well as his voice telling her she was wonderful—if such a picture from her imagination could be real!

Inadvertently her wistful thoughts turned to Fergus, and he wished that somehow she had gathered enough courage to ask him to keep her company this evening. Yet since their quarrel a few days ago, although on the

surface everything seemed much the same, underneath there were dark undercurrents. She was sure of
it. Fergus, she felt, had not forgotten everything she
had said, and she hadn't wished to risk a snub by inviting him to her part.

Which, she decided, not trying to shake off a growing lethargy induced by too much fresh air, a late supper and two glasses of champagne, wasn't much of a
party anyway! Rather listlessly she poured herself
another glass of the cool, sparkling wine which didn't
really taste of anything much but was nice to hold and
contemplate slowly. What, she sighed bleakly, did it
matter if she got a little high? There was no one to
witness such an event—no one but Glen, who appeared to have lost interest in the proceedings.

She left the table and went to sit very still by the fire,
sipping the wine and relaxing in the rosy haze which
slowly enveloped her, soon almost half asleep as she
watched the lazy summer flames flickering softly against
the black, sooty chimney. Quietly she stirred in the vel-
vet-covered, wing-backed chair, her chin drooping to
her breast, when she imagined she heard something.
There was only time to raise her head before the door
opened abruptly and Fergus walked in.

"Talk of the devil—or think of him!" she muttered
stupidly, staring wide-eyed at him. Half an hour ago
she might have welcomed company, now she found
herself resenting it. "Don't you ever knock?" she
asked unevenly.

"Occasionally!" He filled the room with his height
and breadth, and something else she couldn't put a
name to. "Actually," he assured her, "I did knock
once, but there was no reply." His tone was in no way
apologetic and his eyes, as they went over her, were
oddly speculative, lingering narrowly on blue jeans,
pale alluring blouse and pink, seductive mouth.

"I see..." Suddenly Alexa didn't wish to quarrel any more, and she smiled as she looked up at him. The pleasure of the evening, which had started to wane, returned, if vaguely, it always seemed to be there, no matter how she fought it, the longing to see him. There was only his dark, handsome head, swiftly scanning the room before coming back to her face. She could feel her heart thudding and, out of fear that he might guess, she spoke hastily. "Now that you are here you can tell me what you want. I don't suppose you merely dropped in?"

"Why not?" he asked coolly, not aware of her throbbing excitement. "I was passing."

"Passing...?" her voice faded weakly as she tried to concentrate. It could be true. She had no idea what he did in his spare time. It wasn't as if he had his own fireside, a family to occupy himself with. Her lashes fell in some confusion.

"Yes," he stated firmly, his glance leaving her to rest on the table as if determined to find a few answers. "Celebrating?" His brows rose as he noticed the half-empty bottle, the as yet uncut cake with one candle.

He used words with a rare economy! All at once she wished he hadn't seen. The outward signs of her advancing years, when viewed in the cold light of his indifferent query, seemed pathetic. If only she had heard him coming she might have whipped them from sight. "My birthday," she felt forced to say at last, wondering why she was explaining, trying to imitate his intelligence. It was nobody's business.

He studied her another moment. "And so," he said smoothly, "you went to Macdonell's and purchased champagne. Then instead of asking someone to join you in a civilised manner, you choose to sit here and empty the bottle yourself."

Alexa, not prepared for such an attack, blinked. She blinked several times before she found an answer, not caring for what he said—what he implied—one bit. With delicate fingers she brushed the heavy hair from her hot forehead, just giving herself a moment to think. Her voice when it came was faintly plaintive.

"You know I'm more or less a stranger in the district. How could I ask anyone? They might have felt— well, embarrassed. And," she added, with a fine sense of grievance, "you don't have to be so condemnatory about the champagne. I just have one bottle, which resembles fizzy lemonade."

"But not in its effect, I'm thinking." His mouth twitched slightly at the corners as he firmly closed the door without taking his eyes from her slightly flushed cheeks. Advancing to the table, he picked up the contentious bottle with a derisive shake of his head, apparently not impressed by the label. "I'd better join you," he said dryly, "if only to stop you imbibing too much. I shouldn't want to have to carry you to bed."

She flushed at that, colour now running wildly, and stared at him balefully, aware of a mutual antagonism that could not be denied. "Oh, damn," she cried, vanquished for the moment by despair, "please yourself what you do. I don't care! We may as well drown our sorrows together, I suppose."

He didn't reply other than to glance at her sharply—a glance she didn't see. Her eyes were enormous and wild colour splashed her cheekbones, brilliantly contrasting with the whiteness of her blouse. Her shoulders drooped, suggesting listless fatigue, a certain weariness of spirit that belied her couldn't-care-less words. Thoughtfully he filled one of the spare glasses which she had put out as a kind of protest against a lonely fate, then topped hers up, noting that she made no gesture to stop him. "Come on," he said, his voice low with sardonic mockery, "out with it. What's causing the black mood?"

Alexa said nothing, not immediately. The champagne went to her head as she drank it recklessly and she felt sort of floaty, entirely disoriented. Why should this man—this tramp—imagine she was anything else but content? And who was he to question any mood she chose to display? She frowned at him as, uninvited, he took the chair beside her. "I had another letter today from Maxwell. I didn't receive one birthday card! Just a letter from that odious man, and I burnt it!"

"So you burnt it!" For a brief second his fingers tightened around the stem of his glass—it might have been her neck—and his face hardened. Then, as suddenly as it had come, his grimness left him. "Well," he shrugged, "you can have no more doubts about that, so forget it. What's your next grumble?"

"I'm not sure..." Did she have another one? Making a tremendous effort, she tried to concentrate, something she was finding extremely difficult. What was so maddening was that he seemed aware of it. He was so near that if she put out a hand she could touch him. It was his size that was so intimidating, and, as so often before, she sensed in him some thread of controlled anger; this time possibly because she'd been stupid enough to drink too much when she wasn't used to it. "I went for a walk," she murmured, her mind growing impotent beneath his intent regard, "along the shore. I enjoyed it, but I think I walked too far. But that isn't to say I have a grouse."

He smiled slightly. "Why don't you," he asked, "learn to ride your pony?"

"I did try," she protested, "but I fell off."

"I could teach you some time."

Some time? That could be any time—never! She so rarely saw him. "The creature doesn't like me," she announced plaintively. "Have some cake. I made it myself."

Her statement about the pony seemed to put an end to the matter, and amusement lurked in his eyes. They were left with the cake. He considered it afresh, very gravely. "No candles?"

"No candles," she agreed, following the line of his objective glance quite clearly. "At least, just that one. I found it in the kitchen. It doesn't count."

"Well," his voice was filled with amiable derision, "somehow it seems to indicate a birthday, a sort of planting of clues. A deliberate attempt to arouse curiosity. How old are you today? Given the right number of candles I shouldn't have needed to guess."

The idea of having to blow out all those candles imbued Alexa with a fine exhaustion. Even one might prove too much. She was glad she had left the rest where she found them. Fergus talked too much. Rather fretfully she looked fleetingly into his eyes, attempting to organise her thoughts. He had asked how old she was. "I told you," she said.

"No, you didn't." He reached for her glass and refilled it, a hint of devilment lurking. "Have another drink," he added softly, "then you might tell me."

She still had the strength of mind to set the champagne to one side. "I think," she muttered carefully, "I've had enough. If you must know, I'm twenty-one."

"I should never have thought it, but it's comforting to know," his tone was enigmatic. "Twenty-one! Now I can hardly remember..."

"Didn't you have a party, Fergus?" There was that about him which she thought resembled pathos, and quickly she thrust her own troubles from her. Fergus, too, might have suffered from a disrupted childhood.

Yet he surprised her by nodding abstractedly. "Yes, I

did indeed have a large one." He paused, catching her
bewildered glance, and there was silence in the quiet
room. "Forget about me," he said abruptly. "It's your
party, I won't do anything to spoil it."

She laughed lightly. "You couldn't spoil it, Fergus,
by telling me about yours. Nor could anyone, by the
widest use of the imagination, call this a party. But if
you would really rather forget, how about your life
since then? Do you honestly like living the way you
do?"

There, it was out! For weeks she had longed to ask
that question. Now she waited with some trepidation
for his answer, her heart a nervous thud in her ears.

Yet nothing that was happening this evening had
been in any sense premeditated, especially not this
rather frightening moment when Fergus held her captive in his arms. Fear shot through her, cancelling all
else. What did she really know of him? Wasn't she
crazy not to fight him, to push him away instead of
resting nervelessly against his shoulder, as if she
keep it even, held the slight bitterness of reproach.

"You could say that," he drawled, and his eyes on
her wide green ones were cynical. "But I'm not exactly
a hermit, you know."

The hurt deepened, slicing through her. She could
have told him she was well aware of it, but restrained
herself just in time. There was nothing to be gained by
open criticism of what was after all his own affair, but
in striving to avoid an impertinent remark it seemed
she could only produce another equally so. "It probably
comes of living beside a man like Maxwell. I've heard
all about him and his women!"

His smile was ironic, a crisp twist of his well-cut
mouth. "We don't have to go over that again."

"Why not?" Of a sudden she was determined that
he shouldn't have absolute control over the conversa-

tion, tolerating only that which pleased him, discarding what didn't. Yet beneath his taunting regard she moved uneasily, challenging indiscreetly. "He had Lola Lorenzo to stay, and she's a wow!"

"Indeed." It seemed he almost laughed at her expression of incredulous exasperation. Then, sobering, he stretched his long legs, saying lazily, "Can't you forget all these people who bother you, just for an hour? Otherwise you aren't going to enjoy yourself very much."

"Maybe you're right." It seemed a great concession and for a moment Alexa felt almost carried away by her own generosity of spirit. It was clear she wasn't going to get any straight answers, so as he said, why not call a sort of truce? It didn't matter that they were forever making and breaking them. As Fergus said, this was her birthday, and if she didn't make the most of it, well, who would? "I will try," she nodded in agreement, and smiled.

Fergus smiled back, if appraisingly. When he smiled, Alexa decided, he was so much more approachable, and if her pulse beat a little faster when he looked at her like that she could blame it on the wine. "I didn't mean," she continued agreeably, "to raise controversial subjects. Your present position can't be exactly easy. I merely wondered if you enjoyed it, that was all. I was actually ready to sympathize."

"And it's taken half a bottle of champagne to produce the necessary courage?" His dark brows rose mockingly. "You might be grateful that I've restricted myself to one glass of Macdonell's potent liquor, otherwise you might have found yourself listening to all kinds of information you'd rather be without."

Alexa tried to assimilate that without obvious effort, only in her present state of mind it was quite beyond her. Fergus sat there—her eyes travelled slowly over

him, so cool and calculating in his light slacks, the fine
shirt beneath the casual pullover. She envied him if the
life he led produced such an uncaring frame of mind.
Of course, as she had thought before, his confidence
might just be skin deep. Underneath might he not
sometimes long for all the conventional things, a wife
and home of his own, for instance? Everything his
rather aimless wanderings denied him. "You might
tease me about the champagne," she said suddenly,
"but you must know what it's like to have no one. No
card on your birthday, no sign of affection from anyone!"

Her voice rose childishly, and, horrified, she found
herself almost in tears. Flushing scarlet, she jumped to
her feet. "I'm sorry," she gasped, "please take no notice."

Fergus had the nerve to laugh, his eyes glinting on
her hot face, and came swiftly to his own feet, one
hand steadying beneath her elbow, the other fishing
obligingly in his pocket to produce a clean white handkerchief. "You were complaining," he prompted,
carefully drying an overflowing tear, "of a lack of affection?"

"Well, I meant no outward sign." Ineffectively she
tried to escape his restraining hand, not caring for the
flicker of familiar flame that shot through her at his
touch. "Edith," she muttered, "did send a card a few
days ago."

"But a card," he said, watching her closely, "doesn't
compensate for people who aren't here."

Alexa shivered in his hold. "I'm not sure I understand."

"Of course you don't. You're just a confused child.
Yet you've totted up a certain number of years that
must count for something. Don't you have a boy-
friend?"

"You mean like Colin?"

"Young Macdonell—what did he teach you?"

She didn't like the way his tone hardened, and her voice caught. "What a question!" she cried. "I scarcely knew him. There wasn't time."

"What has time to do with it?" His eyes were examining her face, as if looking keenly for outward signs of some hidden experience, not willing to merely accept her word.

"You asked me that once before," was all the reply she could think of. He was too near, and only amusing himself with her tale of woe. She had been crazy to mention anything. His mouth was too mocking. Why, a few minutes ago she'd felt sorry for him, which must be the craziest thing!

He spoke again, his voice pure tyranny. "I should have thought by now you might have come up with a few answers. I've seen your problem whirling in that beautiful head, but in some cases one needs help to visualise the natural conclusion."

She tried to break away from him, suffocating with indignation. There was an undercurrent of tension beneath the lazy banter, but she chose only to be aware of the latter. Her glance was stormy as she retorted swiftly. "In any circumstances you are the last person I would go to for help of any kind!"

He laughed, watching the colour come and go under her smooth, satiny skin. "Come here, Alexa," he said. "A twenty-first is quite an occasion, allowing a little licence, to be sure."

Instinctively alarmed, she backed away from him, only to find his hand tightening on her wrist. "You're complaining," he smiled smoothly, "as I was saying before we somehow lost the theme, about a lack of affection, which translated, I suppose, means that no one has kissed you on your birthday. A state of affairs which can easily be rectified. I can at least supply some outward sign of this commodity you seem to crave.''

Wildly she asserted, "I didn't mean that! There are other things.''

"But nothing else exactly on hand, so we can only give what we have, which must suffice until we're able to purchase a more orthodox if less satisfying present." The muscles of his hand went taut as his arm slipped around her, drawing her closer, and they came together with a sense of shock. There was no logical pause in which she might have voiced some sort of protest and the fact that none entered her mind after that first hypersensitive second, didn't afterwards provide any sort of comfort. Neither did she seem at that particular moment very addicted to the straighter, narrower paths which Edith maintained were the only possible ways for nicely brought up young ladies.

Fergus's intentions, in those first hazy moments, were very clear; but he had kissed her once before and if nothing else it had aroused a curiosity within Alexa regarding her reactions should he do so again. About that first occasion her feelings were mixed, the ratio definitely muddled. There had been anger and despair— low smouldering flames of desire and an instantaneous if totally reluctant response. As to which of these emotions had been predominant, it hadn't been definable, and the futile searching for an answer had haunted many midnight hours. Until, as she now realised, there was only one possible way of solving something which had rapidly been becoming an obsession.

Yet nothing that was happening this evening had been in any sense premeditated, especially not this rather frightening moment when Fergus held her captive in his arms. Fear shot through her, cancelling all else. What did she really know of him? Wasn't she crazy not to fight him, to push him away instead of resting nervelessly against his shoulder, as if she couldn't—or wouldn't—help herself? She could feel his hand against the silken curtain of her hair, holding her still while his fingers laced through it, examining the texture as if it fascinated him a little.

"Such wonderful hair," he murmured soothingly, as if he was well aware of her need for reassurance and was willing to supply it. "Such a weapon for male destruction. How could a mere man resist it!" His face came down to the soft, clean smell of it. "Like violets in the rain," he teased, "and just about as irresistible."

Alexa stood quite still, forgetting all about the need to struggle. While his voice held a hint of amusement she had a vague feeling that he was making love to her, and suddenly she was possessed by an overwhelming fear that he might stop. Her breath held as unconsciously she pressed a little closer, her own arms sliding with a kind of desolate acquiescence around his body. Fergus, she felt instinctively, might be capable of many things, but he would never intentionally hurt her, and surely the gods would not wish to deny her a little consolation on a day such as this! Fergus, it seemed, could arouse feelings she hadn't previously been aware of, and, like the very young experimenting innocently with danger, she chose to ignore the warning lights for the dazzling, enticing picture which flickered irresistibly on a sort of mental screen.

Then as feeling rose like a swiftly oncoming tide between them, his hand slid under her chin, turning it up gently as he found her mouth with his own. She drew a long shuddering breath and yielded completely against him.

He seemed to kiss her mouth for a long, long time. Gently at first, his arms moulding her to him, moving carefully across her back, one hand returning again to her hair, clasping a great handful of it so as to tug her head firmly back to his shoulder, the pressure of his lips increasing when he met with no resistance. Once, when he looked up, she pulled his head to hers, losing all sense of reality, all conscious awareness of what she was doing. She could only feel his mouth beginning to hurt, as it had done on that other occasion when he had kissed her, and it was like drowning, like going off on big rolling waves. Like being swept away by tumbling surf, entirely out of control.

Her arms were around his neck and they were very close, their lips and bodies touching and clinging, tenderness now forgotten as they discovered a deep need for each other. In one blinding instant when she stirred, almost dragging her mouth from his, like some belated gesture of self-preservation, he caught her ruthlessly back to him. "Stop it," he said cruelly, his fingers marking her fragile skin as he held her prisoner.

"No more—please," her voice was a soft moan.

"Kiss me," he commanded thickly, "it was you who wanted it."

She couldn't reply, unable to find within herself the strength to argue, and obediently her lips parted beneath his as everything about her seemed immediately to disintegrate. She was only aware of the hardness of his arms, the wildly responsive beating of her heart which he must surely feel beneath the thin fabric of her blouse. When he paused for another minute her eyes were as green as glass beneath her half-closed lids and her hair hung, golden like ripened wheat, across her shoulders. His eyes went over her, shaken by her new urgent beauty.

"Alexa?" he spoke slowly, his voice seeming to hold a question. As if he understood something better than she did and was prepared to be patient with her—up to a point.

From a long distance she heard her name on his lips. There was within her the urge to focus, but she couldn't, not right away, not while she felt so unwilling to return to mundane normality. Yet there was also the need for some discussion. When Fergus kissed her all her former muddled impressions resolved themselves clearly. Wasn't she lonely living here by herself, just as surely as Fergus must be, tramping the country without any home? When he kissed her she knew it would be good—just the two of them. She didn't know much about such things, having had little chance to gain any sort of knowledgeable experience, but surely if they felt like this after one brief embrace they could do even better on a more permanent basis? But it would be up to her. In spite of the occasional egotism there was probably an outsize inferiority complex, something she would have to deal with. It wouldn't be easy.

She stirred, taking a deep breath. "Fergus," she began carefully, rather tremulously, "have you ever thought of marrying, of settling down?"

Whatever else he had in mind it didn't appear to have been this. Bitterly, she reflected later that she might easily have shot him without achieving the same degree of shock. Not that this was immediately apparent, but it could be ascertained by the abrupt way in which he straightened, putting her abruptly from him, and she felt slain by his dark, glittery look.

"Such things," he assured her, watching her narrowly, "never enter my head."

Alexa had heard of people wishing that the ground might open and swallow them up. Now it had happened to her, and she felt terrible. Totally humiliated would perhaps be a better way of describing it. She was scarcely aware of Fergus pushing her firmly back into her chair, the gentleness of his hands belied by his wholly cynical expression.

"Tomorrow," he promised lightly, "I'll tell Macdonell exactly what I think of his champagne!"

Wild colour flooded Alexa's cheeks as she stared blindly down at her shaking hands. He was being diplomatic, holding out straws which she must grasp even if every inch of her rebelled: for her pride's sake if nothing else. "It's not Macdonell's fault," she said obligingly, "that I drank too much."

"Next time," he advised, the tenseness of his mouth easing a little as he obviously rated his chances of escape higher, "I should stick to lemonade. It keeps one more responsible."

It was then that something inside Alexa gave way, as anger and misery strove with discretion and the latter didn't win. Suddenly she didn't care any more. It was of no use trying to be clever by attempting to apply a different construction to what had turned out to be little more than a fiasco. He knew only too well what she had been about to suggest, and had more or less flung her offer back in her face! He would be laughing all the way to Glenaird! She wouldn't put it past him to relate the whole sorry tale to Maxwell.

Mortified, she scrambled to her feet, temper and embarrassment removing the hurt tears from her eyes. Chin up, head flung back, she glared at him, not prepared to pretend an indifference she didn't feel. "Just get out of here, Fergus," she flung at him, "and don't ever bother to come back. I'm probably not the wisest girl on earth, but neither am I, I hope, the most senseless one! Why, I wouldn't marry you if you were the last man on earth!"

She was almost to the top of the stairs before she remembered that he hadn't even asked her.

The remainder of that night was bad enough, yet the days which followed seemed even worse. In spite of her bravely defiant words Alexa found herself thinking almost continually of Fergus. She kept busy; each night she filled the house with visitors as the season began to get under way. They came from all parts of the country, some from abroad, and to stay on a real Highland croft was, they assured her, one of the high spots of their holiday. She enjoyed having these people—apart from any financial gain she appreciated their company. Having no immediate neighbours could be lonely, and her tourists kept her both busy and amused.

The work, however, was especially hard now that Fergus didn't come any more, and she found herself getting easily tired. She lost weight which in turn must have affected her nerves, as she felt inclined to burst into tears at the least little thing. Very occasionally Fergus did come to milk the cow, but he always contrived to do this extremely early in the morning, leaving the milk beside the kitchen fire to keep warm. And while once she heard him moving about, pride forbade her to move from her bed until he was gone.

If he really wanted to see her, she decided stubbornly, there were other times, and he knew where to find her, but he made no other attempt to contact her and Alexa's heart grew heavier as the days lengthened.

She spent hours along the seashore and walking in the hills with Glen, trying to convince herself she didn't really care for a wild Scotsman like Fergus, but all in vain. Memories stored away came back, refusing to be dislodged, and she drifted somewhere between reality and pain. There were his arms and his lips, his voice, so surprisingly gentle; all blending so harshly with the ruthlessness of his rejection, a state of affairs she found difficult to come to terms with.

At the second letter from Inverness she made a great effort and went to see Robert Kerr as he asked her to. It was a long way to go, there and back in one day in the

little car, but she made it. She took in her Bed and
Breakfast sign, left Glen plenty to eat and drink after
exercising him well, and set off.

Robert Kerr was brief and dour and seemed in no
way to approve of her decision to stay at Invercraig.
"I'm still of the opinion," he said, referring heavily to
his last letter, "that you would be wiser to sell the land.
You could keep the house, in fact Maxwell appears
quite keen for you to do so."

"Really?" Alexa shrugged indifferently, not at that
moment ashamed of her ill-manners, so incensed was
she by the man's obvious deference to Maxwell.

The man smiled, striving, it seemed, for patience.
"You might never again get such a chance, my dear,
and my client is not a man to be played with."

He made it sound as if she was under some kind of
threat. That little bit on the end was surely not entirely
ethical? Why must people persist in treating her as if
she were five years old? To begin with Robert Kerr had
refused to reveal the identify of his revered client. Now
he waved the name of Maxwell in her face as if he
expected the very sound of it to strike fear into her
heart.

"I have no intention," she assured him coolly, "of
playing with a man like Maxwell. You may tell him I am
refusing to sell, once and for all."

Which sounded pretty decisive whichever way you
looked at it, she considered with some satisfaction, rising to her feet. "If there's nothing else," she began,
but he waved her back to her seat, to her surprise pressing a bell for coffee.

"I think it might be advantageous to you if you could
spare me a few more minutes, Miss Alexa, to hear exactly what I have to say ..."

Afterwards, before she left Inverness, Alexa did
some shopping, buying among other things several

new tops and another pair of Levis, which she found so useful on the croft. There was also a new bottle of her favourite perfume, which she tried to convince herself she couldn't do without.

The day was still sunny in the late afternoon with cloud shadows chasing each other over the landscape. The lochs and rivers sparkled, but when the sun went down the coolness of blue water and green trees struck a peculiar chill, filling Alexa with an odd foreboding, a sense of prevailing disaster she couldn't account for. And, much as she tried to shake it off, it stayed with her all the way home.

Glen was delighted to see her, playing happily with the hard rubber bone she brought him after enjoying the special tin of dog meat which she opened as an extra present for being good. He shared his meal with the small cat, whom Alexa still hadn't found a name for. Later, after she had made herself a cup of tea, she was well aware that he expected to go for a walk, because he sat by the door and stared at her and wagged his tail, but she felt too tired. "Tomorrow," she promised him aloud, "we'll go a long way."

The next afternoon, shortly after lunch, they set out. Instead of keeping to the shore where she thought there might be people picnicking, Alexa decided to follow the track through the mountains on the southern side, until she arrived at open country. It wasn't so far and Glen would enjoy romping in the heather.

She hadn't gone more than a few hundred yards before she noticed, to her surprise, that the ground was covered with small marks, easily seen where the recent rain had left wet patches of mud. It didn't take her long to realise they were the tracks of sheep. The impression of their cloven hooves was unmistakable, and so numerous as to pull her up short.

Alexa stopped and frowned, staring anxiously. For

almost the whole of yesterday she had been away from home. Had Maxwell seized his chance and driven a flock over the pass when there was no one here to stop him? It seemed the only, and obvious, explanation. Angrily she walked on, following the evidence until, on a corner where the track curved sharply and widened out, she came upon half a dozen sheep and lambs.

It really was the limit! she thought furiously as at the first sight of her the animals took off as if she were the devil himself. Yet was it possible, she wondered, that the culprits were merely this handful of strays, even though the incriminating evidence spoke of hundreds?

At a distance the sheep stopped, milling around each other before turning to regard her with a nervous curiosity.

She stood motionless for a few more frustrated seconds, then was just about to turn and leave when, to her amazement, Glen flew past her and gave full chase. Aghast, she stared as the usually docile little dog turned himself into a positive bundle of fury. Loudly he barked, herding the sheep with their bleating young lambs into a sort of clearing among the trees where his continuous yapping filled the air distractingly.

Alexa, suddenly finding her wits, raced after him, but long before she reached the spot they had disappeared around the next corner, although she could still hear Glen. Then to her horror, she heard a shot, followed by an ominous, frightening silence. Then nothing more until seconds later Glen came howling back around the side of the mountain, taking absolutely no notice when she shouted and going almost faster than the report she had heard from the gun.

CHAPTER SEVEN

ALEXA swung swiftly around as Glen hurtled past her, her heart thudding wildly. Loudly she yelled for him to stop, but he didn't seem to hear her and kept right on. Fading, as he disappeared into the distance, came the last notes of his wild indignation, and Alexa's heart froze. Maybe he was hurt?

So filled with apprehension that she failed to hear the heavy footsteps behind her, and suddenly found herself face to face with a very irate figure, presumably the shepherd, carrying a gun. For a moment she almost sighed with relief because she had thought it might be Fergus.

Her relief, however, was short-lived when the man asked angrily, "Your dog, miss?"

Like most of the men in these parts he seemed too big, too strong to be easily intimidated, so Alexa didn't even try. Numbly, she found herself nodding evasively, aware of a hard knot of fright in her stomach. "I suppose he is, but he doesn't exactly belong to me. I have him from..."

"Fergus!" the man broke in sharply. "I knew it!"

Mixing strangely with her terror came a strong resentment. "You can't possibly blame Fergus," she cried, "when he's not here!"

"I've told him before," the shepherd exclaimed, ignoring this coldly, "to keep that damned dog under control. The trouble is Maxwell himself is too lenient!"

Fergus—Maxwell! Was she never to escape them? "I've told you," she said bleakly, "Fergus isn't responsible this time. And there was no need to shoot the poor little dog. He was only chasing sheep."

The man stared at her as if she had taken leave of her senses, a fine sense of outrage on his face. "Just chasing them indeed! 'Tis well seen you were not brought up in the country! Even chasing sheep can do untold damage! That dog can't resist sheep, and one of these fine days he will be catching them, worrying them! I have heard himself telling Fergus that much."

"Well, I'm sorry," Alexa gulped, seeing the point of his argument if not entirely in agreement with his methods. Nor did she care for his tone of voice when discussing Glen.

"Poor little fellow," she rebuked him, "you almost scared him out of his wits!"

"Indeed, miss," the man was still impatient, "you might be thankful it is only fright he would be receiving. It was too careful I had to be for fear of hitting an ewe."

"There was still no need," Alexa asserted, "to go about things in such a primitive manner! I'm sure something less disagreeable would have proved just as effective. As it is I don't know what Fergus is going to say. Poor Glen might never reach home!"

"At the rate he was going it's surprised I would be if he has not already passed it," the man declared sourly, his tone indifferent, but he watched Alexa with increasing interest. "How is it that you have a dog belonging to Fergus?"

"My uncle, Angus Lewis, owned the croft," she explained quickly, instinctively feeling this man had already guessed her identity, "and Fergus helps."

"I see, miss," the man became a shade more respectful, even to the extent of lightly touching his cap.

"I knew Angus well, but he was never a man," he added, "to let a dog chase sheep."

A fault, a transgression in his eyes, that could not be easily rectified. Alexa sighed, preparing to leave him, still anxious about Glen in spite of the shepherd's sarcastic assurance that he would be home. She was surprised when he called as she turned away.

"You don't happen to have seen Fergus lately, have you? I would very much appreciate a word with him."

See Fergus? Alexa halted in her hurried flight, glancing at him swiftly. She was just about to retort that she very rarely saw him when something else crossed her mind—something which should have been mentioned earlier. "Have you," she inquired coolly, "been driving sheep through the track while I've been out for the day?"

If she had hoped her abrupt query would produce immediate signs of guilt she was doomed to disappointment. Very little could be ascertained from the man's sombre, weatherbeaten face. There was merely a wary narrowing of his eyes, which might have indicated many things but not one conclusive clue.

"That," he shouted civilly, "is not a question I could be answering. Nor might it be very wise for a girl like you to be asking it. What Maxwell does or thinks is his own business. He's easy enough unless something gets in his way."

Threats, dire warnings, hidden in words! Fuming silently, Alexa stared after him. These people—these Scots! They were too smart by far! One could never, it seemed, catch them out, no matter how one tried. It was awful, and how could one lone girl hope to fight them when no one in all their entire history had ever been able to do that for long? Not with any notable success anyway, and it wasn't likely that she would triumph where others had failed.

A day that starts badly might be expected to improve as it goes on. This one only got worse. After her unfortunate brush with the shepherd Alexa went home. She looked out for Glen on the way, but there was no sign of him anywhere, nor could she find him at Invercraig. Diligently she searched the house and buildings without result. It seemed he had disappeared completely and she grew very anxious, her fury against Maxwell's shepherd increasing.

After she finished her evening tasks she boiled an egg for her supper but could scarcely eat it. She could only conclude that the little dog, in his fright, had run straight back to Fergus. Dogs were fundamentally creatures of instinct, and it would be to his master that one would surely run in times of trouble. There was little doubt, Alexa assured herself, that could she find the courage to go to Glenaird, she would discover him safely established.

Of course the very thought of going personally to Glenaird was not to be so much as considered and, as she had no telephone, there was really no way to contact Fergus. As she ate her supper she worried over it. She had grown fond of Glen in the short time she had had him, and she missed his company, but that might have been endurable if she had known he was safe. Surely if he had returned to Glenaird Fergus would have let her know? He couldn't surely assume she had lost interest in the dog and thrown him out!

All this was very distracting, and so preoccupied was she with such thoughts that she was unaware of a loud knocking on the front door, until it seemed that whoever was there was almost prepared to knock the door down.

Alexa glanced up from the table, suddenly startled. It was nearly ten o'clock and the light was beginning to fade. It was even beginning to rain lightly, the overcast sky wrapping the surrounding mountains in eerie shadow. She couldn't think who it could be at this time of night. It wouldn't be Fergus—he wouldn't have used the front door, neither would he knock. It surely couldn't—her heart missed a beat—be Maxwell, come to complain about the dog chasing his sheep?

Well, there was just one way to find out. Screwing up her fast-failing courage, she left the kitchen and stumbled across the hall, only to find when she dragged the stiff old door open that it was two men searching for accommodation.

For a few seconds she could only stare at them, dragged down by the weight of an anticlimax. She remembered putting her Bed and Breakfast sign out again after lunch, but she had quite forgotten about it. It was late. She had known people come later, but not two men on their own.

Gazing at them reluctantly, she felt herself draw back unconsciously. Usually she stuck to married couples, people with children, or girls like herself; not because she felt there way any need for such extreme caution, but always recalling Fergus's warning about using ordinary common sense.

This evening she had no time, and was in no sort of state to find a reasonable excuse when the two men on the doorstep greeted her politely and asked for rooms.

"If you have anything, miss," one of them said, "we would be grateful. I'm afraid we've left it a bit late."

It was here, Alexa realised afterwards, where she ought to have told them she was full up. The thought did occur, but a lack of cars in the yard wouldn't have borne out such a declaration, and her wits at that particular moment didn't seem up to inventing a few carless hikers or mountaineers. "I suppose I could manage to find you something," she replied hesitantly, as they walked past her into the house.

Numbly she closed the door before glancing at them again in the brighter light. They appeared to be men in their late twenties, rather carelessly dressed, but then they were, she presumed, on holiday. In spite of their untidy appearance they didn't exactly look like rogues, and if she refused to have them they might not find at this hour anyone else who would. "If you like, I'll show you your rooms," she said.

Tourists usually asked to see their rooms before agreeing to take them. Alexa had learnt this soon after she had opened. Private homes, not being subject to the same rigorous rating as hotels, occasionally offered a very poor standard of accommodation. So someone in the village had told her, and people spending a holiday in this way were only being sensible in reassuring themselves.

So now she suggested a tour of inspection right away, and so far she had had no complaints. This evening this purely routine task filled her with nervous apprehension for no good reason she could think of. Fergus had eventually been persuaded to fix the generator, but the light still flickered too much on a windy night like this one and was far from satisfactory. The hall and stairway were dim and the two men giggled and muttered behind her, barely glancing at their beds, seemingly more interested in herself as they announced themselves satisfied. Long before they were downstairs again she became aware with some dismay that they had both been drinking.

It just wasn't her day! Despairingly she slumped by the kitchen table, her head aching. She had left the men in the sitting room and prayed fervently that they would stay there while she made some coffee which she hoped might sober them up. She made the coffee black and cut a plate of sandwiches, then putting the whole lot on a tray she carried it in.

The coffee, however, did little to sober them up. They grew extremely talkative and asked a lot of questions about the croft. So many, in fact, that in the end Alexa felt forced to invent fictitious parents, who, she assured them nervously, would be returning shortly, and that she herself was going to bed. It was small comfort that her story about other people living here besides herself appeared to give them something to think about.

Nightmares, when viewed in retrospect, usually seem worse or not as bad as they actually are at the time. This one, Alexa was sure, would never even bear thinking of.

It was late when she went upstairs and fell into an uneasy sleep. The two men were still talking in the sitting room as she passed. Some time later she awoke, she didn't know why. Maybe it had been the sound of rain against the window, together with the distant rumble of thunder. Yet her eyes turned, in her first conscious moments, not to the window but the door. Outside she heard the low murmur of voices, low-pitched laughter, then to her horror, someone tried to open it.

Panic-stricken, she sat straight up in bed, staring at the door like someone hypnotised, watching the knob turn again very slowly, as if whoever it was who was out there was trying to get in without wakening her up. The door was locked, of course, but the lock itself was flimsy, and likely to give way before the first heavy push.

Suddenly terrified, Alexa leapt out of bed, knowing she hadn't a moment to spare. What did she know of those two men? Even her life might be at stake if she were to stay here any longer. Swiftly, without putting on a light, she belted a thin mackintosh over her short nightdress and slipped out of the window.

The back of Invercraig, like many old houses, had been built almost into the hillside. Cautiously Alexa opened the window, lowered herself over the narrow ledge, and tried to creep carefully over the uneven grey slated roof made slippery by the heavy rain. There was a drop of only a few feet at the edge, but with fright driving her on she jumped too quickly, and when she picked herself up off the rough cobbled path one ankle hurt.

Alexa, scarcely aware of it, glanced fearfully over her shoulder back across the scullery roof to her bedroom window. There was no sign of the men, but she knew they might appear at any minute, and could probably run faster than she could, especially with a sore ankle. Convulsively she shivered as she turned and disappeared into the night.

There was only one course open to her, she realised. She must go to Glenaird and find Fergus. If the weather had been finer she might have hidden successfully in the hills, but on a night like this she could never hope to survive. In her short stay in the Highlands she had at least learned that much. How she would find the courage to face him after the chaos of her birthday party, when she had practically asked him— or been on the point of asking him—to marry her, she didn't know. She must just pretend it had never happened. In any case she didn't seem to have any other option, and anything must be better than to stay at Invercraig with those two men!

The night was wild. For June she couldn't really believe it. The rain, driven by a rising wind, fell steadily, soon soaking through her light coat. There was a moon, but it came only with a break in the clouds, and because of this merely added to the weirdness of the atmosphere. She took the path through the hills to Glenaird, as she dared not risk getting her car out and going by the road; besides, her keys were in the house and she couldn't go back there.

The track wasn't particularly easy even in daylight, and in the dark she found it well-nigh impossible. Since that first time with Colin she had come quite often, supposedly to take Glen for a walk, but liking to sit on the higher ground and look at Glenaird. She had never gone further than the distant belt of trees, but something about the place drew her in spite of herself. Now, as she hobbled along, dragging her sore leg, she wondered anxiously if she would ever get there, and where, if she did, would she find Fergus? He used to tell her he never retired until the early hours, so perhaps she would find a light. If she was unfortunate enough to bump into Mr. Maxwell he need never know who she was. Fergus surely couldn't refuse to help. He could say what he liked, she knew she wasn't acting very wisely, but how many people did when they were half scared out of their wits! And it could have happened to anyone, so it would be no use him saying she had no sense!

Arguing with herself in this almost hysterical manner, Alexa blundered on. The sound of thunder seemed to be coming nearer, interspersed by occasional flashes of lightning which appeared to skip across the mountain tops, illuminating them brilliantly for frightening, infinitesimal seconds. By the time she reached the highest spot of the incline her heart was pounding painfully and she was drenched to the skin, and her face was red and scratched where the wind had blown the branches of the forest trees against her. Never had she imagined the day would come when the solitary chimneys of Glenaird would seem the most welcome sight in the world.

She didn't stop to think: situations like this never evolved from thought. Even one sliver of the commodity might have sent her hurtling back to Invercraig, but

Alexa's legs for the last hour had been propelled by
fear, common sense having long since deserted her.
The house, as she approached it, towered above her,
huge and seemingly menacing, waiting to swallow her
up.

Her intention had been to go around the back, but it
was here that the rain and darkness finally defeated her.
On rounding the corner of the house it met her full in
the face and she could see nothing. There seemed only
one possible thing to do, to try the front entrance.
From the momentary glimpse she had had of it, it was
too imposing to be called a mere door. She would ask
for Fergus. Someone must still be up, as lights were
still shining; there would be no need to explain who she
was.

Unable to find either knocker or bell, she banged on
the door with both clenched fists. Banged on it so hard
that when at last it was wrenched open she almost fell
through it, and would have done if she hadn't been
saved in the nick of time by a pair of steadying arms.

There was a momentary, incredulous silence, before
a voice, a hard masculine voice, exploded in her ears.
"Alexa! What on earth are you doing here?"

Dimly, because she could scarcely see, she realised it
was Fergus. "I've been knocking and knocking," she
reproached him wildly. "You do take your time!"

"Alexa!" He bit off her name like a threat. "Stop
talking such damned nonsense and try to answer my
question. You don't arrive at a man's house at this time
of night for any ordinary reason. And look at you!" His
hold on her arms tightened and he almost shook her,
his eyes icy with rage sweeping her soaked clothes, her
hair plastered to her scalp with rain. "Just where the
hell have you been?"

Alexa's voice, like her senses, seemed to have disappeared. She could only stare at him, which seemed to

anger him even more. His language, she thought dazedly as it numbed her ears, was quite something on occasion. Especially when he wasn't using any restraint, and he didn't appear to be using any now. She listened, slightly bemused, almost fascinated, thinking oddly that Edith wouldn't have approved, and on that thought she almost giggled.

"And you can take that expression off your face immediately," he ground out tersely. "Of all the brainless, senseless, half-witted females it's been my dubious privilege to know, you just about beat the lot!"

"Fergus!" she interrupted, her voice too shrill, bordering, had she but known it, on hysteria, "I only thought..." She stopped, unable to go on as her mind hit a peculiar blank wall. "I only thought..." she repeated stupidly, bewildered by her apparent inability to concentrate, by the way in which the room, the ceiling and floor and everything, was wavering up and down. Her teeth were chattering so hard she couldn't get anything further out. "If I could just get warmed," she half sobbed.

"Damn fool girl!" he exclaimed, suddenly sweeping her up in his arms, furious beyond normal reason if she had been able to figure it out, which she wasn't. All she knew was she felt ill. Nothing would focus properly and her leg hurt so much that she was almost grateful when he picked her up and she didn't have to stand on it any more. Fergus was angry, but he was here and at least she was safe. Anything else was beyond her. "I never," she gulped, delirium hovering, "gave you your tobacco!"

He ignored this. She wasn't sure that he had even heard, as her voice, little more than a croak, was muffled against his chest. His arms were hard and not at all sympathetic, but they held her close and nothing else seemed to matter.

"Fergus," she heard herself entreating frantically, "don't ever let me go!"

"Shut up!" Where previously her silence had incited harsh fury, now he commanded her with equal authority not to talk. Futile tears ran down her cold cheeks, mingling with the raindrops as she clung to him.

She had no idea where he could be taking her, only that they had entered a room and it was warm. Not that the warmth actually penetrated. It was an illusion of bright lights and flickering fire and deep carpets, because there was no noise as he strode over them to lay her down carefully. When his arms left her the cold returned. Her whole body felt frozen and chilled to the bone. "It was those men..." she muttered irrationally, sinking nervelessly into the soft settee.

"Stay there." His voice hardened, the only indication that he was aware of what she said.

"Please, Fergus—" She struggled to sit up, but again a peculiar dizziness overtook her and she couldn't see properly. Did Fergus intend to walk out and leave her? If he did... "Maxwell," she choked, following aloud the frightening trend of her thoughts. "I don't want him to find me here—I don't want him to know...!"

"If you don't shut up I'll murder you, and that's no idle threat, you little fool." Fergus was back beside her, a glass of brandy in his hand, still, it seemed, in a foul rage. He grasped her head, forcing it up against his arm, and made her drink. She spluttered and coughed, but he took not the slightest notice, refusing to let go until she had swallowed the lot. "Now," he said curtly, "what men are you talking about?"

From a distance Alexa heard the question as the effect of the brandy hit her queerly. Men? Unsteadily she blinked, rubbing her hand numbly over the brandy-wet lips. "There were two men," she frowned. "They tried to get into my room. I went out of the window."

For an apprehensive second after that there was nothing else. Only the snap of Fergus's teeth as they closed on a deep breath. Almost instantly he shook her, as if determined to extract the sliver of sense. "Alexa, did they touch you?"

Bemused, she tried ineffectively to escape his hurting hands. "No," she cried. "I told you, I went through the window!"

"Just like that!"

"I had no other choice," her voice slurred.

"And you ran all the way here without shoes?"

"I had shoes! Or I did have them. I put them in my pocket. I might have lost them when I fell from the roof."

"These men..." He seemed to be having some difficulty in containing his temper, which Alexa was uncomfortably aware seemed solely directed against herself. "Had you given them, promised them, rooms?"

Rooms? She made some attempt to nod, to continue what must be a rational conversation, but her clothes were soaked and she began to feel sick and not able to concentrate on Fergus's silly questions. As she visibly shuddered his arms left her abruptly, his glance sharpening on her fever-flushed cheeks. "I'll be back in a minute," he said, straightening quickly. "Don't try to move."

That, Alexa decided hollowly, must be the joke of the century! She didn't think she could move even if she wanted to, which she didn't. She was cold and miserable and had nowhere to go. Her face felt stiff from dried rain when she touched it with her fingers, and the skin hurt where the tortuous branches had caught her, but the most terrifying thing of all was the way in which everything about her remained hazy, as if she had been blinded by her prolonged attempt to penetrate the stormy darkness outside. It would be punishment indeed if she should lose her sight!

"Here." She was startled almost out of her lethargy to find Fergus wrapping a towel around her streaming hair. "Give me your coat," he ordered tersely, "and get into this. Then to bed, and I don't want to hear another word!"

Swiftly she felt him undoing the belt of her raincoat, dealing with the buttons which her numbed fingers couldn't cope with, before hauling it back across her bare shoulders. Vaguely she heard his further exclamation as he saw how little she wore underneath. "For heaven's sake, girl, do you usually run around half naked?"

Her hair was tangled and the towel hurt, and wildly she resented his taunting tones. All thumbs, she managed to push him away. He got the message, although the signals were weak. "I'll turn my back," he countered coolly, doing just that while she fumbled herself out of the few scraps of sodden nylon into the light robe which he had flung roughly down beside her. "I was in bed," she explained needlessly. "I don't know why you're being so horrible!"

"If you could only see yourself, you might realise why," he retorted cryptically. "I've seen better scarecrows, and it's not how I want you running about."

At that she lost the last bit of control which she had so desperately hung on to, and began to sob. Rather wildly and loudly, not at all prettily, her slight body shaking with the force of her outraged emotions as she buried her tear-stained face in her hands. "I think I'm going to die," she moaned.

"Come on, then," his voice was at last surprisingly gentle, almost coaxing as he picked her up once again in his arms. "If you mean to do that you may as well do it in comfort. I'll give you a couple of tablets and you won't know another thing. Not until the morning."

Alexa knew the sun was shining before she opened her eyes. She could feel the warmth of it on her closed lids, but she was also aware of voices discussing things she failed to understand, and instinct strongly advised against making it immediately apparent that she was awake. There was the polite, slightly astounded, query of a stranger asking with some displeasure where he should place the tea, and after a moment, pregnant with disapproval, if he should bring another cup.

For some reason not yet clear, Alexa's breathing stopped, and she shrank back against her pillows wishing fervently that she might become invisible. Then Fergus spoke—she would recognise his crisp tones anywhere—but what he said was wild, totally way out!

"My fiancée, Miss Lewis, stayed the night, McFarlane. She had an unfortunate accident and, along with other things, got wet. She was running a fever, so I put her in here; you didn't happen to be around to air another bed and I wasn't risking pneumonia. As it is she looks none too good."

There came another extremely startled silence, as if this incredible piece of news was more than poor McFarlane could take in. Or so it seemed to Alexa, almost frozen to the sheets with indignation and terror.

The man replied stiffly, obviously resenting Fergus's veiled criticism. "If you remember, sir, it was my night off, and I usually stay with my sister." Another pause, then, slightly warmer, "Would it be in order to congratulate you, sir? I had no idea..."

"You may, McFarlane," Fergus drawled. "And I had no idea myself until a few hours ago, but an engagement isn't usually considered like a wedding, which rates a preliminary announcement of one's intentions."

"No, of course not, sir. I will hope that you and the young lady, Miss Lewis, that is, will be happy. And now, if you will excuse me, I will fetch another cup."

"I'd be obliged, McFarlane," Fergus agreed.

The door closed with a thoughtful click and Alexa opened her eyes.

"About time," Fergus said suavely, his eyes intent on her face. "I was beginning to think you never would."

For one long minute she just stared at him, her wide, shadowed green eyes horrified and full of unconscious apprehension. He was sitting, dressed merely in a dressing-gown, in a chair beside the bed, his legs stretched carelessly before him. The room was spacious and well furnished, and certainly not one usually found in a cottage or bothy. In fact, one glance was enough to tell her that it was an apartment in some large house. Glenaird—swiftly she remembered.

"Who are you?" she whispered, her eyes returning to his, entreatingly, as though begging for an answer other than the one which she instinctively knew she would hear.

If she was already half submerged in a peculiar dark terror, his reply threw her completely under. "Maxwell," he supplied briefly, without removing his cool gaze from her face. "If you'd been a little brighter, my dear, you might have guessed long before now."

She sat bolt upright; the shock, even though she'd been momentarily prepared, was great. "Maxwell!" Even to her own ears her voice sounded hoarse.

"Fergus Maxwell. As my fiancée you'd better be clear."

So she had heard correctly. There had been no mistake. "How dared you!" she gasped, completely stricken. Sharply she twisted in the bed, not prepared for the quick pain which shot through her ankle as she moved. Yet the physical discomfort was nothing to the mental torment. It was frightful. What an absolute fool she must have been—but how could she have known?

"You say," she accused him stormily, "that I should have guessed? How could I?"

He took his time, his eyes exploring, although she was scarcely aware of it, her lovely flushed cheeks, the mane of shining hair which tumbled thickly, in wild disorder, about her slim shoulders; the flimsy négligé which did little to hide the attractive contours of her softly beautiful body. Her anger was apparent, flashing through her remarkable eyes, but her agitation seemed to arouse only a surpreme indifference. His voice came with cynical amusement. "I suppose I was referring to a woman's intuition. Something which you fortunately lack."

Alexa was consumed by a fine fury, and so many questions and accusations were crowding her mind that she scarcely knew where to start. "You're being quite ridiculous," she flung at him shrilly. "There's a difference, surely, between mind-reading and intuition! I'd been told there was a man called Fergus. How was I to know you weren't the right one? It would have been simple enough to explain!"

He laughed, his laughter full of smooth derision. "Never mind. No irreparable harm has been done, in spite of such an omission."

"No harm!" She positively stuttered. "Apart from everything else, what about that man—McFarlane? I heard what you led him to believe?"

"And you pretended to be asleep," he mocked. "And here I was, about to propose in the recognised, traditional fashion."

She could tell by the glint in his eyes that he had known she was awake all along, and she hated his brilliant sarcasm. "I wouldn't marry you if you were the last man in the world," she retorted.

If her reply lacked originality, his didn't. "I doubt, in that case, if you would stand much chance," he mused.

"I mean, considering the competition." He rose to his feet, going to the door as if he had anticipated the quick knock even before it came. "I'll take the cup, McFarlane, thank you," he said, leaving the man outside.

Slowly he moved back to Alexa's side. "Before we shock poor McFarlane any further I think you should drink your tea and get dressed."

"But you let him think..."

"My dear," he said at last, after pouring her tea, "I might have put you in a room at the other side of the house, presenting you as the irreproachably respectable Miss Lewis, but who would have believed me?"

"Why, you..." Alexa ignored the tea. She felt too upset to even look at it; she would have liked to have thrown it through the window. Inside she felt like splintered glass.

"Believe me, Alexa," he cut in smoothly, "this way you won't suffer from a tarnished reputation. McFarlane has the odd fault, but disloyalty is not one of them."

That whole statement, she considered, was highly contestable, and it wasn't so much what McFarlane said as what he thought. His discretion might prove cold comfort if she didn't get this little lot sorted out. "There was nothing to stop you," she declared hotly, "from taking me back to Invercraig."

He flicked a strangely taut look at the still-red scratches on her fine, pale skin, at the perspiration beading her short upper lip, the slight, betraying tremble of her tightly clenched hands. "In your condition you might never have stood the return journey. As it was I didn't give much for your chances when I first let you in. I wonder if you have any idea what you looked like?"

"I was wet," she stammered. "I didn't think I was ill."

"You were incapable of standing up," he assured her, "and half out of your mind."

"Because I ran almost all the way and it wasn't **a** good night. Surely, in such circumstances, it's understandable that I was a bit distraught. Not that I can remember much of it..." She stopped, staring at him cloudily, her head whirling painfully as with an effort she recalled being terrified of losing her sight. Well, her sight seemed all right, even if her head still ached and her face felt sore. "Anyway," she went on irrationally, "it wasn't really any of your business. You weren't, after all, the man I was looking for. You could have taken me home. Nothing could be worse than the mess we seem to be in now."

"I don't," he commented with a wholly diabolical grin, "consider we're in any sort of a mess at all. I did all I possibly could do in the circumstances."

"And twisted them to suit your own purpose, I've no doubt!"

"Well—it's a thought, although it's often referred to as making the most of one's opportunities."

"You could have let me go!"

"I did try." His eyes lingered on her bare arms, his mouth twisting regretfully. "You clung to me, Miss Lewis, as if I was a sort of barricade against the approaching enemy. Until the tablets I gave you began to work, it was quite an enthralling experience."

It was difficult to remain calm. She bent her head quickly so that he might not see her fraught expression. He mocked, but she could only lie there feeling so vulnerable, because while her emotions were involved his weren't. She could only whisper, her heart pounding, "You didn't stay here all night?"

"Most of it," he said, "apart from the short time I spent at Invercraig."

"You went back?" Rather desperately she snatched

and took a gulp of the now luke-warm tea which she had thrust to one side. It didn't bear thinking about. What on earth was he up to?

"You talked of two men," he reminded her. "I didn't imagine you would thank me if I left them to burn the place down."

She stared at him as everything came back in every detail; everything that had been hovering in the background of her consciousness since she woke up. Something she had told herself wasn't important in view of the new crisis which confronted her. How mistaken she had been! The terror and fear of her flight from the croft were too real to push lightly to one side. "What did you find?" she asked, her voice a mere thread of apprehension.

"Just those two men," he told her briefly, "but no sign of anything else, not even your dog."

Stupefied, her eyes widened, dismay washing over her. "Didn't I tell you last night about Glen?"

"No," his voice darkened before the anxiety in hers, "you did not! You never mentioned him."

"It was entirely the fault of your shepherd," she retorted. "He actually had the nerve to shoot at him, although he said he didn't hit him, but the poor little thing got an awful fright."

Fergus frowned and she felt momentary gratitude that he didn't find any humour in the situation. Not that he seemed unduly alarmed either. "I expect he would run home to the bothy. Fergus is away but he probably managed to get in, and will no doubt only be nursing hurt feelings. Chasing sheep is one of his bad habits, I'm afraid."

"You might have told me!"

His lips tightened with impatience. "He's not as bad, Alexa, as all that. Fergus, not being as young as he used to be, is apt to be careless, but it's years since the dog gave any trouble. I agree the mistake was mine, but only in removing him from his familiar surroundings and leaving him at the croft.''

He was talking about Fergus. The real Fergus—the tramp! Gazing at him bitterly, she recalled how the local people had always bewildered her by giving the impression that Fergus was an old man. Maybe Maxwell was right when he said she could have been brighter, but it just hadn't occurred to her that there might be some mistake. If it hadn't been that Maxwell wanted to get his hands on her land, none of this need have happened. It seemed he would go to any lengths to achieve his ends, even to the extent of forcing her into a false engagement. Well, if Maxwell considered himself smart, wasn't it up to her to prove herself smarter? Only it would take time, and a clearer head than she seemed to possess at this minute. It would certainly be the shortest engagement ever heard of— she was at least clear in her head about that!

CHAPTER EIGHT

"You might have things on your mind," Fergus conceded mildly, "which might be none of my business, but I'm not given to long silences when there is definitely much to be discussed. However," he flicked back his dressing-gown cuff, glancing with raised eyebrows at his watch, "I suggest we continue over breakfast, that is if you feel well enough to get up?"

"If you'll just get out," she retorted, not noticeably polite because she was eager to be rid of him, and failing for a minute to remember he was not the familiar Fergus of old. With him she had always needed time to marshal her thoughts, to get ready for the next phase in the battle.

"You happen," he drawled, with a glint in his eye, "to be ordering me from my own bedroom. Of course one of these days it will be yours too."

He indulged in a sort of perverted revenge against every wrong word spoken. "Get out!" she choked, her cheeks burning, her heart reacting in a most startling manner as he rose abruptly to his feet.

For a big man he moved swiftly, catching one of her slender wrists, careless of hurting her, his fingers taut on the frantic beat of her pulse. "One of these days," he threatened, "you won't be able to run, nor have the breath left to order me to be gone. What then, my beautiful Alexa?"

Her eyes flew open wrathfully, her too bright glance resting on the determined mouth above hers. "I know

I hate you," she cried, knowing nothing of the sort but wholly rebellious.

His brief laughter smote her, brilliantly sardonic, as his other hand lightly touched her cheek. "And hate," he mused, "gives such a wild rose colour. If I were you I'd think again."

She almost snatched herself from his grip. "That's exactly what I'm going to do, when you leave me," she assured him. "I shall think of a way to escape."

"Your sense of the dramatic intrigues me," he murmured with cruel irony. "One would imagine, to hear you go on, that the idea of a husband and family doesn't appeal to you."

He was referring, she guessed immediately, to that other night when she had almost made a fool of herself, and her face whitened with an impotent fury as he turned indifferently and walked towards the door. When he chose he used a fine sarcasm that hurt. "I'll see you downstairs in half an hour. I collected a few articles of clothing from the croft, but if you require anything further you'd better consult McFarlane." Without giving her the chance to comment on either statement he disappeared with a casual lift of his hand.

After the door closed Alexa threw back the sheets and almost tumbled out of bed. His bed, as he had had the effrontery to point out, and she couldn't leave it fast enough. Undoubtedly all her affairs were in a vast muddle, and there was no comfort to be gained from the knowledge that it was mostly her own fault. By coming here as she had done at midnight she had achieved nothing, merely played into his hands. And while the shock of learning his true identify was bad enough, this bogus engagement was even worse.

Alexa, in spite of her momentary flash of energy, found to her dismay that she had to grab a chair for a few minutes until the room stopped spinning around her. The strain of the previous evening seemed still with her. She could, she admitted, be worse than she'd thought. Maybe she should give Fergus the benefit of the doubt; perhaps it was her reputation he was chiefly worried about. She couldn't have been in a very fit state last night to travel home, and he might be only teasing her regarding the croft. After all, it wasn't so long ago since she had practically offered him her house and land together with herself. Her cheeks still burned to think of it, but she also remembered his rejection, which was surely peculiar if this had been his sole aim. A few days, he might decide, would tide her over this minor indiscretion, then their engagement could be broken without attracting undue publicity.

Feeling somewhat better, apart from an extremely sore ankle, she limped to the bathroom which Fergus had told her was en suite. Recalling how often she had felt sorry he was forced to sleep in a barn, she was inclined to view the whole set-up sourly. She had been wasting her pity, it was plain to see. Everything here hinted of luxury—a fine apartment, beautifully appointed, if slightly austere as probably befitted a man. It spelt money, money, money, in large capital letters, which made it all the more ridiculous to imagine he was after her scrappy bit of land.

She tried to hurry. There were still many things she was far from clear about, much that she wanted to say and ask. Fergus hadn't yet told her what had happened at Invercraig, and she had still to discover why he hadn't revealed his true identity when she first arrived. She washed unconsciously, like a sleepwalker, patting her face carefully dry though trying to ignore the scratches. When she went downstairs she must try to be methodical. The confusion in her mind was no excuse when her whole future might be at stake.

In the brown paper bag which Fergus had indicated

she found a clean pair of Levis which she recognised as her own. There was also a softly patterned blue blouse; no underwear, but this was too much to expect. He must have decided she would manage without it, which she did, if not very well. She felt distinctly cool and not a little uncomfortable where the seams of the trousers caught her skin, and she was thankful that in a little while she would be returning to the croft.

She had managed to struggle downstairs and was sitting at the bottom clinging to the carved oak banister when McFarlane came to her.

"Mr. Maxwell has been called outside," he explained, after introducing himself formally. "He would like you to go in to breakfast as soon as you're ready and will join you in a few minutes."

"Thank you," she smiled uncertainly, and was overtaken by the disconcerting feeling that she was back at school. There the steward, trained by Edith, had presented the same precise demeanour, and the knack of making one feel always at fault!

With a dismal sigh she remained where she was at the bottom of the stairs. She could see McFarlane was surprised.

"I think, McFarlane," she glanced at him meekly, "I happened to hurt my ankle on the way here last night. I would rather Mr. Maxwell didn't know about it, and I wondered if you had such a thing as a small bandage. I couldn't see anything upstairs."

She had no idea how appealing she looked, sitting there gazing up at him with her wide green eyes and soft fair hair. McFarlane's self-disciplined face softened in spite of himself. "I have certificates in first aid, miss, which I acquired during the last war." He bent down. "If you would be so kind as to let me see, so I can ascertain the extent of the damage."

Obligingly, without undue fuss, Alexa hitched up

her trouser leg, displaying an ankle swollen to twice the normal size.

McFarlane frowned. "However did you walk downstairs, miss?"

"It does hurt," she confessed.

"Just wait here," he commanded. "I'll bring something immediately."

Later she hobbled into the breakfast room, McFarlane assisting by her side. In some way she sensed her sprained ankle had reassured him about some detail that had bothered him. She wasn't sure, but she did feel he had changed his mind about something and she now had his approval, which seemed quite a small victory in itself.

She could only manage coffee and a little toast. McFarlane tut-tutted, but Alexa knew she couldn't have swallowed any of the various dishes he kept hot on the sideboard, delicious though they seemed. He was out answering the telephone when Fergus Maxwell strode in and helped himself to a large mixed grill. "After we finish," he announced, "we'll talk. I rather guess you have plenty to say, but will do so more comfortably in the library."

The problem, Alexa realised, glancing at him quickly, was how to get from here to anywhere else without him guessing about her ankle. She had supposed they might discuss everything over the breakfast table, after which he would leave her free to make her own arrangements, and she might have coped. This was not to be so.

Playing for time, she declared she would like to return to the croft. "Perhaps," she murmured, "you would let McFarlane drive me?" Once there she would be safe, and could more easily terminate this crazy engagement. No one need ever know about it if she managed it cleverly.

"You're not going to any croft," he replied, "unless it's with me."

Her hands clenched with anger beneath the table. "You're a busy man," she pointed out, more reasonably than she felt.

"Of course I am," he agreed with exasperating composure, "but I can spare some time. I'll probably be busier in future. There'll be a wedding to arrange and time to set aside for a honeymoon."

"Oh, don't be ridiculous!" Alexa cried, flushing hotly as she jumped to her feet, completely forgetting about her ankle. "Ouch!" she almost screamed, clutching air wildly as she lost her balance and fell.

"You've hurt your foot—let me see!" He was beside her in a trice, catching her, dumping her back in her chair, flicking up her trouser leg with scant patience. "So," he blazed softly, "somebody's been busy. You didn't put that bandage on yourself."

"McFarlane..."

"McFarlane, indeed!" Authority bristled as he swept her into his arms, striding with her through the door, taking no notice of her struggles. "Be still," he rasped, "be quiet! The time is past, Alexa, when you may run to the servants before me."

"How was I to know my ankle would be swollen when I got out of bed? You didn't wait to see.".

"Should I have done?" his voice rang with sarcasm. "You were hanging on to your sheets like a lifeline. Fat chance I had of seeing anything, let alone your feet. But don't lie to me, Alexa, don't ever do that. That ankle was giving you hell long before you got up."

His mood was black again, his mouth tight with anger. Alexa glanced apprehensively from the corner of her eye. He was a fine one to talk about lying when he'd been doing it himself for weeks! "You needn't think you can frighten me," she hissed in his ear.

Fergus didn't appear to hear. He was shouting for McFarlane to bring his coffee into the library. "Just so we can get things straightened out to my satisfaction," he added, with an emphasis on the last two words Alexa didn't care for.

"It could be easier to buy me a wheelchair," she muttered, trying to match his dryness, her limbs like water as he laid her slowly down on the settee.

"Not with your weight," he eyed her speculatively, not in any great hurry to let her go. "I could carry you all day." He bent his head and kissed her suddenly, a swift, hard pressure on her parted lips. "Put the coffee down, McFarlane," he said, "over there."

Alexa looked fleetingly into Fergus's eyes, heat rushing through her entire body. "The weather is changing," he remarked smoothly, apparently for McFarlane's benefit as he straightened. McFarlane agreed, it seemed approvingly.

Alexa flushed, her nerves taut, her lips still stinging, and thanked McFarlane for a second cup of coffee which she didn't really want. The man withdrew.

"You don't have to go to such lengths," she breathed rapidly. "I'm sure McFarlane understands."

"And just what is that supposed to mean, my so mysterious Alexa?" He came a step nearer again.

"I mean," she choked, "he must know our so-called engagement is too sudden to be absolutely genuine, so there's no need to over-act."

"McFarlane," he retorted, "knows nothing of the sort, and is a romantic beneath that rather grim exterior. He probably derived almost as much pleasure from that brief salute as you did."

"Why, you—" she began, amazed at his temerity, about to deny it.

"Enough," he cut in, not prepared to allow a different opinion. "We came in here to talk, you and I, not argue. We had got, if I remember rightly, as far as the croft."

Instantly diverted, she exclaimed, "You'd better tell me exactly what you found."

"Just the two men," he grunted, "fast asleep in your sitting room, looking particularly innocent, I must confess, of any great crime."

"In the sitting room?" She stared at him with startled eyes.

"I woke them up, so I should know," he assured her. "I seemed to gather they imagined I was an irate father, as they gabbled quite a lot about a daughter which I don't think I possess. Apparently they had been imbibing too freely before arriving at Invercraig, and when it came to the time, couldn't remember which was their bedroom. They had tried one door—yours, I presume—but it was locked. They were too nervous of making another mistake to try any more, so decided to spend the night by the fire."

"So," she whispered, viewing with bitterness her own folly, "I made a mistake!"

"A lot of mistakes," he agreed.

She hung her head, despair winging through her. If only she had waited! The men had meant no harm, and even if they had, the ultimate outcome couldn't have been worse than this! "What did you do?" she asked, twisting her hands nervously on her lap, her heart quaking.

"Nothing," he replied suavely. "I merely did nothing to disperse their belief that they faced a rather furious member of your family. They decided to go, there and then, and I'm afraid I did nothing to stop them. They didn't appear to like the look of me."

"No, they might not." She lifted her head again to gaze at him. She could imagine Fergus standing there, like some Highland fighting chieftain of old. His very

height and breadth was frightening, to say nothing of
the granite-like sculpture of jawline and mouth, and occasionally the line of his brows could give him a dangerous look. Her voice was bitter-sweet. "It's quite
easy, isn't it, when you know exactly how to deal with
people and situations."

His expression was a curious mixture of arrogance
and amusement. "I suggest you forget about that particular pair."

"Everything switched on and off to order?"

He ignored her slight impertinence. "I forced your
bedroom door as I have no liking for creeping in windows, and found everything as you described it. It can
all be straightened out later."

"I'm going back, right away."

"Oh no, you're not." He was studying the sensuous
curve of her chaste mouth with some speculation. "I'm
not a very patient man, Alexa, so don't weary me with
that theme."

"It might take me a while to puzzle this all out," she
countered, her eyes stormy with rebellion, "and I refuse to be told what I can and cannot do. I don't want to
take up any more of your precious time, so, as you say,
we'll forget about the men, but now perhaps you
wouldn't mind explaining why you didn't tell me who
you were when I first came to Invercraig?"

"You didn't give me much chance, if you remember." His lips quirked laconically.

"You were," she retorted, "to all intents and pur-
poses, the man Robert Kerr led me to expect. You were
in the barn, were you not? What were you, the great
Maxwell of Glenaird, doing there, and where is the real
Fergus? He must exist, as people talk about him."

Amusement deepened his voice although his eyes
didn't leave her face. "He certainly exists, my dear,
but he's an old man, and his presence at Invercraig

wouldn't have presented problems with the conventions, as mine might have done if it had become known how much time I spent there alone with you."

Their eyes clashed; she felt ready to explode. "Don't make it sound something it wasn't. Besides, no one saw you."

The dark eyes mocked her. "But everyone knew. You talked a whole lot about Fergus, and even took it upon yourself to fetch his tobacco. I had it from Macdonell. Now what would they think if they were to be told that he was called away suddenly to assist a sick sister, on the very day you arrived? That he's been hundreds of miles away during these past weeks?"

"Hundreds of miles away!" She was aghast.

Fergus Maxwell nodded, quite willing, it seemed, to supply every detail, not deterred by her expression of dismay. "The old man worked for me, too, remember. He was here at Glenaird when the call came. I took it personally and at his request had him on his way to catch a train within half an hour. I drove him to the station myself. I've known Fergus all my life, you see; he's really a very interesting old chap in spite of his unconventional ways. No one knew he had gone, as McFarlane was out and we left in a hurry. Fergus is extremely fond of this sister and I doubt if he will come back here even when she recovers."

It was beginning to take shape, though not in a way Alexa cared for. "And since Angus died...?"

"The two of them were very close friends. I don't think Fergus cared to be here after Angus went."

"So," she said hardily, "you took him to the station?"

"Yes," he replied, his eyes narrowed against her silky tones, "and I was foolish enough to promise to call at Invercraig when I returned. The stock, what there was of it, had obviously been neglected. I took pity on your cow as it was too late to arouse one of my men. Actually I'd almost forgotten how to go about it. I'd never tried milking since I was a kid." He shrugged wryly. "If you'd arrived at the barn a few minutes earlier, I'm afraid the air was blue."

"I seem to recall," she retorted, "there was something wrong with it. Something wrong with the entire set-up, if only I'd stopped to think." She glanced at him sharply, her smooth brow wrinkling. "You'd almost forgotten a lot of things, hadn't you!"

"Nothing," he taunted, "that really counted."

She ignored this as if he had not spoken, accusing him wildly, "You pretended to be this other man because you were well aware I wouldn't accept help from Maxwell. You wanted my land and would stoop to anything to get it!"

He grinned openly at her wrathful countenance, her sparkling green eyes. "I was only looking after what was rightfully mine," he protested mildly, "but I could have saved myself a lot of trouble. You played into my hands so nicely in the end that I'm more than furious with myself."

"You can't be serious—not really," she stormed. "No one knows, or need know, of this ridiculous engagement!"

"You're quite wrong," he assured her, without moving a muscle. "I happened to mention to my manager that my fiancée was staying, and much as I regret it, he is not a man noted for his discretion in some things."

"And you told McFarlane!"

Her obvious bitterness left him unmoved. His eyebrows flicked upwards. "McFarlane could be trusted with state secrets, but in this instance I can see he will be unable to contain himself much longer."

"You couldn't hold me to it," she cried, amazed by

his treacherous arrogance. "I shall just go back to the croft and deny it ever happened."

"No one will want to know you, not when the true date of Fergus's departure becomes known. My people have a sense of fitness about such things. They aren't narrow-minded, but they dislike anything that displeases me."

This was beyond anything! Alexa, in spite of incredulous disbelief, felt also a cold twinge of fear which was, she told herself, ridiculous. He might threaten, but she still had one card up her sleeve. "I'll sell the croft, then, but never to you!"

"No one would buy it. It's too well known that I want it. No agent would touch it."

She glared at him, distraught. Could this be true? Had she the time to find out? Well, there was one more thing she could do. She could go back to Edith!

"Edith wouldn't have you," coolly he appeared to read her very thoughts, "not after what I should tell her."

They stared at each other for one long glittering moment. Whichever way she turned, Alexa realised, he could match her—beat her!

"Look," he said, coming down to her, grasping her shoulders, "Invercraig is important to me. I bought the land on the other side only because Angus agreed to let me have the croft when he died. He was a kinsman and we'd always got on well together. I had no reason to doubt his word. I'm not too proud to admit he tricked me. However, no Lewis will make a fool of me twice!"

"He might have had his reasons, unbeknown to you," she protested. "He was only a very distant cousin."

"As you are," Fergus Maxwell's hands tightened on the fine bone of her shoulder, "but even a thin trickle of blood should be thicker than water. No mat-

ter, this way there will be no mistake. All of a sudden
my problem is satisfactorily solved. I acquire a wife
and the croft; freedom from any future worry about
the all-important right of way between my two prop-
erties. I'll get Robert Kerr to draw up a contract immediately."

"With everything to your advantage!"

"But no, my dear," he smiled, and relaxed his hold a
little, adding dryly, "You won't lose out. When you
consider what you're getting in return, I'm sure you'll
agree you're getting the better bargain."

Such colossal nerve—such an absolute flood of un-
paralleled villainy! Alexa felt she must explode with the
force of indignation surging through her. Yet before
she could collect herself to so much as open her
mouth, there was McFarlane again.

"Miss Helen has just telephoned from Inverness,
sir," he said, after a little polite knocking and coughing.
"She'll be arriving at the Kyle on the evening train and
wishes to be met."

Maxwell slowly removed his hands from Alexa's
shoulders, if not his gaze from her face. "Do you realise, McFarlane," he exclaimed, without turning,
"that for once in her life my aunt is contriving to arrive
when she's actually needed? I shall meet her later,
myself!"

It seemed to Alexa that from that moment onwards
everything was taken from her hands. Miss Helen descended like a miniature whirlwind, a smaller but
forceful edition of her nephew, but with much less fi-
nesse. Or so Alexa decided, after the first few days.
Singly they were formidable. Together they presented
an impregnable front against which Alexa soon admitted the futility of pitting herself.

Miss Helen, or Cousin Helen as she wished to be

called, was delighted with the engagement. "I had long since given up," she confided in Alexa one day on finding her alone. "Goodness knows Glenaird needs heirs, but it's always so difficult to make people see reason. I've paraded in front of Fergus every pretty girl I know without success. I never thought he would actually fall in love."

Alexa felt her cheeks grow pink and was glad Cousin Helen appeared to have no great sensitivity. How could she have received such an impression? She was obviously making the common mistake of assuming that an engagement was absolute evidence of inner affection. True, Maxwell was a superb actor! Wasn't he forever putting an arm around her and kissing her fondly in the presence of others, and, before her ankle recovered, hadn't he made a great show of carrying her from one place to another? When she tackled him about it he merely grinned. It was necessary, he said, that they should present a loving front, and he must have her co-operation.

He made it sound very much like a threat, and until she was better able to sort things out, she had raised no further objections, even if she refused to show any great enthusiasm. It became comparatively easy, with practice, to hold herself rigid in his embrace, to pretend her emotions were not involved, and to ignore the faster beat of a traitorous pulse. It was her one consolation that they were never alone together. Alexa was confined to the house and Cousin Helen seemed possessed of a jack-in-the-box type of figure which popped up everywhere.

She was saying now, with a frankness that made the pink in Alexa's cheeks stain to a much deeper colour, "My brother, Fergus's father, only had one son. If anything had happened to Fergus it would have been a disaster; Glenaird would have been sold. My sister-in-

law disliked children and refused to have more. I
hope, my dear, you won't want to make the same mistake."

Alexa had the greatest difficulty in restraining a
sharp retort. She wanted very much to shout that she
didn't even intend to marry Fergus Maxwell, let alone
have his children, and if she was shaken somewhat at
the thought, it was just because this was all getting too
much for her. Even so, it could be more difficult to
explain to someone like Cousin Helen that she just
couldn't run—give up Invercraig without a fight. Which
was her sole reason for staying! She wasn't so naïve as
to imagine she couldn't walk out if she pleased. Physically Fergus couldn't hold her, and she could always
find a job, yet why should she flee like someone with a
guilty conscience, leaving him the croft for whatever
he chose to give her? If she bided her time a solution
would present itself. There was always one somewhere,
and when it came she must simply arrange to be craf-
tier than he was. There might, if she was patient, be not
merely a way out of her dilemma, but also some form
of revenge which she could collect as compensation for
all the humiliation she was having to bear. Cousin
Helen with her obsession for genetics, for instance!

Probably with this in mind, Helen sided with Fergus
regarding an early wedding.

They were sitting in the library after dinner. It
seemed the most used room in the many-roomed
house. It was long and low with book-lined walls and
comfortable chairs, and while Alexa could understand
its appeal during winter, in summer she would have
preferred the drawing room, where wide windows provided panoramic views of the mountains, moorland
and sea. The library seemed too intimate for her present mood, holding as it did the faint fragrance of old
leather, musky heather, log smoke and tweeds. This

evening the logs smouldered but provided a welcome warmth against the showery weather outside, Alexa, appreciating the overall cosiness, was resentful of her inability to relax, and with frowning concentration began to scheme how she might contrive to visit Invercraig next day.

So engrossed was she that the trend of the conversation between Fergus Maxwell and his aunt penetrated only slowly. It was with some consternation that she heard Fergus mention late June or, at the latest, early July, which was just about three weeks' time!

"Oh, no!" Alexa cried, involuntarily shocked, her eyes swinging indignantly to Fergus. "I mean—I haven't yet told my family about my engagement!"

"I did," Fergus forestalling Helen's astonished exclamation, informed Alexa glibly. "I knew you hadn't got around to it because of your ankle. I'm just waiting for a reply before asking Helen to arrange an engagement party. Then we'll be married shortly afterwards. There's no reason to wait."

"Who is this family of yours?" Helen turned to Alexa after nodding her complete approval of the wedding. "This cousin—have I heard of her?"

"My mother's cousin," Alexa forced herself to explain, but briefly. Further words caught in the tenseness of her throat. How dared Fergus do this! She hadn't intended to tell Edith anything, hoping that with everything quickly solved, it wouldn't be necessary to do so. She glanced at him furiously, but he only returned her stare coolly, and to her utter chagrin, left his chair by the fire and came to sit with lover-like solicitude beside her on the wide settee.

She was even more mortified when, deliberately it seemed, he reached out an arm to pull her against him, giving the impression to a delightfully-interested Helen that they were very much in love. Through the thin-

ness of her silky dress Alexa felt her heart beating
wildly. It was becoming a habit with him lately to drop a
brief kiss on her cheek, to embrace her lightly when he
came into a room and she was there, but this was the
first time he'd actually drawn her close to him on an
evening in front of the fire. As she tried discreetly to
free herself his arm merely tightened with a warning
pressure which did nothing to steady her already racing
pulse.

"You'd better elucidate a little more clearly," he said
softly, as she paused and Helen obviously waited, "she
would really like to know."

"There's nothing much to know." Rather desperately Alexa kept her eyes on Helen's face, trying to
ignore the traitorous inclinations of her body. "Edith
brought me up, after my parents died."

"What about Angus Lewis—didn't he have any say
in the matter? He was your father's cousin, was he
not?" Helen expressed surprise.

"Only distantly," Alexa replied. "Edith did write
twice, but he didn't apparently want anything to do
with me."

"Hmm…Perhaps therein lies the mystery of the
croft," Helen mused enigmatically. "I expect you
know that Angus Lewis's grandfather married a Maxwell?"

The honour, her tones clearly proclaimed, was all on
the side of the Lewises. Alexa nodded, not trusting
herself to speak.

Fergus's firm mouth quirked at the corners, his
glance on her mutinous face. "She's quite aware of
this, Helen," he assured his aunt, "just as she's aware
that history is about to repeat itself. As soon as we hear
from Edith, you can go ahead with everything else. A
party with all the expected trappings, including," he
added softly, "a ring." With one hand he lifted Alexa's

frozen fingers. "My grandmother's ring would fit you beautifully. I think you would like it."

Quickly Alexa pulled her hand away. She could at least manage that. In front of Helen she couldn't very well say it, but a ring was the last thing she wanted. From the jerk of her hand she hoped he received the message loud and clear!

Helen said, "I think she ought to have it without delay, before the party. I wonder you haven't given it to her already."

She—she—she! Almost as if she wasn't actually sitting in the room. They talked over her head, as if she didn't exist, or as if her opinion was of no consequence!

At her side Fergus stirred, his voice very dry as he noted Helen's question. "Maybe because," he said pointedly, "we can never find an appropriate moment. It's not exactly something one does in a crowd."

For once Helen seemed remarkably receptive to a hint. With one hand she swept up spectacles and knitting, with the other a notepad and pen. She smiled brightly, as if an idea of some importance had only occurred to her. "I think I shall have an early night. Perhaps I'll sit up in bed and make out a list for the party. Alexa will have to draw up her own, of course, but we'll have to ask..." Murmuring abstractedly, she left the room.

"Goodnight, Helen," Fergus said firmly, closing the door.

"Now," he announced, moving swiftly to his desk, "we shall have to make up for lost time."

Alarmed, Alexa jumped to her feet. "You don't have to pursue this thing to such a ridiculous extent! Nor do you need to work so hard at fooling Cousin Helen. She only sees what she wants to see, and is convinced enough as it is. You apparently intend to get married, something she's wanted for years. She isn't going to bother studying the finer points, now that everything seems settled!"

Maxwell lifted his head, in his eyes an element of danger as they narrowed on her transparent face. "Unless you're deliberately trying to create a diversion, you could try explaining yourself a little? Have I transgressed in any way? I consider, under the circumstances, I've acted admirably."

Alexa found herself almost unable to put it into words. His expression jolted her a bit, and a wave of pure feeling ran through her. She managed at last, "If putting your arm around me on every possible occasion..."

"Oh, that!" he cut in smoothly, his glance changing to one of patent mockery, "that was just a little rudimentary experiment. We've never got beyond the preliminary stages."

She stared at him, her breath coming sharply. "How do you mean?" Her face paled. It was almost as if he threatened her, that his light caresses to date were merely a sort of introductory offering!

"We are engaged, remember? But as yet you aren't very wide awake. With experience you'll be everything a man wants. Marriage will be the best thing that ever happened to you, only first you need time to get used to the idea. But you tell me how to explain this to Helen? Rather than demand she stops following us around with a permanently anxious look on her face, I imagined some small outward show of affection would serve to convince her that ours is a perfectly normal engagement, and in this fashion, it wouldn't put any great strain on you."

A tremor swept through her, fierce little waves of resentment—and something else. Some emotion which his words aroused, which she dared not think about, yet she doubted her ability to blot it out. His appeal, she tried to tell herself, was that of the senses, and he had no right to use his wealth of experience as a means of pointing a finger of ridicule at the lack of it in her. The way his eyes ran over her, she felt stripped to the skin, exposed to everything she just wanted to run from.

Almost choking, she said, "Why don't you confide in Helen that ours isn't a normal relationship? That all you're interested in is Invercraig? Perhaps this would stop her plaguing me about the size of our future family—if she might turn Invercraig into a sort of dower-house, things like that!"

"Oh dear!" Through his eyes flicked a hint of amusement. "Well, that sort of speculation is normally tied up with engagements and elderly ladies, who are apt to view marriage as a licence to buy a pram. It's nothing to worry about."

She flared wildly—rather desperately, her nerves strung tight, "Being a mere man...!"

He made a sound of complete impatience, his chis-elled mouth hardening as he surveyed her heightening colour, the translucent despair in her thickly fringed eyes. "As such, you think I'm never at the mercy of my emotions," he interrupted sardonically. "Perhaps I've just grown a thicker skin to hide them. I really can't advise you specifically. I can only suggest you ignore such remarks. There's no need for Helen to know more than she does at present."

"I didn't expect you to sympathise," she stared coldly back at him. "Helen is nice, but she has so much on her mind."

He grinned suddenly, turning from his desk with something held in his hand, his dark face inscrutable. "I think if you were to wear this ring it would set her mind at rest. I can't promise miracles, but it might just do the trick."

CHAPTER NINE

FERGUS stood by her side, the ring in his hand, asking her to try it on. Did he intend, she wondered, to use force? He was cool and suave, very sophisticated beneath the tough chieftain image, but wholly determined, if there was a way to fight him she hadn't yet found it, and her wits at this moment seemed entirely scattered.

"Please, no," Alexa heard her own voice as if from a distance. Unconsciously she clenched her fists, hiding them behind her back as she stared at the ring, hypnotised. The size and beauty of the emerald astounded her, but the implications were frightening. Mere words were one thing, a ring on her finger quite another. This seemed much more irrevocable than the talk, a few minutes ago, of an engagement party, which was after all in the future and might never happen. Wildly she clutched at straws. "I couldn't be responsible," she gasped, "for anything like that. I could lose it!"

"No, you wouldn't. Don't be silly." His voice came low, oddly persuasive, and surprisingly he didn't seem annoyed. "No one has worn it but my grandmother," he told her. "My mother didn't care for it."

She felt lost, her confidence ebbing. "I still would rather not," she said tensely.

Maxwell's eyes were like a shaft of cold steel. "If I really tried you couldn't resist me, but I don't care to resort to force."

"Physically you're stronger."

"And in other ways, but I wanted you to come to me of your own accord."

There was silence as they looked at each other. Alexa fancied she caught a flash of anger like lightning in his cool grey glance. A faraway impression, blending with a hint of arrogance, spelling out a heart-stopping message; a silent declaration of what could happen to a girl who was foolish enough to resist his stupendous charm. Stubbornly she kept her hands where they were.

"Come here," he said, and she knew a moment of sheer panic as his arms reached out.

"You're hurting me," she cried.

"I don't want to," he retorted, taking her slight weight when, with her hands clenched behind her back, she lost her balance and tumbled against him. He locked one arm around her narrow waist, his hand hard on the enticing curve of her hip, and twisted her head ruthlessly with the other. His eyes studied her mouth for what seemed a long time before he kissed it. "Such bravado," he murmured softly, as his lips descended.

For Alexa it was too much. There was nothing she could do against the wild sweep of flame that tore through her with the sensuous pressure of his mouth. Helplessly she felt the wildness of her own vivid response as her body pressed against him, driven, it seemed, by almost visible waves of sensation. She was consumed by unwilling excitement, a stormy, reckless responsiveness, which, in his arms at the mercy of her ardently aroused emotions, she was unable to hide. Slowly her locked fingers relaxed, seeming to hesitate, then with a will of their own they slid up around his neck, feeling shattered by the hard, smooth muscles of his back.

His mouth moved, whispered something against

hers, and she replied incoherently, her lips parted, feeling his breath deepening, her own coming unevenly. Faintly she was aware that he was kissing her with one end in view and she had neither the strength nor inclination to resist him.

His head lifted and he stared down at her, but she couldn't meet that taut, assessing glance at all, nor control a sudden trembling. "You're not frightened, are you?" he asked, his eyes dark with a passion he didn't try to hide on her warmly seductive mouth.

She had no breath left this time to answer, or what little she had was doing strange things in her throat. Dazed, she shook her head, not sure exactly what he implied but not able to care, only certain that she could no longer fight the heavy clamouring of her senses. She heard his low utterance of satisfaction and wasn't sure she understood that either, but she didn't dwell on it. Instinctively she realised that she cared for this man more than it was wise to admit, and such moments as this were to be held intimately, treasured against the day when memories would be all she had left.

She murmured blindly, her face drooping against his chest, "Don't leave me."

"I have no intention of leaving you, you foolish girl." His glance sought her face and mouth, her soft creamy throat. She looked fragile, but he sensed a sensuality which matched his own. He pulled her roughly to him again and kissed her mouth. Then he picked her up in his arms. "Come and sit with me by the fire," he said.

He lifted her and everything else seemed to fade as he carried her back to his chair and sat with her across his knees. He wasted no more time on words but continued to kiss her, his hands pushing to one side the slender straps of her bodice as he bent urgently to caress the smooth, warm skin of her shoulders, his lips spreading a trail of fire through the whole of her slender body. It seemed he was trying deliberately to scatter the last remnants of her control, using his lips and hands as sure weapons of destruction.

His lips on hers became a pain, the hard strength of his body a torment as pressure increased, and when she tried half-consciously to protest he merely smothered the words against her mouth, moulding her inexorably closer, as if even the faintest hint of dissent aroused a latent desire to inflict suffering, to take a subtle revenge.

It wasn't until she was holding him tightly, half sobbing with frustrated longing, that his arms slackened slowly and he let her go. Reluctantly but gently he slid her from him. "I shouldn't want you to have any regrets," he muttered, his face suddenly grim.

Alexa could only stare at him dizzily, knowing nothing of the sort, a peculiar sickness rising within her. How could there be any regrets about anything if he intended to marry her? "Surely," she choked childishly, "under the circumstances..." A fine fury attacked her so she couldn't go on.

"A few kisses are permissible." Dryly he finished the sentence for her. "But we weren't merely indulging in a few kisses, Alexa, and well you know it."

She hated his hard, calculating tone. He could kiss her insensate and come out with that! It was irrational, idiotic that she only wanted to be back in his arms when he was telling her clearly, if not in so many words, that her maudlin innocence didn't interest him one bit. "Why did you start something then?" she queried, with all the frank ingenuousness of her age.

One dark brow raised ironically as his eyes slid over her. The fresh Highland air of the last weeks had endowed her with a wonderful glowing vitality. Her long tawny hair had escaped its restraining ribbon and fell in heavy waves across her shoulders, and her eyes were mysterious green pools. Her mouth, naïve and untaught, shook. Swiftly, a metallic flash in his eyes, he swooped, drawing her up on to her sandalled feet until her smooth, luminous face was only inches from his own.

"You're enough to make any man lose his head."

"But not you?" Unwisely she asked, feeling desperate somehow to goad him further. She didn't care to be feeling as she did and have him standing there completely indifferent.

"Not completely." His gaze was still intent—but wary, as if he trusted his own constraint little more than hers. "If you hadn't," his voice deepened, "been such an infant."

"Without experience, you mean?" Her voice came swift, breathlessly challenging. "There's only one way I could get that." Reaction had set in and she was trembling, shuddering with the contact of his fingers suddenly taut on her wrist.

"In a week or two," he said softly, "we'll be married. There's no need to worry about something you'll have to come to terms with soon enough."

He talked in riddles, and she felt hostile and moved fretfully with a small jerk away from him. She couldn't—wouldn't marry him, a man who didn't love her. There were other emotions, she was well aware, but these were only of the senses and didn't last. Marriage to Fergus Maxwell was merely an inconvenience he couldn't afford to be without. It would solve the problem of Invercraig, provide a hostess for his house now that Helen was getting older and keen to retire. All this extravagance of feeling was nothing but an illusion; love had never been for him the motivating power behind the emotional drama of the last hour.

Swiftly this went through Alexa's mind as she flicked

towards him one last green-eyed defiant look before turning to escape.

"One moment, my dear Alexa." The order was crisp, slightly weighted, as though he knew quite clearly what was going through her head.

She stopped, tense, her back to him, on her way to the door. "Yes," she said.

"You've forgotten your ring, madam." He gave the *madam* a sarcastic quirk and before she could flee he was behind her. Catching her left hand, he slid the emerald over her third finger. There it glowed, a glinting reflection of her eyes.

"Like it?" he taunted, viewing the sparkling stone on her slim white finger with the cool appreciation of a connoisseur. "The atmosphere," he grinned suddenly, his eyes on her indignant face, "might not be quite right, but I'm sure you'll agree it's very nice."

Hastily, after one helpless moment, she snatched her hand away. She knew an urgent impulse to tear the ring off, but dared not. It might only amuse him further. "Goodnight," she cried, with what she hoped was a little dignity, before she fled from him through the door.

She fled to her own room, one well removed from the one she had occupied on that first night at Glenaird, and flung herself across the bed. Fighting Fergus Maxwell was an exhausting, humiliating business, like crashing one's head against a stone wall and almost as painful. Somehow she had to beat him at his own game, but daily it became more difficult to find a way. Just as it was becoming rapidly more doubtful whether, in spite of his callous treatment, she really wanted to! She must take herself in hand and concentrate on finding a weak spot; only from whichever angle she viewed him, Maxwell didn't appear to have any, and even should she find one, this was no guarantee that in the event of a showdown she would meet with much success. She might simply appear more ridiculous in his eyes than apparently she already did, and the possibility didn't appeal to her one bit.

Alexa tossed and turned, too exhausted to be wholly aware that she was crying softly, or that the hand with Fergus Maxwell's ring was clasped closely beneath her cheek as she fell asleep.

Several days later Alexa took Glen and visited Invercraig. The little dog, she had been relieved to find, had returned home after his brush with the shepherd, and was now temporarily established in McFarlane's kitchen. One day soon, she believed, Fergus was to send for him, and he seemed quite content with the arrangement; but a trip out, Alexa decided would do him good.

Maxwell had gone to Inverness where he had business to attend. He had asked her to go with him but she'd refused, pleading a headache. The headache hadn't been entirely fictitious. Recently she had felt curiously restless, and exhausted herself trying to keep out of Maxwell's way, yet at night she was unable to sleep. To her surprise he didn't appear annoyed that she wouldn't accompany him, but he did insist she saw him off, and she watched him leave with mixed feelings.

They had had word from Edith, who had arranged to speak to Maxwell over the telephone. Frank was in hospital where he had just had an operation, so they wouldn't be at the party. She hoped he would be recovered for the wedding in three weeks' time.

Alexa, who had hopefully expected Edith to raise any number of objections, had been dismayed. Edith had simply allowed herself to be charmed by him and raised not one. In vain Alexa pleaded that there was nothing which couldn't be postponed, at least for a little while, but Fergus was inexorable. There was nothing to be gained by postponing anything, he said. Edith and Frank would be there for the wedding and afterwards could visit Glenaird whenever they wished.

His attitude wasn't reasonable, Alexa had declared, giving in without notable grace. Since that night in the library he had left her severely alone although she tried to convince herself it was the other way round; not even when other people were around did he attempt to make the smallest outward sign of affection, although he was always studiously polite, and while she tried to believe it was all for the best some traitorous part of her missed his solicitude. It was just as if, she thought resentfully, he considered his ring on her finger absolved him from any further effort.

If anyone had advised Alexa that she was considerably mixed up she might have told them they were crazy. That she did not care one jot if Fergus Maxwell never so much as patted her hand. Instead of brooding about such an insignificant matter she kept herself occupied about the house. She soon discovered, however, that it was no ordinary house and that her efforts in this direction were not really appreciated. In the kitchen McFarlane reigned supreme, along with a woman who came occasionally from the village to cook their main meals. There were others, mainly stockmen's wives, who cleaned, and a man who gardened and did odd jobs. All this, with Helen supervising, left little enough for Alexa to do. The opportunity seemed to present itself when Fergus went to Inverness for her to escape from the place for a while.

She had only once been back to the croft and that had been the day after she had come to stay at Glenaird, when she had pleaded with Maxwell that she must fetch more clothes. He had taken her eventually, but her ankle had been so painful she hadn't been able to do anything. He had taken her by car, by road, and she had noticed that someone had removed her Bed and Breakfast sign. Fergus had told her quite decisively that he was responsible. He had also instructed his men to take her stock to Glenaird until she decided what she wanted to do with it. Which must have been as good as a public announcement that he was acquiring Invercraig along with herself!

This being the first time out with her car since her ankle recovered, she drove carefully. She had, with great daring, smuggled the key to the croft from Fergus's study, mentioned to Helen she was going out for a while and closed the door firmly on her anxious protests. Helen might be in an awkward position—she had probably promised Fergus to keep an eye on her—but Alexa knew a sudden longing to escape for a while from the majestic precincts of Glenaird. She assured McFarlane, when she collected an excited Glen, that she wouldn't be long gone.

Invercraig she found very much as she had left it, but the loneliness of the deserted house made her feel immediately guilty—so much so that she decided to light a fire and stay for a while. There were things to be tidied up and her eyes fell on the pile of dry but obviously dirty dishes in the sink. When the water was hot she would wash them and stack them away. It would look better, if nothing else.

She was on her hands and knees trying to get the fire to burn when Colin Macdonell walked in. She was so surprised to see him she couldn't restrain a slight gasp.

"I thought you were in Edinburgh," she said, glancing swiftly up at him over her shoulder.

"I have special leave for a couple of weeks. The old man hasn't been well again," he added by way of explanation, his mind clearly not on his unfortunate father.

Alexa paid scant attention other than to murmur perfunctorily that she was sorry. For no special reason she could think of she felt enormously pleased to see him. "But how did you know I was here?" she asked.

"I didn't," he replied with a grin, seeming to find nothing odd about her question, "I was merely passing and saw what could be likened to smoke signals escaping your chimney."

"Idiot!" She made a face and laughed.

"You don't mind?"

She screwed around, sitting back on her heels and gazing at him more eagerly than she knew. He was a familiar face, but not one connected with the tension and trials of the past weeks. "Oh no," she shook her head emphatically, "not at all. I've just had an awful job getting this fire to burn. When the kettle boils," she added, "I'll make a pot of tea."

"Let me have a look." He pushed her gently to one side, kneeling before the reluctant flames himself. "Your chimney's probably damp," he said.

"You could be right," she shrugged, watching him coax an unwilling flicker into a blaze. As the kettle began to sing she reached for the teapot. For the first time in days she could feel herself beginning to relax. There was nothing complicated about Colin; he bore no resemblance to Fergus Maxwell. Maxwell was a trauma she must escape from. If this wasn't possible then at least she could forget him for the next few hours, and Colin's presence would help.

Yet it wasn't altogether easy. In the rather awkward silence that followed she realised that Colin must have heard what had happened. His reference, for instance, to the chimney being damp seemed to indicate that he knew she had been away. In small communities news always travels fast and Maxwell, Alexa supposed, would be news. It might be better to mention it straight away—but how to begin? "Just hang on a minute while

I wash my hands," she said, to give herself a moment to think.

He rose to his feet, following her to the sink, and leaned against the wall, frowning narrowly at her over-anxious face as she turned on the tap. There was a burnished sheen about her he hadn't noticed before; her hair and skin, even her mouth seemed vividly alive. In a year or two she was going to be quite something. How, he wondered, with hard dislike, had Maxwell achieved so much in so short a time? Although it was common knowledge that he never wasted any. So far as women went he could be a determined brute when he chose, but Colin had never heard of him being seriously interested before. The speculation and excitement in the village was rife.

Thoughtfully he picked up the emerald ring from the top of the sink where Alexa had hastily placed it before starting work. Didn't the girl realise how much it was worth? "It must have been sudden," he said.

She didn't pretend to misunderstand. "It was..." She ran the tap harder.

Carefully Colin felt his way, not happy about the slight shake to her fingers. "This will make a big difference, I suppose..."

Alexa nodded dumbly as she reached for a towel. Colin turned off the tap.

"You'll have to do something about the croft?" He didn't hope she would be happy or anything like that.

It was an omission she didn't appear to notice. She blinked vaguely, drying each finger with undue care. It wasn't something she wanted to talk about. "Perhaps— in time," she prevaricated eventually.

There was a slight pause. "You wouldn't consider selling it to me?"

"You!" Almost stunned with surprise, Alexa stared at him.

"Oh, I know there are other people who would like it. I'm probably too late."

"But you're still a student!"

"My grandmother left me money. I could afford it. Being a student has nothing to do with it."

"Yes—but..." Alexa's voice and legs simultaneously gave way and she sat down hard on the nearest chair. Colin arriving like this, his unexpected offer, was all too much! If there had been nothing between Colin and herself before he'd gone back to college, he certainly seemed to be viewing things differently now. He held Maxwell's ring as though he disliked the sight of it.

"Here," he muttered, seeing her apprehensive glance, "you'd better put it on. I shouldn't care to be responsible for losing it, although I expect it's fully insured."

"I expect so." She took the ring and slipped it back on her finger, feeling curiously naked without it. She contrived not to look at Colin.

"Do you think he really cares for you?" Colin's query was so dry as to be impertinent.

She flared. "Is that so impossible?"

He actually had the nerve to consider. "Well, I suppose not. You're a whole lot different from the rather deprived little mouse I first knew, and even then when you let your hair down you weren't bad."

"Thank you!" If his voice had been dry hers was more so.

His eyes were keen on her face. He didn't hear her tones. "Something's different, that's for sure. You're not only changed, you're quite a wow! A butterfly emerged from the chrysallis." His voice deepened with cool suspicion. "You don't happen to have fallen in love?"

"Please," she said, assuming a briskness she didn't

feel as she opened a tin of milk and busied herself among the tea-cups, "I'd rather not discuss it." Rather tautly she changed the subject. "You talked of buying the croft."

"What about Maxwell?" he asked shrewdly.

"What about him?"

"Doesn't he want it?"

"He might not," Alexa declared, "be interested in buying."

Colins' eyes narrowed again as he sipped his tea thoughtfully. He wasn't so dim-witted he didn't sense something wrong somewhere. Alexa was too wound up, the casual demeanour overdone, but he also sensed that she might shy like a nervous filly at a lot of questions. Caution would seem his best bet, he would play her along. Lightly he shrugged. "If no one actually does want it, perhaps we can come to some arrangement?"

Alexa stared at him, her breath coming quickly. It was happening, the opportunity she had longed for of revenge! Fergus Maxwell only wanted to marry her for one reason—the croft, with its all-important right of way. But their bargain was only verbal, there was nothing signed. To let Colin have it would be total payment for all the humiliation she had suffered. Determinedly she strove to ignore the fact that it would be history repeating itself, and that Maxwell trusted her and she was about to betray him. This way she would have enough to disappear quietly and start a small business somewhere. Colin didn't like Maxwell, and while he might not be a match for him in many ways, he'd been well enough educated. The sale of one small croft should present no problems. He probably knew exactly how to go about it without anyone being any the wiser.

Still, she must be careful. Colin, she decided fiercely,

must never know all the sordid details. Things were bad
enough as they were, and she didn't know how much
more she could take! "I'm not sure," she hesitated,
her eyes wide open, "I don't really want to upset anyone. Perhaps if you could get something drawn up,
some advice about a private sale so that no one would
know about it until it was over?"

"You're really serious?"

Her fingers clenched, understanding the doubt in his
face yet resenting it. Her proposal had obviously come
as a shock. She didn't really understand it herself,
whatever it was that drove her on, and given time to
think she might regret it. To consider the matter logi-
cally was something she refused to do. Only to herself
could she acknowledge the unexplainable antagonism
she felt whenever she was with Fergus Maxwell.

"I'm quite serious," she told Colin.

"Right, then..." he paused reflectively. Colin's
grandmother had made a lot of money out of property.
A clever woman, her motto had always been: strike
while the iron is hot! She had approved of Colin only
because she believed he had inherited her intelligence.
She hadn't minded when he chose one of the profes-
sions after she had paid for his expensive schooling; a
second string to one's bow had been another of her
clichés. He could come back to property one day. With
this at the back of her mind she had taught him quite a
lot about it. At least she could make sure he never
served behind a counter as his father did. She had been
a snob of the first order, and had never forgiven her
daughter for marrying, as she considered, beneath her.

Alexa had been so right if she had but known. The
dispersal of one small croft would be to Colin's pleasure, not a problem. Invercraig would be a pleasant
source of income—a superb piece of good fortune!
How Alexa would square it with Maxwell he neither

knew nor cared. Maxwell, he'd made sure, would pay dearly for the privilege of driving his stock. Should the man make other arrangements and go elsewhere, well—land was always a good investment, and if Maxwell got mad and threw Alexa out, he wouldn't mind marrying her himself. In fact, Colin's pulse suddenly quickened as he stared at her, it could be his best idea yet.

Rather carried away, he continued jubilantly, "If you could give me a few days I'll see what I can do. Perhaps we could meet somewhere?"

"I think," Alexa swallowed nervously, "I believe Fergus—Maxwell, that is, is going to London for a short visit. Not long. I do remember him saying it wouldn't be worth my while to go with him."

"Long enough." Colin frowned in concentration. "We could have dinner somewhere and discuss any snags—if there are any, which I doubt. There could only be one or two, nothing to worry about. If you could in the meantime decide on a price, then I could give you mine, tell you how much I thought it was worth."

Immediately she could see it wasn't going to be so simple. "How would I know how much to ask?"

"You could trust me."

Could she? Of a sudden Alexa wasn't so sure, but her uncertainty, she tried to tell herself, would rise naturally from her own ignorance. She was aware that she ought to get a proper valuation, some professional advice, but of course there was no time. Besides, if she were to do that Fergus would be sure to hear of it! However, a few thousand would be enough. Even a few hundred and the pleasure of being able to snap her fingers at him. Silently she nodded bleakly, thinking this would settle the matter, but was startled by his next question.

"There's talk in the village of a large engagement

party soon. I'm not sure that I could get everything concluded before that."

"How long?" Alexa knew a cold shiver of dismay. She had forgotten about the party.

"How long?" Colin lifted his eyebrows. "Oh, not long on the preliminary data. After that—perhaps a couple of weeks."

"Then it will have to be afterwards." Alexa felt her cheeks pale. She had wanted to avoid this.

Colin, who was shrewdly one step ahead as to the implications, was determined to make it afterwards. Maxwell was going to squirm, and he wouldn't miss that for all the tea in China! Smugly he almost smiled. "As soon as Maxwell departs for London," he instructed Alexa, "give me a ring. From there on everything should be easy."

Afterwards Alexa was to remember those words with derision. Nothing for her ever seemed particularly easy, she was just beginning to realise. Not that she believed in self-pity, or allowed herself to indulge in it, but fate did appear to have a liking for knocking those who were down!

She managed to escape from Colin after agreeing to do as he asked, and wondered vaguely why she should think of it this way when she should be feeling only gratitude. The truth was that she hadn't the courage of her own convictions, and was absolutely terrified that Fergus Maxwell would discover what she had planned to do with the croft.

Not that he had appeared in any way suspicious on his return from Inverness. His mood had been surprisingly pleasant, and not even when she'd confessed to having visited Invercraig did it change.

He joined Helen and Alexa in the library and discussed the forthcoming party, and mentioned that he intended going to London the following week, which should give him plenty of time to settle the final details when he came back.

Alexa, momentarily forgetting her assignation with Colin, almost begged to be allowed to accompany him. She would have loved to have seen Edith and Frank; Frank and she had liked each other immensely. It did seem rather callous that while he was ill and the opportunity had arisen to visit him she didn't avail herself of it.

"Could I..." she began.

"No, you could not—not this time." Guessing what she had been about to ask, his voice was emphatic and just a little punishing. "You have enough to do here. Such a trip would merely tire you out."

"Of course," she murmured, hastily remembering about the croft, her promise to meet Colin while Fergus was away. Yet her heart was tight beneath a weight of misery as she stared at him. Was it possible to love someone as she did Fergus Maxwell, and betray him? Why was it a thing she felt forced to do?

Fergus, mistaking her apparent dismay, said coolly, "Don't start getting homesick, my dear girl, at this late stage."

His astringent tones hardened her wavering resolution. "I'm not," she cried rather wildly, jumping to her feet. And because she felt ready to burst into stormy tears, she fled.

"Pre-wedding nerves," she heard Helen remark soothingly through Fergus's bitten-off exclamation. Which must have sufficed, as he made no effort to follow her from the room.

Shaken unexpectedly to the depth of her being, Alexa flew upstairs and slammed her bedroom door. Without being fully conscious of what she was doing she turned the key and collapsed on to her bed, pounding the pillows with small clenched fists. Why was Maxwell so imperious? She couldn't even think of him as Fergus. Since she had discovered his true identity nothing had been the same!

Blindly she raised herself on an elbow to gaze out across the wide expanse of heather and trees towards the sea. All around was wild country. Lonely and hard, but a land to love, as she was beginning to love it. Maybe some things were hereditary? The blood of her father might surge more strongly in her veins than she realised. There could also be pride, remnants of the old love–hate relationship between the Lewises and Maxwells, all an inherent, unconscious part of her which she wasn't experienced enough to deal with. She only sensed these things, like a fleeting breath of something beyond her comprehension; like wind moving the water on the surface of the loch, but gone before she could reach out and grasp it. It aroused all the turbulent, untried emotions struggling within her, giving her no peace. Maybe Fergus Maxwell could see his way clearly, but she could not!

Fergus departed for London and on the following evening she met Colin, who took her to Ullapool for dinner. Alexa, who had never visited Ullapool before, gazed around with an interest which momentarily removed her mind from her own troubles. Her eager eyes saw a fishing village of some size, cradling Loch Broom, a long sea loch glinting in the slanting sun of a northern summer night. There were rows of white-washed houses set against the blueness of the water, a harbour and a harbour road with shops and hotels clustered down the side. The streets, as Colin pointed out, were named in both Gaelic and English. It was a scene impressive in its rugged simplicity.

Colin parked the car and, noting her interest, insisted on taking her to the Loch Broom Highland Museum with its items of local origin, housed in one of Ullapool's original buildings. "It will help you to relax," he grinned, "and enjoy your meal. Otherwise you probably wouldn't know, or care, what you were eating."

Alexa glanced at him swiftly. When he liked he could be remarkably astute. While she was still determined to let him have the croft, the whole business was growing daily more distasteful. His proposed tour of the museum might serve its purpose, but not completely. Nevertheless she smiled, for the fault lay in herself, not Colin. Nothing could be accomplished by making him feel as miserable as she was.

After the museum they wandered to the harbour and watched the boats. A passenger ferry was unloading and Colin told her that it linked Ullapool with Allt na h'Airbhe on the opposite shore of Loch Broom. Alexa was fascinated by the beauty and wildness of the rugged coastline, softened only by great sandy beaches. Over the edge of the harbour the water lay deep but crystal clear, and while staring down at it she overheard a sailor describing to a tourist a trip to the Summer Isles which lay, he said, twelve miles up the coast to the north-west.

"I should like to come here again when there's more time," she cried wistfully, as Colin dragged her away.

"You might not think so if we miss dinner," he teased. "One doesn't usually connect a place kindly with an empty stomach."

"I suppose not," she laughed, allowing herself to be guided towards a very smart-looking hotel, beginning to feel better. Ullapool, Lochinver, Gruinard Bay, Durness, these were all magical names of the north-west — names to be printed on her memory.

The hotel not only looked good, it was good. The dining room was comfortable and they ate well, although Alexa discovered she had little real appetite.

Colin trod carefully, fully aware of the tight-rope atmosphere reflected by the tension in the girl's taut face. Silently he cursed the fact that no property deal could be completed in five minutes. Something would blow, he was sure of it, unless he could get this one through in a very short time!

They were at the coffee stage before they discussed a price. Or rather Colin stated one and Alexa agreed. It wasn't, she thought, terribly generous, but it was something. The first snag came when he asked about the deeds.

"I haven't received them yet," she frowned. "Actually I forgot to mention them to Robert Kerr."

"Which just about throws a spanner in the works," Colin grunted wryly. "Never mind," he hastened, noting her alarm, "it will only take a little longer. You can always send for them. It's nothing to worry about— you've only just got engaged."

"How do you mean?" she quivered, not able to bring herself to tell him that Maxwell insisted on an early wedding.

"Well, there's plenty of time to get it all sorted out before you get married. That is," he added softly, watching her downcast face, "if you really intend going through with it?" It was a shot in the dark, but Colin had something to say and such an approach was unavoidable.

Alexa stared at him, her cheeks growing white. "I'd rather not talk about it."

He ignored this. "You could always marry me."

"No, of course I couldn't..." Aghast, she gazed at him with an unflattering astonishment. Colin must be crazy!

"You could," he assured her relentlessly as she paused, bewildered. "It's not so impossible. I might suit you a lot better than Maxwell."

"I think," Alexa said, stumbling blindly to her feet,

"we'd better go home. To come here this evening was a mistake."

"Don't be silly, Alexa." Muttering softly beneath his breath, Colin tore after her. "I'm sorry if I blundered, but it wasn't exactly an insult, surely? Say you'll forgive me?"

Silently she nodded. She supposed he was right, but she was aware in that moment that there was only one man she could ever marry, and he was going to hate the very sight of her when he discovered what she was up to!

CHAPTER TEN

THE days before the engagement party were, for Alexa, fraught with a peculiar tension. It was ridiculous, she told herself, that she should feel bothered by a guilty conscience. There was just no other course she could take. If Fergus Maxwell had so much as hinted at a stronger emotion that the almost casual friendship he had shown her, all might have been different. But to be considered part and parcel of a business proposition was totally unacceptable, and while circumstances might have placed her in a difficult position they surely weren't strong enough to keep her tied to it.

She didn't say anything to anyone about her evening out with Colin Macdonell. She had merely told Helen she was going to the croft for a few hours, and Helen, in the throes of a violent headache, had only asked to be left in peace.

The bit about the croft had been partly true as she had left her car there and Colin had picked her up. Such contrivances were necessary, he had assured her, if Maxwell was not to get suspicious. He hadn't thought it necessary to add that he wanted nothing at all to do with Maxwell until he had everything tied up.

On the next day, as Fergus was still away, Alexa had gone to Inverness herself, making the excuse that she must have a new dress for the party. In a way this was quite true as she had nothing very suitable with her, but this had only been a secondary consideration.

The new dress had been quickly purchased, costing

more than she could really afford, but there had been little time to search the town for something cheaper. Robert Kerr's office had been her true destination and, although her failing nerve had driven her shopping first, the time was soon past for further procrastination. When she did arrive, however, it seemed according to what she learnt that her journey had been wasted.

She listened, concealing her impatience, to the man's politely expressed good wishes, conscious of his more genial manner with unwonted derision. All due to Maxwell's influence, she had no doubt! It was several minutes before she got around to the deeds of Invercraig.

"I'm sorry, my dear," he had murmured, his sober face inscrutable, "I'm afraid I haven't managed to get as far as this. If you could wait a little longer—"

"But it's almost three months!"

"So it is." He had glanced at her mildly. "But very few estates could ever be settled in so short a time."

She hadn't quite known what to make of it. Vaguely she remembered overhearing acquaintances of Edith complaining about the time taken to complete some legal matters, but she hadn't paid any great attention. Colin, also, had hinted of snags. She hadn't told him of her proposed trip to Inverness today, apprehensive that he might insist on accompanying her. Now she realised that in telling him, she might have saved herself a lot of trouble.

"It might be wiser," Robert Kerr went on while she brooded, "to leave everything until after your marriage. I'm sure Fergus will deal with everything. He's more than competent to do so."

Alexa tensed, knowing a swift suspicion. "Did he," she choked, "see you last week?"

Robert's face was suddenly guarded, although not nervously so. "Yes," he nodded evasively, "but then he usually does see me when he comes to Inverness.

On an estate such as his there is almost always legal work to be done."

"I see..." Bleakly, without further satisfaction, Alexa had left. It had seemed quite clear that she wouldn't learn anything more, but she knew a growing conviction that Invercraig had been discussed by the two men, although it seemed neither likely nor desirable that she should prove it.

Robert Kerr did, as he shook her hand, assure her that if it was at all possible he would forward the deeds without too much delay. Which, she felt forced to concede was something—in fact all she required! Momentarily, before she had time to consider it, she had known a surge of relief.

When Maxwell returned from London he surprised her by declaring that he had news which might interest her, if she cared to hear it. She was walking in the quite extensive grounds around the house when he found her, and she was startled to learn that he had met Edith.

"She came into town and we had lunch together," he said. "It was convenient in the middle of the day, as she spends her evenings visiting her husband."

"Frank?" Alexa stared up at him, scarcely aware that he had taken her arm and was holding her close to him. "Is Frank," she asked, in some confusion, "keeping better?"

"I believe so." With some interest he studied her face, so near his shoulder, his mind obviously not wholly on what she was saying. "Missed me?" he murmured, watching intently the tide of colour which suffused her cheeks, his own dark face inscrutable.

Impatiently, trying to ignore her quickening pulses, she nodded. "If only to argue with," she said, "but I should like to know why you met Edith."

"We talked," his eyes glinted sardonically, "and I can assure you that before we parted she was reasonably convinced that I'd make you a satisfactory husband.''

Impulsively Alexa grinned, the smile lighting her slender face. She could well imagine the scene. Edith would treat it with the same grim determination as she did her most serious interviews. Only in a man like Fergus would she more than meet her match, and she could well conceive Edith being eventually charmed by him. ''I do wish I'd been there,'' she spoke unthinkingly.

''Next time you will be.'' Suddenly, as though her nearness affected him strangely, he bent his head, kissing her deeply on her soft pink lips. ''You didn't answer my question properly,'' he teased.

''I don't remember—'' she began, trying weakly to free herself while his arms swept her closer, stilling her feeble protests. ''Oh, Fergus,'' she gasped, not aware that she used his name as his lips, moving over her face and throat, sent odd little shock waves all through her. For one crazy, impossible moment, she let all her basic impulses hold sway, and she twisted entirely into his arms, feeling her body respond madly against him. Her own arms curved to his neck and she allowed her mouth to be crushed beneath his, bruised by his hard strength but in no way inclined to escape.

When he slackened his hold, putting her reluctantly from him, her limbs shook with taut rigors so she could scarcely stand. He smiled softly, holding her gently, seemingly well satisfied with something as he tilted her chin with one firm finger as his eyes explored her flushed face. ''You're tired,'' he said, his voice low, tracing a faint shadow on her cheek. ''What have you been doing with yourself while I've been away?''

''Why, nothing,'' but unhappily her eyes widened, then fell before the slightly frowning query in his. How could she tell him—ever?

"Go to bed," he advised suddenly. "There's nothing like an early night. I can't have my bride looking like a ghost. If you like," his voice deepened, "I'll see if I can scrounge some hot milk from McFarlane's kitchen and bring it up. Then we can talk."

Along with other things, his inflection seemed to say, as he pulled her gently close again, his lips exploring her mouth.

It was more than she could stand without giving herself away completely, and fiercely she pulled herself from his arms. "I'm going to bed," she cried, "but I don't want any milk, nor you in my bedroom, thank you. We can talk tomorrow, not that I can think of anything more which needs to be discussed."

Alexa couldn't think that after her outburst Fergus would have anything more to say to her, ever, but he made no attempt to cancel either their engagement or the wedding, and went ahead with everything as if all was entirely as it should be between them. There was only at times something definitely tigerish in his manner to indicate he had things on his mind.

McFarlane told her that when they held big parties at Glenaird it was their custom to open the small ballroom and engage a local band. She noticed he didn't say group.

"The ballroom is very pleasant," he smiled.

"But it needs cleaning and tidying after the New Year festivities," Helen declared, coming up behind them. "You had better give Miss Alexa some rags, McFarlane, and she can help."

No one appeared to notice the paleness of Alexa's cheeks or the unenthusiastic movement of her hands as she polished. Her lack of excitement was not reflected in the faces of those around her; to the staff on the estate this was an occasion to be looked forward to with pleasure. How much different it all could have been if Fergus had loved her! Her heart ached, and no amount of elbow-grease seemed to make any difference.

All too soon the evening arrived, and with it the upheaval of such an event carried out on a large scale—large, Alexa considered, by her standards, if not those of Glenaird. She felt she scarcely recognised the house anymore. Fergus appeared to have huge numbers of relations and friends and apprehensively she began to realise the full implications of such a gathering. To terminate their engagement at this stage would be a major embarrassment for Fergus, to say nothing of the possible humiliation, and somehow in spite of her firm resolution, Alexa shrank from it.

Several of the guests were staying in the house, as they lived too far away to return home that same evening. Every nook and cranny seemed to be occupied, and Alexa had felt sure they would run out of beds. Altogether there had been an enormous lot of work and Helen looked tired. Was there any real reason, Alexa asked her anxiously, to have celebrations on this scale, especially in such inflationary times?

"Nonsense!" Helen had been quite cross. "There is this huge house, just ready-made for such occasions, and actually the fare we provide nowadays is very much scaled down, and most of it is home-produced. Much of the wine is home-made too," Helen went on, with a more kindly glance. "McFarlane and I put gallons of it down and it comes in very useful. It's quite potent stuff, as good as anything you could buy over the counter."

"I'm sorry," Alexa said, aware that she had blundered.

"Don't worry, child, you'll learn," Helen's smile

was forgiving. "We still like to think we can enjoy a little socialising in these parts, and after all it's the thought that counts. It's the keeping in touch with one another which breeds and fosters a community spirit. Once the old customs are allowed to lapse they can seldom be revived."

It was true, Alexa admitted to herself as she dressed. She had only been here a short time, yet it had been long enough to discover a positive enthusiasm for such things in the area. Anything that could be was celebrated, and sometimes parties were held for no special reason at all, other than that of getting together. But if people sometimes played hard they certainly worked harder and possessed an indomitable spirit which Alexa admired and envied.

Swiftly, pushing such thoughts to one side, she bathed. Considering the crowd in the house she might never get near the bathroom again, even though there were two more. Back in her room she slipped quickly into the silky chiffon dress she had bought in Inverness without pausing to admire the way it fitted her slender figure. The milky white material seemed to reflect the pureness of her skin as it lay gently strapped across her slim shoulders, falling in a cloudy swirl about her ankles and almost covering the high-heeled silver sandals on her feet. Her hair lay heavy, the gold very pale beneath the lights. Colour seemed only to be found in her wide, tilted green eyes above the vivid pink of her mouth, and of course in the great sparkling emerald on her third finger.

Running downstairs, she found McFarlane, who told her that Fergus would like to see her in the study. To her surprise it was still early, so there seemed no reason why she should object. Reluctantly she followed as McFarlane, with a hint of the ceremonious which she suspected he liked to adopt on such occasions, led the way and opened the door. "Miss Alexa, sir," he announced.

Fergus stood inside the room, dressed as she had never seen him before, in the kilt. Wide-eyed, Alexa paused to stare at him. In school idiom he looked super—magnificent! He took her breath away.

"Wait until you see me dressed for one of the great Highland balls I shall take you to in the autumn," he grinned, reading too easily the startled admiration in her eyes and obviously amused by it.

Alexa made no immediate reply. This evening, she thought, was enough. Her eyes refused to leave him. He wore a dress kilt and a short jacket of fine wool with silk lapels, the cuffs flapped and decorated with silver Celtic-design buttons. The vest he wore was also buttoned in silver, and with this he wore a white shirt and black bow tie. His evening stockings were plain with tartan cuffs, and on his feet his shoes had a silver buckle at the instep. In his stocking he wore a dress *skean dhu* with a handle of carved black wood set with a cairngorm. His silver-trimmed sporran was made of sealskin with silver-mounted tassels.

"Why don't you wear it more often?" she managed at last.

He grimaced wryly. "I do quite often wear the kilt, but this little lot takes too much time to put on, more than I care to think about. I'm afraid I haven't normally the patience."

"It seems a shame," Alexa was still speaking disjointedly, trying to control the erratic thud of her heart which she was sure must be visible through the thin material of her dress. "I don't notice many men wearing it."

"Highland dress," he told her, "isn't generally worn for many reasons. First, tartan, kilt and bagpipes were forbidden in the '45 rising. True, it didn't last long, for the edict was repealed in 1785, but in forty years many of the old patterns of the tartans were lost, a lot of the old weavers having died. And worse still, the Highlander got used to trousers."

"Couldn't the fashion be revived?"

"For a lot of people it's a matter of money. Granted it lasts a lifetime, but it can be very expensive." Fergus shrugged, his eyes brooding. Then suddenly, it seemed, he had something else to say. Swiftly he came to her. "I didn't bring you here to discuss the vicissitudes of our national dress. You look more than charming yourself, and I have something to give you."

His hand slipped to her nape and, before she could protest, had fastened a diamond necklace around her slender neck. Against her white skin the stones lay glinting. Gently he turned her to the mirror so she could see.

"It's beautiful..." She could say no other, more words refusing to come. Only her eyes, meeting his in the glass, appeared to convey to him everything he wanted to know. A curious magnetism held her, compelled her. She could not break away, could not turn her eyes from his. How could she accept anything from him under the circumstances, yet how was she to escape?

He lowered his head, his lips clinging suddenly to her bare shoulders, his hands hard on the subtle curves above her waist. Then just as quickly he was putting her from him, his firm fingers sliding down to clasp hers. "Come along," he said, "we must inspect the ballroom—before I forget you don't want me in your bedroom and carry you off."

Alexa was surprised to find she had only been in the study for a few minutes and there was still plenty of time. As she almost stumbled along by his side the house was still quiet. "It won't be in half an hour," he assured her, teasing her a little, with scant pity when she blinked nervously. "Don't worry," he said, "you're going to be the belle of the ball."

In the ballroom the small pipe band had already arrived, and as the tuning up was a bit deafening they stayed by the door. The other small group, comprising a fiddle, accordion and drums, was still to come. To Alexa the music of the pipes was yet a mystery and Fergus tried, when she asked about it, to explain a little.

"The music of the pipes," he said briefly, "is divided into two types. The first is the Piobaireachd or Ceol Mor. This is the great ancient classical music. The second type is the Ceol Aotrom, the kind of music most people associate with the bagpipes. These are the marches, the reels, the strathspeys, the jigs and the hornpipes. It's the great music of the glens and the mountains. Music, Alexa, to stir the blood, that has led men into battle."

He quoted softly in her ear.

"Pibroch of Donuil Dhu,
Pibroch of Donuil,
Wake thy wild voice anew,
Summon Clan Conuil."

"Oh, yes," Alexa breathed, her eyes shining, "we learned it at school and it was always a favourite. The girls used to tell me it was my Scottish blood." She finished it off for him, her clear young voice resounding.

"Cast your plaids, draw your blades,
Forward, each man set!
Pibroch of Donuil Dhu,
Knell for the onset!"

"Which is what we had better prepare ourselves for," he smiled, his eyes on her tremulous face. "Sir Walter won't be here to help us explain if Helen has to head the reception committee alone."

Fergus was beside her and at her other side, Helen. McFarlane stood behind, sombrely watchful. The guests arrived, slowly at first then in a positive stream, and soon Alexa's hand felt limp. Cars parked five deep in the drive, and through the glitter of lights people flocked through the great front door into the open drawing rooms. Beneath such an absolute invasion Glenaird seemed to change completely. The beautiful old house rang with laughter and the sound of excited voices, and in the distance, from the direction of the ballroom, the first strains of music added to the general air of anticipation.

Alexa smiled until she was sure it would be permanently fixed to her face, and all the while she was conscious of Fergus at her side, sometimes with his arm slipping around her possessively, as if he adored her and was determined everyone should know it. Yet there were other moments when, glancing up at him, she caught a disturbing glimpse of a slightly sardonic smile, as though he was well aware that fundamentally their relationship was based only on mockery. While Alexa assured herself it was all part of the game, she felt herself growing as cold as the diamonds about her pale throat and wilfully resistant.

Back in the ballroom Fergus and she led the first dance. She went into his arms, feeling them close around her, and was conscious that here was where she always longed to be; she might hide it from him but never from herself. She was so hopelessly committed as to feel the futility of struggling against it any more. All her small inner furies, her hot-headed opposition, were pointless. She was drawn to him like a magnet, along an irresistible path.

The dance was lively and she knew she danced well, and Fergus, for so big a man, was surprisingly light on his feet. For several minutes they were alone on the floor, an attractive couple, Fergus's dark good looks being a perfect foil for Alexa's fair beauty. They caught and held an admiring attention until the others joined in.

"It would seem you are approved of," he murmured laconically.

She pushed back against the arms which still held her although the dance was over. "Wasn't it all part of the bargain," she muttered back fiercely beneath her breath, "that I should give satisfaction?"

A flame licked in his dark eyes, his fingers tightening cruelly. "You'll pay for that little speech," he promised, "before this night is over."

To the onlookers perhaps he might appear devoted, unable to leave her, but she knew better. With a light laugh she dragged away from him, allowing herself to become the centre of an ever-changing circle. Fergus, she had quickly seen, was very popular with the ladies, many of whom she acknowledged unhappily were much more sophisticated and glamorous than herself. One particular dark-haired beauty he danced with several times, enough, she decided with an unhappy twist of her heart, to cause comment.

Alexa wasn't exactly idle herself, being almost swept off her feet by a positive queue of partners, but though she smiled and looked gay and was poised and lovely, every round of the floor meant absolutely nothing to her without Fergus.

Then suddenly, with a devastating swiftness which took her breath away and rendered her helpless to protest, Colin Macdonell claimed her! In that first instant of surprise she couldn't speak, nor do anything to hold back as he swirled her away. Almost certainly he hadn't been on the list of guests, but surely he hadn't come uninvited? Fergus would be furious!

"I didn't know you would be here," she gasped as he whirled her against him.

"You wouldn't," he said grimly, "but I had to talk to you."

"You mean you've gate-crashed!" It was worse than she'd thought.

Colin shrugged, his lips compressed, his eyes indifferent. "If you like. Actually I came with the other band, the accordion and fiddle. Occasionally when I'm at home I run them around. They're friends of mine."

"I see," Alexa said, but she didn't. Colin had been so emphatic about preserving the utmost secrecy regarding their relationship because of the croft, that she failed to even begin to understand it. Their dancing together like this would immediately arouse Fergus's anger and suspicion.

"It's about the croft I had to see you," Colin muttered, as if reading her thoughts. "Otherwise I wouldn't be here. I'm not a complete fool, but I had to risk it."

"The croft?" she whispered.

"Yes, the croft." His voice held a dry bitterness. "My old man has come to hear of it. Don't ask me how—but the deal is off."

"I didn't—" she began, wild relief stirring in spite of the shock of his announcement.

"I'm not accusing you of anything, least of all of telling my father," he cut in, anticipating what she had been about to say. "Maybe nobody told him. Sometimes I think people around here are psychic. They sense these things."

"So you've told me before." Not wholly convinced,

Alexa's voice was sceptical. One could believe only so much. Colin had never seemed a man to be dominated by his parents; if anything, she suspected, he had been spoiled. She hinted at this, though not in so many words. "You've always seemed quite independent."

Colin sighed ironically. "I'm afraid the old man's ill, and I'm not sure if he'll recover, otherwise I might not have taken much notice. On top of this I happen to have been in a spot of bother lately, and I don't want to upset him any further."

Curiousity stirred as she glanced up at him. "Why should the selling or buying of my croft affect him one way or another?"

The tempo of the band quickened as Colin sighed. "Need you ask! It all ties up with Glenaird. Maxwell, as you must know, has a very great influence around here. It's more a matter of loyalties than money, but I can't really afford to be mixed up with it. Besides, if anything were to befall the old man because of it, my mother would never forgive me. And that means a lot."

Though Colin's whole demeanour was a mixture of despondency and resignation, the relief within Alexa positively surged. Even if Colin hadn't changed his mind, she now knew quite clearly that she couldn't have gone through with it. She couldn't have hurt Fergus in this way. "I don't think I can say that I'm sorry," she choked, unable to hide her feelings, "but why was it so urgent to see me this evening?"

"He, my father, threatened to see you himself unless I came and made it quite clear. You can imagine what that would have meant! If Maxwell should get to know he would never forgive you. He would never stand for it—and I have an ever-growing suspicion that you're in love with the man, although you might not know it."

Horrified, she stared at him, her green eyes darkening with anguish. Evasion seemed impossible. "Surely," she whispered, "it doesn't show?"

He shrugged wryly. "It's not too difficult to guess, but you are supposed to be in love with him, you know. I can't imagine that your guests would be surprised. And this is why I'm here, you little chump. I think too much of you not to come and warn you."

"You think it would make a difference?" Unhappily she appealed to him, seeking a reassurance she didn't receive.

"I shouldn't like to bet on it," he muttered. "Why do you think a man of Maxwell's age isn't already married? Hasn't he ever mentioned his previous engagement?"

Alexa's face went chalk white. "You must be mistaken!" She heard her own voice rise, shrill with a kind of devastating shock.

Colin, if he noticed, ignored it as he enlightened her, cruelly cancelling any former kindness. "Apparently he broke it off because she had dinner with another man. He has something of a temper, your fiancé. This is what I'm trying to shield you from. Since then he's certainly played around but there has been no other serious attachment until he met you."

"Please..." Alexa struggled from his arms, not caring if anyone noticed. She couldn't stand any more of it. "You'd better go now."

"I didn't intend to linger, only long enough to see you. Goodbye, Alexa..." His voice mocked yet was curiously regretful as she turned and left him.

"What did that young fool want with you?" Fergus wanted to know as they went in to supper. His jaw was set and his eyes, as they went over her, held a peculiar glitter.

Alexa, still almost trembling with the shock of

Colin's disclosure, was scarcely aware of his disapproval. The thought of Fergus and another girl was a refined torture, something that eclipsed all else. Why had he never told her? "Nothing," she answered, attempting to palter with the truth, "he came with the band. I knew him at the croft—he was just being friendly."

"Judging by the way he stood looking after you friendship couldn't have been further from his mind! From now on, my dear," Fergus said hardily, "you'll have nothing more to do with him."

Fergus's tone was hateful. She immediately rebelled. "I refuse to be other than polite."

"A formality one reserves for one's guests. You can take it from me young Macdonell was not invited."

Alexa suspected he was being deliberately pompous. Stoically she kept her eyes on her plate. Helen had declared that there would be nothing extravagant, yet how otherwise could one describe all this lovely food? Rather blindly she glanced around the table, concentrating feverishly on the varied array of cold meats and sweets.

"It's much too lavish," she exclaimed with a determination born of an unexplainable bitterness.

"It's not every day," Fergus remarked mildly, "that I celebrate my engagement."

"Didn't you do it this last time?" It was out before she had time to think, and she would have done anything to have left the words unsaid. She did not need to look at him to see his mouth tighten grimly, the narrowed anger in his eyes.

"Come dance with me," he commanded in a low voice, aware that the people around them need not exert themselves to overhear what was being said.

"I'm not sure..." Alexa hung back, searching frantically for some excuse. Anything to avoid being alone with him, even on the dance floor.

He took no notice and his hand under her arm brooked no further argument. Back in the ballroom he pulled her roughly to him. "Macdonell," he ground out, "is that what he came to tell you?" His voice held a cold contempt.

"No—yes..." she stuttered. In another minute her backbone would crack beneath the pressure of his fingers! "You didn't have the honesty to tell me yourself!"

"And you're annoyed?"

"Surely I had some right to know—and it would have been easier than hearing it from someone else!"

"If you remember," he interposed smoothly, "ours is not a normal engagement."

She ignored this. "And your other one was?"

His head went back, his dark brows raised, his eyes glinting on her vividly flushed face. "If you consider the fleeting passion of a boy of twenty-four, I suppose it was. It was well over ten years ago and I had almost forgotten."

"Many men of twenty-four are married, with children!"

"Quite possibly," he didn't deny it, "but the capacity to feel deeply only develops with the years. At least in my case."

Alexa wasn't sure she understood. "If you were engaged why didn't you marry her?"

He actually grinned wryly. "I might have done, even though I discovered quite quickly that my feelings were far from permanently committed. Perhaps Lydia sensed this, as she sought the consolation of another man."

"She broke it off?" To Alexa this sounded incredible.

"She did. I seem to recall a flaming row, and that was that."

A cold shudder ran through Alexa, stiffening her

body, paling her hot cheeks. Were his feelings still as transient, his temper still as impetuous? How much chance would she herself have when she confessed what she must—when he knew that she too had deceived him, if in another way? She must tell him about Colin and Invercraig, this much was suddenly quite clear. What sort of relationship could she hope for otherwise, based on deception? She had been crazy ever to imagine that she could live with such a cloud about her head!

Yet she couldn't possibly tell him until the morning, until everyone had gone home. Might she not then have this one evening—just these few more hours before she bared her soul? Fergus wasn't in love with her but neither, she guessed, was he entirely indifferent. If he wanted her he could have her. Paradise might still be hers, if only for a short space of time!

When his hold tightened she let herself go limp against him. The waltz was dreamy and his lips whispered against her cheeks. "Am I forgiven?"

Her heart beating wildly, she nodded, her fingers creeping and clinging to his strong neck, silently begging to be held even closer. She nodded and helplessly the words escaped her hungry lips. "Love me, Fergus," she whispered, "please, Fergus, love me a little."

For one dramatic moment he went taut, his arm like an iron band about her trembling body. They were near the long windows which led on to the terrace and there was no hesitation in him at all as he swept her through them. "If this is all it's taken," he exclaimed, "to bring you to your senses, I've a lot to thank Macdonell for!"

Once on the terrace his arms momentarily left her in order to avoid a couple deep in conversation. The man spoke lazily to Fergus who from politeness was forced to answer, and suddenly Alexa could stand it

no longer. How dared she presume on time to which
she had no right? She could neither confess to Fergus
nor belong to him completely. An agony of distraction
overcame her, lending near-panic to her heart and racing impulses to her feet. Without a word, apart from a
strangled gasp, she fled from him, deaf to his half-
smothered exclamation as he turned and came after
her.

Along the terrace was a door leading to a small ante-
room, a forgotten, long-neglected place which she
thought might once have connected with one of the
larger lounges. Here she had sought refuge on other
occasions, and instinctively a subconscious sense of direction seemed to lead her to it now. It was deserted
and dark and in a whirl of confusion she sank down
into the deep shadows of an unlit corner.

"Alexa!" It was Fergus's voice, hard with restraint.
"Where are you?"

She gasped—was there no escaping him? Silent as a
mouse she sat, but the faint musky scent of her perfume came to him and he pounced. Like a hunter of
old his movements were sure as he came down to her
on the wide downy sofa where she crouched, dragging
her to him. He was like a man aroused, without mercy,
and at his touch she lost control, her heart shattering
wildly as he forced her head back and his lips crushed
hers.

He kissed her deeply and possessively, his body hard
over hers until there was no sense or reason in her any
more, just an irresistible clamouring of fiery senses.
Her mouth burned as he forced her brutally to him,
and his name became a passionate moan on her fever-
ish lips. His hands were holding her, controlling her
with difficulty. "If nothing else you've given me the
right," he said.

"Fergus...no." There was only a thin divide between this and total possession, and her whole body shrieked that she could deny it. Why did one minute, scarcely tolerable part of her mind have to remind her? "Fergus," she gasped, "don't you understand? I was going to sell Colin the croft!"

Fergus halted, but slowly. His hand went out tilting her hot face to him. "Darling girl," his low laughter came to her softly, "I know all about your little adventures. You met him at the croft and had dinner with him at Ullapool, so I won't waste time on recriminations. You're quite a little fighter. This I recognised to my cost, at the very beginning of our somewhat stormy acquaintance. I never expected you to give up so easily as you appeared to do. I merely took the precaution of keeping one step ahead."

Something inside her was breaking into a fine misery. She was scarcely aware of his teasing tone. "He came this evening and told me he couldn't go through with it."

"And neither could you." There was in his voice total confidence. "Am I right, my darling?"

Tears came, warm on her cheek. "I thought you didn't care."

"Darling Alexa, I love you. From the start. From the moment I saw you, like a small avenging angel, challenging me at Invercraig."

"But..."

"Listen to me." Abruptly he silenced her. "The land, the track, is important, but you are my life. I saw you and loved you, it was as simple as that. You thought I was another man and impulsively I decided to play along. Maxwell of Glenaird doing that! It was unheard-of, but after just five minutes, you little witch, I was a desperate man. It would give me a chance to get to know you; something I doubt you would have allowed if you had known who I really was."

"Yet you stayed away after my birthday?" She felt his handkerchief gently drying her tears which flowed freely when she remembered her bitter unhappiness.

"Until then," he said slowly, "until I kissed you properly, I tried to convince myself that my feelings couldn't be seriously involved. It wasn't so easy to face the truth, or to find a way of telling you exactly who I was. Not without evoking your hatred, something I was reluctant to risk. Then, on the night you came to Glenaird in such a state, I completely lost my senses. I had to have you and didn't really care how I achieved it. The thought of the danger you'd been in made me see red. I had to have you under constant surveillance."

Alexa lifted her head to look at him, her eyes wide with the wonder of it all. "We nearly lost each other. Why didn't you tell me the whole truth instead of only so much?"

"Because, my darling, I thought it would frighten you. You were so like a small, fragile bird. I didn't believe you really cared, and I knew if I didn't keep a tight rein on my feelings I wouldn't be able to restrain myself."

"Oh, Fergus," she exclaimed, her sweet, low voice greatly daring, "as if I should have minded!"

"Why, you shameless little hussy," he grinned, shaking her gently until her hair tumbled about her cheeks and her eyes darkened. He drew a deep breath and again gathered her close, kissing her lips until her mouth shook. "Alexa," he muttered, his hands passionately persuasive, "I hope you aren't going to mind now. I love you and want you so much."

"I love you," she whispered, leaving him in no doubt that she shared his feelings as her arms went around him in complete surrender. She loved him, there could be no one else for her, ever. Here at Glenaird she was at home.